ABOUT THE AUTHOR

Lexie Winston has been an astronaut, rock star, princess and time traveller. In her dreams. But none of the dreams have lived up to what becoming an author has been like. She gets to live in a world of pure imagination, and her heroines get to do the things she's always wished she could.

When not writing books, Lexie is a mother of two gorgeous teenagers and the wife to a patient and understanding man. They live in Western Australia and are lorded over by a black toy poodle. She loves camping, reading and if her iPad was stolen, her world would explode. (It has the kindle app on it.)

And check out my website at lexiewinston.com

And you can find all my links at
https://linktr.ee/LexieWinston

Galaxy Circus

(Sci-Fi Reverse Harem Series)

Apprentice

Stagehand

Whisperer

A Night Most Wicked - Galaxy Circus Novella

Broken Promises

(Dark Poly Romance Series)

Secrets Kept

Lies Untold

M.I.T.H.O.S

(Contemporary RH)

Spies Like Me

Coming 2022

STAGEHAND

LEXIE WINSTON

NEIGHPALM
PUBLISHING

First published by Neighpalm Publishing in 2022

Stagehand: Galaxy Circus Series

Mobi format: 978-0-6450988-3-9
Print: 978-0-6450988-4-6

Cover design by Raven Ink Covers
Content Edited by SCW Editing
Line Editing by Elemental Editing

 Created with Vellum

To all my readers who love a little bit of weird in their kink.

AUTHOR'S NOTE

Stagehand is the second Galaxy Circus novel, a fast-burn RH series that contains some adult situations which may be triggering, such as dub-con.

Galaxy Circus will also contain MM and male appendages of a somewhat interesting nature.

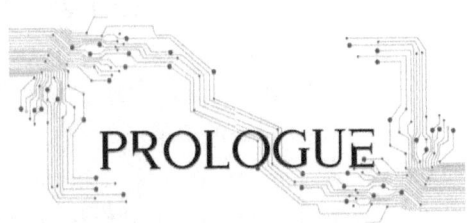

PROLOGUE

"You fucking idiot!"

The backhand across my face from the person standing aggressively in front of me is not unexpected, but it's harder than I anticipated. I'm not prepared for the force of the blow, so I end up sprawling on the ground from the impact. It's grimy and sticky and altogether unpleasant.

This wasn't where I thought I'd find myself when I arrived here.

Working my jaw back and forth, I glare up at them, smoke pouring out of my nose as my teeth clench with barely contained anger. How dare they treat me like this? A growl escapes my mouth, but they're not paying attention, instead continuing to berate me.

"You were perfectly positioned to find the information we need, and now you've fucked that all up."

The shuttle from the Galaxy Circus dropped me off at Fluxx late in the day after I attacked Lila. Link knocked me out when I was about to shift, so I didn't even get a chance to defend myself to the Adams brothers when I woke up.

Nope, it was an instant dismissal because I upset their *precious* granddaughter. That fucking whore took Caspian away from me. Not only had she *mated* him, she'd also given him what I couldn't—babies—and that was an even bigger slap in the face. I'd take physical torture over emotional agony any day of the week. Sure, I slept around, but I had my own sexual needs, and I was waiting for Caspian to get jealous and realize he couldn't live without me. I already had a dragoness lined up to incubate my eggs, and we would have been great parents together.

But she ruined it all.

I hadn't even been on Fluxx for twenty minutes before I was being summoned. I jumped onto a quick transport shuttle and was at the Edalaxian Space Station, a meeting place where people do trades and business of the not so legal kind, within an hour.

When I reached the bar where I was to meet them, I'd been shown to a back room that was typi-cally used for sketchy dealings—all bare bones with a table, chairs, and dim as fuck lighting that gives it a creepy ambience—and I didn't even get a chance to open my mouth before I was being punished and screamed at.

The being in front of me paces back and forth across the room, their hands flying as they continue their tirade.

"What the fuck were you thinking? You were supposed to make nice with the girl and milk all the information you possibly could out of her!" The being pauses, the tension so thick in the air it's suffocating.

There's zero misunderstanding on my part of how royally I fucked this up, but they are not finished.

"Everything we have discovered points at the Unas landing on Skarr, but there is no sign of the orb on the planet. The Galaxy Circus and the Adams brothers have to have it, and if they don't, they know where it is. It's too much of a coincidence that the Unas crash-landed and disappeared only months before the circus was established."

The being in front of me is agitated, their eyes glowing a molten gold as they turn back to face me.

"Well? What do you have to say for yourself?" they demand, and I shrug, pulling myself to my feet and flexing my wings. My own anger pulses, and my beast restlessly writhes beneath my skin, demanding to be released.

"She's useless. I don't even think she's actually Skarrian. There are no signs of power whatsoever. I think the grandpas fucked up. Either she's not their granddaughter, or she's been away from the waters of Skar for too long. I also looked *everywhere* on the ship and pod, and there's no energy signature that is even close to being powerful enough to be the orb."

"We know nothing about it!" the being screams at me. "It could cloak itself or just not emit high readings of energy. Now you have no chance of finding it. You. Fucked. Up."

I shrug, shoving my hands into my pockets. "Sorry," I say, but I don't mean it. I hated having to pretend that I loved that circus. I didn't. The only good thing about it was all the easy ass and Caspian, and it's not like I couldn't get easy ass anywhere else. "I just think you're barking up the wrong tree out of desperation. I'm confident they don't have the orb."

"I don't pay you to think," they snarl at me, and before I can react, I'm looking down the barrel of a laser gun. "You're just lucky I have other options, because *you* are expendable."

I never would have guessed this being would have the guts to kill me, but I'm regretting misjudging them as a shudder of fear rips through my body, and before I can even move, they pull the trigger.

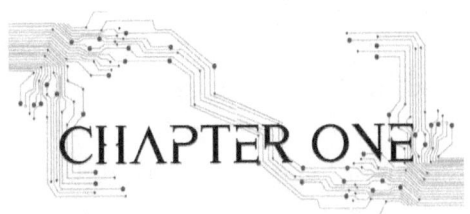

CHAPTER ONE

Lila

Snuggling with Caspian and Link on the couch went a long way to making me feel better, but I still feel miserable a couple of days later. Dylan's nasty ass words hurt me deeply, not to mention the fact that he completely had me fooled, so I guess I'm feeling a little naïve as well.

When I wake up, I'm alone, and I can't say I'm upset about it. It's nice to have five minutes to myself to breathe and process everything that happened. I really haven't had a chance to do it since it occurred, instead falling into bed exhausted every night.

I lie here thinking about what transpired. Dylan's betrayal and false friendship has me picking myself apart and questioning who I've become since I arrived at the circus. I think I've been so desperate for approval and acceptance that I've become a little complacent.

I trusted him way quicker than I ever have anybody else in the past. I mean, we haven't even done a DNA test to ascertain if Eric, William, and John are even my biological granddads. For all I know, they have me in space now and I'm going to be food for Viggy. My brain takes hold of that wild thought and tosses me headfirst down a rabbit hole. What if all those missing people were really victims of alien abductions much more sinister than a simple probe and return? Fuck. Maybe the whole reason I don't have powers is because I really *am* just human. Double fuck.

There is also the mated and pregnant part. Hopefully that means I'm not going to be T-rex food, but I barely know my babies' daddy. Sure, he's sexy and sweet and everything I could wish for in a man, but our relationship went from being annoyed with one another to flirting, having hot fucking sex, and getting knocked up in the span of a week. On top of that, there's the oral sex I received from a cyborg yesterday, all with the blessing of said man. He wasn't just any cyborg though—no, he's basically a sex expert. Sex. Expert. How did my life come to be like this? I have to pinch myself to make sure I'm not actually a mugging victim and lying in a coma somewhere having a fantastical dream.

Eventually, I realize spending all day in bed while letting my thoughts run rampant is not productive. Pushing back the covers, I notice the tightness in my muscles as I move, almost achy from the inner turmoil that's been eating away at me from the inside out. I roll my shoulders and stretch my arms and legs to see if I can get rid of the tension. Stress fucking sucks.

Standing up, I make my way over to the closet to get dressed. I opt for one of the Galaxy Circus uniforms because it seems like the right thing to do. I have to prove I'm taking my role seriously since many performers aren't convinced my grandads made the correct choice by bringing me in. Trying to clear my thoughts, I focus on cleaning my teeth and brushing my hair before calling it good. Sadly, my hygiene routine only distracts me for a few minutes, and now I'm back to square one.

I'm still worrying about the shitshow of the last twenty-four hours when I go out into the kitchen in search of coffee. Link left late last night, and Caspian and I went to bed shortly after. For the first time since we mated, my libido has calmed down, so I went to sleep with his tentacles and arms wrapped around me. I insisted that he take whichever form he is most comfortable with or prefers to be in around me. I would never judge him. For me, I am happiest in my human form and will probably only shift to swim with him, though I can't deny I haven't thought about how sex in that form would be. The anticipation of that happening sends shivers down my spine.

"Hey, baby." Caspian's voice startles me out of my musings, and I feel the blush spread across my cheeks at being caught. Thankfully our telepathy is only active when we're underwater, so he didn't hear those dirty thoughts. I don't think I'm ready to admit them out loud… yet.

He's in humanoid form, though his skin is still his normal mottled blue and purple color. He's sitting at the kitchen counter with a steaming mug of something in front of him. Caspian's smile is large, but it slowly drops when I don't return the friendly greeting. Getting up, he walks over to me and holds out his hands for mine. "Hey, is every-thing okay?" he asks with a small wrinkle of concern between his eyes.

Biting my lip, I shrug and take his hands. I don't want to outwardly reject him. He has experienced issues with women in the past, and I don't want him to think that I'm denying him, but I'm also feel-ing… *lost*.

He guides me over to the couch facing the big picture window and helps me sit down before joining me, wrapping his arms around me, and pulling me into his chest. The immenseness of space stretches out in front of us. The moon is behind us, and there is nothing recognizable before us. Space debris occasionally floats past, but the ship's outer shield protects us from impact.

A sigh escapes me, and I can't deny how good this feels, my body craving the comfort Caspian is giving me. Relaxing against him, I stare out into the seemingly never-ending scenery, trying to come up with the words to express the turmoil I've been feeling.

"Talk to me, Lila." He sounds concerned by the length of my silence, and his arms tighten slightly like he thinks I'm going to flee.

I run my hand over his sexy chest, trying to assure him that I'm not going anywhere. He too is wearing one of the jumpsuits, and I can't deny how spectacular he looks in it. His grip relaxes at my touch, and he presses a kiss to my head.

"Where do I even begin?" I pause, needing to sort through my thoughts so they make sense and aren't jumbled. After taking a deep breath to calm my nerves, I continue. "I mean, Dylan's act really had me going. For the first time ever, I just went with my gut and trusted his intentions. I never ever do that. Like, ever. But I relaxed all of my defenses and let everyone in—you, him, the grandpas, Link. Fuck, I let Link go down on me yesterday because you said it was fine." The words tumble out of my mouth, growing more frantic as I try to get everything out. "Even the grandpas are encouraging multiple relationships, and I didn't once question any of it. But that's not me. I don't trust, and I don't accept everything at face value. I feel like maybe someone's been messing with my mind."

Now that I say it out loud, I hear the truth in my words, and I feel a rush of anger. Is that what has been happening? Did the grandpas have the *warlock* do something to me to make me gullible and compliant? I stiffen and try to pull away, but Caspian won't let me. He tightens his arms.

"No, Lila. No one here would take away your free will, and Dylan is just an asshole. I had no idea his feelings for me ran so deep. I am just as surprised as you are. But if you're so worried about your mind being manipulated, we can get Link to check you again."

"What's to say he's not in on this conspiracy, Caspian? That he's not a part of it? How do I know that the grandpas are even related to me? Maybe I don't show any signs of power because they got the wrong girl..." I started off angry, but by the end of that little rant, I'm despondent. I *so* want to be their granddaughter.

"Link wouldn't lie to you, Lila. He will always tell you the truth, cyborgs can't lie." His words give me some hope.

"Really?" I ask, looking into his expressive, stormy blue eyes for any sign of duplicity, but all I see is love and acceptance. This beautiful creature who has suffered nothing but rejection from the female sex just looks at me like I'm the best thing since sliced bread. How can I not trust him?

"Really, babe." He releases me and stands up. "Come on, we'll go right now. I don't want you to spend another minute more worrying about this. We'll get him to run a DNA test and check for any spells, so when you see Xavier this afternoon about your lack of powers, you won't have to be wary of him." He frowns. "Or no more wary than the rest of us are around someone like him."

I let Caspian help me to my feet. "He's powerful, isn't he?" I ask as he interlocks our fingers and guides me to the door. "He has this magnetic aura that surrounds him, and he practically crackles with static electricity."

"The warlock's one of the most powerful beings in the galaxy," he confirms as we walk to the elevators. This deck is free of people. It's only my and the grandpas' suites up here as well as the flight deck, so there's no reason for anyone to be hanging around.

"How do we know he's not fooling all of us?"

Caspian doesn't blow off my question with a vague answer, and I can see him really thinking about his response before he replies, "Westalins, or warlocks, are an interesting race. They can be devious and conniving, but some also have a fierce streak of honor. Xavier is loyal to your grandpas, but he also wouldn't deceive you on their behalf, especially with both of you having the attraction marks. He's not motivated by greed, and he has everything he could ever want and all the power he needs. One day he will rule the warlocks, and you can't get much higher than that. Although they are a fairly peaceful race and don't go out of their way to start conflict, you can be damn sure they will finish it if they need to."

I hear what he's saying, but it really doesn't reassure me. I get lost in my thoughts, thinking about upcoming DNA tests, seeing the rest of the circus, and getting to know Link better. I don't really pay attention to everything around me, so it's a surprise when Caspian squeezes my hand to get my attention.

"Lila, honey?" I'm shocked to find myself in the waiting room of Link's office. Caspian has a concerned frown on his face, and Josa is sneering at me. I guess I definitely didn't make a friend by asserting my authority last night. The mind-blowing, moan inducing oral probably didn't really help either.

"Here to flaunt the rules again, *human*?" he questions sarcastically, but when I gaze around the room, I see no one's waiting.

"What is your problem?" I snap in irritation, and his eyebrows jump in surprise before he fortifies himself and barks back.

"Link has been promised to me, so keep your filthy fucking hands off him. Sure, you may get him to fuck you, but he can't commit to you, so why don't you do us both a favor and just find someone else." His words are so full of venom that I recoil, and dread sits heavily in my stomach.

Shit.

Have I been physical with a taken man? No

wonder this guy has been so pissy since I stepped foot in here. Should I apologize? I'm floundering, this information adding to my already distressed state, when Link steps out of his exam room.

"Oh, for fuck's sake, Josa, I've told you that I have no intentions of being involved with you. My mother cannot promise my hand in marriage no matter what she thinks." Link sounds exasperated and annoyed, like he's said this to Josa countless times before, but his words are reassuring, and I breathe a sigh of relief. I roll my eyes when the realization hits me. How did I manage to attract two men who have the most fucked up and delusional people interested in them? First Dylan and then Josa. Now, though, I know the truth so I can fight back.

"I happen to like having his hands on me, and his mouth, tongue, and fingers too. I can't wait to get at his dick as well. You might want to block your ears, Josa. Link asked me to be quiet yesterday, but I'm going to let you in on a little secret... I like to be loud." I breeze past him, letting him assume I'm here to fuck Link's brains out.

Link holds the door open for Caspian and me, and as we walk past, I deliberately run my fingers across his stomach, his abs rock-hard beneath his uniform. Turning back, I wink at the jealous prick behind the reception desk. That's right, I'm making friends all over this ship. Thankfully one of the jealous pricks has already been evicted.

When the doors close behind me, I lose the flirty act and jump up on the exam table, taking a seat. I close my eyes and rub my temples, trying to get a handle on my thoughts. It's disconcerting that I've been doubting every decision I've made since I woke up this morning.

"Well this is a nice surprise. I hadn't expected to see you again so soon. What can I do for you both?" Link smiles at us as if the last three minutes with Josa didn't happen.

"Could you please examine Lila to make sure she isn't under any spells?" Caspian requests bluntly, and Link frowns before nodding.

"I can. Is there any reason why she might be?"

Thankfully Caspian is able to coherently express my rambling to Link while I'm so overwhelmed, not to mention my head is now thumping too. I'm not afraid of conflict, but it's becoming a regular occurrence and it's fraying my nerves. I must make sure to drink some more water from Skarr, but I really think it's emotional overload that's causing the pain.

"I'm afraid Dylan's deception and how easily she has accepted all of this has her questioning herself. She says it is out of character for her to be so trusting, and she is worried she's accepting this all without thought because she's being influenced." I can hear the slight hurt in Caspian's words, and it's the last thing I want him to feel.

I shake my head at him. "I didn't mean to hurt you, Caspian. I love what we have despite the unexpected start of our relationship, and I can't wait to get to know you better, but I have to know. I have to know that I am of the Adams' bloodline, and I have to make sure that I haven't been coerced before I go any further." I know I'm not explaining myself properly, and I see the hurt in Caspian's eyes continue to grow, but when my gaze drifts to Link, his expression tells me he understands.

"No, I get it. I heard Josa telling you what my mother has promised him, so I completely understand wanting to have free will. Come on, it's a quick scan, and then you will know for sure."

He parts my legs like he's done the last few times and steps close. I can't stop the shiver of awareness that shoots down my spine at the contact. Memories from the other night flash in front of my eyes like a movie preview, and it's all I can do to grit my teeth and hold in the moan that threatens to escape. His silver eyes swirl as he scans my body.

"My program is designed to pick up physical and metaphysical issues. I never thought to scan for spells before because nobody had given me any reason. I also know how long your grandparents have been searching for you. This is not a small thing. I think the lawyers were slightly incompetent because it has been years, Lila, *years*, since they started looking for you. They'd just about given up hope. I had John in here a number of times over the years for grief counseling for both his wife and your parents, but also because of you. The decision to leave you behind has haunted them. They have been happier this last week than we have seen them in a long time." Link's eyes continue to scan as he talks.

"He's not wrong, babe. They really have been different men this week. All those looks you've been getting while walking around the ship with them were not solely aimed at you, even though it may have felt that way. The Adams men have been unapproachable and decidedly unfriendly for a long time, except to a few select people. Seeing them happy and laughing is probably a big relief for everyone involved. Hopefully they'll be more approachable for the general circus population and we won't have to be mediators." Caspian gestures to himself and Link.

"You've been running interference?" The information from Link about my grandads catches me off guard.

"Yeah. The two of us as well as Xavier and Saxon. It's why your grandpas trusted you with Xavier when he scares so many others. He's basically been a grandson to them, helping them with all aspects of running the ship since he's been on it. People don't argue when he appears, all mysterious and shrouded in mist, crackling with power, they just do as they are told." My heart melts a little more toward the powerful man at this little tidbit. He doesn't sound as bad as Dylan made him out to be.

Link's eyes return to normal, but he doesn't step away from me. His hands come up to my thighs, and he gives them a reassuring squeeze. "Everything is normal, sweetheart. No spells, and no sign of mind manipulation that I can see, because I know that would be your next question. I also ran your DNA results already."

"But how?" I'm surprised, because he didn't even take my blood.

"I took your blood when you first fell from the sky, and its makeup is stored in my memory banks," he jokes, tapping his temple before getting serious again. "When I run it against the boss men's, I can confirm you are most definitely of their blood. I probably should have confirmed that the first time around. I'm sorry I didn't and left you wondering." He sounds genuinely apologetic, and he steps back, looking a little bit embarrassed.

His words have a huge breath escaping me in a rush, and I sigh heavily. All my worries and concerns melt away.

"If you're really concerned about mind manipulation, ask Xavier to have a look. There's nothing that he wouldn't be able to find. Although I can pick up a lot of mental manipulation, the warlocks have a way of hiding their presence from artificial programs. It's better to be safe than sorry."

I jump off the bed and throw my arms around the blushing doctor. His arms come up to embrace me, and I snuggle against his chest. "Thank you,

17

Link. Dylan made me question everything that has happened so far, but now I know I can face the truth. He is a grade-A douchebag."

He rubs my back and gently pulls away. Not wanting to leave Caspian out, I go over and hug my octoman. "I'm sorry, I just needed to know," I apologize, my sense of relief immense, and he returns my hug just like Link. I lean into him a little more, trying to burrow myself in the warm comfort he's giving me.

"It's okay, baby. I completely understand. Just remember there are always going to be assholes, but what you and I have is *real*. There would have been no bond unless me, my beast, and you were all in agreement." Caspian leans down and rests his cheek against my head as I digest his words.

"He's right. I did read up on that, and his beast wouldn't have been able to force the bond without mutual attraction and compatibility. He's also not wrong about assholes. Josa out there is a prime example, and he won't be the last, but you have me and Caspian and your grandpas."

"And I don't think that will be the last of us. You're very likable, babe." Caspian pulls back, winking at me, and once more I'm excited for what's to come. It still amazes me that he can talk so casually about me having more mates without getting jealous. "Come on, I think your grandparents have plans for you to see the warlock today. Xavier's going to see if he can figure out why you're not showing any signs of power, and we can ask him to dig around in your brain too."

A rush of adrenaline spikes through me at the thought of seeing the mysterious sexy warlock. I wonder if he will show me his real form again, or if I will be visiting with the mist-shrouded man.

Disappointment flashes through Link's eyes at the announcement that we need to get moving. I don't want him to think I'm abandoning him for Xavier, so I make the decision then and there to embrace this multiple love interest thing, especially since Caspian assured me that he and his beast are okay with it.

"Link, would you like to meet up for drinks later?" I ask him, making eye contact so he knows I'm being genuine, and his face lights up. His skin and eyes literally start to sparkle like Edward Cullen from *The Twilight Saga*. He's gorgeous.

"I would love to. There's a club on the ship, or a pub or a number of restaurants if you want to get food. Which would you prefer?"

I shrug and look at my mate.

"The club's fun. People really like to blow off steam when we're between shows, but they also don't have the same hang-ups as humans, so you may see things that will shock you," Caspian warns me.

My eyes widen at the possibilities of what I might see. "Is this one of those 'I could be challenged to a duel to the death' things?" I ask cautiously, and both guys shrug, not committing to a direct yes or no answer. Men.

"Don't worry, I'll make sure you're not," Link assures me, but I'm not fully sold.

"Okay, well, I will try anything once. I'd really like to try to fit in. I don't know many of the circus performers yet, and I'd like to change that."

"Great, I'll come get you at eight if that's alright?"

"Sounds awesome. Okay, Cas, let's go find the grandpas, shall we?" Cas does a double take at the nickname, but he looks pleased, his eyes quickly changing to his beast's before shifting back. I'm hoping that means he's happy with the pet name too.

My mood has done a complete one-eighty, and I'm looking forward to seeing my grandpas even more now that I know the truth. *We are family.* Before we leave, I give Link a kiss on the cheek. He holds his hand against the spot I kissed with a look of wonder on his face as Caspian and I leave.

CHAPTER TWO

Link

I stare at the door long after Lila and Caspian leave, lost in my thoughts. I do hear Josa sneer something nasty to Lila, but she ignores the petty shit now that she knows the truth about my mother's pathetic attempt to force me into an arranged marriage. Shaking my head, I take a seat at one of my consoles and skim through all the data I received from Lila's scan. There's still no sign of the ball of energy a Skarrian usually contains within themselves, nor are there any signs of it being contained within a spell or anything like that. I really am stumped. Maybe it has just been too long for her. The Skarrians who landed on Earth originally lost their powers, so maybe that's what happened to Lila, but if that's the case, she's going to be in trouble. The thought alone sends tingles through my nervous system.

The Adams brothers are grooming her to take over the circus, which is a prestigious position to have, whether Lila knows it or not. Giving that role to a human is not going to go over well with the general Skar population, not to mention the rest of the galaxy. The galaxy tends to look down on Earthlings. They find the humans' treatment of their lands abhorrent, and their lack of power makes them inferior in every way. The Adams brothers regularly deal with leaders of each planet, but they have power to back them up to maintain their dominance.

Lila is not going to have this.

The medical doctor in me acknowledges she does have *some* shifting abilities, even if she can't go full kraken, but for now, that's enough to cling onto. I think about the other marks on her shoulders. To be honest, it probably wouldn't hurt for her to have a few powerful mates to back her up. Both my and the warlock's marks have shown up, and between us, we both wield a fairly substantial amount of political power as well as physical power. Xavier is the crown prince, so there's basically no one more powerful than him apart from his parents. I'm not completely sure about the warlock's psychic feeding needs, however, and I'm not sure if Lila will be happy if Xavier needs to keep his harem. I should probably do research on what will sustain him so I can advise her of these things if need be.

Although I don't have any magical abilities, I am the heir of one of the largest companies in the galaxy. Political power is practically at my fingertips. If I have to leave the circus and take up the mantle of Pleasure Bot Industries to help Lila, I would do it in a flash.

I push back from my console, a little surprised at where my thoughts just went. I never had any interest in being involved in the family business before, but I would choose that path for her. I guess it's a testament to how attracted I am to Lila.

I hear murmurs out in the waiting room, so I must have a patient.

Standing, I pick up the subsonic cleaner and run the probe over the table Lila had been sitting on. It's Josa's responsibility between clients to come in and sanitize, but I suppose he's still throwing a tantrum. His outburst the other day did nothing but clue me into my mother's plans, and he is a fool for thinking he had me trapped. Talk about prematurely playing your hand.

I spoke to my father about my source code to see if it's even possible for my mother to gain access, and he was horrified at the thought. He believes she was bluffing or that Josa made up the threat on his own. Although my parents are legally married, they are separated, but because Pleasure Bot Industries is my father's family's company, and my mother is the CEO, it's a tangled web, so they stay legally married for the sake of the business.

He assured me he would investigate her claims and told me to speak to the Adams brothers about having Josa removed as my nurse. Relieving him of his duties would also mean he'd get booted from the ship. It's not like he does anything except sneer at everyone who comes in, so there would be zero hardships.

I hear shouting and growling in the waiting room and hurry out to see who he has pissed off now. Standing in the middle of the waiting room are some of the lightning cats. Their fur stands on end, their pupils are constricted, and their annoyance with my nurse fills the space with palpable tension. As I look around, I realize all of the cats from their streak, bar the female, are here.

"What is going on?" I demand over the noise. The bickering abruptly stops as Josa whirls to face me, waving his arms to get my attention first. "These *pussies* do not have an appointment. Are we just forgetting about protocol now?" The permanent scowl on his face only deepens before he continues. "Need I remind you, Link, that they need appointments first or else they will not be seen? Ever since that *slut* human came aboard, everything we've done in the past now goes out the window."

A low rumbling menacing growl starts after Josa calls Lila a slut, but I can't pinpoint which one the noise is coming from. Who knows? It could have been from all of them.

"For fuck's sake, Josa, get your head out of your ass. There's no one else here, and I know for a fact there's no one on the schedule today. I think you should take the rest of the day off and get yourself together." I step closer to him, making sure my next line is delivered with direct eye contact. "You seem to be coming unhinged, Josa. Maybe I need to run a diagnostic on *you*," I threaten, and his arms drop as he shakes his head, releasing a scoff.

"This human is going to be the end of you, Link. Mark. My. Words." He accentuates the last three words. "Your mother will not stand for you messing with a human. She may be the heir to the Galaxy Circus, but there's no way the Adams are going to hand it to her with no powers, and if they do, there will be hell to pay. People will stop supporting the circus and its mission," he warns, but again, he overplays his hand. He's been snooping in confidential patient files and has given me the perfect opportunity to have him dismissed, which makes me smile.

"Run along now, Josa. I have patients to see," I tell him, and he growls almost as impressively as the cats and storms out. I'm sure if he could slam the office door, he would, but it's just not possible with the sliding doors on the ship, so his attempt at a dramatic exit is anticlimactic.

Turning to the waiting streak, I put a smile on

25

my face. "I'm so sorry for the poor service and wait time. Would you like to come through? Are you all here together, or am I seeing you one at a time?" I look at the five men before stopping on Maxsim. He's usually the spokesperson when Natalia isn't around.

"All of us, if you wouldn't mind." His accent is thick, and his voice is a growly gruff sound that makes your toes curl. Even though my interest lies in Lila, I can't deny how sexy this man is.

"Alright, come on in. I can't say I'm not surprised to see you. You've been with the circus for a couple of rotations now and this is the first time." I don't hide the curiosity in my voice.

This streak of lightning cats has been very distant. None of them have gone out of their way to socialize with the crew, and Natalia becomes a rabid beast if anyone tries to approach them.

I lead them into my exam room. "Please get comfortable. There are chairs, or if you want, you can hop up on the exam table," I offer, and they take a moment to get situated. Maxsim and Echo, the pure white cat, both sit close together on the exam table I just wiped down. Their nostrils flare, so I guess the probe cleaned it but didn't remove her scent as well.

Trace, Fuse, and Sim all take chairs around the room, but they are silent, and they also won't look me in the eye. Something is up with this streak, I just need to wait them out. Trust is not easily earned, and since this is the first time I've seen them as patients, I have to show them I'm trustworthy.

"We would like you to check our birth control, please," Maxsim asks, his voice a quieter pitch than usual. He's looking at the door to the reception like he's worried Josa is going to violate my direct order and come back.

I hold up a finger and go over to the door, pressing the soundproofing button, and the sound-proof barrier flips into place.

"Why would you think that there's something wrong with your birth control?" I inquire, looking around the group. Lightning cats are required to be on birth control until they officially mate or form an official streak. It stops any unwanted pregnancies, which is a huge shame in their society. Some lines within the lightning cat society are puritanical, and breeding outside of mating, or breeding with a different species, would be cause for banishment.

Again, the three sitting on chairs won't look at me, and Echo and Maxsim exchange a glance. Echo sighs. "Natalia wants to force a mating with the five of us, but none of us are interested. She's been especially territorial this week after the boss men's granddaughter arrived." Echo's voice is less growly than Maxsim's and much gentler.

"After being struck on the ass by lightning, she's become even more demanding. Natalia views what Lila accidentally did to her as a challenge to her authority, so she's being even more aggressive in her attempts to seduce us." Sim sounds traumatized. His voice is shaky and he still won't look at me. I can see his visible shudder and then genuine paranoia etched in his features.

What a terrible situation to be in.

"And I take it you're not interested in this happening?" I question, frowning.

"Fuck no!" Trace exclaims without hesitation, and this time he does look up at me. "Natalia was *never* supposed to be on this trip. When the three of us signed up for the circus, it was her sister, Minx, who was originally supposed to be the female." The more he speaks, the more disbelief and frustration coat his every word.

"The five of us are all from the top five streaks in the Laxsus region, which is also home to the Iceen royal family. Natalia and Minx are both daughters of the royal matriarch. Natalia is next in line, and as such, she should not have been allowed to be a part of the Galaxy Circus. Her role is to learn how to lead, but somehow when we all arrived to be transported here, she was there instead of her sister," Fuse explains.

"Are you telling me that we may have an international incident on our hands?" I ask Fuse. My concern as to whether or not the Adams brothers are aware is rising every second.

"No, I made sure of it before we left the planet. Somehow, she convinced her mother it would be better for international diplomacy if she did a tour with the circus," Maxsim explains, his fur rippling in annoyance. "But of course she has barely left our den since she's been on the ship, and when she has, she certainly hasn't made friends or taken any steps to do so." He sighs and looks me in the eye. "Lightning cats are discouraged from having intercourse with the opposite sex until they are a mated streak, and the females are expected to remain chaste. It doesn't always happen, hence the birth control mandate for us. As such, we are encouraged to fool around with one another to see to our sexual needs until that happens. They want us to form streaks of males first and then find a female once we reach maturity, which is usually around twenty-five years." Maxsim pauses to make sure I'm following him. Their complex mating habits are truly fascinating from a medical standpoint. "Trace, Sim, and Fuse are one such streak, and they would have liked to have mated with Minx. That was their plan. Natalia is a jealous bitch and wants to take that away from her sister. She believes that as the future matriarch, she should have the most powerful mates for herself. She thinks that if she can seduce those three, she can bite and claim them. Getting pregnant would solidify her claim whether it's wanted or not. We think she's trying to force a rut, and we would like to make sure that our birth control is reliable so if she does somehow throw us into a rut, there's no chance we can get her pregnant. We shouldn't be able to because she's a beta but who knows what devious plans she's been conspiring."

"Okay, but what about you two?" I point to Maxsim and Echo. "Do you want to be part of her streak?"

Echo shudders, and Maxsim reaches for his hand, pulling him close. "No, Echo is a very rare lightning cat. He's an omega."

Something prickles in the back of my data banks. "Oh, I think I've heard of this. A male who has both male and female internal reproductive parts. You can have babies, yes?" I raise an eyebrow in question, and he nods.

"Yes, but he has hidden it, and to most people, he registers as a powerful beta. A kind warlock took exception to the treatment of male omegas and has been providing his family and any others since with a spell to hide their desig-nation, but Natalia found out. We're not sure how, but she has been trying to kill him the entire time we've been with the circus. Female lightning cats hate male omegas because it means males have other options. Male omegas didn't tend to last long after puberty, when their designations were discovered. Alpha and beta females kill them so that they don't take away their own mating choices. Echo was lucky in that his parental streak contains both a male omega and a female alpha, and he was protected because of their streak's rank. They are one of the most vicious streaks in Laxsus," Maxsim explains on Echo's behalf, who still looks ill at the thought of being with Natalia.

As much as I try to remain neutral, I can't help but feel a pang of empathy for his situation. Being different shouldn't mean an automatic death sentence for Echo. His rareness as an omega should be embraced, but sadly, their matriarchal society views him as a threat. I take a deep breath to clear my mind and focus on the medical importance of their request.

"We're fortunate that we're all alpha's and Natalia is just a beta. We can order her to stop," Trace adds, "but she still tries once the alpha compulsion wears off. They get a couple days of reprieve before she tries again. Natalia is relentless, but what infuriates her the most is that they are a couple. Ultimately, though, Maxsim is her end game." He pauses to look at Maxsim as if to apologize for stating what he believes is obvious. "His family is the one that would give hers a run for their throne if they were so inclined."

"And you two are a couple?" I ask, gesturing between Maxsim and Echo, wanting to make sure I understand what Trace is saying. They both nod, and Echo snuggles into Maxsim's side. "Do you not want a female mate as well?" The medical doctor in me is digesting as much information as possible to help them if needed.

"We're not opposed to it, but so far we haven't

found anyone both our cats agree on," Echo says quietly.

"Okay, so what I'm hearing is that Natalia needs to be returned to Iceen, because taking away someone's will is wrong, not to mention it goes against everything the circus stands for." Even if there are some races who are more than okay with taking away free will. "I'll check your birth control and inject you with a rut prohibitor. Then, with your permission, I will speak to the boss men and see if we can make a trip past Iceen after we leave Earth to boot that bitch off this ship."

I wait to see what their responses are before I move forward, because I want them to know I take patient-doctor confidentiality seriously and won't break their trust. Looking at each cat, leaving Maxsim for last, I receive nods of confirmation. Their facial expressions have changed from worried to relieved and relaxed. I feel determined, more than ever, to help the cats be free of Natalia, so I rummage around in my supplies and insert the right capsule into the injector.

Going over to the exam bed, I activate my internal scanners and scan both Maxsim and Echo. Stopping over Echo's stomach, I marvel at the makeup of his reproductive organs. They really are fascinating. Slotted behind his bladder are ovaries and a womb. The uterus connects to the rectum with a single direction flap to allow sperm to pass into the uterus to fertilize the eggs. The baby then develops inside the womb and is delivered through a birthing channel that sits behind the testicles on the male omega and only opens when the male omega is pregnant. At all other times, this channel is sealed closed. Before this, I never would have thought I would have to brush up on my knowledge of all the different breeding rituals for the species on our ship. First the krakens, and now the lightning cats. I need to add the information from the onboard database to my memory banks. I should probably read up on all the other species on board too, because I'll never know when I might need the knowledge.

Once finished with their scan, I inject Maxsim with the rut inhibitor and Echo with the heat inhibitor.

"Luckily for you, if Natalia is a beta, then she can't go into heat, but it can't stop her from artificially triggering a rut, though I'm not sure how or why she thought you were all going to breed with her. The three of you are alphas too, aren't you?" I ask Trace, Sim, and Fuse, and they nod. "Well, don't you need to be able to knot your partner to breed?"

"Yes, and her sister is an omega. Natalia actually needs a beta partner to be able to breed herself. It's the *only* way they can breed, but she's a little bitter at the fact that she's not an omega and refuses to acknowledge it. We also know that there are ways around a beta getting pregnant by alphas in this galaxy. She's probably been injecting herself with omega hormones or something. The six of us never would have naturally worked as a streak," Fuse continues to explain.

Trace shakes his head and snorts as if it's the biggest understatement of the year. "Well, the five of us would have with Echo, but us three already have a thing with Minx, and those two have a thing with each other," he jokes, gesturing to the lot of them. "Natalia hates that. But if she is injecting herself with omega hormones, all it's going to do is change her scent. Even if she manages to trigger a rut, she still can't physically take our knots, so there will be no breeding. That's why omega hormones are illegal. The stupid betas end up being damaged when the alpha ends up hurting them through no fault of their own."

Silence descends over the room as all of us become lost in our thoughts.

I concentrate on the task at hand and run the same scan on the other three. I inject them with the rut prohibitors as well before tossing the injector back onto a tray. "Okay, your birth control is fine for all of you, and I injected the rut prohibitors. Just get through the next few performances on Earth, and then we can take care of your problem. If we send Natalia home now, we won't have time to get a new cat up to speed on the act. Only three more stops to go—Vegas, Asia, and Australia—and we're done. I think you'll find Natalia will be too distracted by Lila to worry about you five, which should help you in the short term. The boss men want her to start working with the acts sooner rather than later."

"Ah yes, the powerless human." Maxsim grunts. "That's going to go over well." I don't miss the sarcasm in his voice.

"The warlock is having a look at her today. I have a funny feeling that Lila isn't as powerless as Dylan told everyone she is. I think she's going to surprise people," I bluff, hoping it's true.

Echo and Maxsim exchange a look. "Well, let's hope so for her sake. I wouldn't put it past Natalia to use her lightning on Lila." Echo sounds worried, and with good reason. That lightning would be deadly for her.

"I'll mention it to Xavier and see if he can give her some kind of protection from any attacks, whether physical or mental."

"She's going to need it," Maxsim says like he knows something I don't.

I deactivate the soundproof barrier and follow them out, waving goodbye without uttering another word. Josa has returned to the reception desk, and he's filing his nails.

"What was that about?" he questions, nodding at the cats as they leave.

"Patient-doctor confidentiality, Josa. I can't tell you."

His eyes slide to the console, so I go back into

my exam room and check over my firewalls on the client files just to make sure he can't get into them. I wouldn't put it past him to snoop, just like he did with Lila, and then tell Natalia what occurred. He would revel in that kind of discord. Once I'm assured it's secure, I step back out, locking the door to my exam room behind me.

"I'll be out for a while. Message me if there's an emergency," I tell him.

He sits up straight, his eyes wide. "Where are you going?" he demands, but I don't respond. He's still sputtering when the door shuts and I leave him behind me.

CHAPTER THREE

Lila

I t's like a weight has been lifted off my shoulders as Caspian and I go in search of my grandpas. I feel lighter now that I know for sure there's no spell manipulating me. I'm still disappointed in myself for trusting Dylan so easily, but I made the decision to throw myself into this wholeheartedly, even though it makes me wary about trusting my other budding *friendships*. Link, Xavier, and Magenta all fall into that category, and I hate that there's now doubt involved.

At least I know Caspian and I are solid, and I have one person I can completely rely on. In hindsight, it's actually a little reassuring that his beast forced the mating even though I was initially upset when I found out. Where I would still be distrustful of Caspian the man, I'm a hundred percent sure of his beast, which helps settle my concerns about the two of us. Our relationship is tangible and comforting.

"Do you feel better now?" Caspian asks as we make our way around the ship, his hand in mine.

"Yeah, I really do. I'm just still trying to wrap my head around the whole Dylan thing. It really makes me think twice about who I can trust now, and I kind of feel sorry for those who are genuine. They don't deserve my distrust, yet here we are."

Caspian grimaces when I look at him. "Yeah, me too. His whole reaction kind of blindsided me. Never once did he insinuate he wanted more except during the confrontation. Not that I would have given it to him, I didn't feel that way about him. Clearly he was delusional enough to think I'd reciprocate those feelings."

"So you're bi?" I question, wanting to know more about him.

"You'll find that most alien species are a little more sexually fluid than humans. You've experienced this yourself. Sex is natural, and who cares which species or gender you're intimate with as long as it's consensual? As for reproduction, that differs from being to being."

I take a moment to think about his words, appreciating that he's being honest with me. It's almost like he's telling me it's okay to be interested in all species and genders. It's just people taking care of their needs, and I am all for it, but it's the reproduction piece that's caught my attention.

"I did wonder about that. I mean, you tell me you planted eggs into my womb. How exactly does that work? Are they just your babies? Do you fertilize them and I'm just the incubator?" I ramble, trying to ask as many questions as possible. I can't say I'm prepared to hear this, but I'll be sad if none of my DNA ends up in these babies.

"Lila, forget what you know about human reproduction, because that's not how it works with kraken. When my beast gave you the mating bite, it made your makeup compatible with mine. Kraken males lay the eggs, and kraken females incubate them. The fluid they are floating in is what fertilizes them, so if we compare it to human reproduction, you're doing what the male would normally do."

I'm silent while I let my mind wrap around that new bit of information. "So the babies will be half mine?" I ask quietly, needing him to confirm it.

Caspian slides his arm around my shoulders and gives me a side hug. "Yes, sweetie, they *are* half you. Hopefully they are crazy smart, kind, and loving like you too."

I warm at his reassurance, and we keep walking. I'm lost in my thoughts as I think about this pregnancy thing a little more. "Do you turn into a moody, raving bitch when you're ovulating? Because this may be a problem if we sync up," I tease, and he chuckles and shakes his head.

"I only ovulate when I want to, or to be more specific, when my beast wants to. He forced that ovulation. He'd been chomping at the bit since we caught your scent that first night. You sent me straight into ovulation, which is part of the reason I was so bitchy toward you. I thought there was no chance you'd be interested and I'd have to shed the eggs. Imagine my surprise when you weren't horrified at the sight of me."

"Nope, not at all. I thought you were sexy as fuck," I tell him honestly, and he smiles as we make our way through the ship. My grandpas have an office on the same level as Link's clinic, but it's on the other side of the ship. It's nice, though, just walking and talking with my mate.

"I know. When you gripped my tentacle, I could taste your need through your skin. My beast tried to force his way through. That's why I got out of there so quickly." He shudders at the thought. "Otherwise he would have taken you right then and there in front of the whole crew."

"Ah, yeah, not my idea of a good time. I don't mind a little bit of voyeurism, but that would have been ridiculous." I giggle. "I can't believe you could taste my horniness. I'm slightly mortified."

"Don't be ashamed of knowing what your body wants, and just know I won't be the only one. A lot of species have senses that can feel different emotions."

"Like the warlocks?" I inquire, still curious

about my mysterious new friend. Can I call him a friend after one interaction? Possible friend maybe?

Before Caspian can answer, we reach my grandpas' offices. They use these rooms to do all the admin work that goes with the circus, including the diplomatic stuff as well as the trade deals. They have three desks in a triangular shape with a large holoscreen in the space between them. All three are able to use it together, or they can separate it into three individual work spaces. They look up as Caspian and I enter. On the screen is what appears to be a human male, but I could be wrong.

"Ah, Lila, there you are. We were just telling James about you." John gestures for me to come over. Although I can see the being on the screen, I'm pretty sure he can't see me until I step in front of John's desk. "James, this is our granddaughter Lila, she will be taking over management of the circus when we retire. Lila, this is James Smith, our Earth liaison. He and a team of agents monitor all the alien beings that choose to visit Earth or make it their home."

Holy shit, he's a real MIB agent. My excitement at meeting him is not mirrored on his face. He seems to look down his nose at me in disdain, which is impressive in itself.

"Nice to meet you, James," I say politely, smiling at the man. Sometimes you have to kill dickheads with kindness because we all know it irritates the fuck out of them. It's obvious he doesn't like what he sees because he doesn't respond for a moment. Instead, James just studies me like I'm a science experiment gone wrong.

"I knew your parents, Ms. Adams. They never mentioned you to me." He sounds disgruntled, but I'm reeling at what he called me. Holy shit. My real name isn't actually Lila Jenson.

I'm still floundering a little bit, and William must realize it because he quickly takes over.

"James, we will get back to you to finalize arrangements to transport that one detainee. As for any others, we have no one who wishes to stay this time around."

"Very well. I will await your call," James tells William, even though his eyes haven't left mine. Awkward.

The screen blinks out, and I shudder. "Holy fuck, he was creepy. What race is he?" I ask as I shake, trying to rid myself of the unease I felt while he was staring at me. It's like my body is screaming, *Stranger danger! Stranger danger!*

"Human," Eric replies dryly, as if the answer was obvious, but I noticed none of my grandads responded to my James is creepy as fuck comment. He's something I'm going to have to figure out when or if I take over.

"Are you okay, babe?" Caspian asks from his seat in a chair outside of the office. He must notice my tense shoulders and pinched eyebrows.

"Ah, yeah, I was surprised to hear him call me

Ms. Adams. I had forgotten that the lawyer said my name had been changed. It was brain overload with everything he piled on me that day, so it had completely slipped my mind until just now when the creepy dude mentioned it."

"Would you like to know what your birth name was?" William inquires, his eyes twinkling with delight. He's such a pain in the ass.

"Does a bear shit in the woods?" I deadpan, and he snorts.

"Liliana Adams was your birth name, and your parents called you Lili. Liliana was your grand-mother's middle name. I guess changing it to Lila kept it close and less confusing for a toddler."

"Liliana." I roll it over my tongue, and I feel a spike of familiarity in my soul.

"Would you like us to have it officially changed back?" John asks with hope in his tone.

"Yeah, I'd like to reclaim that piece of me, but do you think we could just stick to calling me Lila?" I ask my grandpas. Even though I love the name Liliana, I feel like my identity is linked to Lila.

"I think it suits you better. Liliana sounds like a lady," Eric agrees with a cheeky grin on his face, "and we already know you're not that."

I stick my tongue out at him, but a pleasurable warmth flushes my cheeks. Joking and messing around with my grandpas is so much better than I thought it would be. I was expecting stuffy old men, but thankfully, their personalities are larger than life. It's almost like having three built-in besties.

"So are you ready to visit the warlock?" Eric gets to his feet and stretches. It really is disturbing to look at this man who appears to be in his late thirties and know he's old enough to be my grandpa. He doesn't even look old enough to be my dad. I really must ask them about the whole aging thing. I don't think anyone has actually properly explained that to me.

"Yeah, I guess so. Are you coming with me?" I ask my mate, and he shakes his head.

"No, I need to talk to John and William about our act now that Dylan has been booted, and then I need to go speak to the rest of the troupe. The rumors will be flying by now. I should have told them the day Dylan was banished, but I didn't want to leave you. Is that okay? I can cancel and do it later if you want," he quickly back tracks, as if his answer would offend me, but I shake my head and sit in his lap.

"No, that's fine. Eric will be with me. You do what you need to, and I'll see you later, right?"

He taps the communicator watch on my wrist. "Just call me on this." He waves his corresponding one on his own. "The only reason I won't answer is if I'm swimming in the pool. If I don't, just come and find me there."

"Okay." I give him a quick kiss on the lips and

slide off his lap. Before I can get away, he grabs my hand.

"Have fun, okay?" He winks suggestively, and I feel a small blush cross my face.

Eric snickers and leads me out of their office. I mean, I can't be *that* predictable.

"You're awfully cheerful," I snap at him as we make our way to the elevator. "It was not all that long ago that you were screaming at me about mating the kraken and getting knocked up."

He looks a little sheepish as he presses the button and we start to move. "Ah, yes, I'm sorry I may have been a wee bit irrational."

"You think?" I huff, and he finally meets my eyes.

"I'm just worried we're going to lose you like we lost your grandma and your parents. You're going to have to be patient with us because we will fuck up again, I guarantee it."

I can see how earnest he is, so I let it go. "What's the warlock going to do?" I ask, and he shrugs again.

"To be honest, I don't really know. The ways of the warlocks are a mystery to most of us, but you'll be in capable hands. Xavier is no novice." Based on how much my grandads respect him and the confidence in Eric's response, it seems like I have nothing to worry about.

"So where are we meeting him?" I question as the elevator comes to a halt.

"Oh, he asked me to bring you to his living quarters, which I'm a little surprised by. He doesn't usually want strangers in his space. He has trust issues about whether they want to be his friend or want to say they are friends with 'the warlock.' I do need to warn you about his harem though."

Eric steps out of the elevator, but he doesn't go any farther as he waits for me to join him. I don't say anything, just gesture for him to continue.

"You've been told how warlocks are psychic feeders and feed on emotions, yes?"

"Yes, Dylan explained it to me, but I kind of wonder if it was the truth. He was overly aggressive and sulky when he found out that Xavier's mark was on my shoulder."

Eric grimaces at the mention of Dylan. "Xavier is one of the ones Dylan never managed to seduce. That pissed him off because the man has a harem, so he figured he wasn't all that fussy. Rumor has it he was bitter and his reaction had nothing to do with you but with Dylan himself."

"Ha, so you pay attention to the gossip too, do you?" I joke, trying to ease a little of the tension that's risen at the mention of the dragon.

"When you're in such close quarters for long periods of time, it's very hard to keep a secret." Eric starts to walk again, gesturing for me to walk beside him. "Xavier's harem will probably be territorial. He's the only reason they are here, and they get comfortable. They don't have to work, they get paid well, and from what I heard, the psychic feeding feels good if he's feeding off lust." He pauses briefly, trying to collect his thoughts on how to explain as much as he can in a short amount of time.

"Some of them are low-level warlocks who either have no power or are not powerful enough to need a harem of their own, so they feed from him as he feeds from them, but he requires feedings more often. While they only need it once a week or even less, he needs it every day—or that's what I've gathered. Like I said, it's all very hush-hush. The more powerful the warlock, the more harem members they need until they find their intimate. That's the person that is like their soulmate whom they can choose to bind their life with. Once this happens, the less powerful person becomes as powerful as the other, and they can feed equally off one another. It's also why he is with the circus. He got sick of people throwing themselves at him in the hope he would mate them... or that's what his parents said when they asked if we had a position for him."

Wow, Eric is a fount of knowledge, and I'm hanging onto every word coming from his mouth. "Xylene and Cronus were close friends of your parents and asked us for a favor. They were worried he was going to insult someone with his apathy toward finding an intimate. They are the King and Queen of Westalin, and they are equal rulers."

"You said *people* were throwing themselves at

him, not only women. So he's bisexual?" I ask, not able to contain my curiosity.

"Yes, and warlocks are not particularly fussy about what race they feed from either. It's more of an emotional attraction than a physical one, so be aware that his harem members may surprise you. He picks them for how their emotions taste, but not solely for that. I'm almost a hundred percent sure they all have a sexual relationship too. It's supposed to make the feedings better."

"Can you at least give me a heads-up on what to expect?"

"His harem is a mixed bunch, but I know he has a Morpheian, a Rasque, a Dionall, and a Milobar, as well as a few warlocks."

"That's not telling me much," I point out to him and he stops, turning to look at me.

"Have you still not done your alien research?" He's frowning at me like I'm a wayward school child who hasn't done their homework.

"Of course I have, but there are a lot of different races, and I don't have a photographic memory." I cross my arms, feeling defensive.

"Okay, quick rundown." He drops his voice and moves closer. "Morpheians are metamorphs. They can take on any form you or they truly desire, but their original form is humanoid with no features, so they are shaped like you or me but there are no distinguishing characteristics. They are a blank slate and completely gray, but don't mistake their lack of eyes, nose, or mouth for lack of intelligence, because they can see and hear everything. Oh, and they are hermaphrodites, with both male and female sex organs in their natural shape, but they can shift into either male or female forms."

"That is so cool." I drop my arms and lean in, wanting to hear the rest.

"The Rasque is humanoid in form, but they look like a giant grasshopper, all armor plated with segmented arms and legs. They have two sets of arms and wings, and they are shades of green. Vegetarian species. They are a little frightening if you don't realize this."

"And the other two?"

"The Milobar is a little like an Earth stingray. He has a triangular head and body with arms and legs. He has the same features as a stingray as well, and the whip-like tail can be deadly. Lastly, we have the Dionall." I can see him thinking about how to explain this one to me. "You know that Marvel movie that has that plant-like creature that can only tell you his name?"

"You mean Groot?" I love that movie.

"Yeah, that's the one, so the Dionall are kind of like him, except they are all green and they have two forms—their humanoid one which allows them to move around, and the one they assume when they are sleeping or eating, and that one is more like Earth's Venus flytrap. They are carnivorous blood-suckers. They can be violent, vicious creatures, but I hear they are also extremely protective and loyal. Xavier has had him in his harem for a few rotations now."

Holy shit, that sounds terrifying, and I'm ultimately screwed if they are possessive of Xavier, but thankfully Eric can't see my unease.

"Come on then, game face on." Eric steps forward and presses a bell on the door in front of him. It barely rings before it slides open.

"Come on then, Lila, don't be afraid." Xavier's musical tone mocks me, even though I can't see into the dimly lit room. "Step into my lair."

I square my shoulders and brace myself as I step into the warlock's living quarters. The door slides closed behind me, leaving Eric on the other side. I whirl around, trying to open the door, and I feel Xavier's mist against my back. "Lila, your fear is delicious, but I'd much rather receive a different emotion from you. Come now, I promise you'll be safe. Eric knows not to come into my home, but he also knows you'll be fine. I would never insult them by feeding off their granddaughter without permission. I like enthusiastic consent. Tell me, Lila, will you give me enthusiastic consent?"

CHAPTER FOUR

Caspian

I watch Lila walk out the door with Eric before turning back to John and William. There's a small ball of nerves in the pit of my stomach for Lila, and even my beast is a bit restless, but I know that Xavier will take care of her. His attraction mark is still on her shoulder, and it wouldn't be there if he had nefarious plans for her. Hopefully he can give her some answers as to why she has no powers so we can put her mind at ease.

"What are we going to do about your act, Cas?" William asks, leaning back on his chair and throwing his feet up on his desk. John frowns at him, like he wants to slap his feet away, but he waits for my answer.

"I think we need to hire a new dragon or even a

different shape-shifting creature. When I shift, it really blows the crowd's mind. We probably should have had Dylan shifting too and flying around the dome. They'd just think it was a hologram or something." The thought of Dylan sends a quick rush of fury through my veins, but I compose myself. There is zero need for the grandads to see how much his betrayal as a friend and the way he hurt Lila affects me.

"Do you have an idea about who or what?" William raises an eyebrow, jerking me out of my thoughts. I roll his question around in my mind a bit, surprised that he asked for my input.

"What about a Naga shifter?" I think about my childhood friend and former lover, Silac. I'm not sure what he's been doing since I left Fluxx, but I bet he'd be interested. He has always been adventurous, and he would think working for the circus was a blast.

John and William exchange a look. I swear the boss men have telepathy. I can practically feel the thoughts flying between them.

"Do you have someone in mind?" John inquires casually, and I nod.

"Yes, I have a friend who would possibly be a good fit."

"Okay, well how about you contact that friend and ask if he would like a trial run? He can do the shows in Vegas, Asia, and Australia. We can reassess after that. We have a transport coming from Fluxx with a new dragon." My eyebrows jump in surprise at this announcement. "The head of the dragon clan was not happy with Dylan, who is his nephew, and has offered up his son as a replacement to smooth over relations. If your friend can get to the transport, they can make the trip together."

Before I can answer, the doorbell rings. When it opens, Link's on the other side. He comes in and takes a seat next to me.

"Good morning, Link. I hope you've got better news to make up for the Dylan incident," John asks but I can already tell from the strained look on Link's face that he doesn't.

"Not really, no."

William sighs, knowing that Link's presence is not going to make his day any better. He holds up a hand. "I need coffee before I get any more bad news."

He gets up and goes over to the replicator on the wall and programs himself a coffee before asking us if we want one. He could have done it telekinetically, but I get the feeling he needs to be doing something. All three of us say yes, and so it takes him a few minutes to do that. Once he sits down again, we all have a steaming hot mug in front of us. When I take a sip, I almost choke at the flavor. William chuckles then winks. "It's an Irish coffee kind of morning." He takes a sip of his own and sighs happily. "Okay, Link, hit us with it."

"Two problems. The first being my nurse," he starts, and William rolls his eyes.

"What has that weaselly little asshole done now?" William knows about Josa's issues from when Lila gave Link the night off. Was that only a couple of nights ago? Shit, it feels like Dylan attacked her weeks ago.

Link tells them about Josa's threats. "I'm almost a hundred percent sure my mother can't get at my source code, but my dad is looking into it. I think he also has plans to appeal to the board to have her replaced. As for my immediate issue, I would like to petition for Josa's removal from the circus. I don't even really need a nurse, and all he does is upset my patients anyway." William and John know this goes beyond Josa's outward disgust with Lila since he's rubbed others the wrong way before she arrived.

"That's fine. We have a transport coming in from Fluxx tonight, so he can use that to get back to Cybertronia." John leans in and types out a message on his screen. "I'll just send him his termination of contract. That will give him time to pack."

Link heaves a sigh of relief, and I can see that it was really weighing on the poor guy. "Thank you. My mother's getting more and more demanding. She keeps sending mates that are suitable in her eyes to be my nurse, but they are really useless. Can you just tell her we have no need of one? In reality, they are really only her spies." The tension I saw leave Link's body only seconds ago has returned in the tiniest form in the pinching of his eyebrows.

John and William exchange a glance. "We can…" John trails off and flushes red, and William grunts. "But we have a business relationship with your mother that we are reluctant to shoot down in flames. She is not an easy woman to get along with, especially when she really doesn't want you here. She sees our allowing you to be in the circus as a betrayal. We appease her by allowing her to send whomever she wants for your nurse. We figured there was no harm in that. We can now see how wrong we were, and for that we are truly sorry."

Link cocks his head to the side. "What business arrangement?"

"Since our wife disappeared, and the bond was not broken, we have been using a Pleasure Bot subscription to take care of our needs. We wouldn't dream of cheating on our wife, so they are a good alternative. Your mother is who we've been dealing with."

"Of course you do. Over twenty years is a long time to go without, and a high-tech sex doll is definitely a better idea than cheating. If Mom cuts you off, I can arrange for you to have new ones when you want to change them out," Link assures them, and I see the brothers relax minutely.

Pleasure Bot Industries has a program where you can swap out your bots for new ones when you get sick of them or want to try something different.

The robots are then subsonically cleaned and ready for the next person. It's like a sex library.

"Then of course we can tell her we don't need a replacement. We don't need her using our ship or our show to spy on you or us." William waves his hands around in aggravation.

"What's the other problem?" John asks, ignoring his brother's outburst.

"The male lightning cats came to the clinic."

William stops waving and sits upright. He doesn't bother hiding his surprise since he knows how private the tigers are, which makes my explanation a bit easier to communicate.

"What is the problem with them?" He sounds curious and isn't afraid to hide it, but John looks like he's bracing himself for bad news. The grip on his coffee cup has his knuckles turning a little white, his jaw clenched with tension. Their reactions are polar opposite of one another, which causes me to suppress a laugh.

"They haven't mated, have they?" John's eyes become a little wild as his imagination sends him spiraling. "Fuck, that's just what we need, them returning to their home planet. We do not have time to train a new streak as well as a new dragon and a naga in a few days." John wrings his hands before downing his mug of spiked coffee. Although I can understand his concern, I have a feeling that what's about to spill from Link's lips will be worse. I run a hand through my hair, waiting to see if

John will calm down, and his body finally relaxes a little.

"No, but Natalia is trying to force a mating. They think she's trying to force them into a rut, and none of them have any interest in mating with her. Trace, Sim, and Fuse are actually interested in her younger sister, Minx."

William nods behind his mug as John gets up to make himself another one. "Yes, Minx was who we were getting originally. She's a spare heir, so to speak, but she is an omega, so she is in high demand. Her matriarch wanted her to get some life experience but was sending the male cats she wanted her to form a streak with as well. Those five males are from the most prominent families on Iceen."

"But then Natalia showed up with them. She's in line for the matriarch role as she is the oldest, but she's a beta. We're pretty sure the matriarch was going to overlook her for her younger sister, the omega being a more attractive option because she will have powerful alpha mates. It wasn't until three days after we had left Iceen and were on the other side of the galaxy when we got a missive from the matriarch telling us we had the wrong daughter. How were we supposed to know that? Natalia had a forged letter from her mother telling us about the last-minute swap," William grumbles, and his agitation over getting played is obvious. "That's not our problem, but theirs. It turns out Natalia knocked her sister out and tied her up in a closet, and they didn't find her for a while because they weren't looking for her. The matriarch assumed she had left with us."

Fuck. Who would have thought we'd have such an international shitshow on the ship? I can't believe Natalia managed to get one over on the three brothers. It shows how crafty and cunning she is, which lends credence to why the male tigers are worried about her forcing a rut.

I'm just glad I'm not in Link's shoes right now, because how he maintains his cool professionalism when talking about something this screwed up is beyond me. But I have a feeling this story is far from over.

"And because the female lightning cats are rabid bitches, the matriarch decided that Natalia had shown initiative, even though she lied, and if she could convince these men to mate with her, then she would be suitable to be the heir. So I guess Natalia is getting desperate now that we are close to returning to Iceen, which is the deadline," John adds from between gritted teeth. If the guy was a cartoon, steam would be coming out of his ears.

"Holy shit, thank God I have normal parents. Mine don't care about anything like that. They just hoped I wouldn't mate with a kraken female who would kill me after breeding her." I shudder at the thought, and William holds his mug up to me in a salute.

"Cheers to not being eaten by your wife, Caspian."

Eric's not here to make a sly comment, but I hear one in my mind anyway.

"The other issue is that Maxsim and Echo are a couple. Apparently Echo is a very rare male omega."

"Holy shit! They almost never make it past their declaration. The female alphas and betas usually kill them." John's outburst is quite out of character for him, so I guess his Irish coffee is kicking in quickly. He sits back at his desk with another one in front of him, though I can't say I blame him. The mating rituals of the lightning cats are new to me too, and I almost need a drink after the drama that has unfolded.

"His parents were very protective. Apparently one of his fathers is also one, so they protected him and were able to mask it somehow. He appears as a beta, but Natalia found out and has been trying to kill him." John and William don't look surprised to hear that, so they definitely know more about their mating rituals than I do. I'm pretty much speech-less. "She wants Maxsim, though her being a beta is going to make breeding hard but not impossible. There are ways of triggering it if she's using omega hormones. I'm not sure how she thinks she can take an alpha knot though." Link frowns in thought, and I smile at his complete lack of guile.

"Maybe she likes pain," I comment.

"Maybe."

I look over at him to gauge his expression. He looks thoughtful before his eyes go blank like he's scanning his memory banks, and he's silent for a moment.

"Well shit, I guess we're going to need a new troupe of cats," William says to John as we wait for Link to do whatever it is he's doing.

"Or you could just swap Natalia out for the original female," I suggest. "It sounds like half the group wants to be with Minx. And maybe once Maxsim and Echo get to know her and she them, they might gel too. It sounds like it would be dangerous for Echo to return to Iceen, and if he and Max are a couple, I doubt he's going to want to either. Not to mention Lila didn't do herself any favors when she accidentally hit Natalia in the ass with lightning. Getting her to perform for Lila may be near impossible."

The two men can't hide their snickers. The door to the office opens and Eric walks in.

"But it was strange how Natalia wasn't able to absorb it," John muses. "I thought that was a lightning cat thing."

"It is, but it depends on the frequency. Some lightning cats can absorb other lightning, but if it vibrates at a different frequency, it can also be used as an attack. I guess Lila's differs from Natalia's. It could have been worse though. If it had hit someone else, it might have killed them," Eric points out, taking a seat.

That sobers us all up as Link's eyes come back into focus. "According to my search of the darknet, there is a black market drug that makes it possible for a beta to emit omega hormones that can trigger an alpha rut. This works with a lot of different species that have that biological trait. There also seems to be a high demand for betas who don't mind if an alpha forces his knot. It seems that there are quite a few people who get off on giving and receiving that pain."

"Do I sense a new line of Pleasure Bots in the making?" I joke as he makes notes on the screen on his arm.

"I got the feeling that maybe the betas weren't there voluntarily. The forum I found had people talking about how they liked it best when the betas struggled." Link's words have a feeling of disgust washing over me. I guess it doesn't matter where you go in the galaxy, there are dangerous people everywhere. "If we could provide them what they need, we could eliminate the need for betas to get hurt—unless they wanted to. We can even program in a struggle if that's what they like about it. It's disturbing, but there are people who like their bots to fight and scream." He has that distracted look that he gets when he's busy with a new idea.

Link really is perfectly situated to be part of the research and development division of the Pleasure

Bots business. He sees all the different species throughout the galaxy and can learn from their needs and desires. Even though he works as our doctor, he still sends notes back to his father with suggestions. "I'm not actually sure why we haven't designed a bot that can take an alpha's knot. That's definitely overlooking a big market and something that we should rectify."

"Okay, so I guess that means it is possible, and if Natalia has her hand on that drug, then they are in danger. I will message the matriarch and tell her that Natalia is not a good fit for our show, and that we would like the original female promised. If she refuses, we'll tell her that we will go with a new clan and offer the guys refugee status if they wish to stay. But their families are powerful, so they should be protected from any backlash. We may even threaten to tell them about what Natalia has been trying. The matriarch wouldn't want them to pull their support from her. I think her family only rules by the smallest of margins." John sighs. I know he doesn't like confrontation, so I'm sure one of the other brothers will end up dealing with Natalia's mother.

"Wait, why are you back so soon?" I ask Eric, suddenly realizing he was taking Lila to Xavier. "Where's Lila?" I sit up, a rush of worry prickling my skin.

"Relax, she's with Xavier. He'll protect her from anything. He wanted to see her on her own without an audience. Though I would have loved to see her reaction to his harem. She's still behind on her species research, and it's going to be a real eye-opener for her." He turns to his brothers. "I would like to arrange for Lila to see Saxon for some defense training either this afternoon, depending on how long Xavier takes, or tomorrow. I need to know she can defend herself physically if he's not able to trigger any of her magic. What happened with Dylan has made me worried about her safety. She's pretty much defenseless at this point."

"Josa is kind of aggressive toward Lila too, and the more Link shows an interest in her, the more aggressive Josa gets. Lila and Link are having drinks tonight, and I'm not sure if Josa overheard those arrangements or not," I chime in, feeling much like Eric does about her safety. Link's nurse is batshit crazy. Between the two of us, we haven't been very lucky lately with non-relationship drama. Hopefully Lila and Link work out. I would like Link as a bond mate, and it doesn't hurt that he's pretty on the eyes too.

Link squirms a little as Lila's grandpas study him carefully before Eric claps his hands. "That's awesome. I approve." His brothers both murmur their agreement before moving back to the subject of Lila's self-defense.

"I will speak to Saxon and make arrangements for tomorrow. That will be soon enough. And Link and Caspian are capable of protecting her from

Josa in the meantime if he tries anything, not to mention he should be on that return transport after it drops off the shifters from Fluxx." John sighs and runs a hand through his hair, his frustration evident in the movement. "You mentioned Lila isn't up to date on the circus species? Does she know about Saxon being a vampire?"

They all look at me, and I grimace. "I think so, but I will bring her up to speed tonight, or Link can during their date." I try to cover for my mate, but I don't think I'm fooling anyone.

Eric chuckles. "Let's not assume anything. I had to give her a heads-up on Xavier's harem."

Link finishes with his notes and rejoins the conversation. "I can do that. I probably have the most unbiased information to give her."

"Let's also put out a crew-wide announcement, something along the lines of aggression toward fellow crew members will not be tolerated and is grounds for instant dismissal. That should clear up any inquiries about Dylan and preempt the other dismissals that are coming. Both Natalia and Josa have been overheard being aggressive to other crew members before Lila arrived, so it shouldn't come as a surprise that their behavior toward Lila was the final straw." William sounds as irked as John looks. "We need to make sure Lila is protected at all times. We should probably assign her a bodyguard, but that would make her look weak."

I stand up and pace back and forth, trying to

come up with a solution that would help Lila while also preventing her from being a target. "What if we asked Xavier to be her bodyguard? Nobody would cross him. She has his mark on her back, so we could say they are exploring the attraction. Between him, Link, and me, Lila would never be alone."

"That's a good idea. I'll speak to him once they finish examining her powers. It actually wouldn't be a bad thing for her to take him as a mate, because then it wouldn't matter that she didn't have Skarrian abilities since she could potentially get some of his." Eric is in scheming mode.

"Hang on. Getting powers is not a good reason to mate someone," John cautions, narrowing his eyes on Eric. "I don't want that for Lila."

"Yeah, I don't think you have to worry about that. Lila is the *last* person we have to worry about mating for powers. She's still wrapping her head around the fact that she can be attracted to others even though she and I are now mated. The power thing isn't even registering with her." I try to reassure John, even though it's probably breaking Lila's confidence a little bit, but I'm sure she would hate for him to worry.

"Did she get shape-shifting powers?" William raises an eyebrow at me.

"She can take half form, but she wasn't able to fully shift into a kraken." I sit down so they can't see my dick harden at the reminder of what she looked like partially shifted. She was gorgeous. Her skin changed color, but unlike my mottled purple and blue complexion, she was pink and purple. Her tentacles weren't as thick as mine, and the top half of her body remained the same except for the color change. Her nipples were colored purple, and my mouth watered to wrap around them, but a first shift is not the time or place to scare her with my needs.

I must have gotten lost in my thoughts, because I jump when William claps his hands together. There's a little twinkle in his eye as he hears that his granddaughter can partially shift. "Well that's something at least. Maybe there's hope for her. Okay, Cas, make that call to your friend and let us know how it goes. I think we've got Lila's protection and education organized for now." He takes a deep breath, mentally cataloging the next steps as we all listen like school children. "Link's going to help educate her on the different species, and Eric, you speak to Saxon about defense training for Lila. I'm going to contact Iceen and do the ship-wide announcement to cover our asses. John, you're going to keep drinking your whiskey and relax, we've got it sorted. How about we all touch base this evening to update everyone?"

Now that William has given us our marching orders, we all agree on the game plan, and with that, Link and I leave the brothers to sort out the lightning cat situation.

As we walk down the corridor together, I can tell that Link has something he wants to say. He's been worrying his lip between his teeth so hard it's cracked open and I can smell the blood, so I stop and turn to face him. "Just say what's on your mind, Link. We've been friends for a long time now, nothing you say is going to upset me."

"You're really okay with her and me having drinks or more tonight?" he murmurs, as if saying the words any louder would impact my reaction.

I put a hand on his shoulder, and his eyes widen in surprise as I rub it lightly, trying to reassure him with my touch. Shifters are a very touchy-feely group, and even though Link isn't one, I'm hoping it will reassure him anyway. "Not at all. I knew the moment I saw yours and Xavier's attraction marks on her shoulders that this wasn't going to be a traditional one-on-one mating. Whether it's you or Xavier or other people entirely, I'm going to have to share her, and I'd much rather it be with people I'm friends with."

"Okay, well then, I plan to pursue her fully then," he announces matter-of-factly, wearing a skeptical look on his face like he's waiting for the fallout from his statement. Instead, it's the complete opposite. I'm *happy* for Lila and need to communicate my approval more clearly. My hand drifts from his shoulder to his cheek.

"Enjoy, my friend, and make sure you take good care of our girl." I wink and continue on to my living quarters. I need to make a call to Silac then pack up all of my belongings to move into Lila's place. The thought alone has my body and my beast thrumming with excitement. I want to be back before she returns from seeing the warlock. I bet she's going to need a drink after having her human mind blown.

CHAPTER FIVE

Lila

Xavier's voice caresses my ear, yet his mouth isn't anywhere near it. The sensation tingles down my spine, and I try not to shudder from the feeling. I spin to face the room. The mist I felt at my back is now gone, but I can *feel* him watching me. I can also hear murmured voices and make out shadowed forms, but no one steps forward to speak to me, which adds to the slight discomfort I'm now feeling. My heartbeat is racing and my adrenaline is high as I step farther into his living quarters. There's a strong aroma of incense, spicy and heady, in the air, and there's a hazy quality to the room, but I don't see an incense stick burning anywhere.

Looking around, I notice there's a meal area off to the side of me, but as I walk farther in, my eyes catch on the same kind of picture window that I have. Directly in front of it, however, is a sunken pit with cushions scattered about instead of a sofa like I have. Lounging on some of the cushions are the owners of the voices I heard. There are two women and the being I am assuming is the Milobar, and all of them are naked. The male Milobar is reclined on the cushions with his hands behind his triangular head, and he's very vocally enjoying a blow job from each of the girls. Yes, each of them has a cock in their mouth. This dude has two dicks, and not side by side like an Earth stingray, but one under the other. Looks like a fun time. A little prickle of desire floats through my body at the thought of double penetration.

"Oh yes, Lila, the taste of your arousal is exquisite." Xavier's words tickle my ear again. I drag my eyes away from the show and look around the room. I still can't see him, but I guess the group in the pit hears him because they finally realize they have an audience.

"Who the fuck are you?" the Milobar demands aggressively, pushing the women off of him and standing up. His raging hard-ons point straight out in front of him, and his whip-like tail flicks behind him. "No one is allowed in these living quarters." He climbs out of the sunken lounge and starts marching toward me. I'm frozen to the spot, my eyes locked on his impressive hard-ons. It's hard to take someone seriously when they look like this guy does, but self-preservation kicks in and I back up quickly, holding up my hands defensively in front of me. I know Xavier is watching and waiting to see what I'll do. I'm sure he's expecting me to cower, but I don't. I straighten my shoulders and stand my ground. This guy's a naked stingray, and besides, I need to show people I can't be easily intimidated. I've got this.

"I'm Lila Adams, and I'm here to see Xavier." Well, one would assume that I said something shocking with the way the two women in the pit gasp. The struggle not to roll my eyes at their outburst is real.

"How dare you speak the warlock's name!" The stingray, I'm going to call him Steve, momentarily halts as he tries to wrap his head around me casually talking about Xavier like we've been lifelong friends. He sneers down at me. "You aren't worthy of the air he breathes, you pathetic human."

I shrug off the disappointment and hurt. "Maybe not, but he invited me, the *human*, here." Then I really put in the screws to this arrogant asshole. "Maybe he's grown tired of the same old meal day after day and wants a taste of something different and unique." He chuckles quietly in my ear but still doesn't appear from wherever he's hiding to help me out, and I guess Steve the stingray doesn't hear him.

Fuck my life.

A flash of jealousy flares in this guy's eyes, and both of the women are now out of the pit standing next to him. I was so taken in by Steve and his raging double hard-ons that I hadn't even seen them move. There's no denying it, I was dick-matized.

They have features very much like Xavier's, as well as high cheekbones, pointy, decorated ears, and similar skin tones. Theirs is a washed-out version of his pretty lavender skin, and they don't have anywhere near the amount of silver markings he has. Both of them wrinkle their noses at me like I smell bad. The temptation to sniff myself to see if I really *do* stink starts to feel like an itch I need to scratch, but I can't let them bother me.

"Please, he would suck you dry in no time. You have no discernable power at all," the pretty redhead says, looking me up and down, and I can tell she's not impressed with what she sees. I return the favor, and I can tell you the drapes do indeed match the carpet, or should I say shag pile rug. Do warlocks not believe in grooming?

"As long as he sucks the right things, I really don't care if he has a mouth like a hoover. I'd rather experience death by orgasm than anything painful."

I watch as the two girls scowl at my response, clearly not liking where I'm going with this.

"He wouldn't lower himself to put his mouth on you. He'd only have to put a finger on your skin and you'd be a hollow husk." This is the other girl. She's a petite little thing who looks like a dark-haired

Tinker Bell. I almost want to shake her to see if any fairy dust will fall out.

"I'm good with fingers too, or tentacles or dicks, whatever he wants to put on or *in* me." I shrug casually to show that I am far from picky and have an appetite for anything.

"How do you know about that?" Tinker Bell asks, and I'm momentarily confused, but before I can work out what she's referring to, the Milobar comes at me again. I think he's fed up with this entire conversation, but I could keep going back and forth for days if it continues to piss off Xavier's harem.

With Steve the stingray coming in hot, however, I have no choice but to shut my mouth and prepare for the showdown.

I brace myself. He gets close enough to grab me, and two things happen at once. First, Xavier's mist solidifies behind the Milobar, and second, I jam my knee into his still erect dicks. Like any male, the Milobar goes down like a sack of shit, groaning loudly, but his tail whips out in response, its frightening barb coming directly for my chest. I close my eyes, accepting my fate will be just like that Aussie dude's, as slight disappointment that I won't be able to see what Xavier has to offer echoes in my mind. But instead of the poisonous weapon burying deeply into my chest, it slams into an invisible barrier and snaps in half, and the Milobar screams in pain. Huh, guess he didn't see that one coming.

There's an aura of fury in the atmosphere, and the two women are now cowering together as the Milobar's body lifts off the ground and begins to hover in the air. Xavier's mist surrounds his form, and the Milobar starts to thrash his arms around. "No, please, wait! I was just protecting you," he pleads, trying to breathe between his shouts of pain. This time, Xavier's voice has lost the soft, caressing tones he used with me, and there is no mistaking his rage. My nerves are a little frayed at the end, and I can feel my pulse thumping in my ears as I watch what's happening to Steve.

"Do you think I need protecting? Am I not one of the most powerful people in the galaxy, or have you forgotten, Mithus?" Oh, okay, not Steve then.

"I just thought—" Mithus argues, but Xavier cuts him off.

"You are not here to think, you are here to be my food. You are nothing more than a meal and occasional cum receptacle. Do not mistake my previous use of your body as affection. You are not powerful enough to be my intimate. None of you are."

He aims that last statement at the two women who are now sobbing, their hair rising with the sheer power Xavier is pushing out. Cuts appear across their bodies as his power pulses all around us. Their faces twist in pain, which is weird because it feels like a tickle of pleasure to me, and I almost giggle.

"I'm sorry. Will you please forgive me?" Mithus begs the still shrouded Xavier.

Xavier says nothing, but Mithus's back arches in agony. "Please don't drain me, *please*." I watch as Mithus starts to shrivel in front of me, kind of like a time lapse of a dead body turning into a mummy. It's agonizingly slow, and I cringe away from the squealing sounds he's making. It's too much, so I shove my hands over my ears and close my eyes against the gruesome sight. I try to think of something else that will distract me until the torture is finished, but all I can see is Mithus's body withering away.

There is no mistake about it. Xavier is fucking powerful.

It abruptly cuts off, and a hand lands on one of my arms, causing me to pull my fingers away from my ears. I peek open an eye and find Mithus on the floor in a fetal position, but he still looks to be alive, barely, but he's breathing.

"Get him out of my sight," Xavier says to someone, his hand still on mine.

A group of people have appeared out of a side door and are gathered around, watching the show. A bipedal grasshopper man leaves the group, comes over, and picks Mithus up. Two other women, who give me death glares as they walk past, gather up the two who have been battered by Xavier's powers. Before they can all leave, Xavier speaks again.

"Hear this and tell everyone. Lila is off limits.

She may come and go as she pleases. She is my guest, and as such, you should treat her well. If I find out anyone is mistreating her, what I did to Mithus will be like a space walk." His tone is deadly, and despite not being able to see him, they all cower and nod before hurrying out of the room.

Silence descends, leaving only the sound of my rapid breathing between us as I try to figure out what to say. It doesn't take me long before my curiosity gets the better of me.

"What did you do to him?" I ask as Xavier guides me toward the sunken lounge, but I balk, knowing what had just been going on in there. A burst of power floats through the room and the cushions are replaced with new ones. A table is now in the middle of the cushions, set with an exotic-looking pot and two cups. There's what looks like a hookah bubbling and smoking next to it.

He still hasn't answered me as he helps me take a seat at the low table. Once I'm comfortable, he chooses a seat next to me, still shrouded.

"I punished him, as is my right, Lila. He insulted me by attacking you." There is no remorse in his voice as he waves a mist-covered limb and the teapot floats over to pour liquid into each of the cups.

"Will he survive?" I ask him, not really caring either way, but I am curious. Xavier snorts, sounding disgusted.

"Yes, unfortunately. I didn't think it would be a

good start to our courtship if you saw me kill one of my harem members despite the insults he flung at you," he grumbles, sounding quite put out, and I try to smother a smile. I have come to realize that the alien species I have encountered are quite primal in their ways. It's fascinating seeing him temper his base instinct so as not to frighten me, and I can't say I don't internally squeal that he cares enough to do it.

"Our courtship?" I prompt, wanting to know more about what he thinks is between us.

"Of course!" He sounds surprised that I questioned him. "I assumed that with my mark on your shoulder and yours on mine, you would be amenable to such a thing."

"I'm not saying I'm not, I'm just surprised that you return the interest, especially with a harem." I'm feeling awkward again because it really is disconcerting sitting here looking at mist. "And they were not wrong about my power level, it is nonexistent."

Xavier shuffles closer to me and leans in so that his mist drapes across my neck and shoulder, and a shiver flows through me at the feel of it. "Oh, but *phoeall*, it isn't your power that is delicious, it's your raw emotions—your desire, your fear, your fascination, and your wide-eyed exuberance. I haven't ever tasted anything like it, and I only got a small bite of it the other day. No, you are a smorgasbord for someone like me, and I wish to devour you." His mist dissolves, and I'm left looking at a deliciously sexy man who is staring at me like he's starving. His purplish-blue eyes twinkle with amusement as he calls me that word I still don't understand and my chip doesn't translate.

Xavier is not wearing his armor like he was the first time I saw him. Instead, he has on a flowing pair of black, wide-legged pants and a tank top which lets me see all his lovely lavender skin and silver markings. His indigo hair is down around his shoulders, and the jewelry in his ears, nose, and eyebrows all have turquoise accents today.

"What you did to Mithus, is that what you want to do to me?" I ask as he strokes a finger over my hand before taking it in his. My body shivers with need, but I try to tamp that shit down hard.

"No. I absorbed Mithus's power, which is why he shriveled up like a husk. He will regenerate, but the process is painful. He was punished." He drops my hand and passes one of the full teacups to me. "Drink this, it will help me assess your power levels." He leans back on his pillow, indolent and sensual, and waits as I blow to cool it down and take a small sip of the startling green liquid. It has a fresh minty taste, so I take a larger sip. He smiles, pleased. "No, drinking emotions does not have the same effect as divesting someone of their power. I can assure you I can make it very pleasurable for you and you will enjoy it." It's a threat and a promise all in one.

"You know that I'm mated to Caspian now, right?" I ask, and he smirks.

"And knocked up, if what I hear on the circus grapevine is correct." He grabs the long pipe sticking out from the hookah and takes a drag from it before blowing out smoke rings, which seem to float in the air.

"This doesn't bother you?"

He shrugs nonchalantly before waving a finger through the hovering smoke. "Why would it? You are Skarrian, and polyamory is common amongst them. I'm sure he gave you his blessing when he saw my mark on your shoulder. I don't doubt he gave you blessings for both Link and me." He sips his own tea now.

"No, you're right, he encouraged it, but to be honest, I'm not sure I can compete with a harem of exotic beings. Nor do I want to." His eyes close slowly in a blink, and his face blanks of all emotions. "It will only be a matter of time before you're bored with me and you return to them."

After speaking the words out loud, I can tell I truly meant them as a rock sits lodged in my throat.

"Ah, but won't you do the same? You have a five strikes and you're out rule. It would never be a long-term thing for us anyway," he points out and then he sits up. "How about I make you a deal. I will assess your power problems, and once that is sorted, let me feed from you four times. We will both get something out of it, and then we can say our goodbyes. I will go back to my harem, and you will move onto someone new. I won't have to worry about you growing feelings, and you will get to experience all that being with a warlock has to offer."

His arrogance knows no bounds, but I can't deny I'm not tempted. I mean, what are the chances that I'll develop feelings? But is it considered cheating on Cas if I go into this knowing nothing long term will become of it? How the fuck do Skarrians make a decision about long-term futures in the time it takes to fuck someone four times? Jesus, that could be within a day, and then you have to say see ya. No wonder Magenta gets around. It looks like I may be doing the same thing.

What is the likelihood that he and I are compatible? I couldn't stand to have a partner who had to feed from other people. I know that sounds hypocritical when I may have multiple partners, but Cas and I are mated. There's no *sorry, I'm bored now*, or *I don't like your flavor anymore, time for a new harem*. It's a permanent connection, and from the looks of things when I walked in and the reaction from the three who attacked me, Xavier is not just feeding off the power of his harem.

Then there's his attentiveness to me. His harem certainly seemed surprised when I called him by his first name and had been invited into his personal space, not to mention his very blatant smackdown. It seems like it might be out of character for him, so maybe developing feelings isn't as one sided as he makes it out to be.

I shake my head at the enticing being next to me. "I'm sorry, I'm just not sure. I need to talk to Caspian first. The last thing I want to do is upset him. I'm really happy with him." I won't meet the warlock's eyes, but a finger under my chin has me lifting my gaze to meet his. He has a surprised look of wonder on his face.

"Lila, I have never been turned down before. Everyone is always clamoring to get at my power. I can't say this is a refreshing turn of events." He sounds bewildered, and I smother a smile.

"Why would I be clamoring for your power? I don't know anything about you or it. You could be evil for all I know. And what would I need power for?"

His look of confusion turns to a smirk. "You think I'm evil?"

I take another sip of my tea, thinking of the best way to word my answer. "I don't know. I don't think so because I actually feel really comfortable around you. Your power feels good against my skin when you're using it, but Dylan proved I am a horrendous judge of character. He had me completely fooled."

Xavier's eyebrows jump when I mention his power feeling good. "Did my power not hurt you when I used it against those three fools?" He leans in again, eager for my answer, his chest almost brushing against mine.

"No, it felt like little hummingbird wings were brushing across my body. It tickled."

"Hmm." He rubs one pointy ear, playing with the silver jewelry in it. "Dylan was a man whore and a lying asshole. You weren't the first one to fall victim to his smile. Many crew members did until he got what he wanted, usually sex." He's trying to reassure me, but he fails.

"The thing is, he never implied he wanted sex with me. I thought he was gay and becoming my best friend. I guess I latched onto the first kind voice instead of being wary like I always am. I've learned from my mistakes. I won't trust so easily again."

"Ah, of course, and my proposal sounds too good to be true, yes?" He leans back again, smiling like he's figured things out. "I will prove to you that I can be a friend, and then maybe we can be friends of convenience."

Friends of convenience? Oh. "You mean friends with benefits," I tell him, and he grins.

"Yes, that, four times." He holds up four fingers and wiggles them around, and I roll my eyes.

"We will see. How about we do what I came here to do first?"

"Ah yes, your Skarrian powers that the water is not activating. Okay, let us see what we can do with you."

CHAPTER SIX

Xavier

Seeing Lila in my living space is doing something funny to my insides. I was furious when my harem tried to attack her, and it sparked a rage inside me like I've never felt before. Then, when she told me about how my power did nothing but caress her body when I lashed out at them, I became even more intrigued with this little ball of emotions.

Lila is so open and unguarded, her residual feelings float around her. Just being next to her is a meal for me, and my body absorbs some of what she constantly puts out, which is not how it usually works. I can only imagine what it would be like to actually feed on her when I'm inspiring more intense emotions like anger or lust. She fascinates me like no one else has in a long time. My harem members guard their emotions like a dragon guards its hoard, giving me nothing unless I give something in return. I am so sick of being used for what I can do for them or how I can make them feel. Someday I want what Lila talked about, someone to love me for me and not who I am or what I can do or give them, like what my parents have—true soulmate love. For now, I am happy and excited to entice this gorgeous snack into my bed. My cock hardens just from imagining how responsive she would be.

I see her shiver as the tea starts to take effect. I'm lowering her emotional defenses, her inhibitions, to maneuver my way through the mental layers that everyone has. It makes it easier for me to get into her mind to see if anyone has been in there.

"Link scanned me this morning and said there are no spells on me," she tells me, looking somewhat sad, and her emotions take on a slightly bitter taste which makes me want to remove that sadness.

"No, Link is right, but a cyborg scan can't pick up mental manipulation, and that's what I'm going to check for."

Her breathing increases, and that sadness becomes fear, tasting like mud on my tongue. That's very intriguing. Fear is usually one of the most delicious emotions for me, but from Lila it is not nice at all. I have the urge to change that and make her feel *anything* but fear so I can erase that taste, which again is not something I usually experience, and it leaves me feeling confused.

"Dylan told me to guard my mind around a warlock, that you could take hold of it and control me and I would never know the difference."

Fuck, what a jealous dick. He didn't want her to have Caspian, but he didn't like my interest in her either. I guess that sting of rejection made him petty.

"Yes, a warlock can get into your mind and plant subconscious commands there. I'm not going to deny it, but you would have had to come into contact with one, and I don't know of any who have been to Earth recently, and the only ones on this ship are me and a couple members of my harem, but they aren't powerful enough to do something like that to you. That's why I'm going to delve into your mind a little to make sure no one has."

A floaty smile appears on Lila's face, and I know the tea is definitely working now. I should be able to slip into her mind without any barriers, but I also want to do it with her consent. I wasn't kidding when I told her I wanted her enthusiastic consent, I meant it for everything.

Sitting up, I wriggle closer so my leg is against hers. Taking her hand in mine, I look her in the eye. She tries to dip her gaze away from mine, and I curse that fucking dragon.

"Lila, I need you to look into my eyes. I am going to link our minds, but I promise I'll be gentle and I'll only search for any hidden warlock manipulation," I tell her, and she sways with the sound of my voice. "Before I continue, I want to be sure I have your consent."

"Yes, Xavier, I trust you." Her smile is a little goofy, and I feel something lurch inside my chest at her words. The fact that she says she trusts me means the world, even if she's slightly influenced by the drink. Sure, she doesn't understand that warlocks are master manipulators and love mind games, but I have no desire to play them with Lila. I love how open and accepting she is.

It's refreshing, and I can't deny how attracted I am to her. I'm so tempted to plant a command in her mind to let go of all caution and allow me to fuck her, but that wouldn't be as satisfying as her coming to me on her own. I also promised her I wouldn't do anything nefarious. No, this time I'll let anticipation and the rush of the chase be my appetizer. Delayed gratification has never been something I considered, but people say when you have to work harder for things you appreciate them more.

Her pretty green eyes meet mine, and because of her lower barriers, I'm able to access her mind easily. I try to do the right thing and not pay too much attention as I shuffle through her thoughts and memories, but it's so hard. Her latest memories, the ones that caused her the most recent pain, are right there on the surface. Dylan's aggressive attack and nasty words make me want to gut him, and he needs to thank the brothers because he would not have survived if they hadn't kicked him off the ship.

I would have made sure of it. There are also some hot as fuck images of Link eating Lila's pussy like it's a peach, and her kinky as fuck mating with Caspian. My dick throbs and I groan at those memories. It seems like Lila hasn't got as many inhibitions as a normal human. I guess her Skarrian blood makes her open-minded.

I can't get distracted, and I need to push past these memories and go further back. Getting my shit together, I speed up my scan and Lila's life flashes through my mind as I search for any sign of warlock interference. There's nothing until I reach her early childhood, and it's so small I almost miss it, but there it is, a small spark of warlock interference. I recognize the signature. In fact, I recognize it because it is my *father's*.

I hover over that little spark, but I can't seem to penetrate it, and I don't want to slice into it because there's a good chance it will hurt her, so I try a different approach.

"Lila, honey, what's your earliest memory? Can you remember your parents?"

She slowly shakes her head. "No, though I had a brief flash of something when my grandpas told me a story that my parents had told them. All I remember was a floating stuffed animal. My earliest memory is when I was living in my first foster home. I think I was about five, and they had a party for their oldest child. They had a huge birthday cake for her. I remember wishing that I could have a birthday cake like that too." I'm not sure what a birthday cake is, but the sadness in Lila's tone stabs at my chest, and now I want to make sure that Lila gets one. I will ask John, he will know what it is.

I pick away at the seams of the warlock interference, and I get flashes of memories, but I don't allow Lila to see them just yet. There must be a reason my father locked these memories away, and if they are something traumatic, I don't want her to be upset.

I allow myself to seep into the memory, and I'm shocked to find that both my mother and father, as well as myself, are in it.

"Liliana, these are our old friends, Xylene and Cronus, and their son, Xavier." A blonde-haired lady with the same color eyes as Lila introduces us. The little girl is probably four, and she's hiding behind her father's legs. He's the spitting image of the Adams brothers and has the same dark hair as all of them and Lila.

I'm probably about eight, but I don't have any memory of this meeting at all. Did my parents erase or hide it from me as well? I keep unraveling it.

"Xavier, why don't you take Liliana and show her some of those fun spells you've been working on?" my dad encourages, so I hold out my hand for the little girl. She takes it without any words, but as soon as she does, a flash of purple light wraps around our interlocked hands and all four parents gasp.

I just about drop the memory in disbelief. It

can't be what I think it is. My parents wouldn't erase this, would they?

"Oh my God." My mother gasps, putting a hand over her mouth.

"Is that what I think it is?" Lila's mom asks, and both of my parents nod, wearing troubled looks on their faces.

"Yes, Liliana is Xavier's intimate. I guess soulmate would be the best description, but it is so much more than that," my mom explains.

"No, that can't be. She's in enough danger already, so to be the soulmate of the heir of the warlock empire is just going to put an even larger target on her back." Lila's dad sounds desperate.

"They are too young. He can't feed off of her exclusively. This has never happened before. Intimate bonds are not supposed to trigger until their late teens." My mom sounds shocked.

"Maybe it's because she's in danger. You need to tell us more," my dad says, pressing Lila's parents.

The light dies down between us, and it's obvious that neither of us have a clue what just happened. I'm looking at my parents for answers, but Lila starts to giggle.

"That was pretty, Xavar, do it again," she says in a cute little voice, and I can see myself smile at her butchering my name.

"Go on, just sit over there so we can talk." My dad points to a nearby tree.

I watch on in amazement, stunned at what I'm learning, as young me leads young Lila over to a tree where we sit down. I start to show her how I can make fireworks in my hand, which is the fun spell Dad just taught me, but luckily I was a nosy kid and I listened to the conversation.

"What do you mean she's in danger already?" my mom asks Lila's parents as the four of them take a seat at a nearby picnic table.

I'm assuming we're on Earth, but I don't remember ever going before I joined the circus.

"We're being watched every time we leave the house." Lila's mom sounds so desperate.

"Do you know who it is?" my dad asks, leaning forward, but Lila's dad shakes his head.

"No, we can never see or catch anyone, but I'm worried it's going to escalate."

"Why would they be watching you?" my mom inquires, looking confused, and Lila's parents exchange a glance.

"Can you put up a sound barrier?" Lila's mom requests, and I watch as my dad waves his hand and a barrier appears. They continue talking, but I can't hear a thing.

Fuck! The meeting goes on for a little while, and I can see my parents' shocked reactions to whatever Lila's parents told them, but Lila herself draws my attention away as she claps and laughs.

"They are so pretty, Xavar, can I do that?" She goes to touch them, but I pull my hand away and the fireworks disappear. Her bottom lip drops and starts to tremble, and I see the look of panic cross younger Xavier's face.

"No, no, don't cry," I beg her. "I didn't want you to get hurt." The lip stops trembling, and both younger me and current me breathe a sigh of relief.

Younger me wraps an arm around her shoulders and she snuggles into it. She looks up at my face as she traces a finger across my pointy ears.

At the time, I had no jewelry in them. I didn't get any until I was older.

Her hand drifts to my cheekbones and the light markings on my skin. "You're so pretty, Xavar, and so clever. I'm going to marry you when I get older, and then I can kiss you like Mommy kisses Daddy." She drops her hand and rests her head on my shoulder as younger me wrinkles his nose in disgust, but I don't say anything nasty to her. She closes her eyes and smiles as I watch our parents continue to talk.

How is this memory in Lila's brain? It's not actually hers but *mine*, I realize with shock. It's all from my point of view. So not only have Lila's memories been removed, but this one was deliberately planted, and it must have been one of my parents who did it.

Again, I almost drop the memory at that realization, but seeing the barrier lower, I quickly tune into what our parents are saying.

"Promise me that if anything were to happen to us, you will protect Lila," her mother begs.

"Of course, Alina. We will raise her as one of our own," my mom assures them, but Lila's dad shakes his head.

"No, if the worst happens, wipe her memories and take away her powers. The safest thing for her would be to live as a nobody on Earth. Make sure you change her name so that my parents can't find her either, because they will, and then the target will be on her back again," Lila's dad implores.

"But what about Xavier? Lila is his intimate. He will need her." My mom sounds upset.

"Your son has other options. He can have a harem. Lila's life is more important." He has a stubborn set to his jaw, but his wife puts a hand on his shoulder as my parents gear up to argue.

Thankfully, Lila's mom is more reasonable than her dad. *"Don't be like that, Marcus. When Xavier is powerful enough and ready to find his intimate, you can tell him about her. Now that they have found one another, he won't ever spark on anyone else, will he? I'm sure he will question you two about it one day, and then you may tell him."*

"Then yes, we will do as you have asked." My dad sounds resigned, and that's where the memory stops.

I try to dig a little deeper, but there is no sign of Lila's lost memories, which means my parents must still have them. I need to speak to them immediately.

Sighing, I pull gently out of Lila's mind. She's in a trance-like state, and I don't wake her just yet as I run my hands through my hair in frustration. Why didn't my parents tell me any of this once I was old enough? But then I have never spoken to them about wanting or needing an intimate, and I guess those were the instructions issued by Lila's parents.

Fuck, my thoughts continue to wreak havoc in my mind.

Now what do I tell Lila when she wakes up? I need to speak to my parents before I tell her anything, but she's going to be so disappointed if I tell her I found nothing. Maybe I can distract her. My eyes rake over her body, and I look at her in a whole new way. Before I dove into her mind, I would have been happy to fuck her four times and see her on her merry way, but now that I know differently, a wave a pure possessiveness rushes through me and I squeeze my hands into fists to stop myself from reaching for her. Everything makes sense now. It explains my extreme reaction to her and how I am absorbing her residual emotions, which is an intimate thing, and I don't know how I didn't consider it earlier. All I want to do now is take her into my room and fuck her until I seal myself to her in the Skarrian way then do it again the warlock way.

Do I tell her about this, or do I wait and let her get to know the real me and not the playboy prince I project to everyone around me? Shit, and my harem. I need to get rid of them, but how am I going to feed in the meantime? Saxon will help me out, but maybe I can talk to Lila's mate and see if he is willing to feed me as well until I can get Lila to bond with me.

My emotions are a confused mess when I hear a door open and someone steps into the room. Whirling, I put myself between Lila and the intruder. Standing there is my head harem girl, Elyan. She's wearing a flimsy see-through robe, and I can feel her hunger float through the air. When it hits me, I recoil in disgust. She sees my reaction, and her sexy pout turns to a frown.

"You told me to come find you next time I needed to feed." Elyan is the strongest of my harem and likes to feed from me because she gets a temporary boost, but she's still nowhere near my power levels. In the past I didn't care, but the thought of feeding her now turns my stomach. Shit, that's going to be a problem if I feel the same way about feeding from others.

"I'm busy. Get one of the others to see to your needs," I snap, waving her away. I see the hurt in her eyes, but I have no time to soothe hurt feelings now, especially when I have never asked for feelings to be involved, apart from the superficial ones of course.

She huffs, turns, and flounces back through the doorway, and it slides closed behind her. Thankfully she didn't notice Lila, because she can be a vindictive little bitch if she thinks that my eye is wandering. She's vicious whenever she sees Saxon on the ship. He thinks it's hilarious.

Turning back to my intimate, I help her recline on the cushions and allow her to come out of the meditative state the tea put her in. If I happen to wrap my arms around her and hold her until she shows signs of being conscious, well, we won't tell anyone about it.

CHAPTER SEVEN

Lila

My body is warm and comfortable as I blink my eyes a couple of times. It's like I've woken from a long nap, but the last thing I remember is drinking tea with Xavier. Turning my head, I find the gorgeous warlock fast asleep, his arms wrapped around me as he spoons me from behind. That's why I feel the way I do, and I don't hate the feeling. I know the sexy creature is only interested in a friends with benefits arrangement, but I can't help feeling like I want more with him. There's just something about him that draws me to him, and I want to explore that. I'm just not sure if we can keep sex off the table while we get to know each other. Even now, with his arms wrapped around me in a very nonsexual way, my body rages with desire. This man lights a fire in my pussy, and I think the only thing that's going to put it out is him.

But then I remember what Cas said about my fuck me vibes, and I mentally slap myself. Of course those future children of mine are fucking with my body. I can't wait to gross them out one day by telling them stories about what a horny bitch they made their mother.

I try to ease away from the sleeping man, lest my fuck me vibes start affecting him too. Or maybe they already are and it's the only reason he's interested in me. No, that can't be right, because his mark appeared on my shoulder before Caspian's beast knocked me up. I breathe out a sigh of relief and decide to stay and enjoy my moment with the man. Not to mention he owes me an explanation. I want to know if he found anything in my mind.

"God, Lila, could your thoughts be any louder?" Xavier mumbles, pulling me tighter against him, his dick hardening against my ass.

I freeze, even though I'm dying to grind back against his erection. "Did you really hear my thoughts?" I ask him quietly, not sure if I'm happy about that or not.

One of his hands slips up to cup my boob, and he nuzzles my neck, nipping the tender skin. The throb in my core almost has me moaning out loud, but I manage to stifle it. Stupid fuck me vibes. "No, but I can feel your desire, your worry, and your curiosity," he tells me, his lips brushing against my ear. "And it's all I can do to stop myself from feeding from you. Your emotions are mine to devour, but not without your permission."

What would it hurt to let him have a little taste of me? I wonder what four rounds of sex actually consist of? I never thought to ask. Does oral count? Is it when we both orgasm? Is it penetration, and how would that work for lesbians? Fuck my life, why are there so many questions and who the fuck do I ask?

"*Phoeall*, what are you thinking? You're squirming like a sandar worm." He releases his hold long enough for me to roll and face him. When I do, I almost get lost in his eyes once more. There's a feeling of familiarity and comfort between us that I really don't understand.

I take a deep breath and feel a blush roll over my cheeks. "I'm lost, if I must be honest. One part of me, a big part if I'm honest, wants to ride you like I want to win the grand national, but another part of me, the sensible I want to kick my own ass part, says I have questions that need to be answered, and I think only another Skarrian can answer them for me."

He smirks before leaning in and placing a gentle kiss on my lips, and then he rolls away from me and stands up, adjusting his raging hard-on which is tenting his loose pants. "Of course. Far be it for me to rush you into something you are not ready for. Go and have your questions answered. I will be awaiting your return, but for now, you have awoken a fierce hunger in me, and I must feed." He grimaces apologetically.

His words stab at my heart, and I just about recoil with the pain. Why do I feel this way about someone I'm not even bonded to? It's yet another question to be answered. Is monogamy expected with the appearance of marks? Surely not, because species like Xavier's can't survive like that. So why does it hurt so much to hear him say he is going to feed on someone else? I'm such a hypocrite when I'm going to go find my mate and fuck my frustration out with him.

"Okay, of course, I understand," I tell him and turn to leave, but he grabs my hand and stops me.

"I wish I could feed from a Pleasure Bot, because I can feel your annoyance and hurt, but I can't. They produce no emotions and have no powers for me to feed from. I am so sorry if this hurts you." His eyes are cloudy with concern, but I just pat his hand with my free one, trying my best to reassure him.

"It's okay, I completely understand. Go and use your harem. That's what they are there for, and they'll still be there when whatever we are doing has run its course. You don't want to upset them while I'm trying to figure things out."

Look at that, I can seem reasonable, even if all I want to do is stab Mithus and those two bitches over and over again. I grit my teeth and pull myself away from his hand, climbing out of the sunken lounge and making my way to the door. The lack of a physical connection causes a tinge of pain in my chest. When I turn back, he's looking at me with a frown on his face.

"Don't you want to hear what I found in your mind?" he asks, changing the subject, which is probably a good thing because I'm feeling ragey as fuck. I wonder if this is what happens when the fuck me vibes don't get satisfied. There's no other reason for me to want to go postal and murder anyone who gets near him.

I steer clear of any of his things, lest I pick them up and start throwing them around the room.

"Not right now." I can't help the abruptness in my tone, and I don't turn to look at him so he doesn't see the seething jealousy burning in my eyes.

Before I can take another step, however, the blasted man appears in front of me and grabs me with both hands, causing me to flinch.

"Lila, you're so angry. I have an idea. Would it be okay for me to feed on your anger? Then there would be no need for me to use my harem," he suggests, raising an eyebrow, and I grab the lifeline he just threw me.

I give him a short nod and brace myself, but it just feels like my anger is draining to the place on my arms where his hands touch my skin. Then, with a tingle, it starts to flow into his hands. Xavier closes his eyes and moans, throwing his head back as I start to feel less and less mad. His skin begins to glow like he's suddenly bioluminescent, and his hair starts to float around his head.

My eyes widen in amazement as the fury leaves me completely, leaving me only with a sense of hurt. That's when he takes his hands off of me, even though his eyes are still closed and he has a look of bliss on his face.

"Holy fuck. I never knew it would feel like that," he whispers cryptically as his eyes open slowly and the glowing floating thing stops. He's staring at me like I'm the second coming of the messiah.

"I'm sorry thinking about me feeding on my harem made you angry," he says in a quiet voice, tipping his head to the side. "Would it be better if I asked someone else to help me until you are ready?"

"But who? Who would you feed from who isn't going to make me turn into a hulk with jealousy, and why did that happen?" My rambling is starting to get the better of me, because I understand none of this.

His eyes shutter and he turns from me. Like that's not fucking suspicious. "I could feed off Caspian or Link if they were amenable. Would that be preferable to you, since you wear both their marks as well?"

Okay, he's not going to tell me why, so I will come back to that. I think about his suggestion and how I would feel about him feeding off my mate and potential lover, and the only feeling that inspires is more fuck me vibes. "Yes, I think that would be acceptable." It's all I can do to stop myself from squirming at the sexually explicit direction my mind is heading. I shake my head, trying to compose myself again, and focus on the subject at hand. "But I didn't think you could feed from Pleasure Bots."

He chuckles. "Link isn't a Pleasure Bot. Cyborgs have feelings and emotions as well. They are not all nanotechnology, they have an organic makeup. Pleasure Bots are all nanotechnology, which is just a sophisticated robot that has no feelings and emotions, though they can be programmed to react a certain way."

"Would it be sexual?" I ask, unable to contain my curiosity.

"It would depend on them. It doesn't have to be, as you just experienced, it's just the most fun way to feed."

"Is it sexual with your harem? You have sex with all of them?" I think back to what I saw when I first came into his quarters.

"Yes it is, and yes I do."

I feel that rage and seething jealousy welling up inside me once more. Fuck, I want to slap myself in the face. Why am I like this? Taking a deep breath, I hold out my hand, and he takes it, absorbing the emotions with another moan. His pupils expand like he's getting high, and he smiles goofily. If I didn't know better, I'd think my jealousy was making him happy.

"You are a sensory buffet, Liliana," he coos, and I yank my hand away from him, my anger changing to fear.

"How did you know that was my name?" I ask, and his goofy smile changes to a frown again.

"I'm sorry, I saw it in your memories. Does it upset you? You knew I was going to shuffle through them to see if I could figure out what was going on with your powers."

My fear dies away, and I feel a little sheepish. "Yeah, okay, I'm sorry. Today's been a bit of an emotional rollercoaster. I'm a little more sensitive than I normally am," I apologize, and I can see the sympathy in his eyes.

"And I'm not helping, am I? Come on, Lila, go find out your information so that when I see you next time, you've wrapped your head around it and you can give me an answer. I will refrain from feeding from my harem until you do. I do have another option that will hopefully indulge me until you make up your mind, one that has no significant connection to me or you. Will that make you happier?"

"Do I know this person? Will they be gloating about it to me?"

Xavier shakes his head. "No, I don't think you do, but even if you do, they won't gloat or throw it in your face."

"Then yes, that is acceptable. I will ask Caspian and Link too, but I should have my answer for you this evening."

His face lights up. "Would I be able to see you this evening then?"

"I'm having drinks at the club with Link tonight, but you can join us if you want."

He shakes his head, but his smile doesn't drop. "No, that's alright. I wouldn't want to steal your attention away from the sexy cyborg. He deserves your full attention if this is a first date. I will find you tomorrow and organize my own date."

He escorts me to his door, and I give him a kiss on the cheek.

"It was a pleasure to see you, Lila. I can't wait to see you tomorrow," he tells me. "I will message your grandpas and tell them what I found. I also need to message my parents to ask them about something before I can try to fix what I think is blocking your powers."

"You actually found something?" I ask in surprise.

"Yes I did, and I think it will explain a lot for you, but I do have some questions of my own, so I will get them answered so that everything I tell you will be fact and not guesswork."

"That sounds reasonable. Okay, well, see you then." The door slides open, but it's hard to tear myself away from this man. It's like there's a force inside me begging me to stay with him.

"Why don't you message me when you get home from your date, even if you've got someone in your bed, so I can say goodnight to you?" I get the feeling he's as reluctant to say goodbye as I am. His hands are clenched at his sides like he's preventing himself from reaching out to me. Desire spreads through my veins at his restraint, and I almost give in, but I need to stick to the plan. Questions then answers, and then I can get my hands on my warlock.

"Okay, I will. Bye, Xavier."

I watch as the mist that he hides behind covers his body. "Bye, *phoeall*."

The doors slide closed, and I don't waste any time. I hurry to the elevator, using my communicator to locate Magenta. It tells me she's once again in the rec area where I had seen her during my first tour. I send her a 911 message, and it doesn't take long for her to respond. She tells me to meet her at the same cafe where we had a drink the first day. Was that just yesterday? It feels like a week ago.

I program in the name of the cafe because I don't have a clue where I am, let alone where I need to go. Thankfully my communicator works as a GPS, and when I get in the elevator, it tells me exactly what button to push. Before I know it, I'm seating myself at a table and ordering a drink. I know it's early, but this conversation calls for alcohol, so I pick something new that sounds delicious. They have a scale next to each of the descriptions, ranging from one drink to five. I pick something that has four little glasses next to it, hoping it's enough to give me a buzz without knocking me on my ass.

It's just popping up through the middle of the table when Magenta slides into the chair across from me, her breathing ragged and a sheen of sweat on her face.

"I got here as fast as I could. Is everything okay?" she asks, her look of concern making me smile. I've known her all of twenty-four hours, yet she was happy to drop what she was doing and come running. With Dylan's bullshit, I'm still wary of trusting so easily, but apart from the grandpas, Phillip, and Fiona, she's the only Skarrian I know who isn't related to me. I guess I could have asked Link. If he doesn't know something, he has access to information. I bite my lip, unsure now whether to ask her or not.

Her eyes widen, and she shakes her head, waving a dramatic finger. "Oh no you don't. I saw you second-guess yourself then. That fucking dragon has you questioning your friendships, doesn't he? Look, just because I'm as promiscuous as he was, that does not mean I see you as competition. There are plenty of men and women in the galaxy to go around, as far as I'm concerned. You're going to make a great wingwoman in that you're such a fucking novelty to all these people."

"What, because I'm the freaky human,

supposed Skarrian, who has no powers?" I ask dryly, sipping my drink. My taste buds explode and start weeping as I forcibly swallow and begin coughing at the unexpected kick.

Holy shit, that's strong. I feel like I just inhaled a blizzard. There's a menthol type flavor that makes me feel like I've been sucking on an iceberg, followed by something tart and citrusy. I feel like all my orifices pucker at once.

"What the fuck is that?" I ask, waving a hand at my drink, and Mags looks at it for the first time and blanches.

"Oh no, you got an Iceen freezie. They are especially on the menu for the lightning cats and people from colder climates. Not that the lightning cats ever grace us with their presence. Fucking Natalia wouldn't even spit on us if we were on fire, and she has those boys under her proverbial claws. Sad, really, because I wouldn't mind finding out what it was like to take one of those alpha knots, if you know what I mean." She winks, and I forget about my drink and frozen throat.

"Seriously? They have knots on their..." I gesture to my crotch, and Mags laughs and nods.

"Yup, and supposedly a spur too. It's like you're doubly locked in. You can't get away from a lightning cat. Apparently they can fuck for hours."

Well color me officially interested... and turned on. I'm like a walking, talking ball of sexual need, goddamn it. "Apparently?"

Her smile drops, and she looks disappointed. "Yeah, they very rarely mate outside of their species. Their families tend to disown them if they do."

"Well, now that you've brought up mating, I have questions, lots of questions, and these are not ones I want to ask my grandpas."

"Your grandpas are hot pieces of ass. I wouldn't mind being the meat in their triangular sandwich, if you get what I mean." She winks, and I roll my eyes.

"Yes, unfortunately I do." I gag and she laughs.

"But they are loyal to your grandma, which makes them off limits." Her smile is genuine, so I know she respects their boundaries and won't overstep just to get laid. I'm starting to feel a bit better about her. "Okay, shoot. Tell me what you need to know."

I spend the next hour getting the Skarrian version of the birds and the bees talk, and while Mags tends to overshare, I discover that a simultaneous orgasm is required to count. So hand jobs, finger banging, and oral sex are all still on the table as long as you don't orgasm at the same time. I know I was lucky to get an orgasm from any human guy I slept with, let alone at the same time as him. I guess I never had to worry about it, even if my Skarrian physiology hadn't kicked in, because all the Earth men I slept with sucked in bed.

CHAPTER EIGHT

Lila

A little bit later I receive a message from William asking me where I am. When he tells me I am about to meet Saxon the vampire, and he is going to give me a self-defense lesson, I almost order another drink. Screw the potency. Self-defense lessons with a blood drinking vampire? Now that's something I never thought I would ever hear, but if I've learned anything from my time on the ship, it's that I just need to fucking roll with it. If I worry too much, my brain will explode and leave chunky bits of Lila all over the place, and nobody's got time for that.

I send him my location, and he tells me to wait for him.

"What was that all about?" Magenta asks, leaning back in her chair and studying me like I'm in a damn petri dish. "You look like you're going to have a panic attack."

"William just told me my self-defense lesson, which I was expecting later on in the week, is today. Quick, I need to know everything about Saxon, because my stupid ass didn't finish my species research. Dylan told me a little, but I'm really not sure if I can take anything he said at face value. He told me all sorts of things about Xavier as well, and he's been nothing but sweet to me."

Magenta's eyes just about bulge out of her head at my description of Xavier. "Hold up a minute. Are you sure we're talking about the same person? The warlock is sweet?" She looks incredulous, like I'm telling her Earth is flat or that I have three breasts and six nipples.

"Yeah, and he's cuddly too." The more I divulge, the more her facial expression changes to one of fascination.

"How is mist cuddly?" She genuinely sounds curious.

"Oh no, he removed the mist. He's got these great forearms that feel really nice wrapped around your waist."

I think I could have knocked Magenta over with a feather, because she's speechless. When she finally gets her shit together, the words just burst out of her mouth.

"Powerful warlocks don't show themselves to people very often. I don't think many people in the circus can claim they have seen him in his real form. Maybe your grandpas and his harem. That's probably it."

I wave off her amazement. "Anyway, it's not Xavier that I need to know about, it's Saxon. Please give me the rundown on vampires."

"Okay, sure. Saxon is from the planet Vilax. They are a race of blood drinkers with extraordinary senses and heightened speed and strength. It's what makes them such great acrobats."

"I haven't seen their part of the show yet, but what you've described sounds much like the vampire legend from Earth."

Cool, I've got this shit—crosses, garlic, no reflection in the mirrors, sparkling like Edward Cullen… I am a vampire aficionado. I love me a sexy vampire book with a bit of blood play.

"Yeah, but most of the rest of the Earth vampire lore is crap. And don't call them vampires, they don't like it. The right term is sanguinistas. They prefer night to day because Vilax only gets five hours of sunlight everyday, so they are mostly nocturnal species. They aren't actually allergic to the sun or anything. They live in family clans, and they are born, not made, so they are not dead. They breathe, their hearts beat, and they eat normal food and drink, but they need blood as well. They are also somewhat immortal. They can heal most injuries, even decapitation, if you put their bodies back together, but they will not survive if you burn their hearts—yes, they have two."

She pauses like she's trying to figure something out in her head. "It's weird. They can drink from one another. You'd think that drinking from the same species would defeat the purpose of drinking blood, but it's not the amount that is the issue. They can't process the red blood cells that their own bodies produce, but they can process the red blood cells from either another sanguinista or other species, hence the need to drink blood from another source. They form clans much like a warlock's harem because the blood drinking process is quite intimate. The sanguinista's saliva produces an enzyme that makes it feel good, and if they don't use it, it can hurt. Some of them like the combination of pleasure and pain, and they say it makes the blood taste better."

I can practically see her thinking, because a cheeky grin crosses her face and I brace myself.

"I don't know, I've never managed to catch the eye of one. Maybe I'll make that my mission, and then I'll have some actual facts to tell you instead of hearsay. Velorina, one of the flyers, is super sexy and doesn't seem to be opposed to other species. Maybe I'll invite her out for a drink." She giggles at her pun before leaning forward like she's got a secret to share with me.

"The clan we have here tends to feed only from one another, but I did overhear two of them talking the other day, and they said that Saxon has been getting his blood and sex from someone else. So maybe there really is a chance for me. Oh, and they have their own version of soulmate, or fated mate I guess. They call it their *sanguin rosala*, or their blood rose. Apparently they know from the smell of the blood, but the bond is not sealed until they drink from one another." She is full of the information I need, even though she said it's hearsay.

"So they only mate within their species?" I ask, only slightly curious. I'm already juggling three men, so I don't really need to add any more.

"As far as I know, yes, but so many species like to keep their secrets. There's less chance of being wiped out if no one knows the key to your reproduction. What I do know is that they are super territorial. A lot of the galaxy species are. They are more primal than humans and Skarrians, and a lot less tolerant of other races."

I snort quietly. "No shit! I'm beginning to discover this for myself. Even that cyborg nurse was staking his claim on Link. I read about this kind of behavior in my paranormal romance books, but I can't believe it's true." I blink, not even sure how to process everything she's told me before shaking my head. "I don't have time to care about their sex rituals or who is fucking and drinking from whom, or how they reproduce. The real question is, and I need you to be honest, am I going to get my ass kicked?" She laughs at me, noticing the shift from curiosity to downright worry.

"Oh yeah, most definitely. They are super athletic, and they are all required to do a term in their armed forces. I think it's a minimum two-year obligation, and no one gets out of it. They are considered one of the fiercest armies in the galaxy. You do not want to fuck with the Vilaxians. They are brutal, and because they drink the blood of their enemies, they don't fatigue. They just keep going and going."

She winks when she tells me this, but I'm nearly pissing my pants. Self-defense with a vampire warrior? Yup, my life isn't strange at all. I frown. "They don't sound like tricksters, they sound too noble to coerce someone into giving their blood."

"Where did you hear that rubbish?" she asks, sounding shocked, but then she puts two and two together. "Dylan, right? What a dick. From what I hear, he wasn't opposed to offering himself up as a blood sacrifice to them. Estrella, Radella, and Hale were always hanging out with him. He has always had his eye on Saxon too, but as I mentioned, I guess Saxon has someone providing him with blood as well."

I think back to what Dylan told me.

"They cannot take your blood without permission, but be careful. They are tricksters, and words can often be twisted so you end up giving blood without realizing it. They don't kill

their donors, but they can make it as pleasurable or as painful as they like. It's not up to you which sensation you'll get."

So I guess that was all bullshit. I wonder if the other bit was too?

"One thing you need to know is that although all of us may have a human-like form, we are far from it. Underneath our clothes, things may not be what you expect. Be aware of this if you decide to pursue any kind of physical relationship with anyone. You need to talk to your grandpas about Skarrian physiology too before you do anything like that. Educate yourself before you get into trouble."

I shake off my memories with the promise to take everything Dylan told me with a grain of salt.

"Okay, so is there anything else I need to know?"

She snorts with amusement. "Oh, babe, you've opened Pandora's box. I'm sure there's a million things you need to know, but it's not all going to happen in one day."

A short while later, William is showing me into the gym. It's set up much like a human gym, but on steroids, and this one even has a course much like American Ninja Warrior. A lot of the equipment is occupied, and people smile and wave to us. We do the same in return, my grandpa more familiar with everyone than I am.

He doesn't stop in the main area, instead taking me past everything to a door in the back wall which opens as we approach. When we step through, I can see it's a private but open space. I guess it may be for classes or private lessons, but what catches my attention the most is what I think are two people sparring. They are moving so damn fast my eyes can't keep up. It's like watching everything in fast forward.

"That's not even full speed," William mutters out of the side of his mouth, and the two beings stop all of a sudden.

"Holy shit. Doesn't that make you feel sick?" I ask. One of the guys, who has ice blond hair and bright, teal-colored eyes, winks at me and shakes his head, chuckling.

"Do you feel dizzy when you stop running?" he asks, and I instantly feel a little silly.

"Touché," I mutter, and his grin grows.

My gaze goes to the other man, and this one seems familiar. It's the man with the deep magenta eyes I remember from my first evening. His head is tilted to the side, and he's studying me like a predator studies its prey. I'm not sure if the shiver that runs through my body is from fear or those damn pregnancy fuck me vibes. I hadn't gotten a good look at him when he'd caught me that day, it was just his eyes, but I take a moment to study him.

He's wearing a pair of athletic shorts and nothing else, and it gives me every opportunity to look my fill. I hadn't realized how damn tall he is, he's got to be six-eight maybe, with broad shoulders and a muscular upper body. I move my gaze downward, and I notice he's got muscular *everything* —abs, thighs, calves, and I bet if he turned around, his ass would be tight enough to bounce a quarter off of. This guy's most definitely a warrior. Like many of our armed forces men back on Earth, he is ripped to say the least. Where Xavier is lean like a dancer, and both Caspian and Link have swimmers' builds, this guy is beefy. He looks like he could bench press me, and I'm so here for that, but on the other hand, he might just be about to make mincemeat out of me, and I may have peed my pants just a little.

What skin I can see is pale, and his lips are almost the same color as his eyes. His hair is pitch black and is close cropped. He studies me with the same intensity that I'm looking at him, but I'm not sure I've impressed him like he impressed me. He sneers slightly, and I see a flash of fang.

"Well, as fun as the tension in this room is, I need to jet. Time for me to get something to eat." Blondie flashes some fang at me, and I can't help but gasp and step back. Inwardly, I groan. Fuck, way to go, Lila, insult the vampire. "Unless you'd like to offer up a vein, beautiful?" I think I take too long to think about it, because Blondie's face goes from amused to something different, something almost primal, and he takes a step toward me.

"Hale!" William scolds, and the vampire shrugs.

"Don't blame me, it's not often we get newbies. It's fun fucking with them, but I am sorry if I scared her."

He and Saxon do a bro hug type of thing before he walks over to the door, which slides open, and then he disappears in a flash. My eyes are still trained in his direction, even though the door closed once he left the room.

"Saxon. Thank you so much for doing this for us. I appreciate you giving up your downtime for it. You remember Lila, our granddaughter?" William introduces us, and I turn my attention back to the serious man in front of us and hold out my hand.

"Nice to meet you. I really appreciate you catching me that first night. That would have really hurt if I'd hit the ground."

"Yes, it would have." His voice is quiet, but there's a husky quality to it. Damn it, the man's sexy enough as it is, he doesn't need to sound sexy too. Why couldn't he have sounded like Elmer Fudd or something?

That's all he says, and he doesn't take my hand, so I quickly drop it. Fuck! Did I just mess up? Is offering your hand insulting to a vampire? Why can't Link download all this information into my brain? Hmm, I wonder if he can. I'll have to ask him tonight.

William kept talking while my mind was wandering, but now he slaps Saxon on the shoulder and Saxon smiles at him before he waves goodbye to me. William leaves me alone with the blood-sucking vampire, who doesn't seem to be terribly impressed with me at all. He is also now staring at me again with his intimidating gaze. Shit! No wonder they are considered one of the fiercest warriors in the galaxy. They only have to stare their enemies down and they'll roll over and show them their bellies like little submissives. Or is that just me?

I try another smile. Hopefully it doesn't look like I'm constipated. "So, William said you were going to give me some self-defense lessons. I've done a few before, but it's been a while since I worked out." About two weeks, but I'm not going to admit that. I'm also not going to tell him I'm a black belt in a few disciplines, because I bet that means diddly squat to him. Magenta made it seem like these guys were the elite of the elite, and if he has heightened speed, strength, and senses, my black belts aren't going to be worth a damn.

"Well, I can try, but to be honest, if you have no powers and you're as weak as a human, no amount of self-defense is going to stand up to most galaxy beings," he states, still standing there as still as a statue, showing no emotion or anything.

No, Saxon, please don't sugar coat it for me.

I barely manage to prevent myself from flipping

him off, because holy crap, what a fucking grump he is. I cross my arms, feeling more than a little self-conscious and defensive.

Why is everyone making such a big deal about my lack of powers? And I can't believe William even told this guy. How is something a secret if you share it with every goddamn person on the ship? God, I hope Xavier has some answers for me after he speaks to his parents.

"Yes, well, there's not much I can really do about it now, is there? Look, if you don't want to, we can just give this a pass and I'll tell the grandpas it went well." His eyes widen in surprise, but I have a bachelor's degree in difficult men manipulation from working in a bar, so I'm confident I've got this. "I mean, if you don't have the skills to teach a beginner, that's not your fault, is it? They should have found someone more qualified."

His pale cheeks pinken, but I don't think he's embarrassed. From the look on his face, I know my intended arrow hit its mark. He starts to bluster, but I don't give him a chance to finish because I haven't quite gotten him to where I want him. "Maybe I can carry a weapon for protection. Or maybe, if the grandpas are so concerned, they can hire me a bodyguard. Oh yes, I can just picture it in my mind. Some muscle-bound hunk who would have no problems putting their body between mine and any danger." I look him up and down. "Maybe even another Vilaxian." I put my finger against my cheek and pretend to think. "Hmm, I guess I would have to be willing to share my blood with them since they will be coming aboard without their clan."

I guess that's the last straw, because he explodes. "Of course I can teach you. I can turn even the most pathetic human into a warrior, but you need to be willing to work hard."

Ouch!

I cross my arms. "Excuse me, but where did you get the idea that I wouldn't work hard? I've done nothing but bust my ass since I got to this ship." He raises one perfectly sculpted eyebrow at my rant, but apart from that, his face doesn't move or show any expression. "I bet it was the fucking dragon again. Well, let me tell you something." I step forward until we are chest to chest, my finger poking at the rocks beneath his tank top. "I may have made a bad decision by trusting that asshole, because it turns out he certainly wasn't my friend, but I would have thought intelligent beings would know better than to listen to idle gossip and rumors."

Before I can take another breath and continue to berate the vampire, I'm on my back on the floor faster than I can even comprehend and he's standing over me. A wave of nausea rolls through me, and I clap a hand over my mouth. His eyes widen in surprise, which is then followed by alarm, and within seconds, I'm kneeling in front of a toilet just in time to lose my earlier drink.

I expel the contents of my stomach, while Saxon helpfully holds my hair back, before groaning and sitting back against the nearby wall as the toilet automatically flushes.

"Point proven, but don't ever do that to me again."

CHAPTER NINE

Saxon

T he little human girl groans as she slides down the nearby wall and puts her hands on her head. "Point proven, but don't ever do that to me again."

The offensive smell of everything she expelled from her tiny body is strong in my nostrils—mostly menthol and a tart tinge, but also something like stomach acid—but it's not as bad as a disemboweled karta monster, so I just ignore it.

Feeling a small prick of guilt for pushing her body too far, I use my speed to get her a bottle of water from the fridge in the training room before returning to hand it to her.

"Here." I hold it out and she looks up, her eyes almost rolling out of her sockets with the movement of her head, but she reaches a shaky hand out for it.

"I am sorry. I forgot that your human body has not adjusted to being in space, let alone traveling at such speeds."

"My human body as opposed to my not human body? What else does he think?" I hear the little girl mutter sarcastically, and I'm surprised to find myself smothering a grin.

"Skarrians often have speed and heightened senses too. I forgot the entire reason you are here is because your body does not seem to be developing any Skarrian characteristics," I explain as she takes small sips of water. Her color is starting to return, and I can hear her heart rate begin to slow.

"Yeah, that's right, assclown, rub it in. Everyone loves to hear about how useless they are," she mutters under her breath again, but this time I don't have to worry about smiling.

"You're not useless. We just have to figure out a way to deal with your limitations." Lila's head shoots up, and her eyes widen like she was just caught doing something she shouldn't have been.

"Fuck, enhanced senses?" she asks, and I nod, fascinated with this little girl as she grumbles a little more about nosy fucking men who don't know how to pretend they can't hear shit. I can now somewhat see what Xavier was talking about when he told me about her. We don't tend to talk while having sex, because it's purely a physical exchange, but he was extra chatty after we finished last time, and I can't say the subject hadn't interested me after catching her the first night. Xavier's blood tends to leave me feeling a little blood drunk because of its potency, and having him lie next to me while I recovered wasn't as much of a hardship as I thought it would be. Unlike the members of my clan, he didn't want to talk about feelings or commitment, he was happy imparting all the real gossip as opposed to the trash Dylan had been spreading. Who knew the socially distant warlock was up on the latest drama?

Then I remember something he said. "Aren't you mated to the kraken shifter?"

She looks up at me and blinks like a cute little cirillion fluff ball. "The kraken shifter has a name, but yeah, I am."

"And he *bred* you?"

Bingo.

This gets a reaction, and she scrambles to her feet and steps up again, her finger lifting even though she's still a little pale in the cheeks. I see her look between it and my chest, and she must decide she is going to have another go at poking me regardless of what the consequences may be.

"Now listen here, mister. I don't see how that is any of your business." Her little finger tickles as she stabs it against my chest. I've got to give it to her, she is brave. No one else would treat me like this. It's like she lacks the basic instinct of self-preservation. I grab her finger and cradle it in my palm, knowing that if I squeeze too hard, I could crush it with my strength.

"It is if I am going to train you. Being with child may affect how you react to things. For example, you may have had such a bad reaction to my speed because being pregnant is messing with your equilibrium." She steps back, looking thoughtful, and I drop her finger. "As well as your fragile human body not being able to cope."

The thoughtful look disappears, and she growls at me. Lila makes it too easy to tease her, so her reaction is kind of cute, and this time I can't stop the small smile that crosses my lips, exposing my fangs to her. I expect her to recoil like she had with Hale, but she doesn't, and I find that strangely intriguing. Yes, she has zero self-preservation.

In fact, her eyes seem to lock onto my mouth, and I hear her heart rate pick up again. Combined with the heady scent she's suddenly putting out, I'd say she's definitely not scared but interested, and dare I say turned on. Though I can't say I'm surprised. Earth's fascination with vampires makes me not all that unusual to her, and with the way they sexualize blood drinking, they are not far off the mark.

Her physical response has me thinking. I've never tried human blood before. I'm curious, but not enough to proposition the boss men's granddaughter. I'm not that hard up. I've got Xavier, and the clan if I get desperate, but apart from Hale, I've started to get tired of them.

Our clan formed when we were doing our

required military service. Hale and I quickly worked our way up the ranks to captains, and both of us had our own squadrons. Velorina was in my squad, and Hale had the other two. When our service came to an end, the three girls got out, but Hale and I stayed.

Eventually, we attracted the attention of people higher up in the formal structure of Vilax. The Queen of Vilax selected our clan to perform with the circus, telling us that Vilaxians are always in the circus as protection for the Adams family. Their diplomatic missions are sometimes fraught with danger, and we were to act as their bodyguards and hired muscle during negotiations. The trapeze act is just a good cover. It took some convincing, but eventually Hale and I agreed. Although we saw it as a step down, a demotion of sorts, they assured us it wasn't and that we should consider it a holiday during non-wartime. We still go back once every couple of months and train with our units just to keep our skills fresh.

The girls were delighted to join the circus, since they get all the travel and fun they could want, but now things seem to have shifted between us all. I no longer enjoy Estrella and Radella's company, finding them annoying and frivolous. Velorina prefers girls to men, which is fine, so she spends more time with the other two than Hale or me, and Hale really isn't picky. He will take blood from the clan, or he is happy to find blood from one of the other performers. I think Estrella and Radella have realized the dynamic has changed, so they have started pushing for more. They want us to exchange commitment vows, but I'm not sure if it's about romantic interest or if they like their status in our clan and will use any excuse not to lose that status.

Some clans are so happy they decide to form permanent bonds, much like a human wedding. They get commitment tattoos and go through a whole ceremony, unless they are lucky enough to find their blood rose, which is magically fated and sealed, but I just don't see the point of committing. We have an extended lifetime, and I get bored easily. I don't see myself staying with the same clan forever. Most people don't, and clan dissolution is common, much like the divorce rate on Earth.

"Well, you're just going to have to figure out how to work with this fragile human body." She puts her hands on her hips, and I get a good look at her body for the first time. She's wearing the Galaxy Circus jumpsuit, and it hugs every dip and curve of her figure. My eyes linger on the swell of her breasts, and a number of dirty thoughts fly into my mind about how I could work over her body.

She clears her throat, but I'm not going to feel guilty about checking her out. She'd done the same to me when she first walked in.

"Gun," I say, and her brow wrinkles in confusion.

"Huh?"

"Do you know how to use a gun? That's probably the best option we have, unless your Skarrian powers kick in."

She looks a little unsure of herself but quickly recovers. "Ah, no. I've never needed to know how to use one before, and none of my foster families ever showed me."

"Foster families?" I can't stop the question that jumps out of my mouth, and I can't take it back either. Lila seems taken aback by my question, clearly not expecting me to show any interest in her personal life.

"On Earth, if something happens to your parents when you are young, or your parents are not nice people, you are placed with families who are paid to look after you. When my parents died, and the Adams brothers weren't found, that's what happened to me. I got lucky, because most of my families were okay, but sometimes they are not."

"You lived with strangers who were paid to look after you? You didn't just become part of their family?" My brows furrow, not fully understanding what she means.

"No, that is adoption. Unfortunately, there aren't enough families who want other people's kids, so a lot of us miss out." She doesn't sound too upset, more matter of fact than anything, but I can't help but feel sad for her. You don't often hear of that happening throughout the galaxy. If a Vilaxian chooses to have a child, that child will be looked after by the clan if anything happens to the parent. Most clans are fairly large, unlike our small one. Children are always raised by the clan, it's like having many loving parents. My mother and father's clan was made up of about twenty people, so there was no shortage of people to love me and my brother and the other children when growing up.

I shake my head. I need to stop getting distracted. What is it about Lila that makes me think about clan structure and ask questions about her childhood? I need to get my head in the game.

"Physically, you are no match for most species, especially the ones who have fangs and claws and can shift or are strong and fast. We need to counter that. Come on, follow me."

Lila quickly goes over to the sink and runs the water, cupping her hands and allowing them to fill with water before she drinks from them. She swirls the water in her mouth before spitting it in the sink. She catches me watching her in the mirror and grimaces. "Nobody likes that taste."

Grabbing my shirt from where it was hung, I pull it over my head before leading her out the door and back into the gym. There are still a few people working out in here, but I don't stop to talk to any of them, even though I can see one or two trying to catch my eye. Lila follows closely behind me as we leave the gym and move to another door on the right side of the corridor. This one requires me to swipe my thumbprint across the access panel. In the circus ship, we have access cards we need to use—I think they do it that way for the humans—but everywhere else on the big ship, the restricted areas have biometric scans. Thumbprints, eye scans, and blood sample. One of those will get you access if you are approved, and I am approved for this one. The door beeps as it scans my thumb, and the door slides open, allowing Lila and me access. The room is dark and cold, but sensors activate the lights as I step into the empty room. Lila is close behind me, almost bumping against my back, and as the door closes, I feel her shiver as she adjusts to the temperature of the room.

"Holy shit, it's cold in here." She wraps her arms around her midsection before moving around me and takes in the wide-open space. "This ship never ceases to amaze me. It's like it defies all laws of building on Earth. How were we in a large, normal-sized room on the other side of this corridor, but this room is like a big warehouse?" Her voice echoes in the cavernous space. "What is this for?"

"We are not constrained by human notions, and this is the gun range."

"Why so big?" she asks. "And where are the targets?" She sounds skeptical, and she looks around the space once more in case she missed it.

I go over to the desk that sits in the middle of the back of the room and place my thumb against the control panel once more. It lights up, and I program in a sequence of commands. The room's hologram takes over and creates my icy terrain. Lila's eyes widen in surprise.

"Holy fuck, this is so cool! It's a holodeck," she whispers reverently.

"I don't know what a holodeck is, but this is our tactical hologram console, or THC. It is Vilaxian tech that we use to train our military forces to be adaptable to any environment. We can program it for any terrain, and we give it parameters to mimic different environments. Then we add tactical scenarios. This hologram is Iceen. They are not particularly confrontational, and they don't involve themselves with other planetary squabbles, but it's a good environment to train in because of the extreme temperatures."

She frowns, looking confused. "But it's not snowing," she comments, and I push a couple of buttons, adjusting the temperature commands. The temperature in the room suddenly plummets as the environmental simulators kick in. The wind begins to blow, and snow starts falling from the ceiling.

"Holy fuck." She wraps her arms around herself even tighter, and I see goosebumps break out across her skin as her nipples pebble beneath her jumpsuit. I itch to reach out and stroke my thumb across one, but I keep my hand by my side. Fuck, I don't know what has come over me.

Suddenly, a yalani pops up on the landscape

and roars and starts running toward us. Lila screams and darts behind me.

"What the fuck is that?" she screams, clutching the back of my shirt.

"That's one of the other species that inhabit Iceen. They are an intelligent but highly aggressive humanoid race." I watch the shaggy, hair-covered alien race toward us. Her grip tightens on the back of my shirt as he gets closer, but before he reaches us, I erase him from the scene. She breathes a sigh of relief and slowly releases my shirt.

"He looked like an albino Wookiee," Lila says through chattering teeth.

I quickly adjust the temp controls. "Obviously you are not dressed correctly for a real simulation, I just wanted to show you what the room can do." The room goes back to its normal temperature, and Lila steps to my side, brushing down my shirt awkwardly like she's embarrassed she hid behind me. It's cute, and I struggle to hide my grin. Again. "What is a Wookiee?" I ask, having never heard that term before.

"A character from one of the best sci-fi movies Earth has ever made," she says, smiling.

"Yeah, they probably had an alien advisor on their team and didn't even realize it." I enter in a couple more commands, and the Iceen landscape disappears to be replaced with a traditional shooting range.

"Okay, let's get you a gun and teach you how to

use it. The gun locker is also protected by a biometric scanner, and only certain people are allowed to access it."

The weapons room is actually hidden by a permanent hologram. To the far right of the console is what looks like a wall, and if you were to reach out and touch it, you would meet solid metal, but certain members of the circus can walk straight through it. It's part hologram, part warlock spell. Xavier was under orders from the Adams brothers to code Lila into everything that has security like this on the ship. Xavier was more than a little suspicious when he was first told this, before he had met her, and he built in a failsafe. As long as Lila's intentions and motivations are honest and true, she should be fine. If it doesn't let her through, it means she's hiding something. I'm pretty sure he no longer feels suspicious, but I don't think he's had time to change the spell. I guess we're about to find out if the Adams' trust in their granddaughter is warranted.

"Where are we getting a gun from?" she asks, looking around the room skeptically.

"From over here," I reply and walk through the wall before turning around to watch her. I've disappeared from her sight, but I can still see her. I chuckle at the way her mouth drops open, and I can see her saying something, but the spell blocks out all sound.

She walks forward slowly, putting up her hands.

It's disconcerting walking through a wall when you've never done it before, but as she continues to walk, her hands go right through and appear on my side. There's a huge grin on her face as the rest of her body follows her arms.

"That is so fucking cool," she whispers, spinning around to look at the hologram. From this side it's transparent and a little hazy, and she pokes her arm in and out a few times. I can hear her singing, "*You put your right hand in, you put your right hand out.*"

"Are you okay? Did that hurt your brain on the way through?" I ask, a little unsure about her reaction. Maybe this was too much for her fragile human brain and I broke her.

"No, no, I'm fine." She turns back around, a pretty pink hue on her cheeks from embarrassment. As she looks around the room, her eyes widen at the sight of all of the different weapons. She is so expressive, it's fascinating. Vilaxians learn how to control their expressions at a very young age, while Lila is refreshingly responsive to everything. I wonder momentarily how that would translate in bed, but her excited shout has me pushing those thoughts away.

"Oh my God, it's like a scene from *Men in Black*." She heads for one of the laser cannons and tries to pick it up, but she struggles with its weight. "Holy shit, that's heavy," she complains, and I laugh. I can't help showing off a little, so I make my way over to her and the cannon and pick it up with one hand, putting it on my shoulder where it's supposed to go.

She rolls her eyes. "Okay, fine, you've made your point. Give me the weapon for noisy crickets."

Noisy crickets? "What are these noisy crickets?" I ask, putting the cannon back where it belongs, moving over to the handheld weapons, and grabbing a laser gun for her. "Are these dangerous creatures from Earth that I've never heard about?"

She waves a hand. "No, I was being silly. Ignore me. What have you got there?"

"This is a laser gun, and each of them are coded to the user, which means once it reads your blood, it won't work for anyone else in case you lose it during a fight. This way, no one can pick it up and use it on you."

"Oh, that is a great idea, I like that." She holds her hand out.

"It's shaped similarly to a human gun, and built into the trigger is a little needle-like protrusion. When you wrap your finger around it, it will puncture your finger. You'll feel a small prick, and then it will numb the area. It will not fire unless that needle is in your skin, reading your blood. This is a new weapon, so it will code itself to your blood, and it only needs a drop in the little reservoir in the top. Once it reads it, it will seal closed and the gun's yours. Basically, it's point and shoot, and don't point it at anything you don't want to kill. There is no stun option on this gun, it is set to kill every time.

You may get away with a flesh wound if you hit a limb, but laser injuries are nasty, and if you hit them anywhere on the body, it will destroy anything that lies in its path."

She yanks her hand back in horror. "Nope. No way. Not happening. That's too much." She shakes her head and backs up.

"No, Lila, you saw the yalani. It was coming for you, and this is the type of weapon that will stop it. A lot of alien species run on instinct before logic, and this is your only chance if no one else is around to help you."

She sighs. "Fine, but what should I use to cut my finger to get blood for the top of it?" There's a knife display in one of the cabinets, and she goes over to it and pulls out a Vilaxian dagger. It's standard military issue and designed to never get blunt. She drags her thumb across the point, and a drop of blood appears on the wounded flesh just before a tantalizing smell, spicy and sweet, hits my nostrils and they flare. My cock hardens instantly, and my fangs lengthen and start to drip. It's not my usual venom, but the venom designed to seal two people together for a lifetime.

My blood rose!

CHAPTER TEN

Xavier

After Lila leaves me, I dissolve into mist and move through my quarters in search of my harem. They have retreated to their own communal living space to help Mithus and the two girls recover. Why the three of them were in my space, I don't know, and it's just another thing they have done to piss me off recently. They are under the delusion that they mean more to me than just a source of energy and an occasional fuck. I have always made it clear that a relationship is not in the cards. I'd always held out hope that I had an intimate out there, much like my parents. The anger I feel now, knowing that they hid it and didn't tell me, is immense. There's also a sense of relief, though, like a long wait has finally come to an end. But before I deal with my parents, I need to deal with my wayward harem.

As I slide under the door of their quarters, angry voices greet my ears, and instead of coalescing, I hover unseen to eavesdrop on their conversation. The room smells like sex, so I guess they have started trying to heal Mithus already.

"That fucking bitch. It's her fault that Xavier almost killed Mithus," Elyan rages, not taking my rejection well. "And now he's putting her before all of us. I will not stand for it. She needs to go."

"Elyan, be careful. She is the boss men's granddaughter," Nambra, the redhead who was caught in the Mithus crossfire, rasps from where she's reclined on their couch. Topirey, my Dionall harem member, is giving her head to help her recover from my anger. Her hands are clasped onto the foliage on his head as his long tongue works over her clit and folds. His teeth are sharp and dangerous, but he knows how to use them to create the perfect balance of pleasure and pain. It's why he's in my harem in the first place.

"The Adams are not our boss, only Xavier can dictate to us. You know what he's like. His attention span is short, so if we get rid of her, he will forget about her and put his focus back on us," Elyan continues, freely speaking her traitorous words, and my blood boils.

"I don't think you are right, Elyan," Sinath, my Rasque harem member, tells her, his clicking sounds translating into Skarrian through my implanted translator. His mouth is unable to form words like a humanoid, but he excels at sucking dick. It seems his intelligence may need to be rewarded too. "Xavier has shown more interest in the human girl than he's shown anyone else before. I think you would find yourself dead if you got rid of her."

Mithus groans as Lexus, the dark-haired warlock who attacked Lila, rides both of his cocks. Her ass and vagina bulge as she undulates, her head thrown back in pleasure. Although Mithus does not absorb power nor feed on emotions like a warlock does, Lexus can feed her power into him as they fuck to heal him. So while she heals herself, she heals him at the same time.

The three remaining members of my harem watch on in silence. Zanorn is a metamorph and can take on any form I want him to, and if I had to name a favorite harem member, it would be him. When he's in his natural form, he's a blank slate with no discernible features, just a humanoid-shaped body, his skin a gray color with no markings. He's sitting with Ara and Jastia, the last of the warlocks in my harem. Both women are quiet and unassuming and don't involve themselves with gossip or intrigue. They feel no jealousy and are aware of their role in my harem, and because of this, they are also in my top three. The three of them will survive what happens next, but I am not sure if the others will.

"No, he is only being kind to her because he wants to keep the Adams brothers happy. Why he bows down to the pathetic Skarrians, I have no clue. He could be home on Westalin, living the good life, but instead he's a lackey for this damn circus. He could at least get rid of the Adams brothers and run the damn thing."

Such traitorous words from my harem member, and it sounds like this is not the first time she's had these thoughts. Have I misjudged their loyalty and turned a blind eye because I enjoyed feeding on them?

"Be very careful what you say, Elyan, your words border on treason. If you want to get rid of Lila, then you will need to do it so it looks like an accident, but as for the boss men, I would leave them alone for now," Sinath cautions the devious bitch, and he was doing so well. With those words, he just became a coconspirator.

I continue to listen and see if they will dig themselves a deeper grave while feeding off the sexual energy everyone is putting off. I'm basically stealing it so that the ones who are trying to heal won't be able to. I wonder how long it will take for them to notice they are not healing. I watch as Topirey extends a limb toward Nambra. It changes shape from a hand-like appendage until it is one solid branch. He doesn't bother smoothing off the surface, so it penetrates Nambra with a slightly sharp end and bark-like skin. She arches off the couch, her moan one of painful pleasure as he fucks her with it. His tongue and teeth continue to work her sexual organs. Warlocks are pleasure pain sluts, some worse than others, but we all like it occasionally.

Although warlocks look much like a humanoid species, our genitals differ slightly. While we still have cocks and cunts, we also have additional pleasure organs. The best way to describe them would be small tentacles that sit where a clit would be for human females. They are not long, probably only two Earth inches, and they have the same kind of sensitivity as a human clit, but they are able to tangle with the tentacles of a male warlock, which kind of locks the two warlocks together. The male's tentacles are around the base of our cocks. They caress and stroke each other when they interlock, creating a whole other level of sexual pleasure.

A squeal has me dragging my attention away from Nambra and Topirey and onto Mithus and Lexus. Lexus has started squealing, so I guess the barbs in Mithus's cocks have activated. They pierce the vaginal walls when he gets close to his climax to lock you in place so he can deposit all of his seed inside you. It's quite a painful sensation, but when he comes, it feels amazing, because it's hot and has a chemical in it which triggers an orgasm in the recipient.

She's barely moving, and he's grunting and groaning like an emaciated lastovian hog. It really is the most unattractive sound, which is why I only fuck him when I feel like having two cocks in my ass, and that isn't very often, to be honest. I can also always ask Zanorn to give me two cocks, and that is much more enjoyable. I mainly use him to suck me off. His toothless mouth has the most amazing suction action.

"What kind of accident could we cause?" Elyan talks out loud as I draw in all the sexual energy, gorging on it to punish my harem a little more. I can't believe none of them have noticed that I am here.

"I want nothing to do with any of this," Zanorn announces, standing up and drawing Ara and Jastia with him.

"You are going to get yourselves killed," Ara warns.

"He wouldn't choose her over me. He wouldn't strike out at me like he did them," Elyan declares haughtily as she sneers at the copulating couples on the couch like they are the dirt beneath her shoes.

"I wouldn't be so sure of that," Jastia calls over her shoulder as the three of them hurry toward their sleeping quarters.

Ah, clever boy. Zanorn is looking right at me as they depart and get out of the crossfire.

"Why isn't this working?" Nambra groans as I hold off their orgasms. "Get over here, Sinath, and let me suck your cock." He goes over to her and gets up on the couch, positioning his pelvis before her mouth. I watch as he drops his pants. The armored plates that cover his sexual organs slide back, and the long, spiny protrusion extends out. She runs her tongue up the length of it a couple of times, and I watch as blood starts to drip from where the spiny barbs slice little cuts into it. I stifle a moan. Although I have no inclination to join them, it still builds a desire in me that is going to need an outlet. Eventually the plates separate, and his long, thick, fleshy cock comes out. This one doesn't have spiny protrusions, but I wait in anticipation for what's about to happen. He shoves it into her mouth before the spiny outside plates slam into her cheeks, the barbs digging into her skin and holding her in place. Her muffled scream of pain causes my own cock to throb. He starts to thrust back and forth, not taking any care to be gentle. Nambra's eyes widen, and I can hear her breathe through her nose. Although she knew it was going to happen, it is quite shocking when it actually does.

"Please, Elyan, help us out," Lexus begs. "You're the most powerful of us all, maybe you can help us heal."

"I've never helped you before, so why would I start now?" Elyan's haughty ways have had her rejecting anyone else in the harem. She mistakenly believes she's better than all of them because she is more powerful, but that is most definitely not the case, which she is about to find out. She only ever feeds from me or from residual emotions, just as I am doing right now. She should be able to feel what I'm doing, but she is so distracted by her jealousy and anger she still hasn't realized I'm in the room.

"Please, Elyan, please," Lexus begs again, the pain she's in is all too obvious in her voice. Without Mithus's orgasm, she's not getting the chemical release for his spikes not to be painful. Her pussy is full of a hundred barbs right now, and he keeps fucking her like the rutting lastovian hog he sounds like despite the restricted movements he can make.

I start to chuckle, and it echoes around the room as I manifest my misty, shrouded body in front of them. I make the mist recede, allowing them to see my true form. Elyan's eyes widen, and a smug smile crosses her face. I don't reveal myself until I want to fuck while I feed, so I'm sure she thinks I'm here to join the orgy. Once upon a time, I would have, but not this time, and not ever again.

"Xavier, there you are." She uses my name, which she knows not to do, but her jealousy has made her stupid. She drops her robe, and her lacy lingerie disappears, leaving her slender, toned figure exposed for my eyes. The others keep reaching for their pleasure. "Please use my body and take our sexual pleasure to sate your need." She falls to her knees and reaches for my belt, and I slap her hand away.

"They ask why it is not working, and you are too consumed by your own jealousy to check where all the healing energy is going. How can you be so stupid?" I feel her search the room and watch her eyes widen as she realizes I have absorbed it all.

"How long were you listening for?" she asks quietly, looking up at me with a calculating glint in her eyes.

"Long enough," I tell her, and she decides to cut her losses.

"That human bitch cannot give you what you need. She is weak and useless, and I will kill her so you are not distracted. She probably purchased a spell to catch your eye." She doesn't hold back her disgust, and I'm surprised by her bravery.

"Unless she got the spell from my parents, do you think it would be something strong enough to fool me?" I bellow, my voice shaking the room. "I am the warlock and the most powerful being in the galaxy. I do not need your petty jealousy and pathetic plotting to protect myself. Here, let me show you."

I hold out my hand, much like I did to Mithus, and I start to absorb all her power. Her screams of agony are music to my ears. She begs me to stop, promising to do better and be better, but it is too late. She showed her hand and I'm calling her bluff, or however the human idiom goes. I continue to take, absorbing first her anger and jealousy before moving onto her power until she becomes as powerless as Lila. Unlike the delicious feast that Lila's anger provided me, Elyan's emotions are bitter and rancid, and I can't wait to be done with this. Once I feel the last of her power leave her, I stop and pump energy back into her, making her whole once more, ensuring she will survive what I've done to her so she can suffer the consequences for her traitorous words. Whole and powerless and *nothing*. I thought about killing her, but that would have ended her suffering, and she could be reborn later. This way she has to live a lifetime with no power. I drop my arm down to my side and step back, satisfied with my punishment.

"What have you done?" she screams and stumbles to her feet. She holds out a hand like she's trying to attack me with her power, but I just chuckle when nothing happens.

"You have been punished for your traitorous words, Elyan. You should never have even thought about Lila and the Adams brothers in a harmful way. It is not for you to decide who runs the circus or to dictate what I do, where I go, or who I see. You are a nobody. You are nothing but a warm body for me to use and discard as I needed. And now you are even less than that." I watch as the realization that she has screwed up dawns on her face, and I can't help but smirk. "Now you will not find your way into another harem. You will be reduced to menial jobs, and even then, possibly not because you have no power. Your best bet would be a Celesian brothel. You've always been very good on your back, I will give you that. You have talented tentacles that really know how to stoke a man's pleasure."

Her tentacles might be talented, but that's about the extent of it. She was a rather unadventurous and prudish lay, which is why she would never join in with everyone else. Heaven forbid Mithus fucks her with his double dicks or Sinath clamps his cock into her mouth.

"You will be confined to your sleeping quarters until we are able to organize a transport for you to Westalin or we return there. You will not be given the harem bonus that is in your contract, nor will you be given references so you can find yourself a new harem. The shame of being kicked out of my harem and being powerless will follow you everywhere."

She tries to launch herself at me, and I freeze her mid-strike. I turn to deal with the other five. "As for you five... Topirey, you have a reprieve, for you have not upset me today, but I suggest you step away from the others and return to your room."

He quickly extracts himself from Nambra and hurries away, his raging boner weeping precum because I hadn't let anyone orgasm. He will find that once he gets to his rooms, he will be free of the ban, and if he chooses to take care of himself, I won't care.

Lexus and Nambra are sobbing, desperate messes, and Mithus is not much better, while Sinath is clamped into Nambra. I wave a hand, and both males lose their erections so Lexus is able to clamber off of him and Sinath can pull free of Nambra's mouth.

"Did I give you permission to heal yourselves?" I ask quietly, and they shake their heads.

"But you didn't say we couldn't," Mithus retorts stubbornly as both his hands go to his cocks and he fists one in each, trying to get his erection back.

I raise an eyebrow, and with a wave of my hand, his own hands explode, and because they were wrapped around his cocks, they are caught in the crossfire. His genitals are reduced to blobby mounds of flesh, and his arms have stumps at the ends as his screams echo around the room. Blood runs down his body and onto the couch.

"Mithus, your pleasure has always been under my control, and you know that. I have been lenient and let you use one another, but your contract says you are for my exclusive use only and I have the right to punish you if you do not adhere to this. This is my punishment." His screams die off as he loses consciousness. Lexus is covered in bits of Mithus, and she sobs as I listen to his heartbeat stutter before it ceases to beat any longer.

"Take this for what it is—a warning. You will remain in your sleeping quarters and will heal as slow as a human as a reminder to never cross me again or think you are more than what you actually are. Consider this your notice of termination, and be thankful it's not permanent like Mithus's is," I tell the two female warlocks and the Rasque. "Now get out of my sight." They can't move fast enough, and they quickly disappear, leaving me with a frozen Elyan and Mithus's corpse.

"What a mess," I grumble and wave my hands. Mithus's body disintegrates, and then I use my power to clean up the mess he left behind. The whole entire time, I let Elyan watch. I'm hoping she will be discouraged from trying anything. I would have killed her, but her father is one of my father's advisors. It's why she is in my harem to start with. He's not going to be happy with her lack of powers. Maybe killing her would have been kinder.

I unfreeze her, and she quickly changes her mind about attacking and quietly leaves the room without looking at me. I'm not sure she will stay docile, but I need to make a call to my parents, so I have to trust that she will do as ordered. I will be able to feel if anyone leaves my quarters, though, so I think we're good for now. She's also no danger to Lila at the moment, since she is as powerless as Lila is, or so everyone thinks.

I return to my living area and throw myself into my lounge pit before waving my hand at the picture window. It becomes opaque, and I use it to call my parents. It's always tricky to video call someone out of the blue, but when I work out the time on my home world, I realize it's midday, so I think I'm pretty safe and won't find my parents naked. I take a drag on my water pipe while I wait for the connection. I need something to calm my rage, killing Mithus and stripping Elyan of her power wasn't enough.

"Xavier, my boy, so good of you to call. Your mother has been pining for you." My dad's face fills my screen, and he's wearing his stern, warlock king expression. I must have caught him in the middle of something official.

"Am I interrupting?" I ask casually, not really caring if I am.

"No, nothing important. Hang on a moment, and your mother and I will move to another room." I can hear blustering and insulted tones in the background as my father gets up and moves, taking the communication orb with him. I can also hear my mother trying to smooth over my father's rather rude departure, but it doesn't seem to be going well. My father stops, and there's a pause, followed by my mother's outraged gasp. "Cronus! You can't freeze the Telazion representatives like that," she admonishes as he starts to move again.

"Who's going to stop me?" He chuckles as they move into their private office next to their throne room.

The orb shuffles around a bit, and when it stops moving, my parents are sitting together as my mother beams at me. "Hello, darling. Your dad was lying, of course. It is him who has been lamenting about how horrid and neglectful his oldest son is to his aging parents."

I snort at my mother's exaggeration. "Hardly elderly."

"What can we do for you, my boy?" my father asks, ignoring my mother's teasing.

"I need you to tell me what you did to Lila Jenson."

They exchange a confused look before my mother responds, neither of them knowing Lila's new name.

"Who?" she asks.

"Lila Jenson, or maybe you would know her as *Liliana Adams*."

My mother gasps before putting a hand over her mouth, and my father's deep purple skin pales until he's almost as light as me.

"I see you recognize the name." There's no hiding the annoyance in my tone now, and they both flinch. It's an unusual reaction from them to say the least. Nothing normally fazes the almighty King and Queen of Westalin.

"Yes, son, we do. I guess it's time we told you the story." My dad sighs, and I brace myself for what they are about to tell me. I hope that once my parents are finished, I'm not as furious with them as I was with my harem.

CHAPTER ELEVEN

Lila

I watch as a drop of blood wells on the pad of my finger, but when I hold it out to place it in the gun, I find that the stoic Saxon has been replaced with a nostril flaring, fang baring, red-eyed monster. The sight alone sends my heart rate soaring, and my fight-or-flight instincts feel like they are about to take over.

My blood! Fuck! I would have thought a being who drank blood every day would have better control than this, but when he starts to pant, my immediate instinct is to pull away. I try to move my hand so it's not too close to him, because I'd rather not become Saxon's lunch, but before I can, he has my hand in his vicelike grip. I struggle in his hold, but he growls and I freeze.

Fuck. This is *not* going to end well.

I watch his movements intently and can see a slight shift in his eyes.

"Lila, you need to move away from me very slowly, and I need you to leave the vault and range. Once you are in the corridor, I need you to run as fast as you can and find Xavier. Tell him you are my blood rose, and he will know what to do," Saxon says through gritted teeth, and I can see him physically struggling to hold himself still, even though he's holding onto my hand. His body is practically vibrating, and his shape is getting blurrier the longer we stand here. My instincts are screaming at me to run as terror courses through my body.

He drops my hand and I do as he says. I desperately want to run, but I'm almost a hundred percent certain that would trigger his predatory nature and cause him to chase me. Maybe any other day, that would be appealing, but not when Saxon's barely hanging onto his last ounce of control.

My shoulder burns again with another attraction mark as I slowly back away, not turning my back on the violently contained man in front of me. Of course I'm turned on by how he looks, and I'm surprised the mark didn't appear on my shoulder the minute I saw him. Why has it appeared now? Is seeing his primal side what triggers my vampire kink? That brings my number to four. Fucking hell. How does one juggle dating four men? I think I might need to call Dr. Phil for this one.

My fascination with vampires started long ago

and only grew with each movie or paranormal romance I read or watched, but reality is somewhat of a kick in the face. This guy in front of me is a lethal, bloodsucking machine, and he has caught my scent. My ridiculous sense of self-preservation can't decide if she wants to throw herself at him and offer up my neck in sacrifice, or if she wants to quietly pee her pants and leave the room, the smell of urine marking my trail.

I feel myself pass through the barrier and he disappears from sight, but I know he can still see me, smell me, and sense me, so I don't dare turn and run just yet. Step by step, I cautiously move across the cavernous room. My hip bangs against the control console, but I contain my hiss of pain and slide my way around it, wishing that I had activated the gun already, but nope, that didn't happen because apparently my blood smells good enough to make this highly disciplined man go berserk. Seriously, what the fuck is up with my luck? I guess I need to be grateful that the fuck me hormones weren't misbehaving as well, otherwise I probably would have thrown myself at him instead of backing away calmly.

Although, there is still time.

I internally sigh at myself. My life is in danger, but yet I'm thinking about getting laid. There is something seriously wrong with me.

I finally make it to the sliding door and push the button to open it. It slides quietly to the side and I step through, watching as it closes swiftly behind me. A roar rattles the door as I turn and race toward the elevator, pushing any button on my watch and shouting into it.

Shit. Shit. Shit.

"Call Xavier," I instruct, but I get a fucking message.

"The warlock is on another call right now, please try again later." What the fuck? We have an answering service on an alien ship? My heart is racing, and my legs are moving as fast as they can. As I get to the elevator, I slide to a stop and slam my hand down on the call button. Thankfully it arrives within seconds, and I hop on just as another roar echoes down the corridor. Fuck, with his speed, he will be here in seconds.

"Come on, you stupid, slow-ass, *Driving Miss Daisy* door." It closes quickly, separating me from the rampaging, bloodsucking, sexy man, and I breathe a sigh of relief. I try to control my heart rate so I don't pass out and attempt to think of solutions. If I can't find Xavier, who is going to protect me? I'm assuming he's not just going to stop the moment I'm out of sight because the constant, albeit sexy, roar echoing through the hallways tells me I'm right.

Think, Lila. Think.

Caspian? But would he be a match for the military trained Saxon? Maybe in his kraken form. At this point, my mate is my best option for protection because I doubt his beast would allow Saxon to get close when he's all vamped out. He said he was going for a swim, so hopefully he's still at the pool.

I program the location into my watch and press the floor number. The elevator takes me to the right place, and I don't waste any time getting off and stripping as soon as the door opens. I'm almost naked by the time I hear another roar. Holy fuck, I can hear him already. The elevator opens only onto this space, but maybe there's a set of stairs somewhere on this level. Either way, he's coming, and I think my luck might have run out.

Kicking off my shoes, I remove my bra and panties, not wanting to lose them when I shift, and pray that this works. Doing what Caspian told me, I picture my shifted self in my mind, and I feel my body change as the magic flows over me with surprising ease. Not waiting for the change to finish, I throw myself into the water.

Caspian? I scream through our telepathic bond, but he doesn't respond, and my heart sinks with worry.

He's not here.

Fuck.

I am so *not* equipped to deal with this on my own, but I'm all I've got.

With no one to talk to, questions begin running through my mind at a rapid pace.

What am I going to do? I don't know how long

Vilaxians can hold their breath. Is he going to come in after me?

My finger has stopped bleeding, and if there is any blood, it's now being dispersed in this giant pool. Let's just hope Nikos's friend Sweet Pea doesn't find my blood as tasty as Saxon obviously thought it would be.

I dive deep into the bottom of the pool, hoping that even if he can hold his breath indefinitely, his body can't withstand the pressure at this depth. Swimming through the reef that teems with life, I look around. I can't decide where to go or what to do. There also seems to be no sign of the Aquilian shifters, so maybe they are out and about on the ship for a change. I might just go and hide out in the cave at the bottom of Nikos's place. Maybe his sister, Nixie, is there and we can hang out until Saxon has snapped out of his predatory self. I just need something to distract me until this is over.

Now that I've calmed slightly, I propel myself along with my tentacles. It's kind of weird but also fun and fast. Before I know it, I'm shooting up the tunnel and surfacing in Nikos's pool. Pulling myself up onto the platform, I drag in fresh air and feel my gills automatically seal as I dry off.

My heart is still racing after my close encounter with Saxon, and I find myself having the same thoughts as I try to digest what happened. I'm not sure what to do. Is this a one-time thing where once he's gotten the scent of my blood out of his system he will go back to normal? Or is this a permanent state and he's going to hunt me to the ends of the galaxy?

My sex starved body is telling me to turn my ass around and let him impale me with whatever he wants to. You know, fangs or cock or tongue. I'm really not fussy, but the sensible, values her life side of me is telling horny me to fuck off. We don't want to die today. It's seriously like those cartoons where there's a devil on one side and an angel on the other.

I try to reach Xavier again, but he's still on another call. I'm about to try calling Caspian to find out where he is, because his kraken would protect me from the vampire, but I hear voices in the living area above me.

"What are you doing here, Saxon?" I can hear Nikos's grumpy tone echo down into the cavern. "Why are you in my home?" I look upwards and realize that this pool links to the top through a shaft with a set of stone steps that circle up the wall. If they look over the edge, they will see me. Shit!

"Lila is in your pool. You have her. I want her. Give her to me *now*," Saxon growls, and I hear Nikos click his tongue at him in admonishment.

"No, Saxon. Caspian told me we do not kidnap and ravish females anymore. You must invite them to have sex." I can't help but smile as Nikos repeats the words that Caspian scolded him with. "I also do not think she would want you to drink from her when you are in such a frenzy. Go away and come back later."

"You dare to wave a weapon at me?" Saxon sounds outraged. Maybe it's his dick. With Nikos, you can never know for sure, but I wish I could see what is going on.

"You are not thinking clearly, and when you do, you will be upset if you hurt Lila." Nikos doesn't raise his voice, he just states his opinion in a matter-of-fact way.

A roar echoes down the tunnel. I don't think Saxon is impressed with Nikos's logic.

"What is that racket?" A cute, tinkling voice joins the conversation. "What are you doing in our home, sanguinista?"

"Lila is in the pool, and I want her," he demands again. "Give. Me. Lila."

"Lila? The boss men's granddaughter?" Suddenly, a head with beautiful golden hair and eyes peers over and down the shaft that leads to the pool. It's Nixie, Nikos's sister, and she smiles and waves. I give her a sheepish grin and wave awkwardly. Her face disappears, leaving me to listen again. "So she is. Well, you can't have her. Get your shit together and come back once you're calm. Seeing you like that is enough to frighten anyone, let alone someone who only thought they were human a little over a week ago."

Another raging growl echoes through the pool as I watch the water ripple from the vibration.

I don't think this is going to end well for my Aquilian protectors.

"She is my blood rose, and I am not leaving until you give her to me." He mentions that phrase again, and something tickles the back of my mind. I'm sure Magenta said something about that, but I can't remember what it was.

"Oh, well that explains your reaction." Nixie sounds surprised.

"No kidnapping and ravishing. Caspian said so," Nikos repeats, and I hear Nixie reassure him.

"No, not without enthusiastic consent at least. Sometimes a woman enjoys a good ravishing," I hear her tell her brother.

"They do? Hmm, I will take that into consideration." He sounds thoughtful, and I giggle despite the serious circumstances. I wonder why Saxon hasn't just pushed the two Aquilians out of the way and flashed down. Whatever weapons Nikos wields must be serious, and it's clearly *not* his dick, because Nixie would have reacted.

"Go see Link and ask if he can mute the reaction for the moment. Someone needs to explain what is happening to Lila. The poor girl is having so much thrown at her at once—mated, pregnant, and then that asshole dragon, not to mention lost grandpas, heir to an alien circus, and well, just everything. No wonder she's hiding at the bottom of our pool. I'm surprised she's not curled up like a coloomy shell and sobbing."

I hear Saxon growl once more. "No, I am not leaving. I will wait until she comes out if you won't let me through." I wonder how he got to their house. I didn't hear him enter the water, and I think that's something I would have picked up in shifted form, but there are no dry paths leading to the homes in the middle of the pool. Holy shit, I wonder if he can fly.

"Fine, then you give me no choice. I'm sorry, Saxon."

A beautiful, haunting melody rings through the rock chamber, and I find myself swaying in time to it, my eyes drooping and my body relaxing. My tentacles become pliant, and I flop down. It's so freaking weird not to have legs. I actually haven't had a good chance to explore this shifter body, but I guess now is not the time. I make a mental note to shift at home in our tub and get Caspian to give me the rundown on kraken biology.

There's a shout and a thud, and then I hear Nixie and Nikos again as that dreamy feeling leaves me. "I'll alert Link that we need him. He'll know how to deal with the unconscious Vilaxian and hopefully mute Saxon's need for Lila until someone can explain to her what it means."

"I will go and see if Lila is okay," Nikos tells his sister.

"Fine, but remember consent is crucial, Nikos. Say nice things to her, and smile without your sharp teeth. That's enough to scare anyone who's not Aquilian. And don't be..." She trails off.

"What?" he asks.

"You. Don't be you. Be a nice version of you if you want to tempt this woman to swim with you and maybe stroke your fins."

"I don't want her to swim with me, I want to fuck her." Now that the melody has stopped, I'm more lucid again, and I snort when I hear him say that.

Nixie sighs. "Okay, well, I tried. Good luck with that."

Footsteps make their way down the steps, and Nikos finally appears in front of me. His pastel green skin glimmers in the low light of the rock cavern, and his metallic gold hair hangs long down his back. He holds a golden trident in one hand like Poseidon, but it's the rest of him that startles me. I don't know why. Of course the man doesn't have a tail while he is on dry land, I just wasn't expecting this. The man in front of me is naked, apart from a piece of cloth covering his groin, and it's not doing a very good job of hiding anything. In fact, now that his molten gold eyes are locked onto my exposed breasts, his cloth starts to move as his dick hardens. He places the trident against the wall and steps forward.

"Hello, Lila. I like your breasts." I hear a groan and the sound of a slap from above.

"For fuck's sake, Nikos," I hear his sister complain.

"Ah, thank you, Nikos? I… uh… like your cock?" Although the thing is still draped in cloth, it is now standing at attention, and it looks like it could have nice girth and length, not to mention it's moving around like an elephant's trunk.

"Would you like to suck it?" he inquires. Um, well, okay then. How am I supposed to answer this question? A burning sensation on my shoulder tells me exactly how I feel and what I want to do. Goddamn it, I know I'm attracted to this man, but should I really be sucking his dick? One part of me just wants to embrace this whole Skarrian experience, but the other part of me, the one which is rooted in Earth morals and traditions, is screaming at me for being such a slut.

"Raincheck?" I ask him, and he frowns, looking up.

"It is not raining. It can rain in our environment, but we don't put it in storm mode very often. What has that got to do with you wrapping your lips around my manhood?"

"It is an Earth saying. It means, can we do that next time?" I explain, hiding my grin.

"Yes, of course. Link is on his way, and he will probably bring your mate. He would undoubtedly want you to suck his cock first. I shall wait my turn." Nikos makes it sound like it's perfectly reasonable for me to be sucking a lot of cock, and while I'm tempted, I need answers about Saxon. Why did he react so intensely to the scent of my blood, and will his need to find me continue? I really need him to work with me and show me how to use that gun, and hopefully I can convince him that my body is not as fragile as he thinks so I can work on my hand-to-hand combat skills as well.

"How is Link going to get over to your home?" I ask, hoping the change of subject might make his raging boner go down.

"Can I at least touch your breasts? Maybe I can help you relax while we wait for him to arrive," he offers, stepping closer to me, and I hold up a tentacle to stop his forward movement. Unfortunately, I haven't quite got the hang of them on land. In the water, they function like a breeze and everything happens naturally, but on land, not so much, and it wraps around his cloth-covered dick instead of touching his chest where I had intended for it to go.

"Oh, you have changed your mind?" he asks, sounding adorably hopeful, and as I try to figure out how to remove it, the suckers latch onto the underside of his cock, which is not covered by the cloth, and I can taste Nikos through them. He's salty and tangy and delicious, kind of like a margarita. Fuck me. If giving head tasted like that all the time, I would have been the blow job queen in high school.

He moans and thrusts into my tentacle as I try

to pull it away, but before I can get it to cooperate—the damn thing has a mind of its own—I hear voices in the upper section again, specifically Link's and Caspian's.

My heart sinks, and I pull harder, trying to unwrap it, and Nikos throws his head back and moans, "Yes."

"No, no, no. This is not what was supposed to happen. I'm not even sure what is so good about it! Your damn dick is half wrapped in cloth."

"But your breasts bounce so nicely and your grip is so good." The footsteps come down the spiral rock staircase, and Nikos speeds up his thrusts. I can't get my tentacle to unwrap no matter what I try. It's like it's sentient and refuses to give up control.

Just as the other three step out onto the platform, Nikos shouts and thrusts hard once more, exposing the tip of his cock through the cloth. As he does, cum shoots out and splatters all over my chest, the warm sticky fluid tingling against my skin as my tentacle finally unlatches itself and moves enough so it can suction around the now dripping tip.

I look at my mate and potential lover in dismay. "This is not what it looks like."

They exchange a glance and grin. "Looks like a good time to me," Caspian says, and Link joins in with his laughter as Nixie groans, slapping a hand over her eyes.

"Fucking hell, Nikos. What did you do?"

CHAPTER TWELVE

Link

When Nixie called me to come to their habitat, I was surprised. I hadn't been invited down there before, but when she mentioned Lila being in danger, I dropped everything I was doing and hurried. I messaged Caspian and told him to meet me there, hoping that nothing bad had happened to his mate.

When we arrived at the platform near the door, I was prepared to strip down and swim across, but Nixie activated a floating path that came from the housing section to the platform we were standing on, allowing us to walk easily over to her house. When we got inside, I was stunned to find Saxon unconscious on the floor of the main living area.

"What is wrong with him and why is he here?" I ask, bending down to run my hand over him to scan for abnormalities. Vilaxians don't get sick because their cells regenerate and are constantly healing themselves as long as they get a constant source of blood.

"He was in a blood frenzy. I had to sing him to sleep. He wouldn't leave." I watch concern wash over Nixie's face as she repeats what happened.

"A blood frenzy? What caused that?" Caspian questions, sounding surprised. He pushes a hand through his blue hair, trying to understand what Nixie is telling us. I don't blame him for worrying, it's not often that Vilaxians will go into a blood frenzy outside of battle. The only other time would be if…

"He found his blood rose," Nixie finishes, voicing my thought out loud.

"He did? Well, good for him. Is it one of the Aquilians? That's extremely unusual, isn't it? Aren't they usually Vilaxians as well since they need to be able to sustain each other on their blood? I don't think I've heard of a non-Vilaxian blood rose. It would surely be a death sentence for the other species if that were the case."

I stand up as Caspian finishes asking his questions. I know that Saxon is fine. He is sleeping peacefully, which is probably for the best because he will suffer withdrawals and blood frenzy until he can get his blood rose to consummate their connection. I have a funny feeling that Caspian is in for a rude shock when he discovers who Saxon's blood rose is.

"I will have the hover stretcher come down here, and I will take him back to my clinic and keep him sedated until we can talk to his blood rose," I tell the two of them.

Nixie nods, looking resigned, but Caspian still looks confused. "What is wrong? The two of you look like this is a bad thing. What aren't you mentioning?"

"Because his blood rose is Lila, Cas," I tell him gently. "Isn't it?" I ask Nixie, and she nods.

"Yes, she was hiding from him in the bottom of the pool, but she's in our grotto at the moment. Nikos is with her, but she needs someone to tell her about being his blood rose and what it entails."

"Can she survive that?" Caspian asks me, sounding shaky.

"I'm not sure. Like you said, there has never been a non-Vilaxian blood rose, or not that I've heard of. I will scan my data banks in search of more information as well as Vilaxian archives, which might have more," I tell him, inputting the instructions into my screen so my computers back in my clinic can start the search.

"Come on, I've programmed the stretcher to make its way down here. Let's go check on Lila while we wait."

As we walk down the stairs, Nixie tells us about her brother telling Saxon the same things

Caspian had told him, and we're chuckling when we get to the bottom of the stairs. We stop the minute we step out onto the platform and find Lila with a tentacle wrapped around Nikos's erect cock, with what looks like iridescent cum all over her chest.

A look of pure dismay crosses her face as she meets my eyes. "This is not what it looks like."

I look at Caspian, who is wearing the same grin of amusement that creeps across my face at the humorous sight.

"Looks like a good time to me," Caspian says, and I can't stop the burst of laughter from exploding from my mouth. Nixie groans as she slaps a hand over her eyes.

"Fucking hell, Nikos. What did you do?"

"Nothing, I did nothing. We were talking, and then Lila grabbed my cock. You said she had to initiate things, so who am I to say no if she wants to stroke my glorious manhood?"

Caspian and I laugh harder as Lila tries desperately to pull away from him, but it doesn't have the effect she wants it to. Nikos groans again, the sound of pleasure making my own cock move inside my pants.

"Don't just stand there, help me!" she screeches at us. Her eyes widen in frustration but then turn helpless when she realizes we haven't moved to assist her.

"Oh, Lila, my little crustacean. If you want

your men to join in, that is okay with me. I don't mind rough male hands playing with my anal slit."

Nixie screams in disgust and dives into the water, changing. Her tail sends up a splash of water as she dives deep in an attempt to get away from her brother's sexcapades. The dress she was wearing floats on the surface of the water.

"I can't get my tentacle to unwrap no matter what I do." Her desperate pleas stop our laughter in its tracks. "I was just trying to stop his advances by putting my tentacle against his chest, but the damn thing had other ideas."

We get a hold of our laughter, but I can see it's as much of a struggle for Caspian as it is for me. She said she was trying to stop his advances, though, so we shouldn't let this continue.

"I think maybe you may have an inner beast after all. Although you can't make a full shift, it seems to have taken a liking to the Aquilian and is showing it in the only way it can. Whereas my beast and I can communicate within our mind, it seems you have yet to accomplish that, so it is taking over as much as it can," Caspian explains as he moves over and uses his hand to unwrap Lila's tentacle from Nikos's boner.

"No matter how I tried to move forward to use my own hands, it was like I was stuck in one place. I had control of my upper half, but my lower half was not responding at all, and I couldn't get close enough to remove my tentacle," she says as he succeeds. Without another word, she drags her body away using just her arms and allows herself to fall into the water, disappearing just like Nixie did.

"Are you going to finish what she started?" Nikos's question has me looking away from Lila and back to him and Caspian, whose hand is still wrapped around his erect dick. He releases it and pats him on the shoulder.

"Not this time."

Nikos's lip juts out in a pout before he shrugs his shoulders. "Never mind. Lila was enough, but I can't wait to have those pretty lips wrapped around my member," he comments as he turns and points to Lila's mating mark, which has appeared on his shoulder. "She is not as indifferent to me as she appears."

"I guess that takes her to five," I tell Caspian, who nods but frowns at Nikos. A small hint of worry prickles the back of my mind. Is there going to be enough room in Lila's heart for me? I quickly shake it off. Lila has shown a huge capacity for love just by accepting what happened between her and Caspian, so I'm sure everything will be fine.

"You just make sure if you do anything with her, you tell her everything she needs to know about having sex with you in either form. She has had enough surprises within the last week, and she needs to know everything so she doesn't get hurt." Caspian's lighthearted tone becomes sterner at the end, his protectiveness over his mate overruling any niceties.

"I promise I will tell her everything. She is pregnant with your young, yes? She will need lots of dick to keep her hormones happy, and I'm ready and willing to help out." I half expect Nikos to fall to his knees and beg Caspian to let him participate in keeping Lila sated. Thankfully, he maintains a shred of decency and keeps it together.

"Settle down. Link is courting her tonight, and we need to sort out the deal with Saxon. If Lila desires to pursue a sexual relationship, you will get your chance, I will make sure of it."

Nikos flashes his sharp teeth at us in a threatening manner. "Make sure you do." My eyebrow quirks at his response, because I doubt Lila would take kindly to Nikos threatening her mate or demanding a turn with her body.

"How about you deal with the vampire, and I will take Lila back to our place and put her in a bath, then she can have a nap before her date with you tonight?" Caspian suggests.

"Are you sure you are still okay with us having a date?" I check again. He's been so good about all this, and there hasn't been any jealousy or resentment or anything. I've got to say I'm a little surprised, since shifters are usually possessive as fuck. I expected more of a reaction when he learned about two more suitors. I know I'm a little worried, but he seems to be taking this all in stride. It's a little unnerving, and I hope it's authentic.

"Yeah, man. I'm just thrilled that I was first and that she even wanted me to begin with. There will be occasions when I am selfish and want my time with my mate, but my beast is pretty stoked that she's carrying our young even though it might be a while before we meet them. Our place is solid, but we also understand those fuck me vibes and her Skarrian nature are going to attract other suitors. I'm okay with that as long as she is happy."

I nod, feeling more relaxed by his admission, knowing that I won't be overstepping any boundaries. "Okay, go and look after our woman. She seems pretty cut up about what happened," I tell him, but Nikos grumbles next to me.

"I do not know why. It was a beautiful thing to see her lovely chest mounds covered in my seed."

Anger zips through my veins at his dismissal of Lila's feelings. "Because, man, that was not what she intended to do, and she couldn't stop her beast once it took over."

His chest puffs out. "She has nothing to be sad about. I will find her and explain everything is wonderful." Before I can stop him, the idiot rips off his loincloth and dives into the pool, shifting into his dolphin form before taking off after Lila.

"Fuck, that's not going to go well. Those idiot animals of theirs are even hornier than their humanoid or mer forms," Caspian swears, tearing off his clothes and shifting quickly. "Pick her up around eight, I will make sure she is ready."

"I want to take her for dinner first before we head to the club, so I will make a reservation at Saturn's Rings for just after eight."

"That will be perfect, because my friend Silac and Dylan's dragon replacement are arriving on a transport and are expected at half past eight. That will give me enough time to get to the docking platform to greet them and show them to their quarters."

"I'm not sure what time I'll have her home," I tell him cautiously, and he slaps me on the back as one of his tentacles caresses my leg. I glance down at it in surprise, and when I look back up at him, he shrugs innocently.

"My beast thinks you're cute. Anyway, have fun with Lila. If she stays over, just shoot me a message so I know not to expect her home. Silac was going to use one of the rooms in our quarters for a couple of days, but he can have my old ones instead. And Dylan's replacement will be in his old quarters. I'll give them a late-night tour and bring them up to speed with what is expected of them. I'll probably be late too, so don't worry." He gives me a wave and takes off after Nikos while I climb up the stairs to deal with the wayward vampire. I am hoping I'll have all the information on what it means to be a sanguinista's blood rose by the time I get back to my clinic.

Nixie is quietly singing under her breath as she folds some laundry that has been dumped on a nearby sofa. She must have swum around and climbed out on the surface. She's covered by another dress that ties behind the neck. It's a traditional dress for the Aquilians, much like Nikos's loincloth. It makes changing forms easy.

She looks up when she sees me and grimaces. "Where is my idiot brother? I swear my mother bashed his head against a rock when she was teaching him to swim."

"He chased after Lila when she ran in embarrassment. He wanted to tell her she had nothing to be embarrassed about."

She groans and stands up, dropping the piece of cloth she was folding. "I should probably go rescue her from him. He doesn't integrate himself as much as the rest of us do, and because of that, his social skills leave a lot to be desired. On our home planet, women throw themselves at him because he is a prince."

"You guys are royalty?" I didn't know this, and I'm starting to get a little suspicious now. I can't believe that there is another high-ranking family aboard this circus. With them, Prince Xavier, General Saxon, and the Lords Maxsim and Echo, we have a fairly influential group of beings on board the Galaxy Circus.

Why are all these powerful people working for the circus and not back on their home planets, learning how to rule or lead troops into battle? I must check the archives to see if this is a common occurrence or if this is something that has happened recently.

"Yup, Mother and Father decided that my idiot brother needed a reality check, so they made us come and perform in the circus as part of the mermaid show. I love it. I have so much fun performing and traveling the galaxy. But Nikos did not cope very well, and he sulks at the bottom of our pool instead of learning about different worlds. I think my parents are going to be very disappointed if he comes back and is still the arrogant man whore that he was before we left."

"Hmm," I murmur, but before I can voice my suspicions, Saxon groans. "Oh no, we don't want him to wake before I can get him back to my clinic. Can you sing him to sleep again?" I ask her hurriedly, and she nods.

"Close off your ears so it doesn't affect you." I do so, and my hearing disappears, plunging me into silence. I watch Saxon as Nixie opens her mouth and sings, and he stops moving and relaxes once more. She waves at me to turn my ears back on.

"Done, but you better hurry. You need to knock him out and see if you can find a solution to this problem. Now that he's found her, no other blood will satisfy him."

"You know a lot about Vilaxians?" I question as I lift him onto the nearby hover stretcher.

Her pastel blue cheeks deepen into a darker blue as she blushes and looks away from me. I chuckle. "Hale convinced you to play with him, did he? I'm surprised the girls let him near you."

She shakes her head, still not looking at me. "No, I let Velorina drink from me. I did some research after that about Vilaxian relationships."

"It's good to educate yourself," I assure her with a smile, but inwardly I'm surprised. Skarrians are an anomaly in the galaxy in that they will happily form family units with whomever they are attracted to, whereas almost eighty percent of all other species tend to stick within their own race. An Aquilian princess having a relationship with a Vilaxian woman would be a scandal. It's not that she's a woman, that wouldn't matter, but the fact that she is a different species surely would.

I'm not going to judge, though, because cyborgs are much the same, and once my mother hears from Josa that I am courting Lila, I'm sure I will get disowned. I'm not all that upset about it. My father won't care, all he wants is for me to be happy, and he's the only one in my family who matters to me.

"Alright, I better get him back to my clinic. Thank you for your help with Saxon and protecting Lila. See you around, Nixie."

"Bye, Link, and have fun on your date with Lila tonight. Be on the lookout for Estrella and Radella though," she warns me. "Once they find out that

Lila is Saxon's blood rose, they will be gunning for her."

"I will. I might not look like it, but I'm quite a formidable opponent myself," I assure her, and she looks me up and down.

"Oh yeah, I can see that, and I bet Lila can too." She winks, and I use the console in my arm to move the stretcher forward. Back across the floating pathway we go, and when we stop to wait for the door to open on the other side, it retracts, leaving just an expanse of water with no way across but to swim.

I peer down in the hope that I can see the other three, but they are nowhere to be found, so I move the stretcher out the door, following along behind it. I have to get all the information I can to give to Lila tonight, but I can't wake Saxon to do it, and asking the others is out of the question.

I wonder if Xavier knows anything. I will message him and ask before I go the official route. I don't want anyone to know that Saxon is out of commission for the moment. That could endanger his life.

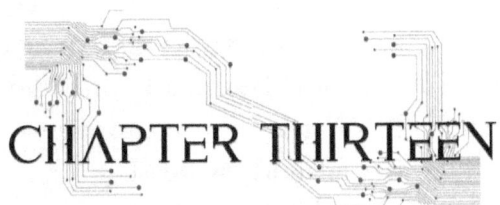

CHAPTER THIRTEEN

Caspian

When I hit the water, I'm still grinning about the shocked look on Link's face when my tentacle caressed his leg.

Robot sexy, my beast tells me, showing me images of a naked Link with our tentacles wrapped around him and our mouth on his cock. I've got to say his imagination is fairly vivid. I don't remember having seen him naked before.

Whoa, what is this all about? Not that I'm arguing, but you have never wanted a man like that before. You were always telling me you wanted to eat Dylan in a completely different way, I remind him.

He bares his fangs at me and hisses at the mention of Dylan. *Bad dragon. Have mate now and can play with mate's other mates. Can have fun.*

Oh okay, so now that we have a mate and she's carrying

our young, you feel secure enough to want to play with others?
I question.

Not others. Mates, mates, he insists and shows me an image of Xavier and Saxon and that idiot Aquilian. I can't help snorting in amusement, and bubbles billow out around my head.

So we're not being choosy now? I ask curiously, and I feel him give me the equivalent of a shrug.

Feels good, who cares? He nudges me in the direction I need to go and fades into the background, so I concentrate on finding Lila.

Plunging downward into the reef, I swim in the direction where I know there's a cave. It's a beautiful spot, and when the light shines through it and hits the brightly colored gems lining the walls of the cavern, it sparkles brightly. It's like a rainbow exploded inside the cave. I discovered it one day by accident. I've been meaning to ask one of the Aquilians about it, but Nixie is the only one I really speak to. The other five, including Nikos, tend to stick to themselves.

Sure enough when I get to it, she's in there, but she's not alone. Nikos is with her, but that idiot is in his beast form, which is much like mine and driven by instinct. I watch him chase her around the cavern, his prehensile dolphin dick chasing her like it's a heat-seeking missile. He swims past her mouth, trying to get her to open it, but she's got it clamped tight. Nikos rubs against her tentacles before swimming under her and trying to stick it into her breeding entrance, and that's when I put a stop to it.

I grow in size and launch myself at him, wrapping my tentacles around his body. He struggles, but I've got him wrapped up tight. If I squeeze him a little too hard, well, I'll never admit to it.

Are you okay? I ask Lila through our telepathic connection. At first I think she's sobbing, so I hold out my arms to her—I can still hug her while my tentacles are wrapped around this horny creature—but then I realize she's laughing.

He's just like the rapey dolphins on Earth, or a Labrador that keeps trying to hump your leg, she chokes out between peals of laughter. *Every time I opened my mouth, he tried to stick his dick in it. And what is up with that dick? It moves like an elephant's trunk.*

Earth dolphins are descended from Aquilia. Much like how humans are Skarrians who have lost their powers, dolphins are Aquilians who have gotten stuck in their beast form.

But they are not colored like them, she points out as I feel Nikos start to struggle. He had been playing possum, but he started to move again when he felt my grip loosen minutely.

Earth's salty water turned them that color, I tell her as I grit my teeth and hold onto the struggling beast tightly. I may have to shift fully and let my beast handle him. I consider injecting him with the paralyzing toxin I can excrete from my suckers, but he has stopped wriggling again, so I don't bother. Just as I'm about to suggest to Lila that we should head home, I feel something near my anal opening.

What is that? Looking down at the animal locked in my tentacles, I realize that when he was wriggling, he flipped himself upside down and is now working his cock into me.

I quickly expel my paralyzing toxin, and he and his roving dick stop moving, so I release him and let him float away.

What happened? What did you do to him? she asks, watching the dolphin and its now floppy member float out of the cavern and away on the current.

He tried to… I trail off, not sure how she will take it. Even *I'm* surprised he tried going there with me in my half form. He and his dick are going to be a problem.

What?

Well, he tried to do to me what he tried to do to you.

Her mouth drops open, and once again peals of laughter float through our connection. *Ha ha ha, he really is a horny dog.*

You're not upset? I ask her, and she shakes her head.

No, we both know you enjoy men as well. I would be horrible to deny you that, especially when I'm just as interested in other people. Though I would probably ask for you to only play with the same men I'm playing with.

I think I can agree to that, my beast was suggesting something similar, but I'm not sure I'm ready to share that with her yet. I want her to make decisions about her relationships without any influence from me. *Now come on. For now, I'm perfectly happy with you, so let's get you home and you can have a nice relaxing bath. I will answer any questions you have about anything that happened today, and whatever I can't answer, Link will tonight, and if he can't, we will ask Xavier.*

That sounds lovely, but is he going to be okay? she asks, pointing in the direction that Nikos floated.

He will be fine. It only paralyzes their external muscles, so he can still breathe, and unlike Earth dolphins, these ones have tiny gills so they can breathe underwater, I inform her, and I can feel her relief. Despite his rapey ways, she still doesn't want any harm to come to him.

I hold out a hand and she grabs it, and together, we leave the pretty little cave behind and swim back to the edge.

B ack in our room, I encourage Lila to hop into the bath while I go get a drink to relax her. She really likes the rilaxious, so I grab us both one of those. When I return to the bathroom, she's splashing happily in the pool there.

Her face lights up with a smile as I pass her the drink, and then I strip off my pants so they won't get wet when I take a seat on the edge of the pool. Both of us shifted back to human form and dressed before we left the Aquilian habitat, not wanting to give anyone we passed during the trip back to our quarters a free show.

She takes a long sip of her drink before swallowing and sighing. "God, I needed that. It has been a long-ass day. My brain is on fucking overload, and I have no clue what the fuck I did to set Saxon off."

"Link's going to give you the rundown on that tonight during your date," I tell her, and she waves her hand without the drink around.

"Good, because I do not want to talk about it right now. Why don't you get your sexy ass in the tub with me and tell me about your day?" She splashes water in my direction, and I quickly get up and strip off the rest of my clothes before stepping down into the tub. Her eyes roam over my body, and her smile changes to one of pure pleasure.

"I will never get enough of seeing you naked," she murmurs as I step up to her and pull her into my arms.

I nuzzle into her neck, and she giggles. "That goes both ways," I reply as I feel her breasts rub against my chest as her legs wrap around my waist, putting her pussy against my rapidly hardening cock. "I thought you wanted to hear about my day," I tease as she grinds against me.

"Caspian, I am so worked up after everything that happened with Xavier, Saxon, and Nikos that I'm about to spontaneously combust. What do you say we multitask? You tell me about your day while I ride your dick."

Sounds like the best kind of compromise to me.

She pants as my fingers slide down to circle her clit, and I take one of her nipples into my mouth, allowing the suckers inside to latch onto it.

"Please!"

Grabbing her hips, I line myself up and thrust deep, and she shouts, throwing her head back.

"Fuck yes."

I take a seat on a nearby ledge and she straddles me. I feel my suckers at the base of my cock latch onto her clit as she starts to writhe on my dick, her inner muscles undulating much like our tentacles can. Whoa, that's different.

"Oh God, it feels so good." She arches her back, putting her beautiful breasts right in front of my mouth, so I don't waste any time showing them love. Nipping and sucking, I tease her nipples while making small thrusts, but she is entirely involved in riding my dick, and it feels too good to fully take over.

Talking isn't going to happen anytime soon as we both chase our pleasure in each other's bodies. The sound of lapping water and our quiet pants echo around the big room as Lila's movements get quicker and the muscles around my cock continue to tighten. It's almost like she has suckers inside her pussy, but I've never heard of something like that before. I have a feeling being Lila's mate is going to come with one surprise after another.

"Why do I have the urge to bite you all of a sudden?" Lila asks, meeting my eyes, and my movements stutter at what I see. She doesn't notice and keeps riding my dick, but her pupils look like they would if she was in full kraken form. They hadn't changed like that when she shifted earlier.

"Your beast is making herself known. If we mated in beast form, she would bite her partner during copulation," I tell her breathlessly as I resume thrusting. This time I take charge, holding her hips in place while I pound up into her. She grabs my shoulders and rests her forehead against mine. Her beast peeks through as the waves splash against us as we move.

"Harder, Caspian, I need more."

I allow my body to shift, and my cock thickens into a tentacle, stuffing her full. She moans her delight as a second tentacle comes around and forces its way into her mouth, a third presses into her ass, and a fourth latches its suckers onto her clit. Lila is completely stuffed to the brim and can no longer move, so my body takes over. In a coordinated attack, the tentacles pleasure Lila, and I almost lose my head at the sensations. Her mouth is sucking hard, her ass is hot and tight, and her pussy's undulating movement is out of this world. Two more tentacles wrap around her chest and suction onto her nipples.

It proves to be too much, and I feel her orgasm detonate through her body. She stiffens and everything tightens as her muffled groan vibrates my tentacle, setting off my own orgasm. I feel my tentacles explode as the beast forces us to come through all of them. He wants Lila filled with our seed so that it drips out of her body when she goes on her date with Link tonight—possessive bastard that he is.

She splutters a little, and some of my cum dribbles out of her mouth, but she does her best to swallow it all. As we both come down from our releases, and I drag my tentacle out of her mouth, I see her eyes widen in panic and change back to human as one of her hands slides down to cup her belly, and I know what she's worried about.

"No, it won't be enough to trigger that. You have to suck them all dry to start the pregnancy process," I assure her, and I feel her relax. She leans her head against my chest, and I remove the tentacles from her breasts. I stroke her back with my hands as I feel her breathing start to even out.

"Such a good girl, taking all our seed," my beast coos to her, pushing me to the side so he can speak to her. "Such a good mother for our babies. You have our seed in you now so cyborg man knows that you were ours first. We should give him our seed, too, so he can be ours also."

Holy fuck, my beast has lost his mind. I think he

just wants to play now that he feels secure of our place in Lila's life.

A small, satisfied smile crosses Lila's lips as she turns her head and caresses one of my tentacles. "That sounds like it could be fun. As long as I get to play too, or at least watch."

She's still stuffed full of tentacles in both her ass and pussy, the beast wanting to ensure that our cum stays where he wants it. I can feel him getting ready to go again, so I push him to the side and take over.

"Come on, baby," I murmur, slowly pulling myself from her body. "Shall we go and have a nap before your date?"

"That would be lovely," she says sleepily. Her eyelids are starting to get heavy, but she looks blissed out. My beast is preening like a fucking peacock because he made her feel that way.

Lifting her into my arms, I carry her out of the bath, changing back into human form and wrapping towels around our bodies before moving into my new room. Although I haven't completely moved my stuff in, the bed is made, and I can't deny wanting to smell her all over my sheets when she's not in it tonight.

Pulling back the covers with one hand, I lay her down, removing her towel before covering her back up. "Are you not going to join me?" she asks as I remove my own towel.

"I am, I just want to set the alarm to give us enough time for you to get ready," I tell her with a wink, grabbing the tablet for the room off the bedside table. I set the alarm and then climb in on the other side.

"Can you shift back?" she murmurs as her eyes drift closed. "I like having your tentacles wrapped around me."

My beast crows triumphantly *again* inside my head, and I allow my body to change once more, gathering her up and pulling her close. Her breathing evens out as I place a kiss on each of her eyes and her lips.

"I love you, my beautiful mate," I whisper, but she's already fast asleep. A feeling of satisfaction rolls through me as I close my eyes to enjoy my nap with my mate.

CHAPTER FOURTEEN

Lila

W hen Caspian and I woke up, I quickly showered again, because despite his beast's best intentions, I was not going on my date with Link while Caspian's spunk dripped out of me.

Wrapping a towel around my body, I have a sudden thought that causes me to panic. "Oh no." I walk out into the living area, looking for Caspian.

"What's wrong, beautiful lady?" he asks as the doorbell to our room rings.

"I have nothing to wear. All of my clothes are in my room in the pod. I only have uniforms, and that's not sexy."

Caspian gets up from the sofa to answer the door. "Actually, babe, you look fucking hot in the uniform, but I already thought about that." He opens the door and takes something from the person on the other side before closing it again. He turns and holds out a dress bag. "While you were in the shower, I messaged Magenta, and she organized for one of the boutiques to send something up. Privileges of being the boss men's granddaughter and all." He sends a cheeky grin my way.

I'm an instant puddle of motherfucking goo. "Oh my God, my mate is amazing. Seriously fucking amazing." I hurry over to him and throw my arms around his neck, kissing him hard on the mouth. He kisses me back before extracting himself from my grip and passing me the bag. "Here, go try it on. Link will be here shortly. I'll keep him entertained until you're ready. In the drawer of the bathroom cabinet is a makeup applicator. Just hold it up to your face and it applies it instantly. Sorry, but there's nothing fancy for your hair, so you'll have to manage that one yourself, but there is a dryer on the wall. If you stick your head up into it, it will at least dry it instantly too."

"Holy shit! The technology here is fucking amazing. Where have these things been all of my life?" I sigh dramatically. "Thank you so much, Cas. That will make getting ready so much quicker, and I can't wait to try everything out."

Leaving him to let Link in, I hurry to the bathroom to get ready. I can't wait to see what Magenta picked out for me to wear. Hanging it on a hook in the bathroom, I open the bag. There's a little note from the devious little Skarrian attached to the dress.

No underwear because you can't wear it with this dress, and hopefully you won't need them anyway. ;)

Magenta

As I lift the dress out of the bag, I can see exactly why I don't need underwear. It's a short, body-con style dress with only one sleeve and a futuristic slash across the neckline. It's made of a shimmery holographic fabric that picks up different colors depending on how the light hits it. It's gorgeous, but it's going to hug my curves, and there is no room for panty lines. Dropping my towel, I pull it over my head. Thankfully, it's tight enough to control my breasts. I shimmy it down my frame, and it hits me at mid-thigh. Reaching back into the garment bag, I pull out a pair of silver heels to go with it. They are only about three inches, so they are perfectly manageable, but it brings me a little closer to Link's lips if he needs, you know, mouth to mouth.

I look around the bathroom. It's the first time I've used the bathroom in my living quarters, so I haven't really had a chance to take everything in. Plus, I'm not currently distracted by a sexy purple and blue octoman who really knows how to use his tentacles. I spy what I'm assuming is the hair dryer. Much like the big ones in hair salons on Earth, it looks like I stick my whole head into it.

I gingerly duck and then stand up inside it. It

covers my whole head, but my long hair is still sitting against my back. I'm not sure if this is going to work, but there's a small screen on the inside giving me instructions. I press the green button, and a mask drops down from the front wall of the machine and covers my face. It's kind of like one of those full diving masks. It suctions on and seals to the skin around my hairline, and air floods in so I can still breathe. Then I feel something start to gently gather my hair. It almost feels like a claw but without the bite. Pushing the blue button as instructed, I hear a humming sound, and then I have a slight moment of panic. Please don't let it fry off my hair, or worse, perm it.

It goes on for about a minute, and then I feel my dry hair fall back around my shoulders before the mask unseals and rises, and the machine's screen flashes that the sequence is complete. Ducking and stepping out of it, I reach up to feel my hair. Sure enough, it's bone dry and silky straight, but the best part? I didn't feel a fucking thing. I decide to leave it exactly as it is once I see it in the mirror. It looks like I've come straight from a salon.

Okay, that machine was successful. *Looking good, Lila.* It's time to find this makeup applicator Cas was telling me about. Opening one of the drawers under the sink, I find another full scuba mask style thing. I'm guessing this is the makeup machine, because there's nothing else that looks remotely like it could apply makeup.

With my heart beating fast once more, I bring the machine up to my face. Again, it's pretty self-explanatory and has great step-by-step instructions. Holding it up to my face, I scroll through styles, but unfortunately it has only a name and no description. Tapping my finger on top of the machine, I consider my options. It's not like it's permanent, right? I can always remove it if I don't like it. Taking a leap of faith, I press "okay" on the style on the screen—Zandarian. This machine doesn't hum like the hair dryer, but it does vibrate ever so slightly. Closing my eyes, I hold still. Through my closed eyelids, I can see a light scan my face before I feel something spraying over my skin. It tickles, and it's all I can do to stop myself from giggling.

At the end, there's a small pause before I hear a recorded voice say, "Your transformation is complete." I pull the machine away from my face and check out my reflection in the mirror. I blink a couple of times at what I see.

Hmm, Zandarian must mean drag queen chic. Blue glitter eyeshadow frames my eyes, with pink rouge highlighting my cheekbones and a bright pink gloss on my lips. Long, feathery false eyelashes round out the look. Holy crap, that's way too much makeup. I look down at the machine in my hand and scroll through the options on the screen, finding removal. Hallelujah! I go through the process again and it cleans my face, and I become a blank canvas once more. This time I try to find an Earth style, and thankfully it's there. A smoky eye look is what I need. Holding the machine up to my face once more, I repeat the process. This time when I pull it away, it looks fabulous.

Placing it back in the drawer, I smooth my dress down, feeling a little nervous but excited. I blow myself a kiss in the mirror and head back to the living area.

Voices in the living area bring a little flutter of nerves to my stomach. I'm still having a bit of trouble wrapping my head around the fact that I'm going on a date with my husband's blessing. My lips spread into a smile at that thought. My husband! I wonder what Cas would say if I called him that. Maybe I could convince him to do a small Vegas wedding with me while we're there. It's something to think about a little later. Right now, I'm ignoring everything but this evening's plans, never mind the other three marks on my shoulders. Nope, tonight is all about the two gorgeous men who both look like they want to devour me when I enter the room.

I can tell by their body language that I interrupted them mid-conversation, but I give zero fucks because the way they are both caressing my body with their gazes makes me feel like a damn queen.

"Whoa," Link whispers reverently, his silver eyes darkening, but my heightened hearing kicks in, and

I hear the word clear as day. I feel my cheeks warm slightly.

The fact that this gorgeous, slightly nerdy, intelligent man likes what he sees makes me feel good. While he gets a good look at me, I take in the tall, sexy cyborg, and it's all I can do to keep my tongue in my mouth. This is the first time I've seen him out of his Galaxy Circus uniform, and let me tell you, it's not a disappointment. He's wearing a black, long-sleeved, button-up shirt that makes his shimmery skin even more noticeable. The top two buttons are open, and the sleeves are rolled up. I'm such a fucking forearm whore, and not even his built-in screen can turn me off. He's paired it with black jeans and a purple tie. He looks edible.

"Wow, Lila, Magenta really picked an amazing dress. Now I wish I was coming with you," Caspian says, licking his lips, and Link quickly jumps in.

"You're welcome to join us," he offers, but Caspian just shakes his head.

"No, tonight is your night. Have fun. I have to go greet the new arrivals."

"Oh, Cas, I'm sorry we didn't get to talk about your day. I was so wanting to hear about it," I tell him, and he smiles.

"That's okay, babe. Have fun, and I can tell you all about it tomorrow." He sounds pleased, and I make a mental note to chase him down and make him tell me all about it.

"Well, if that's the case, can you make sure that

Josa gets on that return flight too? I wouldn't put it past him to try and miss it," Link requests, and Caspian quickly agrees.

"No problem. Lila, just shoot me a message if you're not coming home tonight," Caspian says with a grin, and I feel my cheeks heat up again. My husband is basically giving me permission to get laid.

Best. Husband. Ever.

He presses a chaste kiss to my lips and hurries out of our quarters, leaving me alone with Link.

"You look exquisite, Lila. Here, these are for you." He pulls a bunch of flowers out from behind his back. They are like nothing I've ever seen before, all bright, vivid colors with feather-like petals.

"They are breathtaking, Link. Where on Earth…" I break off and think about what I said before continuing with a little giggle. "Or I guess I mean where in space did you get these?"

"We have a biozone level where they grow all sorts of things. There is a garden shop on the retail level so people can bring a bit of life to such a sterile atmosphere."

I take them from him and bring them to my nose to smell the blooms. They have a complicated floral scent, kind of like peach tea and lavender, if I had to describe it using what I know from Earth. "I'll just find some water for them." I head over to the kitchen area and search for a vase to place them in. After opening a couple of cupboards, I find something suitable and fill it with water, placing the flowers inside.

I really need to spend some time trying to acclimate myself to my living quarters.

"Shall we go? I reserved a table for dinner before we head to the club." Link holds out his arm, and I link mine with his—no pun intended.

"I can't wait. I've been looking forward to spending time with you, just the two of us." We leave my quarters and head for the elevator.

"Me too, and I found out some information for you about why Saxon went feral when he smelled your blood, so we can discuss that too if you want." I remember Caspian telling me that Link would be able to shed some light on the situation, and I'm glad he brought it up and not me.

"As much as I want to ignore it and just talk about us, I would be stupid not to educate myself." I turn my head so I can look at him. "I can't believe, just because I was lucky enough to escape earlier, that it will happen again. I'm surprised he didn't catch up with me once whatever Nixie must have done wore off."

The thought that Saxon could be lurking around the ship, just waiting for me, has my insides churning a bit. I force down the paranoia that's starting to put me on edge.

We step into the elevator, and Link hits the button to the floor where the restaurant is. "Oh, well, that's because he's currently sedated in my clinic. He's no harm to you until he wakes up, and by then, you should know everything you need to."

I step up to him, placing one hand on his cheek and one on his chest. "Thank you, Link. I can't tell you how much I appreciate you and Caspian looking after me. It's been a little bit of a bumpy ride so far, and knowing the two of you really have my best interests at heart is a relief. Between you and the grandpas, Dylan's betrayal hurts a little less."

I take his lips with mine, dragging my tongue along the seam of his mouth so he opens to me. When he does, I slide my tongue in to tangle it with his and kiss him deeply, putting all my feelings into it. It doesn't take him long to respond, and he pulls me hard against his body, taking over the kiss and dominating me. Phew, who would have thought that he had this in him? I guess I shouldn't be surprised, cyborgs are supposed to be the experts on pleasure. How lucky can a girl get?

I'm breathless and lightheaded when he pulls away as the doors open. He wears a smug grin on his face as I try to steady myself, putting my hands against his chest and blinking to defog the pure lust from my mind.

"Come on." He holds my hand, and the two of us make our way to dinner.

Dinner is yummy, despite me not being familiar with anything on the menu. I decided to let Link order for me, and everything he chose has been delicious.

"So tell me more about yourself," I ask before I shovel another delicious bite into my mouth. "I know you're a doctor and have great taste in food" —I wave my hand at the table, and we chuckle— "but I want to know more. Tell me about cyborgs or your family, or even Pleasure Bot Industries. Anything."

I'm practically begging by the end, but I see him thinking, so I keep eating while he gets his thoughts together.

He takes a deep breath. "My family is complicated. Cyborgs don't have fated mates, intimates, blood roses, or anything like the attraction marks the Skarrians have. They rely on nanobot compatibility. I guess I need to explain cyborg reproduction for you to understand. Much like most organisms, sex is required to reproduce, but because of our nanotechnology, parents are able to pick both physical and mental traits they'd like their children to have. Once they decide to reproduce, the parents program their eggs and sperm to contain these necessary trait markers, thus ensuring the desirable outcome in their child. When a cyborg baby is born, their source code, the thing that makes them uniquely them, is copied onto a microchip and deposited in a safe place. That place is one of the best kept secrets in the galaxy. Only the caretaker has access to this secret location. There is much speculation that it's in an alternate dimension. This is to protect each individual, because if anyone were to gain access to it, they would be able to rewrite their programming. Much like I can change features on my body, someone else would be able to control that."

I stop eating and stare at him, completely engrossed in what he's saying. "Hold up. You can change your features?" I ask him, and his silver eyes switch to red and he winks at me. "Holy shit."

"But all of that information is put into our central servers, and from there, we can access people who have compatible codes if we choose to."

My heart sinks. "You don't marry for love?" Link must hear the disappointment in my voice, because he reaches out to grab my hand.

"Some of us do," he assures me, "but some cyborgs prefer perfection over happiness. You won't ever find an ugly cyborg, but you may find ones that aren't as gifted as others. They are usually children of love matches."

A pang of sympathy plucks at my heart for the

gorgeous man in front of me. He has looks, brains, and talent, so I can guess where this is going.

"My parents are not a love match. Although my father's family have all been love matches in the past, he chose to buck tradition. Dad decided he was too busy running Pleasure Bot Industries, turning it into the galaxy wide company it is today, to court a partner, but he desperately wanted a child. My mother was his perfect match, and I am the result of that. Mom signed up on the proviso that she got to sink her claws into the company and become the CEO. I mean, it wasn't a bad decision, she is a business mastermind, but their marriage is cold and loveless, and they both make use of the Pleasure Bots that our company is famous for."

"Isn't that cheating?" I ask, wanting to hear about it from someone who has the down low.

He shrugs. "I guess some people could consider it cheating, but realistically, Pleasure Bots are well-programmed, lifelike robots. They have no autonomy or feelings. They have intuitive programming, so they can react in a way the customer may want them to, but at the end of the day, you switch them off, put them on to charge, and close the door. They aren't programmed to be part of day-to-day lives. They are just like any kind of masturbatory object, just more versatile and capable of talking dirty to you, or anything you want it to really."

I flush a little at the thought of my masturbatory objects, and I can guarantee they weren't talking dirty to me. I know he can't read my thoughts, but from the gleam in his eye, I'm sure I'm giving everything I'm thinking about away.

"So your parents' marriage was unhappy?" I bring him back to the original topic.

"Not unhappy, just indifferent. I was raised by my father and his family, only seeing my mom occasionally until I started to mature and become a possible asset. But by then, it was too late. Dad allowed me to develop my own interests, and they did not align with my mother's hopes."

"So you never saw your mother? That's really sad. You had one, but she couldn't be bothered. I don't know who was worse off, me without one or you with one who didn't care."

"No, it wasn't until I was about seventeen when she popped back into my life. She was furious at my father for allowing me to become interested in medicine. She insisted that I intern at the Pleasure Bot company for six months in the hope that it would change my mind."

"What did she think was going to happen?" I ask, and he blushes, increasing my curiosity.

"Well, she made me a product tester."

"I'm sorry, what?" I question, not sure I like where this is going.

"We have a product testing department to make sure all our designs are satisfactory," he explains, and my eyebrows just about shoot off my face.

"You fucked sex bots for a job?" I'm not sure

how I feel about this. I mean, how am I ever going to compete with perfect creatures who are designed to cater to your every whim or desire?

"Yes, it's a very coveted position in the company," he tells me, unaware of the turmoil in my brain.

"I bet," I grumble under my breath, but I guess he hears me, because he squeezes the hand he's still holding.

"But I hated it. Lila, I can't even begin to tell you how excited I am about the possibility of us. For so long, I've been looking for someone I can connect with on an emotional level, and until you, I have felt nothing for anyone other than some mild interest." My heart melts, and any worry I had slowly seeps away. "I'm more like my father's family than my mother had hoped. Dad's contribution to my DNA must have required an emotional connection, ensuring that I didn't end up like him, because I'm almost certain he regretted his marriage to my mother from day one. I can't wait to introduce you to him. He's going to be so excited to meet you."

"And your mother?" I ask, not sure if I want to know the answer when he grimaces.

"Oh, she'll be polite to your face because she won't want to upset the Adams brothers' granddaughter, but I wouldn't take anything she says at face value. She always has an agenda. Do not trust her," he warns as the waiter stops at the table to ask if we need anything else.

"Okay, Lila, we've had dinner, and we've talked all about ourselves, but we really need to talk about the elephant in the room," Link teases an hour or so later. We just left the restaurant, and we're walking to the club which is on this level but on the other side of the ship. We could have taken the side slip elevator, but Link suggested we walk.

He told me that just past all the retail stores, there's what they call a space walk. It's a tunnel or enclosed bridge, I guess, that is completely made of glass, and when you walk through it, you get a 360° view of space. It kind of feels like you're walking in it. I couldn't wait to try it, so I jumped at the chance, even if my feet were starting to ache in my heels.

"Fine." An exaggerated sigh leaves my lips. I know he's right, but I still want to keep my head in the sand for a little longer, even though I know I can't. "I guess I can't avoid it any longer. Tell me what the situation is all about," I reply, sitting down on a lounge in a little alcove just before the space walk starts. It gives us another fantastic view of the outside of the ship, and I'm pretty sure I need to be sitting down for this conversation.

My body is tense until Link sits down next to me and drags me closer, his arm wrapped around my shoulders as we both look into the vastness of the Milky Way. He's giving me comfort without me even asking for it.

"You are Saxon's blood rose. Do you know what that means?"

I shake my head. "I think I remember Magenta saying something about that when she was giving me vampire 101, but I obviously didn't pay attention."

"A blood rose to a sanguinista is basically the equivalent of a mate for a shifter or an intimate for a warlock. You're his soulmate, his perfect match. Your blood is the one match that can sustain him indefinitely." He pauses and looks down at me to check that I'm alright. "Are you okay so far?"

Am I okay? I mean, I guessed it was something like that, but I seem to be adding mates that have nothing to do with my Skarrian biological wants and needs and everything to do with theirs. It feels like it's all out of my control. I liked the idea of try before I buy and the attraction marks when it was on my terms, but this, just like Caspian, is something that is out of my hands, and I'm really not sure how I feel.

"Talk to me, Lila." Link sounds a little desperate at my silence, and his arm tightens around my shoulders. Shit, I guess I was thinking longer than I realized.

"What do you want me to say, Link? That I'm ecstatic about this? I can't, because *once again*, my choice is being taken away from me."

Link nods in understanding. "I know this is hard for you. Of course it is going to be difficult because you were raised human, and their concept of intimate relationships is so far apart from most of the rest of the galaxy, it's ridiculous. If you had been raised Skarrian, none of this would be new to you. Though I have to admit, Vilaxians don't often have blood roses who are not of their own race, but it has happened. I discovered this today when I was doing my research."

"And what happens to the blood rose if they are not of their own race? Do they survive? If Saxon needs to drink my blood every day, I'm going to run out of it very quickly. And as you know, I will die when that happens."

Link chuckles at my naivete and presses a kiss to my head. "No, sweetheart, when the Vilaxian seals the blood rose bond with the blood rose who isn't Vilaxian, they feed them some of their blood. With the venom in their bite and the blood, the blood rose's system adapts, much like you did when Caspian's beast gave you his mating bite. The blood rose will start producing more blood so they can see to their partner's needs."

"So basically I'm like a never-ending Slurpee for Saxon?" I ask quietly, and Link quickly shakes his head. I close my eyes and take a deep breath, trying to calm the helplessness I feel right now. Fuck. I don't know how much more of this conversation I can take, but Link is giving me the clinical information I need.

"No, it's so much more than that. It's hard to explain to you because nothing like that exists on Earth. It's like falling instantly in love, but because it is one-sided, you have no idea of the feelings that are rushing through Saxon. It's why he was so feral —all those intense emotions on top of the fact that to him your scent, your *blood*, sings to him in ways we can't comprehend."

A shiver runs down my spine. "Can I reject him?" I inquire, weighing all my options, and I feel Link stiffen like I've asked a taboo question, but then he blows out a sigh.

"Yes, Lila, you can reject him. If this was two-sided and you were Vilaxian, it wouldn't even be an option. You would have sealed yourself to him already and the two of you would probably still be secluded in his den. But because it's one-sided, you do have the choice to say no."

"What happens to him if I do? Will he find another blood rose?"

Link shakes his head. "No, he won't. Lila, what you have to realize is it's actually a rare occurrence for a Vilaxian to find a blood rose. They occur for only like twenty percent of the population. The others make do with drinking from anyone, and they never experience the kind of connection a blood rose partnership does."

"And what will happen to him if I do reject him?" I prompt when he doesn't answer my question the first time.

"Saxon will die."

CHAPTER FIFTEEN

Lila

Link drops that bomb, making me responsible for Saxon's life. Holy fuck! How fucking cruel can this universe be?

"He can no longer take blood from another being until he seals the bond with you. It's considered cheating, and their bodies will reject it until his connection with his blood rose is secure."

I remain silent while I consider my alternatives. Not that there is anything to consider now that I know he will die. There's no way I'm going to let that happen, but it feels so sudden. Sure, the man's sexy as fuck, but apart from that, I know nothing other than he held my hair back when I puked from motion sickness. I mean, that was kind, right? Especially with his enhanced senses.

I'm still warring with my thoughts when Link

stands up and holds out his hand. "Come on, you don't need to make a decision today. Remember, I have him sedated in my clinic, and I can sustain him intravenously until you make a choice. His body won't reject that, so we can keep him out for a couple of days."

"I'll need to talk to Caspian, and of course I want your opinion too," I tell him, and he blinks, seeming shocked. "Link, you and I are seeing where this relationship might take us. Unlike Caspian or Saxon, I guess, we have the luxury of it happening naturally without it being forced on me, and I can't tell you how much that relieves me. Of course I want to ask your opinion on anyone else I might be sleeping with or marrying, so to speak."

He yanks me into his arms and hugs me tightly. "Thank you, Lila. I didn't actually really think I had any chance with you with all these magical matings. Why would you want someone as boring as me?"

I pull away but grab his shirt, fisting the fabric as his hands fall to my hips. "Oh, Link, you are anything but boring to me. Come on, let me bury my head back in the sand for another twelve hours. I'll worry about Saxon in the morning. Right now, I want to see what your dance moves are like."

And a few other moves… in bed.

Patience, Lila. Patience.

He grabs my hand and twirls me under his arm before dipping me. "Let me tell you, Lila, my dance moves are on point. My programming won't let me be anything but perfect. I know how to seduce you with my moves, so are you sure you're ready for me to bring the heat?" His eyes twinkle with amusement, and I feel all my lady bits squeal with excitement.

"I can't wait for you to show me what you've got," I purr suggestively, and when the amusement in his silver eyes changes to a hot smolder, I know my night is about to get exciting.

I'm sweaty and breathless and horny as fuck after we spend a couple of hours drinking and dancing. Link introduced me to a few people who came over and talked to him earlier, but he didn't encourage them to stick around.

I can see Magenta on the opposite side of the dance floor, but she's dancing with a tall, athletically built woman, and it looks like it might be getting hot and heavy. They have their arms wrapped around each other, and the taller woman's leg is between Magenta's. She's so engrossed, she doesn't even notice me.

"That's Velorina. She's one of Saxon's clan," Link informs me when he sees where I'm looking.

"Huh, Magenta mentioned she had her eye on

one of them. I guess she managed to catch her interest as well."

"Now that I think about it, they don't know that Saxon is out of commission yet. I haven't told them, but it won't be long before Hale or one of the others comes looking for him. You probably shouldn't go anywhere alone for the next few days. I'll speak to Xavier. He will be able to keep you company when I have to work or Caspian has to work with the new act." A prickle of unease worries at my mind. Link never mentioned anything about me being in danger apart from Saxon, and he's sedated. I almost ask him what he's talking about, but then I remember my mantra for today.

"Nope, we're not talking about He-Who-Won't-Be-Named until tomorrow, remember?" I place a finger over Link's lips, shushing him.

He opens his mouth and sucks my finger into his warm, wet heat, his eyes locking onto mine. My core throbs, and I decide I'm done with vertical dancing.

"Take me home, Link, and show me all those moves you promised me you know."

I don't have to ask him twice.

He grabs my hand, pulling it from his mouth, and then he takes off, dragging me through the crowded dance floor. He rushes us to the elevator, and it takes us up to one of the residential levels. I don't get a chance to see which one, because the minute the door closes and he presses the button, he's on me, pushing me against the wall and taking my mouth with his. He kisses like he's trying to consume me through our connection, but it's not sloppy and gross like other past, regrettable kisses. No, this one has all the right pressure and tongue, and it's nothing short of breathtaking. He lifts me up, and I wrap my legs around him so when the doors open, our mouths don't have to part. I feel us moving, but I'm too caught up in this kiss to care about much else.

I blink and we're in his bedroom. Link drops me onto his bed and looks down at me with a satisfied smirk on his face. This sexy man has me right where he wants me.

His bed is just like the one in my quarters. It's huge, big enough for three or four, and as comfortable as a cloud. I wave a finger at him.

"Strip now, please," I order, propping up on my elbows so I can get a good view of Link removing his clothes. He quickly pulls his shirt over his head. Tonight was the first time I'd seen him out of his uniform, and he looks even better in a shirt and jeans than he does in his regulation clothes, but holy fuck, shirtless Link is even better. I bring a finger up to my mouth to check for drool. Nope, I'm good, and even if I had any, I would feel no shame.

Link is all long, lean, defined muscle covered by that gorgeous shimmery skin. His silver hair is sticking up from removing his shirt, and he has that sexy rumpled look which is different from his everyday, straitlaced, put together doctor persona. And the look in those silver eyes makes my heart pound even faster.

This man is fucking sinful.

His hand goes to his jeans, and I swear time slows down as he undoes the button and pulls down the zipper before shoving them down his thighs. I hold my breath in anticipation. What is he going to look like down there? Caspian's suckers were a shock, but they turned out to be an awesome surprise. I wonder if the good doctor is packing anything different. I mentally slap myself for not asking Magenta about cyborgs as well in our alien birds and bees conversation.

When his underwear hits the floor, and I see what he looks like down there, I blink, unsure what I am seeing. Link is completely hairless and incredibly well-endowed. I wonder if cyborg parents program that kind of thing into their children's coding when they are creating them. Is that how cyborgs are created? Damn, another birds and bees failure.

He pounces onto the bed and crawls up so that his naked body surrounds my still fully dressed one. Before I can reach out to stroke any of that satiny, shimmery skin, he sits back on his heels and drags me up. Next, he grabs the hem of my dress and wiggles it over my butt before pulling it up and over my head. He tosses it away with a flick of his wrist as his eyes rake over my naked form.

"Lila, you're mouthwatering," he praises before leaning in and taking one of my nipples into his mouth. He licks across the tight bud, and as he does, his tongue changes texture.

What the hell? I pull his head back from my breast with both hands.

"Show me your tongue," I demand, and he sticks it out. Sure enough, it has little ridges running across it. "But that's not how it normally is, is it?" I ask him, and he smirks before poking it back out again. I watch as the ridges flatten out and it becomes normal again.

Holy shit! "Can you do that with other parts?" I ask him as I look down at his thick cock. It bobs slightly like it knows I'm looking at it before it slowly starts to change. Little lumps push up all over it and it starts to vibrate, much like my favorite rabbit vibrator does.

I'm rendered speechless, and Link must take that as a sign to continue because he sucks my nipple back into his mouth again. He teases it until I'm moaning in need before swapping to the other one and giving it the same treatment. It feels so good, I grow a little bold.

"Can you show me how it feels on my clit?" I ask, but I don't really give him a choice as I push his head down where I want it to be. His shoulders shudder under my hands as he shakes with laughter, but I'm not going to be embarrassed for taking what I want.

The first lash of his tongue has me shouting, "Holy fuck, yes!" but then it starts to vibrate, and my orgasm bursts out of me before I even realized it arrived. I feel myself squirt all over Link, and I blush with embarrassment and quickly apologize, but there's no need, because the man is licking it all up like it's his favorite meal.

"Lila, you taste so good," he murmurs as he cleans me up and I come down from the unexpected pleasure. "I can't wait to feel your tight cunt squeeze my cock."

Oh, hello! Dirty talk from my sexy nerdy love interest? If I wasn't already screaming with need, that would do it.

"Well, get up here then and take it for a spin," I demand, and he works his way back up my body, placing kisses over my stomach and breasts before taking my mouth with his. He tastes like me, but I'm soon distracted by his tongue, which still has ridges on it as it slides against mine.

I run my hands through his silver hair, the texture soft and silky as he lines his sizable length up with my pussy. I brace myself for him to thrust, but he slowly slides in, and my eyes just about roll back into my head at the feel of all those bumps against my sensitive walls. Finally, he's fully seated, and he leans his forehead against mine, breathing heavily.

"Just give me a minute. It's beyond my wildest dreams. You have internal muscles I've never felt before," he hisses between breaths, and I can't help the smug grin that spreads across my face. I can't believe that me, boring human Lila, is almost unmanning this sex expert cyborg. It's fucking good for my ego.

"Caspian says he thinks I have developed suckers inside from our mating," I tell him, and he groans as I bear down.

"Whatever it is, it's amazing, but now it's my turn." He moves his head back, and I see the molten heat in his silver eyes. He pulls out and leisurely slides back in, and I lose the smile as my mouth opens on a silent moan. He activated the internal vibrations, and that, combined with the nodules, creates a sensation that is out of this world. He rolls his hips slowly, setting a rhythm that has us both rising to a peak.

My hands explore his back as our mouths alternate between kissing and tasting each other's bodies, but the urge for me to bite becomes strong, and I'm not sure what that means. My beast's wants are coming to the surface more and more, and she wants me to mark this cyborg as ours, but I'm not quite ready for that.

"Fuck me from behind?" I beg him, wanting to know what it feels like, and if I'm face down in a bed, the beast can't take control and bite him without my permission. I have no clue if that would mate us like Caspian and me, or if I don't have enough shifter genes for that. He pulls out and flips me over before slamming back into me. I almost orgasm right then, but he does something and his dick shrinks, leaving me feeling empty.

"Agghh!" I scream. "What are you doing?" I feel him pull out, and then his thumb teases my asshole.

"Lila, can I fuck you in both holes?" Link's voice is low and rumbly, and it sends a shiver down my spine.

"You can do that?" I ask, not really caring as long as he sticks something inside me.

"Yes," he answers but doesn't elaborate.

"Okay." I think I would have agreed to anything to get him to keep going, and it's not like I haven't done it before. I feel him dribble something slick and wet over my ass before he uses his fingers to work it into me, first one, then two, and then three, preparing me properly for double penetration. The whole time, his other hand continues to stroke my clit. He's changed the texture of his fingertips as he quickly gets me to the edge of climax again. Before I can topple over, however, he pulls his fingers away, and I feel two heads nudge at both of my holes. I stiffen in surprise.

"Relax, baby, I've got you." He starts to push in, and his fingers come back to my clit and start vibrating. Bit by bit, he sinks deeper, filling me full in both channels. Thankfully he seems to have reverted to a smooth state, because I'm not sure if I could have handled all those bumps as well. I bury my head in the mattress and thrash it back and forth as the pinch of pain in my ass turns into a slow burn of pleasure. Soon, he's fully seated and I'm stuffed full.

"Fuck, fuck, fuck, fuck, fuck," I chant as he starts to move, knowing I'm not going to last long at all. He's gentle for a couple of strokes, but then he works up a rhythm, and soon enough, I'm thrusting back on him, reveling in the sensations that are searing my pleasure center.

My whole body is like one giant exposed nerve, and all it takes is his hand slapping my ass once before I explode, screaming into the mattress as I feel him bathe both of my channels in cum. I feel it seep out the sides and slide down the inside of my thighs as my orgasm blazes through my body in a never-ending cycle of pleasure until I'm a whimpering, quivering mess. Link murmurs words of praise, but they don't register in my destroyed mind.

I'm not sure how much time passes before he pulls out and goes away for a moment, returning with a warm cloth to clean me up.

Once done, he helps me into a shirt and a pair of male boxers. From the scent of the fabric, I know they are his. He lifts me and moves me to a nearby chair while he strips the sheets off the bed, quickly remaking it with a fresh set, before carrying me back and laying us both down. He spoons me from behind, and I think I'm finally capable of producing words.

"What was that?" I ask, rolling over to face him.

"I want to see," I insist, pulling the sheets back to look at his naked body. The sex afterglow has momentarily disappeared in my quest for knowledge.

"My body is made up of nanobots that I can change however I want. I did it with my tongue and my fingers and the bumps and vibrations, but I can also do that with my cock and change the shape of things," he explains, and I watch with wide-eyed fascination as his upper torso grows more muscular before my very eyes before returning to normal. "I can do the same thing with my cock. Some species have different breeding needs, and we are capable of meeting those needs if necessary."

"Show me what you did," I demand, and as I watch, his very nice cock splits in two, and then each thickens to become two whole cocks, one underneath the other just like Mithus.

"Best boyfriend ever," I whisper as I reach out to touch them. They feel exactly the same as each other. "And you come out of both?" I ask, because there was no mistaking the feeling of cum dripping out of my holes.

"Yes," he confirms before pushing my hands away and allowing it to reform into one girthy, mouthwatering dick. Before I can convince him to let me put it in my mouth, though, he pulls the blankets up and snuggles me close.

"Thank you for an amazing evening, Lila."

"It was most definitely my pleasure," I tease,

and he smiles before rolling and picking up his room tablet.

"I believe you need to send Caspian a message before we go to sleep," he says, handing it to me.

"Oh, and Xavier too, if you don't mind." I take it, and he snuggles in next to me as I send my mate, and potential future date, goodnight messages. Once done, I don't wait for them to respond before placing the tablet down on my side table and snuggling into my cyborg boyfriend's arms.

"Goodnight," I murmur, reaching back to touch him. He's slightly cooler than I'm used to, and I shiver. He must notice, because within moments, I feel his skin warm. Sighing, I close my eyes, enjoying being surrounded by the smell and feel of him, and fall asleep.

CHAPTER SIXTEEN

Lila

The next week passes in a blur as I familiarize myself with the ship, spend time with both Link and Caspian, and avoid making any decision regarding Saxon. Xavier is also surprisingly absent, as are my grandpas, but they explained that they were trying to get the new additions to Caspian's act up to speed, as well as deal with the fallout of Saxon being incapacitated. They mentioned another issue regarding the lightning cats, but they wouldn't tell me about it. Saxon's clan did not take the news of his incapacitation well, and I was cautioned to stay far away from them and to not go anywhere alone, but Xavier's absence means I have no protection if they decide to confront me.

His clan wants me to make a hurried decision and are resentful about the fact that I am not ready to. I mean, I don't blame them. I'm essentially keeping their friend in a coma while I work through my objections, but damn it, this is all new to me. Magenta suggested that one side would be happy to make him bond me by force, ensuring his survival, but also that the two women would happily push me out an air lock in the hope that my death would bring his need for me to an end. There's a fifty-fifty chance that he would survive the loss.

I never got my gun lesson, so I slunk around the ship, wishing I had Xavier's mist to hide myself in.

Eventually I became so paranoid, jumping at every bit of noise, expecting the Vilaxians to be around every corner, that I decided to stay within my own quarters for the remaining few days until our next show. Caspian's friend was moved to his own quarters before I had even returned from Link's the next day, so I never did get to meet him. They have all been too busy rehearsing for the Vegas show, but Caspian promised he'd introduce us the moment we got a chance.

Magenta has come to hang out with me a few times, which stopped me from going stir crazy, but mostly I've been thinking about Saxon and what decision to make. Caspian and Link have been completely supportive and said they would abide by whatever I chose to do, but what it comes down to is that I can't let the man die. He can't help that I'm not Vilaxian and don't have the same need to seal our bond. There would be something fundamentally wrong with me letting him die because I feel uncomfortable about something, and it's not like he's hard on the eyes. You wouldn't even need to twist my arm to get me to offer my neck up to him. I've always been somewhat of a vampire slut, even before I knew they were real.

The door to my quarters slides open, and Link and Caspian walk in. Both are busy chatting, so I take a moment to admire my men. Link and I haven't done anything else since that night, the whole Skarrian mating bond hanging over our heads. Sex with Link was amazing, and it would be easy to fall into a sex marathon and find myself mated again, but I'm enjoying taking things slowly with him. It's completely different from my and Caspian's mating, which has just fallen into such a natural rhythm it's like we've been together for years. I wonder if that's because of the mate bond, and it makes me curious if the same thing is going to occur with Saxon.

But Saxon is going to have to wait. Vegas is our destination, and today is the day.

"Are you ready, babe?" Caspian asks when they notice me waiting for them to finish talking.

"God, yes. I can't wait to breathe fresh air again and feel the sun on my face," I reply, and my face must take on a wistful expression, because they exchange a worried look.

"Has it really been all that bad not being on Earth?" Link asks, his tone carrying the same worry as the look he exchanged with Cas.

I shake my head. "No, but I can't deny I'm starting to go a little stir crazy being stuck in my quarters. I wanted to explore the ship some more and get involved in some of the other acts. I haven't even seen the whole thing yet." I run my hand through my hair in exasperation. "Constantly worrying that I'm going to be attacked is a nightmare, and I really shouldn't have to be worried about that, for fuck's sake. It's not *normal*." I throw my hands up in the air and start pacing around. Obviously I'm not as fine as I thought I was. "I mean, what the fuck? I have been forced to stay in my room because two women are having a tantrum about not being the 'chosen one.' Too bad, so sad. If I were a Skarrian with powers, there wouldn't even be a question of me being able to defend myself, but because I'm human and weak then I'm in danger. Well, maybe we need to face the fact that may never change. *Maybe*, just maybe, we need to accept that Fiona and Phillip are the best options to take over the circus, and I should just stay in the US when you all leave."

Fuck, that felt good to get off my chest.

Link's mouth drops open in shock, but it's Caspian's reaction that makes me feel like a selfish bitch. His face pales, and he flinches like I've physically slapped him, before his eyes flick to beast and back. Now I feel like complete and utter shit. We're mated, so of course he's not going to want to let me go.

"Oh, Cas, I would never leave you behind. You could come with me, and I'd find a new job in a bar. Maybe we could stay in Vegas. I'm sure there's a show where you would fit in, or you could stay home and be a house husband. We've got three babies that are going to need someone." I hold my hand over my stomach, thinking about the possibilities. A nice little white picket fenced place with me and Cas and our babies. Sure, we'd have to teach them not to shift or tell anyone what they are, but we could do that.

"Is that really how you feel?"

When I look into his eyes and see the hurt in them, and the same emotion in Link's gaze, I realize then and there that I could never leave them.

I shake my head and sink back onto the couch, wringing my hands in my lap. "No, I really don't, but it's been a lot. The circus, being an alien, and having no powers, and then the mating, the pregnancy, and my attraction to Link and Xavier, as well as being Saxon's blood rose, not to mention the whole thing with the rapey dolphin and Dylan... I feel like everything has been going at a rapid pace between my personal and professional life. It just hasn't stopped. I haven't had anyone to talk to." They start to argue, but I hold up a hand. "Or anyone who is unbiased. Magenta is great and all, but she's Skarrian, and she just doesn't understand my concerns." Something occurs to me, and I sit up, knowing the perfect way to solve my problem. "I need Susie."

"Susie, your best friend?" Link asks, and I melt because he remembers.

"Yeah, Susie is my ride or die. We tell each other everything, and I think she's just what I need. Do you think if I invite her to come visit in Vegas, and maybe bring Mark, that I could tell her everything and then have Xavier remove it all from her mind?"

I hate the thought of messing with my bestie's mind, but I also understand that this information would be catastrophic in the wrong hands, and all it would take is for Susie to get loose lips after a few drinks with Mark or any of her other friends. She'd either be committed or we'd be hunted.

Nope. It's better for all of us if Xavier does his thing.

They exchange another glance before Cas shrugs. "I don't see why not, but it means you're essentially lying to her. Can you do that?"

"I'm already lying to her now. At least this way I'm kind of telling her the truth, even if she doesn't remember it. I need her. Magenta's great, and she suggested a girls' night with Nixie, but I haven't known them for very long. No one gets the human side of me like Susie does, and I need to speak to her." Tears roll down my cheeks as I try to communicate what will help me get through this mental shitshow. The guys crowd in on either side of me, Caspian wrapping his arms around my shoulders and Link taking my hand in his.

"Oh, babe, I'm sorry. We should have realized it was all too much. I can't believe we didn't recognize how overwhelmed you were feeling because you've been handling this all so well." Cas sounds devastated and slightly panicked at my emotional overload.

"It's okay, you've all been so busy the last couple of days, and that's my fault too, as is Dylan leaving and Saxon's absence. And the grandpas have been dealing with the political fallout of those things and something to do with the lightning cats that no one has brought me up to speed on. On top of that, I think Xavier's lost interest. His mark on my shoulder is still there, but it's lighter than it was. I guess he decided that I was too much trouble, or whatever he saw in my mind wouldn't meet his standards."

I worry my lip at the thought of what Xavier might have seen to cause him to pull back.

"Oh no, Lila. I promise that's not the case," Link assures me, and I see them exchange another look over the top of my head. I sigh, pulling away from them.

"This" —I gesture between the three of us— "is not going to work if we keep secrets. And I don't do secrets."

"Xavier has been dealing with his own political issue and the death of one of his harem members. We promise that he wants to come speak to you and probably will once we get back to Earth." He tries his best to placate me, but it does nothing to ease the doubt and disappointment I feel in my heart.

"But how about we do this? Usually the circus will set up in the Black Rock Desert in Nevada, but this year we have negotiated with the Vegas city council to set up just outside its city limits. Apparently they want us closer so it's better for tourism and hotel capacity. We've been given a deal with one of the hotels on the strip. They are offering special Galaxy Circus stays, with priority seating for the people who book those vacations. Why don't we get you a room at the hotel and you can call Susie and invite her out for a few days? The two of you can catch up, she can see the show, and you can get in some girl time. Because after we leave Earth, we won't be back for some months, and depending on solar storms and meteor showers and all sorts of atmospheric interference, you may not be able to contact her for a while."

Caspian doesn't get a chance to say anything else before I'm smothering him with kisses. "Yes, yes, yes! That would be wonderful, Caspian. Thank you."

Both guys start to laugh at my enthusiastic response. Once I finish showing Caspian my appreciation, I turn to Link and do the same thing. I think I surprise him a little because I haven't been over-the-top affectionate with him in front of Cas, but I've decided to say screw it. Both of these guys are in my life, and if it doesn't bother them, then who am I to deny it? Feeling Caspian's hands on my body while I'm kissing Link has me cursing myself for not starting this sooner. It brings a whole new level of intensity to our kiss, and I shiver with the potential. But first things first.

"I have to call Susie." I jump up off Link's lap and start to run back to my room where the communication tablet is, but Caspian doesn't let me get far. He lunges forward and grabs me, spinning me around and causing me to giggle.

"Hold your larnuks, sweetheart. Before you go racing off, your grandpas need you. They want you to experience what we do for setup when we land on Earth in a different spot."

"Now? But don't we need to get to the circus pod and make the return journey?" I'm sure that's what we've been talking about.

"Yes, the pod is about to open for boarding," Link explains, "and I need to transfer Saxon to my clinic on the pod so I can continue to monitor him while we are down there. Now that Josa has been fired and is no longer on the ship, I can't very well leave Saxon up here unsupervised. So I'll see you when we land." Link gives me one last kiss, even though Cas's arms are wrapped around me. Their bodies sandwich me between them, and another shiver of desire goes through me. Oh yeah, I am definitely on board with this multiple mates thing. The potential is limitless. Link's body is slightly cooler than Caspian's at my back, and it creates a nice contrast.

"Okay, I'll come find you later," I promise, and

he pulls away, leaving me momentarily chilled and disappointed. But it's not like we could start anything just yet with the time constraints.

He leaves, and Cas whirls me around in his arms, kisses me hard on the lips, and pulls away, taking my hand and leading me to the door. "When we land, we have to do the reverse process of take-off. We can't very well just appear all of a sudden. People would panic if they saw a ship coming out of the sky. Granted, it usually doesn't matter in Nevada because we're typically in the desert, but this year is different. We'll send down an advance party with the teleporter, and they'll set up holo emitters which show the scene of the circus being erected. It's why there is always a fence around, so that people can't just wander in. Then, at night, we land under a cloak and take the place of the hologram."

He told me this as we moved through the ship, and now we're at the teleporting room. When we enter, Officer Kirk, one of the teleporting operators, is sitting at the desk, and he smiles at us.

"Hey, Lila, Cas. You're here right on time." He gets up and moves to a cupboard, pulling out the holo emitters I remember from my first time before handing them to me. "Here you go. I'll transport you into a nearby alleyway, and then you'll have to walk a few hundred yards to where we need to set them up."

"Are you coming with me?" I ask Caspian, a

little unsure because he's still wearing his natural purple and blue form.

He shakes his head, but before he can answer, a voice does it for him. "No, that would be me again, *phoeall*. I had so much fun the first time, I couldn't help but volunteer again." Xavier's silky timbre sounds in my ear and I jump, startled at the unexpected voice. He chuckles as I spin, trying to see his misty, shrouded form, but he's invisible.

"Okay, I'll leave you in Xavier's capable hands," Caspian tells me, smothering a smile like he knows something I don't. "Instead of coming back to the ship, why don't you book that hotel room and call Susie? Once we land, we can sort out what's going to happen after that. I'll let your grandpas know what the plan is."

I throw my arms around Caspian. "God, I love you," I exclaim, and I feel him stiffen up and think about what I said.

Oh, I said the words.

Is that the first time I've told him? It must be, even though I've felt it basically from the start. Maybe it's the mating bond, but I really don't care. He's done nothing but cherish and care for me since our beginnings in that pod, and I know it's only been just over a week, but it's enough.

His body seems to melt into mine as he wraps his arms around me and whispers in my ear. "I love you too, baby, so much." Everything seems to fade away while we just live in this perfect moment.

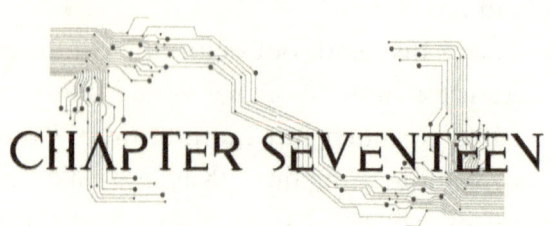

CHAPTER SEVENTEEN

Xavier

I distract Officer Kirk from Caspian and Lila's private moment by making my misty form appear next to him. It works, and he instantly recoils but quickly recovers.

"Jesus, warlock, you scared the shit out of me," he snaps, holding a hand against his chest like his heart is about to fall out.

I chuckle. I do like to get a reaction out of people, and normally his fear would be tempting, but now that I know Lila is my intimate, I don't want to feed off anyone else. Feeding from her anger earlier in the week was enough to sustain me much longer than anything my harem has ever provided, but it's wearing off, and I'll need to feed again soon. With Saxon out of commission, I either need to ask Lila again or absorb some of the residual feelings and emotions around me. If I stand in the circus tent during the show, the humans' excitement and joy should temporarily sustain me.

I slap my mist-shrouded hand on Officer Kirk's back. "I do like you. I admire your bravery for talking to me like that." My words must remind him who I am, because he pales slightly. "No, none of that crap now. I appreciate when people treat me like I'm a normal person, thank you. Now, if I might ask a favor. Would it be possible for you to drop Lila and me a little farther away from the site? I have a few things I need to talk to her about, and I don't want her distracted by the job we are there to do."

He looks a little unsure and opens his mouth to argue with me.

"Don't worry, I have received approval from the boss men, and I assure you the holo emitters will be in place and ready to go when the ship needs to land. And even if the program isn't quite where it needs to be, you just stay cloaked until it is."

"Yeah, okay. As long as the boss men approved it, who am I to argue?" He fiddles with a few buttons on the console. "How about I drop you two blocks over? Is that far enough?" he asks, and even though he can't see it, I smile widely.

"Perfect, thank you. I owe you one," I reply, and

he beams. Having a favor owed by the warlock prince is no small thing, and I rarely give out favors.

Lila and Caspian peel themselves apart. I don't know how he does it. If she just declared she loved me, I would whisk her back to my quarters and fuck her into oblivion. With one last kiss, Cas waves to me and heads off to finish his preparations for reentry.

I hold out my misty hand for Lila to proceed with me onto the teleporting platform. She bites her lip in that cute nervous way she does. "It's okay, *phoeall*. It will feel just like when I teleported you on Earth," I reassure her, and a little wrinkle forms between her eyes.

"Why aren't you doing it this time?" she asks.

"While I can teleport long distances, and traveling across a planet is no challenge for me, the distance we need to cross now is beyond my capabilities." I'm loath to admit there are limits to my power, but it is no secret. I don't know of any being that can teleport across space like that. We all rely on mechanical means to help us.

Lila's mouth forms a surprised O as I wrap my mist around her and pull her into my arms. I make it so we're both shrouded in the mist, but she can see me now. Her eyes widen in surprise as I appear, but before she can say anything, I give the order, "Okay, Officer Kirk, beam us down."

This time her mouth drops open, and I wink at her. "I like Earth movies, and let's face it, I had to watch it to compare it to real life, and I just couldn't help myself considering the officer's name."

Before she can answer, the humming sound of the teleporter indicates Kirk has started it. Between one breath and the next, we leave the ship and appear on the pavement in a Las Vegas alley. I wrinkle my nose at the smell, but Lila is still too busy staring at my face to react to the fact we've even moved, let alone what it smells like.

She reaches up and runs her fingers over my face. "You look human," she comments as her fingertips brush over my cheeks and up to my now curved ears.

"Well, it wouldn't do for me to show up looking like an alien, would it?" I tease, but she continues her perusal of me.

"Not alien, they'd probably think you were fae," she murmurs as she steps away, and I let the mist dissolve. She looks me up and down, studying my favorite glamour. "You look like a punk rock star. I love the way your eyes appear like they are rimmed in kohl, and while this look is great, I much prefer the real you," she tells me when she finishes her inspection, and I practically preen like a jaxa bird.

"Come on, let's walk," I suggest, holding out a hand, but she looks down at herself, wrinkling her nose. "I'm pretty sure that while you blend in, I don't. I look like I'm going to attend a sci-fi convention, and there are no pockets in this damn thing for these." She holds out the holo emitters, and I pluck them out of her hand and make them disappear. "What did you do to them?" she asks.

"I just put them into a sub-space storage hole that I have. You never know when you're going to need something quickly, and I can always access it no matter where I am. They can stay there until we need them, and then I can pull them back out."

"That is so freaking cool. Do you keep snacks in there? I would keep snacks and probably a hair tie and maybe a tampon." Her wide-eyed enthusiasm is so adorable.

"Ah, yeah, sure," I answer, not wanting to tell her I keep all my weapons in there and a few sex toys. You never know when you may need either of those things. "As for your outfit, I can fix that." I wave my hand, and Lila's Galaxy Circus uniform disappears, replaced by a sexy set of galactic lingerie that leaves absolutely nothing to the imagination. The flimsy piece of lavender cloth is see-through, and I see her nipples pucker when the cool air hits them. Her thong-covered ass is exposed, with the tiny piece of cloth skimming across the top of it. She teeters precariously on the heels that came with the outfit.

"What the fuck?" She looks down at herself before looking back at me, propping her hands on her hips. "Seriously, Xavier?"

I feel a sheepish grin spread across my face, and I run a hand through my short faux hawk that I rock in this glamour. "Whoops, sorry. I got my outfits mixed up. You were not supposed to see that one… yet," I explain, a little embarrassed that my fantasy was the first thing that popped into my head when I thought about what to put her in.

I wave my hand, and the lingerie disappears, replaced by a Galaxy Circus T-shirt, a pair of cutoff denim shorts, and leather combat boots. I give her ripped tights and a long-sleeved mesh undershirt below the galaxy circus top, and make her makeup punky like mine. She glances down at herself before looking back at me with a raised eyebrow.

"We match. We look like a couple," she states, and I shrug, feeling smugly pleased at her observation.

"I know." I don't explain myself, instead grabbing her hand and walking in the direction of where we need to be. We stroll in silence for a little while, and Lila leaves her hand in mine, which thrills me more than it should. What the fuck is going on with me? I'm the warlock, I am one of the most powerful people in the galaxy and have a harem of aliens at my beck and call to see to my every need, yet all I want to do is spend time with this little Earth girl who causes my cock to harden just by the feel of her palm in mine.

I'd always been told that the intimate bond is like no other, but thanks to my parents, ours is nonexistent until they can return Lila's memories. It's there under the surface, and it's why we both feel drawn to one another, but it's nowhere near what it will be once we can act on it. Much like Saxon's bond with Lila, it's a surprise that it happened with a non-warlock. Intimates are supposed to be all about sharing your power base as well as a romantic and sexual connection, but Lila isn't able to do that with me. I mean, I'm powerful enough as I am, so that doesn't concern me, but I would have liked to have given her some of mine. That would have protected her from anything that might be coming for her in the future.

When I spoke to my parents, they said it may still be possible, but until we do the intimate ceremony, we won't know. Now I need to explain this all to Lila and pray to every deity in the galaxy she will accept me.

The streets of Vegas are noisy and smelly, but it could be worse, we could be right on the strip. Thankfully we are on the outskirts and nobody pays particular attention to the two of us as we walk hand in hand. I swing our hands back and forth, excited that she still hasn't pulled away, but she's too busy holding her face up to the sun and enjoying being out of the artificial environment to notice.

"You know, you don't realize how much it means to be able to go outside for fresh air until it's taken away from you," she tells me. "And when you are outside, you're so busy running from one place to the other, or trying to protect yourself from the sun's harsh rays, that you don't even stop and take a moment to just enjoy it. I totally get the appeal of sunbathing now, even though I hadn't in the past."

I make a mental note to figure out how we can make it so she can have these things regularly. Once we leave Earth, we don't tend to stay in one space all that often. We can land the circus pod on any of the other planets we visit, and we are free to leave and stay in their hotels or wander around and sight-see, as long as we return every evening to perform in the show, but for the times in between, I'm sure I can create an illusion or program one of the holorooms to provide her with what she needs. First, though, I want to talk to her about what I saw in the memory.

"Lila?"

"Hmm?" She faces me and finally realizes we're holding hands, but instead of pulling away as I expected, she just gives my hand a squeeze and leaves it there. She finally looks around, noticing where we are.

"Oh, I thought we were going to be teleported closer to the site, but it doesn't look like the pod could fit in anywhere here." She strains her neck as she looks behind us without letting go of my hand.

"Oh, no, it's a couple of blocks that way." I nod in the direction we're headed. "I asked Kirk to drop us a little farther away because I wanted to talk to you about my conversation with my parents and what I found in your mind."

Her steps falter for a moment before she hurries

to keep up. I'm not stopping, and I'm not letting go of her hand—partly for reassurance that she's not going to run away, and partly because I hope she doesn't hate me after what I'm about to tell her… or hate my parents. They are absolutely dying to meet her now that I know the truth. They weren't even annoyed to hear about what I did to Elyan and told me they'd tell her father. I wasn't going to argue about them assuming that responsibility.

"Okay, so talk," she demands, and I can't do anything but obey because I've been needing to tell her this.

"When I looked into your brain, I found a hidden memory, but it wasn't one of yours, it was one of mine that had been removed from my mind and planted in yours."

"Holy shit, that's a pretty impressive power. Can all warlocks do that?" she asks quietly. I smile at her because the first sentence out of her mouth wasn't about why my memory is in her mind or why someone planted it there.

"No, only the more powerful ones, and it was my parents who did it. It turns out you and I have met before."

I explain what I had seen, and she listens without interrupting. The only outward sign that she is affected is her hand tightening in mine. When I finish that part of the story, she's quiet, so I don't hurry to continue. I want her to have a chance to absorb what I just told her.

"Okay, so my parents asked yours to remove my powers and memories if anything ever happened to them. But did your parents tell you why? What were they talking about when they put up the barrier?"

I run my hand through my hair in frustration, since that's something I still haven't managed to figure out yet. "No, they wouldn't tell me. They said it was a matter of security. I tried to argue that I couldn't protect you properly if I didn't know why, but they wouldn't budge."

She looks disappointed but quickly shakes it off. "And I'm your intimate? Is this like being Saxon's blood rose?" she inquires softly, and I stop and turn so that I am facing her.

"If you mean that you become the most important person in my world, then yes," I answer, putting all of my feelings into it.

"And I won't feel this until your parents return my memories and the powers they took from me?"

"No, probably not, but I'd like to think that you were attracted to me anyway. After all, your Skarrian attraction marks appeared on both of us."

The frown she had been wearing eases a little, and she smiles. "That is true, but will you still need to feed from your harem until we join? You won't need your harem after that, will you?"

I am beyond ecstatic that she hasn't rejected anything outright and she seems to be accepting this, but I'm probably going to jinx it, because I need to make sure before I answer anything else.

"You're taking this rather well. Are you okay?" I ask cautiously, skepticism lacing my tone, and she giggles.

"Xavier, do you *want* me to freak out?"

"No, no," I assure her quickly. "I guess I just didn't know how you would react, and part of me was expecting the worst."

"In the last two weeks, I've discovered I'm an alien who is going to inherit an alien circus. I'm mated to a kraken shifter, dating a cyborg, and the blood rose to a vampire, so hearing that I'm the soulmate to a warlock isn't any weirder than all of that. I guess I've decided to embrace whatever comes my way. If I don't, I think you'll find me rocking in the corner, chewing on my hair, talking to a ball of lint."

I desperately want to push into her mind and check if she's telling me the truth. If the intimate bond had been activated, then I would be able to feel it, but for now, I'll respect her and leave her mind alone unless she gives me permission.

"Okay, well, as long as you come talk to me if you need to. As for my harem, I will need to feed off others until the bond is activated, because if I fed exclusively from you, I'd probably kill you, or at least leave you looking like Mithus because you have no power to absorb."

"Fuck no," she explodes and starts to wave her hand around. "It was fine before I knew about this. Well, actually it wasn't fine, but there wasn't anything I could do about it." She gestures between us. "But now that I know you're mine, you will not be partaking of your harem again. When we get to your home planet to see your parents, they will be asked not so politely to leave the ship."

I smother the grin that wants to break out across my face at the possessiveness of my intimate, but I contain it. I don't want her thinking I'm not taking her seriously.

"You can feed from me, Cas, or Link. Oh, and I guess Saxon is an option once he and I do whatever it is we need to do to blood bond."

I feel my eyebrows jump. "You've decided you're going to bond with him?" I ask gently, and she growls.

"Of course I will. I can't let him die just because his stupid genetics took the choice out of both of our hands."

"You know how I told you back in my room earlier this week that I had another option to feed from apart from my harem?"

She nods but wrinkles her nose like she doesn't really want to hear what I'm about to tell her.

"Well, Saxon is that option, so once you do your thing, he will be happy to feed me as well as you, if Cas and Link aren't interested."

Lila lets out a sigh of relief. "Yes, that will work for me." She picks up my hand again, and we start walking down the street in the right direction.

"So you and Saxon fuck, do you?" she asks

bluntly, not hiding her curiosity, and again, I barely contain my smile. Lila really is delightful, and I can see that our joining is most certainly not going to be boring, especially because she will have other mates as well. Play time will most certainly *never* be boring.

CHAPTER EIGHTEEN

Lila

My dirty mind is still thinking about Saxon and Xavier fucking when he teleports us to an empty elevator in the hotel the circus has a deal with. Our conversation flowed easily after he shared that I'm his intimate, and our hands were clasped the entire time until we had to place the holo emitters and activate the program. Thankfully the area where the circus tent will be didn't have much foot traffic, so we were in and out with lots of time to spare.

Xavier drags me through the opulent foyer, with marble floors and luxurious drapes strategically placed around the room, to the reception desk, telling them we are checking in before giving his name. The guy behind the desk's eyes widen, and he scrambles around. "Of course, Mr. Colest, we have the penthouse suite reserved for you and your…" He trails off, and Xavier looks at me with a cheeky grin.

I know what he's about to say will either force me to smother him in his sleep or jump him.

"Wife," Xavier tells him with a wink. "We're newlyweds. You know, with the whole Vegas thing, I couldn't stop myself from proposing to the most amazing woman I know. Now we just want some alone time away from the rest of the crew, if you know what I mean." He lays on the act hard for the receptionist, but he seems to buy it. Though I can see him looking at our outfits and judging them.

I giggle but don't contradict him. It's fun pretending, and I guess it's not far from the truth. Instead of freaking out when Xavier told me the story about being his intimate, I decided to just go with the flow. Freaking out and getting upset isn't going to change anything for me or him, but it explains why I felt connected to him at the very beginning. The Skarrian mark only confirms the physical attraction.

I am also looking forward to meeting his parents and getting my memories back. I know they were just following through on what they promised my mom and dad, but did they have to do such a good job of it? I'm feeling anything but kind and generous toward them at the moment, so I'm pretty sure that meeting with the new in-laws isn't going to go well. That's a challenge for future Lila to manage.

"Here are your keys. Just swipe the card and press the P in the elevator, and it will take you right up." He peers over the desk. "No luggage?" he asks, raising an eyebrow, and Xavier shakes his head.

"No, we're going to do some shopping. I want to spoil my new wife as a wedding gift."

"Well, let us know if we can help with anything. If you could just sign here, we can view your credit card." My heart stops momentarily when he asks to see our credit cards. I try to maintain my carefree smile, but inside, I'm panicking.

My purse is back on the pod with my phone and the rest of my belongings, and do aliens even have credit cards? I shouldn't have doubted Xavier though. He just reaches into the pocket of his designer ripped jeans and pulls out a wallet, which he opens before taking out a black American Express card. I guess that answers my question.

Minutes later, the two of us are headed to the elevator hand in hand. The sexual tension between us is off the charts, and there's the giddy feeling of anticipation thrumming through my body. Once we get to our room, I throw myself onto a couch without even looking around, trying to get a hold of myself before I jump him.

"Holy shit, that was nerve-racking. I thought for sure we were going to get kicked out. First, for how we are dressed, and second, for lack of payment.

We'd be out on the streets pandering for money, or I could always strip to pay our bills." I toss an arm over my head dramatically as my imagination goes wild.

"Stripping? No. Oh, Lila, I can't believe you doubted me." Xavier goes to the fully stocked mini bar and grabs a champagne glass before pulling open the fridge and grabbing one of the cute mini bottles of champagne. He pops the cork before pouring it into a glass and returning to me.

"Here you go. Why don't you order some food, and we'll relax for the next couple of hours. Once the pod lands, we can teleport to it and retrieve some of your things. We will have plenty of time to shop over the next few days."

"Now that I'm living on the ship, I'm going to need a few more things. I don't have anywhere near enough to last me months on end," I tell him while taking the glass.

"Lila, we do have shops on the ship, and the planets we will be stopping at all have city centers with shopping opportunities."

I wave my free hand at him before I take a sip of my champagne, the bubbles exploding across my tongue. The flavor is a little tarter than I expected, but not awful.

"I know, Xavier, but there are a few things I can't do without, things I only want specifically from Earth."

"Like?" he asks, sitting down on the couch next

to me. He appears genuinely interested, but it's weird to see him in his glamour, and it takes me a moment to reply.

"Well, chocolate for one, and then there's wine and margarita mix, and I wouldn't mind picking up a kindle and loading all my favorite books onto it."

"Oh, and what is it you like to read?"

Well, fuck, that was an epic backfire. Now I have to explain about my love of monster alien porn and paranormal romance. I clear my throat and pray that my cheeks aren't flushing from his innocent question.

"Oh, would you look at the view out of that window!" I get up, taking my glass with me, and go over to it. "Susie and I always talked about coming to Vegas, but we never got a chance to." I turn back to face him. "Cas said I should call her and invite her to come see the show. Would you be able to get my phone from my room in the pod for me? Oh, and the charger. I'm sure it's dead by now."

Hopefully my word vomit has done enough to distract him, but I can tell by the quirk of his eyebrow and devious grin that I don't have this sexy warlock fooled.

"Don't think I didn't notice you avoiding my question about reading. I look forward to seeing this kindle. I too very much like reading. Maybe we can read together."

Hmm, not sure how much reading we'd actually

get done if he was sitting next to me while I was doing it.

Xavier waves his hand, and an unfamiliar phone and charger lands on the table.

Frowning, I pick it up and look it over. "This isn't mine."

"No, it's a burner. I can't teleport yours from the mothership, and I don't want to leave you to go back and get it. I'm hoping you know Susie's number, but you'll have to charge it first."

Aww, isn't he the sweetest?

Sure enough, when I pick it up, it's dead, so I find a socket and plug in the cord before grabbing the room service menu off the same table.

"Are you hungry?" I ask him before doing a double take. "Wait. Do you eat real food?" I question, because I really don't know if he does or not.

"Yes, of course, it just doesn't fuel my power like emotions do. Order me something, and we will have a nice meal together while I get to know you a little better. You can tell me about growing up in those foster homes and how you met Susie."

I sit down next to him and drop the menu into my lap, biting my lip before I ask Xavier my next question. I feel a little guilty because I will be doing to Susie what his parents did to me, but I really need to get everything that has happened off my chest.

"Xavier, can you take memories away like your parents?" I inquire, playing with the menu in my lap and not looking at him. A finger slides under my chin and lifts it so I am looking at the gorgeous man. It's so weird seeing him look human, and although he looks hot, I miss his true form. "Do you need to hold your glamour while we are alone?" I ask before he can answer my first question.

He shakes his head, wearing a smug grin on his face as he lets his glamour fade, and I breathe a sigh of relief. It was really bothering me that he had to hide himself. I guess Cas will have to do the same if he comes and stays here with me. Maybe it would be better if they all stayed on the ship. I wouldn't want them to feel uncomfortable just because I needed some girl time with Susie.

"As for your question, I can. Whose memories do you want to take away?"

I startle at his question since I didn't specifically ask him to take them away. He clearly saw through my bullshit.

I sigh, feeling a little uncomfortable about asking him for this favor. "Susie's. I want to tell her all about this, but of course I want to protect you all too. I don't think she'd talk, but it is fairly out of this world—no pun intended—and I don't even know if she would believe me."

"You would need to ask your grandpas first, but if it is okay with them, I can remove her memories of your talk once you're done. There is another option though. I can make it so that she remembers but can't actually talk about it to anyone but you."

"I don't know what would be worse, to be honest—to know all those things and not be able to talk about them, or have the memory removed."

"Okay, I'll let you think about it, and you can tell me what you decide. Your grandpas may have an opinion too. They may not approve of you talking about the circus or aliens."

I quickly agree and go back to perusing the menu. I just hope my phone doesn't take too long to charge, because as much as I'm enjoying spending time with Xavier. I need my girl.

"Well, well, well. Look who has finally remembered she had a life before the circus," Susie answers, sounding pissed, and I cringe at the verbal bitch slap I just received through the line.

"Fuck. I know, Susie. I've been a shitty friend. Let me have it."

"A bad friend? Oh no, Lila, you have been a rotten friend. Actually, rotten is even too nice of a word! I got one call two weeks ago to tell me you had arrived, and then nothing. Poof. Gone. No longer to be heard from again. I thought you had fallen off the face of the Earth. I've been calling the police because I've been worried about you! I wanted them to storm that fucking circus and search for you. I thought that maybe you'd been kidnapped and sold into sex slavery or something. They told me I was crazy when I explained what happened." She takes a deep breath before continuing. "You didn't even respond to me via social media. It was like you'd been abducted by aliens." I hear Susie breathing heavily as her rant winds down. She's eerily close to the truth, and it takes everything in me not to snort.

I pause to give her a second to calm down. "Are you done?" I ask just to make sure she wasn't taking a breather before fully unloading.

"For now," she replies dryly. "I reserve the right to continue depending on what you have to say for yourself."

I pick at the invisible lint on my Galaxy Circus top, trying to think of how or even where to begin. But at the end of the day, she's right. I *did* just disappear.

"You're right, I have been bad. In my defense, I have been falling into bed every night exhausted, and the grandpas have kept me so busy during the day I haven't had time to charge my phone, let alone call you." I hear her grunt, clearly thinking I'm spewing bullshit to placate her, so I quickly continue. "But I was wondering if you and Mark wanted to come out to Vegas for a couple of nights and see the show? We can catch up, and there's a room with your name on it in the hotel we're staying at."

I hear her take a deep breath again and brace myself for her rejection. She's quiet for a moment, and then I have to pull the phone away from my ear.

"Squeee! Oh my God, yes! That would be awesome, thank you. I'll call Mark and see if he wants to go. We're off for a couple of days anyway, and we were just going to hang around the house. You know, even if he doesn't want to, I'm coming for sure."

"Okay, well let me know what decisions you make." The relief I feel at her wanting to come to Vegas is instantaneous, and I quietly release the tension I was holding in my next breath.

"I will, and bitch, don't think you're going to get away with not telling me everything. I know when something is going on with you, and I can hear it in your voice," Susie threatens, and I smile. It's exactly why I need her, and I hadn't realized how much I missed her.

"Fuck, I'm so excited to see you. Talk to you soon." I hang up and toss the burner phone onto the coffee table, looking around the suite I haven't had a chance to explore yet. After we ordered food, it arrived quickly and we both ate. I swear burgers and fries have never tasted so good. Xavier asked me questions about my childhood, desperate to know what it was like for me growing up. To say he was not happy by the end of my story would be an understatement, and he muttered filthy curses under his breath about his parents that had me smothering a smile of delight. He said something about how my childhood should have been full of spoiling, and if it had been up to him, I wouldn't have missed out on anything. It was just as good of a first date as the one I had with Link. Yes, it counts. Afterward, Xavier offered to give me some privacy for my call, put his glamour back on, and returned to the landing site to ensure the hologram program was running okay.

The sun has set, so the ship will be landing soon. I'm assuming that Xavier decided to wait until it does. I'm a little disappointed, because I was enjoying spending time with him. Unfortunately for me, he'd been the perfect gentleman, but I'm pretty sure he's going to need to feed soon, and he's not going to be getting what he needs from anyone but *me*. I guess it's going to be up to me to seduce him, but I'm feeling a little inadequate. I saw the members of his harem. They were gorgeous and exotic and different. How is having sex with me ever going to compete with that? Is he truly attracted to me, or is being his intimate affecting that too?

He did tell me that the fact that I don't hide my emotions is a major turn-on for him. His harem learned to keep them locked up tight. They withheld them to ensure that he needed to seduce them to feed. It's why he stopped using them as much and started using Saxon. Apparently Saxon has a lot of repressed emotions, and getting him to react in any way was a game to Xavier, but he also fed Saxon in return so he was getting something out of it as well. The thought of Saxon and Xavier together is enough to make my core throb with need, and when I think about being between them, my nipples tighten and my skin flushes as my body drowns in a wave of desire. Damn fuck me vibes.

Getting up, I head for the master room and the bathroom that is attached. I'm hoping a cold shower will help the sudden onslaught of horniness that my future children just caused.

Stripping off my clothes, I leave them lying on the floor of the bedroom before heading to the shower, praying that it has a detachable showerhead I can make use of.

"Thank you, hotel designer."

I say a quiet prayer as I turn the water on. Although there are a number of heads in this fancy-ass shower, one of them is most definitely detach-able, and I cannot wait to use it. I let the shower heat to the temperature I like and step in. Standing under the spray, I let it wash the dust and dirt and buildup from being in space from my body. Although there's plenty of water on the ship and in the Aquilian habitat, it still doesn't feel quite the same as having a shower here on Earth. I guess our water must be different, and the slight smell of chlorine is comforting in a way I've never noticed before.

I let my mind wander, letting go of all the worries regarding matings, bondings, pissed off harem and clan members, and learning about the show, and just enjoy a few moments of peace and quiet. I wash my hair and body, trying to ignore the constant need that is hammering at me, but when a moan leaves my mouth as I run the soap over my rock-hard nipple, I give up pretending I want anything but an orgasm.

Grabbing the detachable head, I run it over my body, aiming it at my nipples. Up close, it's hard and sharp and slightly painful against the sensitive peaks, and it feels so fucking good that I lean against the wall to prop myself up. Shit, I haven't even gotten to the good bit yet. Maybe I should sit on the bench for this.

Lowering myself to a sitting position, I spread my legs wide and aim the showerhead directly at my clit, but the pressure is so hard it threatens to send me straight over the edge, and I want this to last a little longer. I adjust the stream to a gentler option and try again.

"Oh, fuck yeah, that feels amazing," I mutter as I move the head in a circular motion, teasing my clit.

"Well, it looks like I returned at exactly the right time." Xavier's voice has me screeching in surprise and yanking the showerhead away. I almost drop it as a flush of embarrassment replaces the desire.

"Oh no, please don't let me stop you." I can't really see him through the foggy glass, but I see his outline and hear the buckle of his belt clatter against the tiles as he strips off his jeans. I wait for a moment, but he doesn't join me, so I wipe at the glass to see what he is doing. He holds his cock in his fist as he strokes it up and down.

"Would you like to join me?" I ask. "I could feed you, if you would like," I offer a little shyly and pray that he doesn't reject me. I have nothing to worry about, however, because his eyes widen with delight before hooding with desire, and he licks his lips as he removes his shirt with the hand he doesn't have wrapped around his cock.

He hesitates at the door of the shower. "Are you sure about this? My cock isn't like a human one," he warns, and I roll my eyes, gesturing for him to hurry up and get in.

"Xavier, Caspian fucks me with his tentacles and I love it, and Link's dick can change while it's inside me. You have nothing to worry about."

"Sounds like you've been having a lot of fun, *phoeall*." He closes the door behind him and steps up to me, taking the showerhead out of my hand.

CHAPTER NINETEEN

Lila

Xavier runs the showerhead back and forth over my clit while using his mouth to tease my nipples until I'm a begging, sobbing mess.

"Please, Xavier, please fuck me," I cry out, and he puts the showerhead back before crowding me against the wall.

"Remember what I said, Lila? I want enthusiastic consent. Can I feed from you?" he asks as he slides his hands under my ass cheeks and lifts me up. I wrap my legs around his waist, knowing I probably would have agreed to anything because I'm so worked up, but I really don't mind. I get a feeling of immense satisfaction from being able to provide him what he needs to survive.

"Yes, oh God, yes please," I beg, rubbing my

soaked lips against his cock, which is squashed between our bodies.

"Lila, look into my eyes," he demands, so I do. His gorgeous purple blue eyes start to swirl, and I feel him sink into my mind, our emotions becoming a never-ending loop between us.

"Oh my God," I pant as he adjusts himself and lines up with my entrance. With our eyes still locked and our minds linked, he thrusts deeply into me. "Fuck!" I scream as he stretches me, and then the tentacles at the base start to tease my clit, and I feel my orgasm sweep through my body. He rolls his hips, giving me friction to intensify my orgasm, but then there's a draining sensation as I feel Xavier start to feed on my pleasure. Because we're linked, however, his own pleasure from feeding mirrors back to me, and I feel my orgasm start to build once more.

This time, though, he doesn't take it easy. Thrust after thrust, he pounds into me, my back held firmly against the wall as he works me up once more.

"Harder please," I cry out, and he doesn't even question it, just gives me what I need. His thick length punishes my pussy, while his tentacles caress my clit.

"I'm going to come again," I warn. He takes my mouth with his, and the suctioning sensation starts again. I tumble over the edge into a mind-blowing orgasm and black out briefly from the pleasure feedback, riding the never-ending loop of pleasure.

I feel Xavier's orgasm burst out of him, which just sends me into another. My voice grows hoarse from my screams of ecstasy. His cum tingles as it enters my body, giving me another unusual but incredible feeling, and I pant through one more orgasm.

"Stop, stop," I sob as he continues to leisurely thrust inside of me. "No more, please."

He chuckles before stopping and kissing me deeply.

"Lila, that was incredible. I can only imagine what it will be like once you and I activate our intimate bond."

I rest my head on his chest as he continues to hold me against the wall. His hand caresses every part of my skin he can reach as the water washes over us.

"I don't think I'll survive if it gets better," I mumble before tapping on his shoulder, silently asking him to lower me down. As he pulls out of me, a gush of lavender fluid follows, and I squawk with surprise. "Is that your cum?" I ask as I watch it flow away in the stream of water.

"Yup, and one day when you're ready to have my child, I will fill you full of it and use a spell so it can't leave your body. It will ensure that the seed of anyone else you have sex with while trying to conceive my child will die. It eliminates the competition," he tells me unapologetically, and I have a moment of panic.

"It's not going to hurt my babies now, is it?" I question, cupping my tiny little baby mound that thankfully hasn't gotten any bigger.

"Oh no, I would never do that to you and Caspian. It is benign and no more harmful than Link's or anyone else's you might be having sex with."

He lowers my feet to the floor before grabbing a bottle of shampoo, pouring it into his hands, and gesturing me to turn around. Even though I washed before he arrived, I'm not going to say no to pampering, so I spin, and he proceeds to wash my hair, his fingers working magic on my scalp.

"Oh my God, I feel so spoiled. Mind-blowing orgasms and a head massage. Could it get any better?"

"Only the best for my wife," he teases, nuzzling my neck before washing out the soap.

His *wife*. Why do I like the sound of that so much?

Sometime later, I'm lying on the bed with Xavier curled around me. There's a vague feeling of guilt because I didn't check in with Cas or

Link before I jumped Xavier, but they know his mark is on my shoulder, and they gave me their blessings to explore my Skarrian nature. I'm now sure Skarrian is the galaxy term for slutty, but I'm okay with that. I wonder how Susie is going to take this. Is she going to slut shame me, or is she going to be jealous of all the amazing alien dick I've been getting?

"*Phoeall*, stop with the guilt." Xavier groans, giving me a little nudge with his body. "I'm so full, I can't take any more now."

"Well, I can't just shut off my emotions," I grumble, and he places a kiss on the back of my head.

"No, of course you can't. It's fine, but do you want to talk about whatever is bothering you?" he offers, and I turn to face him.

"I'm just feeling a little guilty about jumping into bed with you and Link and Caspian all at the same time."

"Not at the same time, but I wouldn't be opposed to it," he jokes before getting serious. "I'm sure they will be fine with it. They know the attraction marks appeared on both of us, and if they do have a problem, I'll just tell them you are my intimate and I'm not giving you up for anyone." He presses his lips to mine, but I hear the burner phone message tone beep out in the main room.

I roll out of his arms and hurry, naked, to check if it was Susie responding.

"I can't say I'm sad to see you go when you're naked," Xavier calls after me, and I feel my lips lift in a grin. Picking up the phone, I read the message.

"Whoop, they are coming! Mark's really going all out and treating her. He's rented a convertible and they are driving. They can't leave until the day after tomorrow, but they'll be here in time to catch the show that night," I call back to Xavier.

"That's great," he whispers in my ear before appearing in front of me. He's like the damn Cheshire cat, appearing out of nowhere, and he scares the crap out of me. I step back to get a really good look at his naked body. I was too busy treating it like my own private amusement ride earlier to really pay attention, but the gorgeous silver mark-ings he has on his face flow down all over his body as well. I run my finger along them, tracing down his chest and onto his groin where one of his tenta-cles at the base of his cock wraps around my finger, pulling it toward the rest of them.

Giggling, I untangle it. "Are these natural?" I ask, going back to the markings. "Or tattoos?"

"Natural. They appear on a warlock's body during childhood, and the more powerful the warlock is, the more markings they have." I guess that explains why half his body is covered in the delicate silver marks.

I start to reach for his cock, which is standing straight out in front of him. I mean, neither of us have clothes on, and it would be such a waste of an erection to not do anything with it, but he grabs my hand and tuts at me.

"Uh-uh, Lila, we need to head back to the pod now that it's landed and tell your grandpas about your friend coming to visit, and discuss with them whether or not you can talk to her about all of this."

I push out my lip in an exaggerated pout and drop to my knees. I didn't get to taste him before, and I'm dying to know what he tastes like, especially after seeing his purple cum, not to mention what those tentacles feel like against my lips. I bet they tickle. Looking up at him from beneath my eyelashes, I know I've won when he releases my hand. There aren't many men who would resist a naked woman on their knees, wanting to suck their erect dick.

Shuffling forward, I take it into both hands. Its thick girth and long length are going to be more than I'm used to, but Cas and Link have been good practice, so I think I'm becoming somewhat of an expert at handling big dicks. Putting it in my mouth is going to be a whole new challenge though. I haven't had a chance to suck Link's yet, but Caspian seemed to enjoy what I did to his tentacles.

I run my tongue along the underside of his shaft before licking up the precum that is flowing freely from his slit.

I blink in surprise when I get a taste of him and sit back on my heels, looking up at him in shock.

"You taste like Twizzlers. Is that normal?" I ask him as I watch the slit produce more and more precum. Way more than a human does.

"I don't know what they are, but yes, I've been told that it is sweet by many of my harem members." I bare my teeth at him, and his hands move to cup his junk. "Sorry, sorry. I won't mention them again."

"They better have not come down in the pod. They better be up in space," I growl before pulling his hands away from his cock.

"Three of them are confined to their quarters on the ship, so they wouldn't have come down. Two of them cannot pass as human without a glamour, which I have not provided for them. The remaining three are making the journey so they can do some shopping. Vegas has the best outlets, and they asked for special permission, but I will not be feeding from them," he assures me.

"See that you don't," I tell him before running my tongue over his dick like it's a lollipop, trying to catch all of his precum as it weeps continuously. I hear his breath catch, and then he starts to breathe heavier as I finally seal my mouth around the head and take him deep into my throat.

"Holy fuck, Lila, your throat has suckers," he shouts as he grabs my hair like he's having trouble holding himself up. Hollowing my cheeks, I use my tongue to caress him as I slide back and forth. "Shit, I'm not going to last," he complains as he starts thrusting in and out of my mouth. Every time my lips hit his pelvis, his tentacles stroke and caress, tickling them just like I thought they would. Pulling his dick out of my mouth, I pay them special attention, licking and sucking them, and Xavier's pants turn to moans.

"Oh yeah, baby, just like that. Your mouth feels so fucking good on me."

I smile, because he sounds like he's about to fall apart, and take his dick back into my mouth so I can swallow down everything when he does.

Then something happens inside of me, a small nudging to the side, before something takes control of my actions. *What the fuck?*

I want a turn to make mate feel good. Suddenly, I'm just along for the ride as my inner beast—or at least that's who I hope it is—shifts us so I'm now all tentacles from the waist down. Xavier has his eyes closed and his head thrown back in ecstasy, so he doesn't even notice. When my beast probes a tentacle against his ass, he shouts in surprise. He looks down at me with wide eyes as she works it into his tight ring.

"Oh hello, little one. Have you come out to play? I was hoping I would meet you." His voice is low and seductive, but she continues to control my body as she thrusts in and out of his hot channel and deep throat his dick like a pro.

His thrusting picks up, the hold on our hair tightening. "I'm going to come," he warns, but we don't move—my beast wants to feel him fill our mouth. "Oh God, I can feel your smug satisfaction. Can I feed from it?" he rasps, and we nod as best as we can with his cock in the back of our throat.

It only takes two more thrusts before he's coming like a hose down my throat. We swallow everything, the red raspberry flavor so delicious that I think I will make this a daily occurrence. Who needs actual Twizzlers when you have this on tap? He finally finishes, and I pull away as my beast removes her tentacle from his ass and recedes, happy with how she took care of our mate. I guess she hears everything that goes on. I'm only hoping that one day, I can meet her properly.

Xavier collapses to his knees and pulls me against him, but I balk. I'm half tentacles, and I don't want to freak him out. He frowns at me.

"Don't be ashamed of how you look, Lila," he scolds, and I open my mouth to argue with him, but he doesn't let me. "I can feel it, remember?"

I sigh, called out by the psychic or whatever he is. "Fine, I'm not ashamed. I like how I look, and I know Cas does, but I was worried that maybe you would be turned off."

"Did you see my harem?" he asks, making me meet his eyes. "I'm really not all that fussy." He chuckles before nuzzling into my neck, grabbing some of my tentacles, and wrapping them around his body. I'm not sure if what he said is a compliment or an insult, but before he can get a feel for my confused emotions, I tamper them down. "Besides, you're sexy as fuck like this, and they feel amazing on my body. It's like you're kissing me in a hundred places at once."

I give in and wrap my arms around him, finding his lips with mine. We make out for a little while just like this before I pull away and shift my body back into my human form.

"So your beast took over, did she?" he asks as we lean against the couch, my back to his chest.

"Yes, how did you know?" I question, not looking away from the large window in front of us. The lights of the Vegas strip stretch as far as the eye can see, and I have a sudden thought. God, I hope those windows have privacy tinting, because anyone looking in would have gotten quite a show, what with my tentacles and all of Xavier's lovely violet skin.

"Your eyes changed and looked just like Caspian's do when his beast pushes to the front. Was that the first time you've felt her?"

I shake my head and tell him about what happened with Nikos. He just about busts a gut laughing when I get to the bit about Nikos trying to stick his dolphin dick in Cas.

It suddenly occurs to me how nice this is with the two of us. We're acting like an actual couple and talking about stuff. I snuggle into him, not wanting to get up and go back to the pod, but I know we have to. All I really want to do is stay right where we are, with Link and Cas here too.

I'm suddenly moving as Xavier lifts me and stands before sitting us back down on the couch and stretching out, my body still on top of his. He waves a hand, and I feel a blanket cover us as I lay my head against his chest.

"How did you know?" I ask, and I can practically feel his smug satisfaction.

"Being a warlock comes in handy sometimes. We still need to head over to the pod, but I guess we can do it a little later."

I mumble my assent, but my eyes are already closing, and I know we aren't going anywhere anytime soon.

CHAPTER TWENTY

Link

Saxon makes the trip down in the pod with no adverse effects. I don't like keeping him sedated this long, but I agree that Lila needs time to make a decision.

This has not gone over well with his clan members, Radella and Estrella. They are demanding to speak to Saxon themselves to confirm what I told them about Lila being Saxon's blood rose. They don't believe my truth because it almost never happens with a non Vilaxian.

"I don't know why you two care so much. We know very well that neither of you are his blood rose," Velorina sneers at her clan members. "You can't force that connection. You're just worried about what's going to happen to our clan now that Saxon's mate is not a sanguinista."

Hale looks between the three women with amusement but stays quiet, not wanting to get involved in the argument. Smart man.

"Why don't you shut up, Velorina? Don't think I didn't see you with the slutty Skarrian at the club the other night, and we know you've used that pathetic Aquilian as food too," Estrella snaps.

"Yeah, gross. What does she taste like, fish?" Radella adds, her lip curled up in a sneer.

"Well, at least it's better than pathetically pining over someone who has no interest in you." Velorina crosses her arms over her chest and quirks an eyebrow. "I kind of feel sorry for Hale. How does he feel about you two being so upset over his best friend, yet when he feeds outside the clan, neither of you blink?" The two women splutter but have no good response to that. Hale runs a hand through his hair before finally stepping into the argument.

"I think all four of us know, and Saxon *certainly* did, that this clan has grown tired of each other. Now that Saxon has found his blood rose, the timing couldn't be more ideal for us to start looking for a new one. Velorina isn't happy, and neither are Saxon and I. You two were the only ones who didn't see it, or maybe you did and that's why you're trying to cling so hard to Saxon." The deadpan look he gives them both almost makes me laugh.

"Well, that's for the five of you to work out," I interject, waving my hand around. "But you can sort it out once Saxon is conscious again. For now, the four of you are going to have to work out how you can do your act without him."

"But why can't we just wake him up? He must have made a mistake. I'm sure Lila isn't his blood rose. He hasn't been feeding properly, and he must have just gotten hungry," Radella argues and tries to step around me, but I grab hold of her arm firmly.

"Don't," I warn her. She bares her fangs and steps into me, crowding my space. She's almost as tall as I am, and she has some serious musculature. To be honest I'm not sure I would win in a fight against her.

"Who is going to stop me?" she threatens, and Hale and Velorina step up.

"What is going on here?" a voice behind us bellows. William steps up next to me with his arms crossed and a look of fury on his face. "You weren't threatening my doctor, were you?" he growls, and when a stubborn look crosses Radella's face, I know this is not going to go well—for her at least.

"He won't let us see Saxon, and I demand to, or I will be calling the queen, his aunt, and letting her know that you are holding her general and nephew hostage."

William starts to chuckle, and it's kind of scary. Both Hale and Velorina step back out of the cross-fire. Smart move, because Radella and Estrella start to rise into the air, and when they try to fly back down, they are unable to, because William's telekinesis is holding them in place.

"I have already spoken to the queen and explained the situation. I assured her we are looking after General Saxon, and she was thrilled to hear that my granddaughter is his blood rose. She is sending someone to replace him for the time being. I can easily call her back and request a few more be sent. It seems that maybe your time with the circus is done."

"I'd like to stay," Hale quickly requests, and Velorina chimes in her agreement.

"Very well, and we are happy to have you."

"We are not leaving until we hear it from Saxon's mouth himself," Estrella continues, being stubborn and mouthy. She doesn't know when to cut her losses and move on.

"Very well, then you will stay and finish out the show, and you will wait until Lila decides she is ready to form their blood bond and Link lifts the sedation. I have been given permission by the queen to throw you into the brig if any of you cause problems until we pass Vilax. The new Vilaxians will be arriving at the mothership this evening and will be transported down." He turns to Hale and Velorina. "You have the next twenty-four hours to get them up to speed for tomorrow night's show."

"How many are coming?" Hale asks, nodding his head in acknowledgement. "And do you know who?"

"Yes, Saxon's brother, Xenos, and his small clan." I watch as a myriad of emotions crosses Hale's face. I'm not sure what is going on in his mind, but I watch as Velorina reaches out and puts her hand on his shoulder.

William groans. "Is this going to be a problem?" he demands gruffly, and Hale quickly shakes his head.

"No, it's fine. I'm just surprised. He was originally part of our clan, but they split from us when we got assigned to this ship by the queen. He said it was beneath him to perform in a circus. I'm kind of curious about what changed his mind."

"Fucking hell. I swear if you give me any more headaches, I'll kick the lot of you off and find a new act. I hear the Jelliads are quite entertaining. Now go find John and see which rooms are available for them." He lowers the two girls to the ground. "Remember that I'm watching you," he threatens, and the aerial troupe takes off, disappearing in a blink of an eye.

"Link, my friend, I am getting too old for this shit," William grumbles as we move from my waiting room to the clinic. "All this drama is more than we've had in years. First Dylan, then the lightning cats and your damn nurse. Now we've got two new shifters, a fresh bunch of sanguinistas, a dead harem member, and one who has been stripped of all their powers. It's been nothing but cleaning up messes that all seem to stem from Lila."

Wait, is he saying that the source of all of the drama is Lila?

I bristle, narrowing my eyes on him, and start to defend her, but he shakes his head. "No, you don't need to get upset, I'm not blaming her. She is but a catalyst for people's insecurities and neurosis. It could have been anyone at any time. It's just interesting that she has all these powerful partners," he muses, and that reminds me of something.

"Is that a coincidence? It suddenly occurred to me when I actually took a moment to think about it that the Galaxy Circus has an unusual amount of high profile and powerful people as its performers."

William's eyes shutter, and his eyebrows furrow in a stubborn frown. "If you end up sealing a Skarrian mating bond with Lila, you can ask those questions. Until that happens, I am going to ask you to please keep that observation to yourself. For Lila's safety and all of ours."

Ah, so there is something. I knew I wasn't imagining things, but I respect this man too much to push him, not to mention I want to keep Lila safe.

"Okay," I agree, and he breathes a sigh of relief.

"Thank you," he says as we look down at the sedated Saxon. "How long can he last like this?"

"I think he'll be okay for a few more days. Maybe once Lila has spent some time with her girlfriend, she may feel better about the situation, though she has confirmed she will bond with him."

"Caspian sought us out for permission for Lila's

friend to visit. Of course we said yes, it cannot be easy adjusting to all of this. It feels like she's been with us forever, but in reality, our granddaughter has only been with us for a few weeks." A thoughtful expression passes over his face.

"And what of her plans to tell her everything and have Xavier remove her memories?" I ask, adjusting the flow of blood feeding Saxon in his coma.

"We will do whatever we need to in order to make our granddaughter feel at home, so if she needs this, we will give it to her as long as Xavier is on board with it."

"I don't think you will have any problems with him."

"No, I believe you are right. I was coming to find you because they are due back at the pod shortly. I thought maybe we could have a meal together and talk about her plans for her friends."

A rush of pleasure washes over me at being invited to have a meal with Lila and her family. I guess that means they aren't opposed to our relationship. I didn't think they would be, but there was always a chance. I must not have hid my reaction very well, because William chuckles and slaps me on the back.

"Ah, Link, we're thrilled Lila has attracted so many kind and powerful mates and potential mates. We are happy to welcome you all and know that our Lila will be well looked after and protected in the future." There's something slightly off about his tone, but he doesn't pause for me to question it. "Come on, Caspian is waiting with Eric and John. Unfortunately Saxon can't join us this time, but hopefully next time we have a family meal, he will be back to normal." He leads me out of my clinic, and I activate the locks on the door. That way we don't have to worry about Radella and Estrella getting any stupid ideas.

When we get back to the Adams brothers' quarters, I find Xavier and Lila have arrived, and although there is nothing out of the ordinary about Lila's appearance, I can tell she has been well fucked by Xavier. Maybe it's the lingering smell of his scent on her skin that I catch when she gives me a kiss hello.

"Hi," she says quietly to me as the others make conversation. "I know it hasn't been long, but I missed you."

A smile spreads across my face as I give her a hug. "I know how you feel. Did you have a good time with Xavier? Did he look after you?" I ask, my voice low so her grandpas don't hear it, but they seem to be too distracted by Cas and Xavier to notice.

"Oh my God, he sure did," she gushes, her eyes twinkling. Seeing her so relaxed after her emotional breakdown earlier in the day has put me at ease.

"Did you get a hold of Susie?" Caspian asks,

interrupting our private little chat with an unrepentant grin on his face.

I drag her over to the sofa and position her so she's sitting next to Caspian and then sit down on her other side. We each take hold of one of her hands, and Eric beams at the three of us. Xavier takes a seat on the other side of Caspian and drapes his arm over the back of the couch, playing with Lila's hair.

"Oh, I am so happy. Look at our growing family," he exclaims, and John grunts at him.

"Don't get ahead of yourself. Link isn't bonded to Lila yet. Thankfully they are doing it the sensible way and getting to know each other first. None of this fated mate crap," he grumbles, and Lila's mouth drops open at his outburst. If looks could kill, John would be incinerated.

"Now, John, don't be like that. Ignore him, he's missing our wife terribly at the moment. While seeing you all starting something new is wondrous, it also highlights what we are missing," William explains, and Lila gasps, pulling her hands out of ours and jumping up to hug her grandpas.

"Of course you must be, and here I am being insensitive by flaunting my three mates in your face."

"Three?" Eric quickly latches onto her statement, and all three of them turn to look at Xavier. "Do you have something to tell us?"

Xavier doesn't wilt under the glares of the three

men, and instead calmly explains about searching Lila's mind and finding his hidden memory that his parents removed and implanted. You could have knocked the brothers over with a feather when they heard about their son and his wife appealing to Xavier's parents for help. That reaction couldn't be faked, so they definitely knew nothing about it, and my heart hurts for them.

"And Lila's powers and her memories will be returned to her when we get to Westalin?" John sounds hopeful, and when Xavier confirms it, I see tears well in his eyes. "Well, thank fuck for that. I've been so worried about her always being in danger."

"Care to explain a little more about that?" I press, hoping that he may be more forthcoming than William.

"No," William responds, snapping his gaze to me before John can, and I can tell by his tone there will be no arguing. "As much as I want to say screw Earth and let's go straight to Westalin, we can't. We have that deportee being delivered later in the week, and we can't leave without him.

"And Susie is coming now. I need to see her if I'm not going to be able to see her for months," Lila chimes in almost desperately. The relaxation I saw on her face moments earlier has dimmed, and she's nibbling on her lip, waiting for her grandpas to comment.

"Of course you can see your friend. You can tell her whatever you need to, and as long as Xavier agrees to the plan, he can either take away her memories of the conversation or make it so she can't talk about it to anyone but you," Eric reassures her with a soft smile. "But as a compromise, how about you give her the option of which choice she would like? That way you won't feel guilty about taking away her choice."

I notice Lila's spine stiffen slightly. It's similar to something she mentioned earlier about having no choice in who her mates are except me. "Yes, that is a great idea. Thank you for recommending the alternative." Lila breathes a small sigh of relief. I guess the decision was eating her up.

"First things first. Tomorrow, you need to see the rest of the show. I can't believe you've been with us for over two weeks and haven't seen the whole thing yet," William mutters.

"In my defense, a week of that was spent in space, and it's your fault for running me ragged that first week," Lila argues and sticks out her tongue.

"Okay, how about we get some dinner and sit down for a nice meal?" Eric suggests, standing up and brushing off his pants. "I don't know about everyone else, but I want to hear more about Lila's life when she was growing up. We've been so busy with all of the circus stuff, we haven't really had a chance to learn about that."

"I'm not sure what you want to know. It wasn't very exciting," she tells him, and he waves a hand.

"I want to know about your first boyfriend and

hobbies and activities and all that stuff we would have known had you been in our lives."

She giggles, and I raise an eyebrow.

"What's so funny?" I ask her.

"I was just thinking about who or what my first boyfriend would have been if I had actually grown up in the circus. I bet it would have been very different than the one I had."

"It would have been me," Xavier growls. "If my parents had not interfered, there would have been no way I would have let you see any other boys."

She giggles harder. "Funnily enough, your Earth glamour kind of looks like my first boyfriend did. All punk rock and angst. So I guess you're not far off the mark."

He growls again as the rest of us chuckle and settle in for an evening of family time.

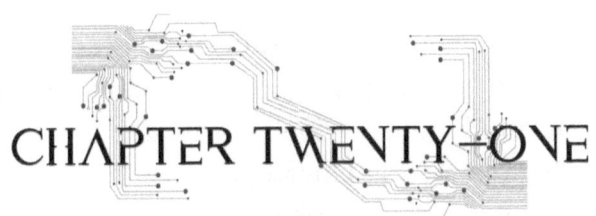

CHAPTER TWENTY-ONE

Lila

The morning was spent hiring crew to handle the concession and souvenir stands. It didn't take long, and the ones we hired had previously done the same job at other times for the circus, so thankfully, interviews weren't needed. I ran around supervising the unloading and displaying of the merchandise, as well as the setup of the food vendors and equipment in the catering kitchen. The grandpas kind of just threw me on headfirst with very little instruction, and even if it's tooting my own horn just a little, I think I did an amazing job. I was originally worried I'd have to stop people from trying to sneak backstage, but they were all professional and knew the drill. I deflected a few questions from one or two newbies, but the majority were just happy to get on with the job. The newbies realized that their questions weren't going to be answered, so they gave up after a while too.

Our merchandise ranges from stylish shirts and hoodies to plush lightning cats and ridiculous tentacle plushies that doubled as scarves. I can't deny that one of the latter may have found its way around my neck, but I plan on hiding it from Cas later so he won't tease me. It's nothing like the real thing, but it helps ease the ache I feel from not seeing him all that much over the last few days.

The sun starts to sink, headlights begin to pull into the parking lot, and the arena starts to fill up slowly. I take that as my cue to get out of the way. The excited buzz of the patrons was enough to get my own adrenaline pumping, and when I took my seat between Eric and John, I couldn't wait for it to start.

"I'm so excited to see the rest of the show," I tell Eric as I hand them both a beer that I grabbed on my way down. Our seats are in the front row, and I have an up close and personal view of the performances. Although I wish I could be watching strictly for pleasure, my future role as owner of the circus requires this to also be a business meeting.

"The beginning looks a little different now too," he replies, taking it from me. "Caspian has worked hard to revise it, and both of the new shifters have integrated well. I'll make sure that you get a chance to meet them later."

"Yes, although it is still juggling, fire breathing,

and knife throwing, they added another element to it. It's a fake fight between the two new shifters. Anyway, you'll see. I think the audience will like it." John sounds just as eager as I am about their new performance.

Like before, my new senses kick in, but this time it's easy enough for me to block out the scents and sounds of the excited crowd. Instead of being over-whelmed by it all, I find it fun to people watch as they take their seats and wait for the show to start.

The lights dim and the show begins with William appearing in a flash of smoke and lights in the middle of the arena. Eric sighs.

"He just doesn't have the same pizzazz I do. I keep telling him he needs to be showier." Eric gestures wildly with his hands like he's putting on his own performance in the crowd. He's not wrong though. Unlike Eric's sparkly outfit, William's is more sedate, missing the sequins and glitter, but he still looks the part of ringmaster.

He does the opening spiel, getting the crowd hyped up even more than they already are, and Caspian's troupe comes running out to start their show. This time instead of Dylan and Caspian wandering through the crowd, it's Cas and two other men. One of them breaks off from the group as Cas and the other do their juggling acts.

He starts to pace around the ring, looking at all of the audience members. I'm so busy watching what he's doing I miss Cas's transformation, but I hear the gasp of the crowd when it happens and quickly turn back to see my gorgeous mate juggling a whole crap load of knives. I clench my hands into my pants as I watch, holding my breath until he's finished and unharmed.

In fact, I'm so distracted with worry, I don't notice that the other performer has stopped right in front of me. Cas puts down his knives, the dragon blows out his fire batons, and they both stand and watch.

"What are you doing, Silac?" Cas calls, and Silac paces back and forth in front of the audience.

"I am hungry," he calls back.

"But you can't eat our audience. I won't allow it," the man standing next to Caspian tells him. He's Dylan's dragon replacement, but so far, he's holding his human form.

The audience rumbles at his words, a bit of unease and curiosity rippling through the tent.

"Eat us?"

"Why would he want to eat us?"

"Maybe he means he wants a snack from the concession stand."

"Damn, he's hot. I volunteer as tribute for him to eat me."

"Don't do it, man. We can get you something to eat once the show is finished. How about you come back here and finish our act so the next one can go on? You're supposed to be throwing knives at a member of our audience," Cas reminds him, but

Silac ignores him and steps in front of me, and I finally get a good look at the man.

Like Cas and the dragon, he's only wearing a pair of sparkly black pants and his feet are bare. His body is all sleek, lean muscle, much like Xavier's physique, and he has a ring through each nipple. He has short, tousled, emerald green hair and a bit of scruff around his jawline. It's his eyes, though, that have me staring. They are reptilian, with a black pupil and orange sclera. They look like Halloween contacts, but I'm almost a hundred percent sure they are not.

"No, I want this one!" he calls back to them without breaking our stare down, and with another flash of smoke and light, he shifts into a ten-foot-tall snake man. From his waist down, he has the tail of a snake, and a hood like a cobra's now flares out over his head, replacing his hair. His scales are emerald green with orange, horizontal stripes running across his body and black diamonds lining the length of it intermittently. His tail, which must be at least fifteen to twenty feet long, is thicker than my waist until it tapers daintily at the very end.

The audience gasps and screams, but they don't run in fear. Caspian's change has already prepared them.

Instead, it only amplifies their anticipation of what will happen next. I can see people beginning to stand, trying to get a closer look at Silac as he plays the rebel performer.

Silac slithers closer, his gaze locked on mine in a way that holds me hostage. His tail flicks out, and before I can say *snake*, it wraps around me. It feels cold and dry against my skin, and I try to struggle, but it just tightens until I can't breathe, so I stop resisting and it eases slightly.

Fuck my life. This is what I get for sitting in the front row. I'm being strangled by a snake, and although it would be a fascinating scenario in bed during most days that end in Y, it's far from a turn-on right now. My throbbing core and tight nipples probably make me a liar, but it's not true unless I acknowledge it, and I'm not sure I'm ready to acknowledge that I'm turned on by a snake man.

Eric and William are on either side of me, beating furiously at the snake shifter's tail, but he ignores them and lifts me into the air before slithering back into the middle of the circle. I'm not ashamed to admit the scream that leaves my mouth is not at all dainty. I go full serial killer victim and thrash my arms around, but with a quick flick of his tail, I'm suddenly face-to-face with this exotic, albeit terrifying, creature, and my frenzied movements stop. He brings me closer to him, close enough that I can reach out and touch his naked torso. Now that I'm closer, I see he has a tattoo all over his body that is the same pattern as his scales. Unable to stop myself, I reach out to see if it is skin or actual scales, and his mouth drops open in surprise. I snatch my hand back, kicking myself for my curiosity, as his fangs extend and he pulls me closer to him. His pupils dilate and contract, and a forked tongue slithers out of his mouth and licks up my cheek. A shudder runs through my body as he leans in and sniffs me.

"Who are you?" he asks, unable to hide the confusion in his voice. He sounds as surprised about his reaction to me as I am about my reaction to him.

"I'm afraid I can't let you continue to lick our audience volunteer," the dragon tells Silac.

"And what exactly are you going to do about it? Throw one of your puny knives at me?" the snake sneers at him while he holds me immobile. I try to turn in his hold so I can see what is going on, but I'm well and truly wrapped up, and it's actually not uncomfortable. His scales have taken on the heat of my body, and it's warm and cozy, so I stay still, waiting for this to play out. I'm seriously hoping this is part of the show.

"No, but I can do this." Unfortunately I'm facing the wrong way, but once more the crowd gasps and I listen to their responses to learn what's happening.

"Holy shit, is that a dragon?"

"How are they doing this?"

"It's got to be an illusion or special effects."

"Maybe it's animatronic, like the dinosaurs and other animals are."

"You think your dragon is a match for me?"

Silac bellows and loosens his tail. I start to fall, but he snatches me out of the air before I can go anywhere.

I'm now chest to chest with him, our breathing erratic, and as he slides me gently down his body, just past his pelvis, I feel twin bulges that make my eyes widen. He smirks at me before my feet finally hit the ground. Does he have two dicks? Is he like Steve the stingray—I mean Mithus, and have them permanently, unlike Link who can just whip two up at my whim? The possibilities are mind-boggling, and I'm very glad they are hidden within his body, because what I felt was not PG at all. He tries to gently move me out of the way, but the dragon lunges at him, and I get tossed to the side by his tail. I land hard, the breath whooshing out of my lungs, and it takes me a moment to recover. I hug my hands around my belly, worried for my babies.

"When I defeat you, I will not eat the girl. I have decided she shall bear my young."

What did he just say? His voice also changed then, and I'm slightly concerned that Silac's beast has come out to play, much like Caspian's does.

The crowd gasps once more. Fucking hell, there are kids in the crowd. He needs to keep that shit PG. It's okay to want to eat *me*, but not everyone appreciates monster porn and has a breeding kink.

I scramble to get up as Silac and the dragon whose name I don't know engage in a battle with flames, flying, hissing, and striking. Caspian hurries over to me on his tentacles, helps me up, and brushes me off before holding me close as we watch the epic battle in front of us.

"The babies?" I whisper, and he squeezes me reassuringly.

"They will be fine. They can take a lot more than that. Are you okay? You're a little bit flushed, and you are putting out some major fuck me vibes," he whispers.

My eyes widen. "Oh. That would explain all the weird things I was experiencing. He must be sensing those and reacting to them."

"Lila, honey, don't sell yourself short. You also don't need to be embarrassed about the fuck me vibes. Much like your Skarrian mating marks, the vibes will only activate when they find an attractive and suitable mating partner. It doesn't happen with everyone. Think carefully. When you were with any of the other crew since we mated, did they do anything to you?"

Now that he mentioned it, they really hadn't. I shake my head.

"No, because they are selective and in tune with your own wants and desires. Instinctively, and you can probably thank your inner kraken for it, those fuck me vibes will only entice beings that you are turned on by."

"But how many more times is this going to happen? Damn it, Cas, I already have three, four including Saxon. Is there a limit to this?" I ask, hearing the desperation in my voice, but before he can answer, a loud bellow echoes out through the arena, and we both duck the stream of fire that got a little too close to us.

The dragon, which is as big as a house, is a holographic pink color in some light, but then he looks almost black at a different angle. The crowd shouts and cheers for the dragon as he defeats the snake monster, and Caspian whispers in my ear.

"What do you think of the new show? Silac and Tirrian think it's a hoot. They came up with the idea themselves."

I watch the pink and black dragon as it takes the Naga in his mouth and shakes his head before tossing him to the ground, defeated, where Silac lies before another flash of light and smoke has him changing back into his human form. The crowd cheers as the dragon changes back into a man who hurries over to Caspian and me.

He bows before kneeling at my feet and taking my hand. "I am forever your servant, my lady," he announces before placing a kiss on my hand.

The crowd erupts into applause as I look down at the man holding my hand in his, but I almost stumble back when I meet his eyes. In them is a cold fury the likes of which I've never seen before. Whoa, I wonder who pissed in his Wheaties. He stands up and escorts me back to my seat before helping Silac up, and the three of them take a bow before exiting the arena.

"Wasn't that fun?" John beams at me.

"You could have warned me," I grumble at them, and Eric smirks.

"What would be the fun in that? You should have seen your face when he shifted. I just wish I'd thought to take a photo, because it was everything we'd hoped for."

I flip him off as William returns to center stage to give the crowd a warning about the barriers and the temperature drops in the arena.

The lightning cats storm into the arena, their roars sounding out as lightning flashes. The crowd oohs and ahhs as William puts the cats through their paces, but one of them breaks off from the group and stalks toward us. Slightly smaller than the others, this one is a pale icy blue with large, gleaming white fangs. The tiger gets to the other side of the glass from where we sit and pounces at it, scraping its claws down the glass barrier. I flinch as the crowd around us screams at the sound of nails on glass.

"Get away, Natalia." Eric bangs his fist against the glass. Out of the corner of my eye, I see movement just before she's tackled from the side by Echo, the pure white tiger. The two of them claw and spit, rolling around on the ground until the largest of them, Maxsim, uses his huge paw to cuff Natalia across the head. She rolls over the frozen landscape, and I watch as blue blood drips off both her and Echo. Neither of them was pulling any punches, and that certainly wasn't part of the show.

"Holy shit," I murmur as William pulls a whip out of thin air and cracks it in Natalia's direction. An arc of lightning travels across the arena from the end of it and hits her, and she screeches before running back out the way they came in.

Maxsim licks Echo's wounds on his face while William finishes off the show with the other three cats.

"William is going to be pissed." Eric sighs as he sits down. When I look at John, I can practically see the steam coming out of his ears, so I nudge his brother and nod to him.

"I don't think he's the only one." I can't help but feel sympathetic for him. All these changes are a lot to take in.

"If the Vilaxians even place one foot wrong during their performance, I am going to go ballistic," John fumes quietly, his face turning a few shades of red. "I'll fire everyone and hire a whole new lot of performers. There is no shortage of people who want to be involved with us."

"They came down from the ship yesterday, didn't they?" I ask them, trying to distract my furious grandpa.

"Yes. Hale assures me that they have their act worked out, but I know Radella and Estrella are particularly, how should I say this kindly... unhappy at the moment. I wouldn't put it past them to cause problems."

"I can't wait to see it and all the other acts I missed the first night."

The three of us sit through the next couple of acts, which I have already seen—Magenta and her silks, and the Nengh clowns—before we finally get to the part I haven't seen yet. Once the clowns clear the stage, a hush falls over the arena as smoke starts to drift across the audience. Where it's coming from, I really can't tell. I'm sure Xavier is working his mojo somehow.

"That's Xavier's mist. It has people getting a little foggy on the details regarding the pool's arrival. It's convincing them they are watching the floor open up and a pool rise out of a hidden hatch underneath," Eric whispers quietly as the three of us, unaffected by the mist, watch the pool beam down. It's huge, almost as big as the arena itself, and it rises just enough to be sticking up from the floor. There are glass panels all around so we can see what's going on under water and a platform in the middle of it. Flashes of pastel-colored shapes swim back and forth too fast for the eye to see. Standing in the middle of the platform is Nixie in her human form. She's wearing a wetsuit, but the skin we can see is still pastel blue. She has on a headset, and she's waving to the crowd.

"Hello," she greets everyone with her musical voice, "and welcome to the wet portion of the show.

If you are sitting in the first couple of rows, there are plastic ponchos under your seats. Now would be a good time to put them on if you would like to stay dry."

She gives the crowd a few moments to do as she asked. I reach under mine, but there isn't one. I look at John and Eric, and neither of them have one either, so I don't stress about it.

Nixie continues to talk, weaving a magical story about mermaids, dolphins, and true love that mesmerizes the crowd as the five pastel-colored dolphins leap and spin and perform when given instructions from her. They balance balls, tail walk, and launch Nixie into the air when she gets into the water with them.

She asks the crowd to again look under the chairs, and if they find a colored hoop, to stand and hold it up high. I play along, and sure enough, there's a pastel green hoop under my seat. Picking it up, I stand and wave it high as requested.

"Now I'm going to send the dolphins to collect them. They need to get the one that matches their color." She's facing me when she says this, and when she winks, my heart drops in dread. Fuck, I have a feeling I should have looked harder for something to cover me.

Quick as a flash, the dolphins speed for their colored hoops. All of them slow as they reach the person who has theirs—except mine. Nope, it does the dolphin equivalent of drifting, and I watch as a wall of water comes flying toward me. I get soaked, and the crowd around me starts to laugh as I glower at the stupid animal. He nods his head up and down and even blows a couple of fountains of water, which also hits me. Water drips down my back and into my underwear as I look at both my grandpas who are bone dry and grinning at me.

"What better way to get to know the show than by being a participant?" John remarks as Eric snickers. How the fuck did they stay dry? I bet they used some of their Skarrian magic. Assholes.

"Oh my goodness, are you okay?" Nixie calls to me, not even trying to hide her grin. "I'm so sorry Nikos got a little enthusiastic. He must like you very much. Why don't you step closer, hand him his hoop, and give him a pat?" she suggests, and I hear mischief in her voice, but it's not like I can refuse in front of thousands of people. So I step forward and lean over to drop the hoop over his nose, but before I can, he lunges.

CHAPTER TWENTY-TWO

Nikos

I finally have her in my grasp. She got away from me last time, but I'm hoping now that she's in the water with me, I can convince her to stroke my fins. My beast has the same idea, and he and I wrestle for control. If he takes over, the crowd will get a show that is not appropriate for children's eyes, so I keep him buried deep down.

Lila tumbles headfirst into the water next to me, and I hear the crowd laugh and cheer around us. When she resurfaces, she's trying to fix her beautiful brown hair, and when she does, all I can see are her bright green eyes glaring at me as she splutters quiet obscenities.

Ah, so she wants to play hard to get. I can do this too.

This act must be for the crowd. She happily wore my seed on her skin the other day, after all, so she must be interested in mating with me. I also have her mark on my shoulder in human form, so maybe this is a form of courting for humans. Well, I am intrigued and up to the challenge.

"Oh goodness me," my sister scolds, swiftly adapting to the small change I made to the act. "Well, I guess you should bring your prize over here, Nikos. Would you all like to see him tow his new friend through the water?" she asks the crowd who, of course, answers enthusiastically. I swim around Lila a couple of times, trying to get her to hold onto my fin, beyond excited to feel her grip it in her hand. Our fins are directly connected to our sexual organs, and it's going to take all my control not to get an erection in the pool. The Adams brothers would probably castrate me if I did, so when she does, I speed as quickly as I can back to the platform where Nixie helps her climb out. The crowd cheers and I do a quick lap of the pool in celebration, splashing all the smiling children as I go. I love children and hope to have many of my own one day.

This has me thinking. Lila is already with child, so I know she is not opposed to breeding. If I can convince her to breed with me, then she can't ever get away.

Nixie continues on with the scripted part of the

show, telling everyone she'd like to introduce us. This is where we change into our mermaid form and surprise the crowd by launching ourselves up onto the platform like that. The other four Aquilians in the troupe have recently become a family pod, so I think this will be the last stop on Earth for them. They will get off when we pass Aquilia. Joaquin is already showing signs of being with child, and they will want to be in our home waters when they give birth.

I hear the cue, and the five of us dive deep, the other four changing shape before leaping into the air to the oohs and ahhs of the crowd before splashing back down. We all swim over to the platform and use our tails to get out, but the audience can now see I'm still in my dolphin form.

"Oh no," my sister cries. "Nikos must be cursed like the mermaid in our tale. We all know what fixes a curse, don't we?"

"A kiss!"

"True love's kiss."

"A wizard."

The children all shout.

"Yes, that's right, do you think that maybe our audience member here can give Nikos a kiss and break the spell?"

The crowd cheers, and Nixie looks at Lila, who rolls her eyes but crouches down. I must remember to buy my sister something nice as a thank you for helping me out.

"You're going to pay for this," she growls at me before she places a kiss on the end of my nose, and with a flash of lights and smoke, I change my form before grabbing her and sealing my lips to hers. She squeaks in surprise and holds onto my shoulders to steady herself before sinking into my kiss. I've been very careful not to cut her with my jagged teeth, but I do manage to draw blood, and it sears my very soul as it races through my system. Oh yes, this is the woman for me. Her very essence sets my whole being alight, and again, I struggle to keep my cock within my sexual slit. My beast is smug as he crows his triumph in my head.

"It worked!" Nixie cheers, and the crowd applauds loudly as Lila pushes me away and hisses at me. I ignore her and roll so she can see my tail, wanting her to see how shiny and sparkly the green and gold scales are. It's always been something that has attracted females in the past.

That was my problem the other day. I should have shown her my tail underwater, and maybe then she might have let me put my cock in her breeding hole. I don't care if it's the one in human form or the one when she's in half shift. She's sexy either way.

I wave and smile to the crowd when Nixie gets to my introduction, my sharp teeth exposed for all to see, and the crowd gasps before some of them wave back.

"Now how are we going to get our fabulous and

patient audience member back to her seat?" Nixie muses out loud.

I hear a child shout, *"Make Nikos swim her back. It's his fault really."*

That tiny human just became my second favorite after Lila.

"What a wonderful idea! Well, that's the end of our show. Next time you're out on the ocean and see a dolphin, remember they might be a mermaid waiting for true love's kiss." Nixie waves, and in a flash of light and smoke, she too changes, much to the delight of the crowd, and they all jump into the water. I sit on the edge of the platform and gesture for Lila to join me, but she shakes her head, and the crowd laughs.

"How else are you going to get back to your seat?" I ask her quietly, and she glares at me again. Is this her way of trying to arouse me?

"I will swim myself."

"Come on, my little seashell. Don't disappoint the children." I nod to the audience, and she sighs and joins me on the edge.

I lift her into my arms before launching us into the pool. I use my powerful tail to keep us both above water as I swim her back to her seat. Eric steps down to help her out of the pool, handing her a towel.

"Kiss him!" the same child from before demands, and she quickly goes up again in my esteem, but I

can't very well put her in front of my love so she can be equal.

I pucker my lips, and I see she's about to refuse, but Eric gets involved. "Come on, Lila, don't disappoint the crowd."

"I hate you all," she mutters under her breath, then leans forward and presses her lips to mine. No tongue this time, but I'm okay with that. I keep my teeth to myself in front of the boss men.

When she pulls away, I whoop in delight before diving under the water with a splash of my tail in her direction, sharing my habitat with her so she knows how important she is to me. She must be so thrilled that I have shown her all this affection and nearly swooning with delight. If the single females on Aquilia could see her now, they would be boiling with jealousy. They would demand to fight her for her right to be my breeding partner. I would love to see Lila fight for that honor. The thought nearly catches me off guard, and my erection almost slips out of my sexual slit again.

I dive down deep as the pool beams back onto the ship. We need to climb out, and then Nixie and I will beam back down for the final parade.

"You idiot!" my sister screeches at me once the pool arrives back on the ship and we shift forms and climb out. The other four say a quick goodbye and disappear out of Nixie's line of fire. Cowards.

"No, Nikos. Don't you dare look at them." She smacks my chest as we both put on our modesty clothes. "They weren't the ones that went rogue during the middle of the show. What were you thinking?" She continues to smack me, though the hits barely register as anything more than an annoyance. I grab hold of her hand and press it against my chest.

"Wasn't it wonderful? The crowd loved it. I was a star," I crow, almost bending into a bow, but she just rolls her eyes.

"You better hope that the boss men liked it. They have enough trouble with the performers, if the rumors are true, and we do not need to add to their worries. It's bad enough that Dorado confirmed Joaquin's pregnancy and that they will be leaving the show once we get back to Aquilia. I don't want to go, I want to stay with the circus. I like it here."

"I think maybe it's a certain female Vilaxian that you like, and maybe you don't mind the male one either." I raise an eyebrow at her in challenge. "Don't think I didn't see you sneak both of them and that Skarrian woman into our house the other night, Nixie."

She huffs. "Fine, but I also like this way of life. I don't want to go back and be expected to find a partner and have a brood of babies."

"It will be fine. Everything will work, you'll see, and soon Lila will be taking my cock into her breeding channel."

"Goddamn it, Nikos, you're an idiot," my sister

snaps and slaps me on the back of the head before heading for the transport chamber to return to Earth.

I follow behind, happy with my plan that I'm sure will come to fruition soon.

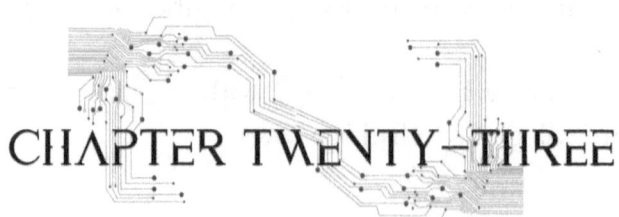

CHAPTER TWENTY-THREE

Lila

"That fucking can of cat food," I mutter to myself as I use the towel Eric provided to dry myself the best I can, but I eventually give up trying.

"That was marvelous. Did you have any idea they had changed the show?" John asks Eric who shakes his head.

"No, but it was amazing, and the crowd loved it. We got so much engagement from the children! We need them to do it for the rest of the shows on Earth." They both look at me with expectant expressions.

"Oh no, no way. Uh-uh. I can't. Susie will be here for tomorrow's show." I shake my head vehemently, but John just pats me on the leg. I'm interpreting his move to say, *Be a good girl and take one for the team.*

"And I'm sure she will enjoy seeing you as part of the show."

"But now I have to sit here wet for the rest of it," I complain, scrunching up my nose. Nobody likes wet underwear.

John puts a finger to the earpiece in his ear. "Can someone tell Xavier to meet Lila in the bathroom near our seats?"

Just then William announces a short intermission, and the crowd starts to leave their seats in droves. I watch as the kids bounce up and down, tugging on their parents' arms in excitement. The look of wonder on their faces is nothing short of adorable, and my frustration with Nikos eases slightly.

John sighs. "Actually, tell him to meet her in our office."

He turns to me. "Go on then. Xavier will dry you off with a spell, and then you can return to watch the rest of the show. Viggy is next, you're not going to want to miss that."

He's not wrong. I've been dying to get a better look at the dinosaurs, but being cooped up in my room all week has made exploring impossible. When we get back on the ship to go to Asia, we'll get another week off in between, so I'm going to get one of the guys to show me their habitat.

I hurry out of my seat and head to my grandpas' office. I need to use the elevators to get up there, and as I hurry toward the staff one, I think about my cousins. They have been scarce since they saw me get off the pod with Caspian. Neither of them has tried to seek me out to get to know me, but then I haven't either. Not after the way they treated my mate. I wonder if there's going to be a problem when it comes to me seeing the dinosaurs.

Xavier is waiting for me when I reach the office, and he grins as he looks me up and down. My Galaxy Circus jumpsuit is dripping wet and sagging in places where the water has pooled due to gravity. "Drowned kala mouse is not a good look on you, *phoeall*."

I cross my arms, inhaling deeply to maintain my composure. Maybe I should volunteer Xavier to participate in tomorrow's performance, then he can fully understand my attitude.

"Were you watching? Did you see what that idiot did? The grandpas thought it was *wonderful* and want me to do it for the rest of the performances on Earth," I complain, and he waves a hand, instantly removing my wet clothes so I'm standing here naked.

"What the hell, Xavier?" I screech and look out the big picture window, covering my important bits with my hands. "Dude, I don't need to be flashing everyone my tits and ass." He just grins and steps toward me. I back up, holding up my hands, but he quickly has me pressed against the window.

"It's mirrored glass," he whispers as he bends down and takes the skin on my neck between his teeth and bites down hard, just shy of breaking the skin. My knees buckle from the sensation, and he catches me as I cry out.

"Why? What are you doing?" I ask him, and he shrugs as if we were just casually talking about the weather.

"Marking my territory so that idiot Aquilian knows *you are mine*," he states possessively as he pulls away from my neck and admires his handiwork, brushing his thumb across the mark. I'm sure there's a perfect imprint of his teeth in my skin now.

"Well fuck, you could have given me a little bit of pleasure at the same time," I grumble to him, and he steps back. I watch as a range of emotions flicker across his features—arousal, anger, sadness, and longing—but he finally settles on one, if the glare he gives me and the clenching and unclenching of his fists is anything to go by.

"Lila, it is taking all of my power to hold back my anger at the moment. Until we can secure our intimate bond, I'm afraid my emotions may be all over the place. It is the only time a warlock is ever out of control. It's why intimates bond very quickly, and I thought I had a handle on the way I'm feeling. I was okay seeing you with Link and Caspian, but his immaturity and lack of social etiquette by attempting to claim you in public has my blood boiling. My need to eviscerate and flay him is riding me hard."

Xavier clamps his mouth shut, working his jaw as fury and jealousy radiate off him in turbulent waves. I can see why people fear the warlock, but I'm incredibly turned on by the thinly veiled violence.

"Whoa, okay then." I reach out and stroke his cheek, hoping to ease some of his concerns. "It's okay, but if you need to mark me in the future, maybe giving me an orgasm at the same time might make it easier for me to take. I like angry fucking."

My soft gesture hasn't relaxed him yet, so I scramble to think of a solution that will help calm and reassure him, but I am coming up blank. This is a situation where communication is key.

"I need to mark you, and I need you to mark me with your scent," he pleads almost desperately. Gone is the cool, sophisticated, powerful warlock, and before me is a desperate, needy man.

I look around the room, my eyes catching on the couch. "Okay then, come on. I think I have a few more minutes before the show starts." I drag him over and gesture for him to lie down on the couch. "Do your thing, get naked," I demand, waving a hand at him, and in an instant, his clothes are gone, and his big, thick, purple dick waves at me for attention. Licking my lips, I climb my naked body over his, presenting my pussy at his mouth. "Make it quick. We do not want my grandpas coming to find us sixty nining on their couch."

I feel his hands on my hips as I lower myself down, and then his tongue swipes through my folds before he goes to town on my clit. Grunting, I can't help but ride his face for a moment or two while I stroke my hand up and down his dick. I'm not great at multitasking, I tend to get lost in the pleasure, but I am going to do my damnedest to give him a blow job that makes him come hard.

Leaning forward, I press our bodies together and take him deep into my throat, hollowing out my cheeks and sucking. I do this a couple of times before pulling back and spitting on my fingers, returning my mouth to the head of his cock while I probe his ass with them.

He groans when I finally insert them, the vibrations tickling my clit and bringing me close to the edge.

There's no noise in the room except for sucking and slurping sounds as the two of us race to get each other off. I feel Xavier start to feed through his hands. It's not as intense as it was when our eyes were locked. I can't feel his emotions, but the sensation of him feeding is enough to tip me over the edge. I moan my pleasure around his cock, and soon he comes too, but as I feel his first jet, I pull back and let the rest of it cover my face and tits. The warm lavender spunk tingles against my skin, and I rub it in as I continue to ride his face, milking as much pleasure out of my orgasm as I can while covering him in my essence as well.

Once I feel my orgasm ebb, I dismount Xavier. "Do you feel better?" I ask him as I continue to rub his cum into my body. It actually soaks in much like moisturizer, leaving me with a lavender shimmer all over my tits.

His eyes are hooded with lust as he watches me, his erect dick not going down one bit despite his orgasm. "Yes, for now."

"Can you dress me?" I request, and he waves a hand, putting me in a dry version of the same outfit I had been in. I quickly check myself in the mirror on the wall. That lavender shimmer is all over my face. "Are my grandpas going to know what this is?" I ask him, and he gets a smug ass grin as he nods.

"Yup."

"Well, can you remove it?" I question, and he shakes his head.

"No, I want everyone you come in contact with to smell you and see that you are mine." There's a stubborn set to his jaw, and I don't think I'm going to be able to convince him otherwise.

"Can you at least make it so they can't see it?" I request, and he waves his hand again.

"Done. I have protected your grandpas' fragile sensibilities. Though I'm pretty sure they wouldn't have cared. It is a common thing for alien species to mark their partners and lovers with their seed."

"Yeah, well, okay, but I don't really want them knowing what I've been doing up here, you know, in their office. Also please hide the bite mark from human eyes," I deadpan, and he rolls his eyes before getting to his feet, his naked body distracting me for a second.

"It has already been done. Lila, you worry too much." He kisses me hard before clothing himself and leading me out of the office by my hand. "I am looking forward to drying you after every performance," he announces as he pushes me into the elevator. It's only then that I realize he hasn't been shrouded in his mist. In fact, I haven't seen him shrouded since we came to Earth together.

"How come you're not all misty?" I ask him, waving my hand at his body as he leans nonchalantly against the wall.

"You are my intimate, you don't hide yourself from your soulmate," he states casually, but my heart skips a beat in pleasure at hearing him call me his *soulmate*.

"But what about the other night at dinner? You weren't shrouded then either."

"They are my friends and also family now, I've never hidden myself from them." I hear someone talking farther down the corridor, and the mist suddenly forms and he winks. "But we wouldn't want anyone else to get the wrong idea."

The doors close, and I hear him chuckle quietly as he floats in the direction of the voice. I'm sure he's going to give some poor backstage worker a fright.

I head back to my seat and place my butt on it just as the house lights go down again and William is lit up. The arena is now a leafy jungle landscape. William's outfit has changed from ringmaster to big game hunter, and he carries a big rifle.

"Who's ready to go on a safari?" he asks, wearing binoculars around his neck and ridiculous, poofy khaki safari pants on his legs.

"I am *not* wearing that," I tell my grandads. My tone leaves no room for argument.

"Oh! Look who's back. What took you so long?" Eric asks, his eyes twinkling mercilessly.

"Nothing, just took Xavier a little while to get me dry," I lie, not even bothering to look him in the eye, knowing I won't be able to hide my guilt. I hope Xavier went back and cleaned the sofa.

"Liar," he whispers as John pats my leg.

"Don't worry, we will find you something suitable to wear. Now quiet, the both of you, this is my favorite part."

"Does anyone know what we're hunting?" William asks the crowd, and I hear a little voice pipe up.

"Bears?"

William shakes his head. "Nope, bigger."

"Elephants!" another little boy shouts, and William shakes his head again.

"No, even bigger."

"What's bigger than an elephant?

"There isn't anything bigger than an elephant!"

"The only thing bigger than an elephant is a whale."

"Please stand back while we erect the barriers once more," William commands, and the crowd quickly does as he says.

This time they go up a lot farther and it's a double barrier—first the glass and then power lines on the inside, creating an electrical fence.

"Please refrain from touching the glass. It should be safe, but we wouldn't want to risk it."

The crowd sounds confused, and it's then when giant, loud footsteps start to shake the arena. The large door on one end slides up, and in lumbers Viggy.

"Ladies and gentlemen, I give you the tyrannosaurus rex." The crowd surges to their feet in a wave of panic, but Fiona is sitting on Viggy's back. She is miked up and dressed in an outfit somewhat similar to William's, but more feminine. "Okay, I'd wear that," I tell the brothers, my eyes locked on the sight in front of me. I've seen him before, but it really is incredible to be so close to an extinct animal.

"Don't be afraid. Viggy is practically an overgrown puppy. Who would like to see him play fetch?" she calls into the crowd, who seems to have calmed down and are starting to take their seats again.

She reins Viggy to a halt, climbs out of the

basket she was sitting in, and gingerly walks down his back and tail before jumping to the ground.

"Do you want to play catch?" she asks, and his tail starts to beat up and down. He wiggles just like a Labrador, and the crowd laughs, still a little uneasy.

"Okay then. Sit, Viggy," she commands, and he sits back on his haunches with his little T-rex arms out in front of him. He waits patiently, his tongue hanging out over his giant jaw and teeth. Really, he just looks like the dinosaur from the *Night at the Museum*, just full bodied as opposed to skeletal.

Fiona skips to a trunk on the side of the arena, and William goes over and helps her open it. Together, the two of them pull out a big ball.

"How is that not going to pop?" I ask the grandpas, not taking my eyes off what is happening in the arena.

"It's made of a special material. It's kind of like those Kong toys for Earth dogs, but obviously rated for dinosaurs," Eric explains.

"Oh yeah, obviously," I reply sarcastically, and he flicks my ear.

"Such disrespect to your loving grandpas. How will we ever cope with such an ungrateful granddaughter?" he and John chuckle to themselves.

Fiona rolls the ball across the arena. The thing is almost as big as she is.

"How is she going to throw that?" I ask when she gets to the other end. What I hadn't noticed before is a catapult device, which she loads the ball into. She steps away and raises her hand.

"Come, Vigorish." The T-rex lumbers to his feet and rushes toward Fiona, shaking the arena with each step. There's another rush of people screaming and getting to their feet, but Viggy slides to a stop in front of Fiona and sits again. "Good boy," she coos, and he wiggles with delight.

"Alright, so you can probably guess that there's no way I can throw a T-rex size ball, so I'm going to use this machine, and Viggy is going to get it and retrieve it for me. Are you ready?" she calls to the crowd, and the response she gets isn't very enthusiastic. She mimes a frown. "Oh no, Viggy, that wasn't very good, was it? Come on, show him you want to see what he can do. Are you ready?" She cups a hand to her ear and the crowd's response is much more enthusiastic this time. "Alright, let's count down from five. I want to hear you all! Five, four..."

"She's a good showman," I mutter mostly to myself, but the brothers hear it.

"Yes she is," John replies as the crowd gets to one and she presses the button on the machine, launching the ball to the other side of the arena where it hits the barrier and drops to the floor. Viggy rushes after it, his footsteps once more shaking the ground. "It's the only reason we've kept them both in the show, but only barely. Their personalities are horrible. But they are your grand-mother's sister's children, and we wouldn't dishonor our wife by rejecting them."

"Nasty attitudes aren't enough to be kicked out, unfortunately. Up until now, they have done no harm and caused no real issues yet." Eric sounds disappointed.

The act continues as Fiona shows the crowd that she has Viggy trained as well as a performing poodle.

Finally, she wraps it up. "Now who do you think would be faster in a race? Good old Viggy here —" She pats his shoulder, and he flinches slightly. It's the first time I've seen it during this performance, but it's there. I lean forward and feel the brothers lean with me. "Or a velociraptor?"

"They are going off script," John mutters, and Eric shakes his head.

"Maybe I spoke too soon. What the fuck has gotten into our performers? First Nikos, which worked out okay, thankfully" —I give my grandpa a scathing look to show how much I disagree with his statement— "and now this. This could go badly. That animal is a menace. I want to send it back to our zoo in Skarr and bring one of the other dinosaurs instead."

The crowd shouts back with its answer, and Fiona claps her hands together. "Alright, I propose a race!"

The big back doors open again, and in comes Phillip riding Htaed. The raptor pulls and tugs on his restraints, and Fiona's smile wobbles with worry until Phillip gets him to line up next to Viggy. She then climbs up Viggy's back so she's sitting in the little saddle strapped to him.

"Once around the arena. On three." She starts the countdown, and the crowd joins in, but Htaed breaks away before they get to go and takes off, leaving Viggy in his dust. The raptor races around the barrier, his eyes on the audience all the way around. Suddenly he stops and throws an almighty buck, launching Phillip over his head. Phillip hits the ground hard and doesn't get up. Htaed starts to dash toward him, but William is there, standing over Phillip's unconscious body while brandishing a pole that sparks at the end. Htaed veers away and continues his mad dash around the barrier without his rider.

"Get Xavier down here now. That raptor is out of control," John barks into his earpiece.

"That's like a taser," Eric explains as John shouts into his earpiece again, "but it's not enough to drop him. Xavier will hopefully be able to grab his mind and direct him back out the doors."

Poor Viggy is starting to pant like a dog, so Fiona pulls him to a stop. Htaed just continues to run in circles, swinging his head back and forth between William, Phillip, Fiona, and Viggy. All of a sudden, he charges Viggy, deciding he's an easier target. Viggy sees him coming and bellows an almighty roar, which has Htaed veering off again.

This time he charges the electric barrier, throwing his body at it. The raptor hits it and it sparks, pushing him back, but he just shakes his head and tries again. Once more the barrier sparks, but the lights in the arena dim ever so slightly. Again Htaed shakes off the electric charge and lunges at the barrier in the exact same spot, which is just down from where we are sitting.

"Holy shit," Eric gasps. "He's shorting out the electric barrier. It's not going to last much longer if he keeps that up."

Suddenly, in a flash of light and smoke, Xavier appears in the middle of the arena with a purple cowled robe over him. He holds up a hand, and Htaed slides to a stop in front of him. Within seconds, Xavier must grab control of his mind, because he turns and calmly walks out of the arena.

The crowd cheers wildly, not vaguely aware of the danger they were in. Xavier disappears again, and Fiona waves goodbye to the crowd as she and Viggy leave the arena to a thunderous applause. William helps a dazed-looking Phillip to his feet. He is whispering, and from the look of fury on William's face, I don't think he's speaking words of praise. A stagehand runs out from the side and puts Phillip's arm over his shoulder before helping him out of the arena. William brushes off his outfit and composes himself before he addresses the audience once more.

"Wow, was that something or what?" he asks.

"Phew, that could have been a disaster." John sags next to me, and it's my turn to pat his knee.

"Thank goodness for almighty powerful warlocks, right?" I tease him, and he shudders in relief.

"Shall I tell him you said that?" Eric asks, and my head swings to him.

"Don't you fucking dare."

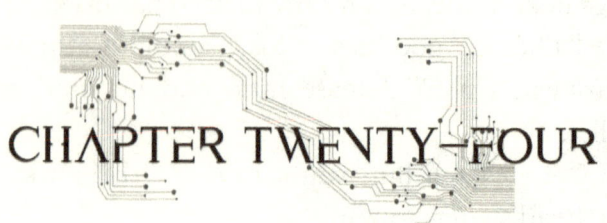

CHAPTER TWENTY-FOUR

Lila

Eric and John settle down once more now that the dinosaur danger has passed. I can't believe that I'm even thinking those words. My life has become bizarre and unbelievable. William takes to the center of the ring again, still wearing the stupid hunter hat and outfit and holding his gun.

"Phew, that was a little close. I almost thought I was going to need my gun," he tells the crowd in a joking manner, but I could hear the truth in his voice.

"I think you would have needed a bigger gun, buddy," someone yells at him, and William tips his hat in his direction.

"You may be right, my friend. But after that heart-stopping act, are you ready to see another?"

The crowd cheers, and the same heckler yells, *"Am I going to almost shit my pants at this one?"*

William chuckles. "No, this time all you have to do is keep your fingers crossed that the act doesn't have slippery hands. I give you the Volans."

The spotlight shines toward all the rigging that is located at the top of the arena and down the flimsy ladders that lead up to it. We watch as seven people climb to the top to stand on tiny little platforms on either side.

I lean into John. "How come there are seven of them? I thought Saxon's clan only had five people. And what does Volans mean? Is it Vilaxian?"

"Volans is Latin for flying. We decided to stick to Earth words when we are here in case people used Google to look it up. As for the number of people, we are not happy with the remaining members of Saxon's clan," John murmurs quietly as music fills the arena and the trapeze act begins. "With Saxon down, they were short a catcher, so we needed someone in a hurry. The queen sent us Saxon's brother and his small clan to cover. That's who the extra three people are."

"And by Saxon's clan, he really means Estrella and Radella," Eric adds. "I'm pretty sure that clan is on the verge of collapse, especially with you being Saxon's blood rose. William said that Hale and Velorina basically confirmed it. So once we finish here on Earth, that is another thing we have to deal with. I've got to say, Lila, things really have been boring until you got here." The stupid man chuckles and claps like an excited child. "This is the most excitement we've had in *years*."

I send a fake glare my grandpa's way for insinuating that I attract all of the drama in the circus.

The crowd oohs and ahhs and gasps as the aerialists flip and turn and swing. The act is so mesmerizing that when it finishes, I startle in surprise. I was so engrossed, I hadn't noticed that over half an hour had passed. One by one, they drop down to the safety net hanging below them before flipping over and landing gently on the ground. The seven of them take a bow and wave to the crowd before running off. The arena goes dark as crew members come out and tear down the net, the spotlight highlighting William as he banters with the crowd once more.

"Is everyone ready to go home yet? Or would you like to see one more act?" he asks the audience, who obediently shouts their enthusiastic response.

"Who likes to ride on the carousel when you go to the fair?" People in the crowd raise their hands. The children are more eager than the adults, but that's to be expected. He waits a few seconds to let the anticipation build.

"Would you like to see our carousel? We don't just have horses on ours, however, we have larnuks. They are a special breed of alien horses." He gives an exaggerated wink and the crowd chuckles.

"What's a larnuk?" a little girl asks boldly.

"It's a unicorn with wings, but ours aren't colored like your horses on Earth. No indeed," he tells her, rising up, strapped to a harness, as the floor of the arena seems to open again. Up out of the ground, much like the pool did, an old-fashioned carousel rises, with a roof and center pole, but the wooden horses are missing. The center pole is painted in bright colors with fantastic-looking creatures all over it, as is the top of the carousel.

"Where are the horses?" a child yells.

"Ladies and gentlemen, I give you our larnuk mistress, Zala, and her larnuks," William shouts as the sound of thundering hooves fills the arena. The big door opens, and six of the most magnificent-looking animals I have ever seen come running into the arena.

"Oh my God, they are gorgeous," I murmur as I take in the sight before me. Built like a Friesian, with long flowing manes and tails, these animals have wings tucked into their sides and sparkling horns sticking out of their foreheads, and each and every one of them is a bright jewel color. They are emerald, violet, gold, scarlet, and sapphire and copper. They toss their heads and snort as they canter around the arena. Atop the gold larnuk is a curvy, dark-haired female who looks like she has colored streaks in her black hair. They seem to match her horses.

"When she bonds with each creature, it creates a streaked lock of hair, that's why she has all the different colors in it." Eric leans forward, as mesmerized as I am by the creatures. "They really are magnificent creatures. They breathe fire, and their main food source is precious and semi-precious gems. You should see the vault we have on the ship that holds their supplies. If an Earthling found them, they would think they hit the jackpot."

"Rilu is a desert-like planet with little oases dotted all over it. The Rilus are a nomadic race, and they use the larnuks for transport. The planet is riddled with gem mines, which they use to feed their animals and to trade with other species. That drink you like is made from the rilax berry, which only grows in their mines," John explains as the mistress sends the horses to stand in a specific spot on the carousel.

"It takes extreme courage and bravery to become a larnuk master or mistress. To bond with them, you need to allow them to bite you. You can't see it, but Zala is covered in silver scars from where her horses bonded with her. Most Rilus will only ever bond with one or two horses in their lifetimes. Being a larnuk master is equal in power to the tribe leader. She has four more horses, but she only ever uses six for the show. She swaps them in and out." Eric eyes Zala with admiration, but it's not sexual, just full of profound respect.

The animals all start to move in synchronized formation, round and round, just like a carousel. Their high stepping movements get faster and faster until all of a sudden, at her command, their wings snap open and start to flap as they get even faster. At her accented order of, "Fly," the six of them take off into the air to the gasps and shouts of wonder of the crowd.

Round and round they soar as the whole carousel floats into the air and moves to the top of the arena before they descend back down to the wild cheers of the audience.

"Holy shit. How is that happening?"

"There must be some rigging, but I can't see it anywhere."

"They can't be real, they must be animatronic."

The crowd cannot believe what they are seeing but are no less impressed by the whole spectacle.

She herds the horses off to the side and the carousel returns into the bottom of the arena before it closes up again. She has them trot around the arena in formation before they line up across it. With a wave of her hands, the six of them rear up onto their hind legs before she has them canter around the arena once more. She walks over so she's in line with them, and as the gold one passes her, she grabs hold of its mane and pulls herself up onto the moving animal. She tucks her feet in behind its wings, which then snap open once more, and she and the animal soar into the sky. The others take flight behind them and then they fly out the large double doors once more.

The applause in the circus tent is thunderous, and the crowd is on its feet, cheering and shouting.

"This is the best show I've ever seen."

"The special effects are amazing."

"I am definitely getting tickets for tomorrow night."

William runs out to wrap up the show, thanking everyone for attending and reminding them of the merchandise stands in the foyer.

"Now, everyone, let's show the performers how much you enjoyed the show as they all return to the ring for the grand parade!"

Marching music fills the dome as the giant doors open and the performers come out. Caspian, Tirrian, and Silac are all still in half form. Magenta smiles and waves from the back of a truck, swinging on an aerial hoop. A couple of the ice tigers are in a cage, snarling and growling at the audience, causing the children to scream with delighted fright. The clowns run in and out of everything. The smaller mermaid tank, with Nixie waving and Nikos in beast form, is being pulled by another truck. I see Viggy and Fiona, with no sign of Phillip and Htaed, and the aerialists, who are waving and walking in formation, occasionally flip and cartwheel. Lastly is Zala and her golden larnuk.

"Come on, let's get out of here before the crowd starts leaving," John says, helping me to my feet. As the crowd shouts and cheers around us, the grandpas and I make to leave, but not before the mermaid tank passes us and I feel a wave of warm water cover my back.

Shouting, I whirl and see Nikos's damn beast laughing at me just like an Earth dolphin can, his sharp teeth shining in the light.

"He is so dead," I grind out between gritted teeth as the audience laughs when they see what happened.

If only they knew how much I *wasn't* joking.

E ric, John, and I make our way backstage to the big area where everyone gathers at the end of the parade. I'm talking to performers, congratulating them on their show, when all of a sudden I see the dragon storming toward me, still in half form, with his wings out and steam pouring out of his nose. Now how did I know this was going to happen? He wasn't afraid to hide his hatred of me earlier.

"So you're the Earth bitch who got my cousin kicked off this gig," he growls, stepping right into my personal space. Unlike Dylan, who was pitch black, Tirrian is more like an oil slick black. He has a shimmer to his skin that flickers from green and gold to pink and blue. He's holographic depending on what angle you view him from. Pink scales continuously shift back and forth across his skin in an agitated manner. He's much larger and more intimidating than Dylan was as well. The guy is basically one Targaryen family member away from going full *Game of Thrones* dragon on me. I feel my beast take over in defense of the unexpected threat, and I start to shift, growing rapidly, but this time it's not just my bottom half, *everything* moves, and I get pushed into the background.

"Holy fuck. Tirrian, step back, you idiot, before she eats you in one bite," Caspian shouts, putting himself between us and the puny dragon who looks like he might be tasty.

Dragon just like old one. Should have eaten him. Will eat this one.

No, no, no, I beg my beast as I hear her inner ramblings about eating Tirrian. *Please don't eat the dragon.*

Caspian steps forward, the brave man, and we tower above him. We must be at least as big as Tirrian's dragon form was, which was huge. He takes one of my tentacles in his arms and starts stroking it, murmuring soothing tones, and my beast forgets all about the stupid dragon and starts purring like a cat to her mate. His soothing sounds lull her into a sort of sleepy state, allowing me to push her back out of the way and force our shift.

I'm naked when I make it back into human form. Xavier steps out of the crowd of performers who gathered around and waves a hand, quickly clothing me, but not before the dragon gets a good eyeful.

He sneers. "You're just a pathetic, mate stealing Skarrian who has no powers and needs to rely on what your mate shared with you. You're no better than a human. You should just go back to where you came from."

I can feel my beast begin to shift in her slumber. This is so not going to end well.

"That is enough," William bellows as he and his brothers join us. "Tirrian, your father assured us there would be no more problems. Don't pick up where your cousin left off, or you may find yourself in a very difficult place. Your father will not be happy if you cause an international incident when you don't have the full story. I suggest you go cool off before you do irreversible damage or irreversible damage is done to *you*." William's tone allows no room for argument, and a couple of the performers from his act drag him off, leaving me with Caspian who is looking at me with wonder.

"You have a full form, and she's beautiful." He pulls me into his arms and hugs me tight as I try to get my bearings. "I can't wait until we can swim together. My beast was trying to push his way out, but that would have done us no good. Hopefully she won't actually want to kill me when they meet."

He pulls back, and I shake my head. "No, she was pretty thrilled with your attention. But maybe we should ask Xavier to be on hand when they first meet just in case," I suggest and turn to the warlock who has been not so subtly listening.

"Of course I will. Are you okay?" he asks and nods in the direction Tirrian went.

I shrug. "I guess so. It was just words, and none of it was true. I'm sure there are hurt feelings about Dylan. Maybe I just need to sit down and explain what happened to him."

"Yeah, I think for now it would be best for you to avoid him." William's frown is fully in place.

Yay. Another person I have to avoid.

"I think it may be time for a circus meeting. We haven't needed one for a while, but with everything that has been going on, I think it would be wise. I will not tolerate all the unacceptable behavior that has been happening." John types some things into the tablet he's carrying. I'm assuming he's sending a circus wide message.

"Well, I'm not staying on the pod, so avoiding him won't be any problem. Tonight has been a bit much, and I am ready for my bed. If Xavier wouldn't mind taking me back to the hotel room, you and Link can join me when you finish up," I tell Cas, and he beams.

"You want us to come too?" He sounds surprised but happy.

"Of course I do. That is if you don't mind wearing your human form in public. I totally want you to meet Susie. All three of you." I include Xavier in my request. The guys look like I handed them the keys to the Playboy Mansion. Beyond thrilled doesn't even describe it, and a comfortable warmth spreads through my chest. I never realized that these simple gestures would mean so much to them.

"I'll take Lila now and come back and get the two of you when you are ready," Xavier tells Caspian who quickly nods.

"Oh, Lila, before you go, come meet Silac. I'm sorry we sprung that on you, but we thought it would be fun to surprise you." He drags me over to his Naga friend who is still in half form after the parade. I was so mesmerized by him during the act, and there was so much going on around us, I didn't really get a good look at him before I was wrapped up in his tail, but holy fuck! Seriously, is every performer in this circus smoking hot? Even that rude as fuck dragon was gorgeous, not that I would ever admit it or do anything about it.

Silac's upper body makes me want to lick all the lines and ridges, and where his scales start at his waist, I just want to run my hands over them and feel the texture. I feel myself reaching out like I did during the act, determined to figure out if that skin is smooth and if that pattern is a tattoo or scales as well, but Caspian quickly grabs my hand.

"Silac, stop mesmerizing my mate."

Silac holds his hands up in defense. "No, it wasn't me, that was all her." Caspian gives me a funny look, and I grimace, feeling guilty as fuck, even though we had already discussed my reaction to him.

"Lila, I'd like for you to meet my best friend, Silac. Silac, this beautiful woman is my mate, Lila." I hold out my hand for him to shake, and he slowly reaches out to take it. As my eyes meet his, I wobble a little, feeling faint all of a sudden. His reptilian pupils seem to swirl, and I can't take my eyes away from him. It's like when Xavier sank into my mind to look for my powers but different. It's almost like I can catch a hint of his thoughts.

Beautiful... sssssssexy... Cassssspian... sssssso lucky...

They cut off abruptly and he pulls his hand away, frowning. "Nice to meet you, Lila," he says and then quickly slithers away from us.

I look at Caspian in dismay. "What was that? Did you hear that? Did I do something to insult him?"

His brows are furrowed as he watches his friend disappear. "I'm not sure. What did you hear?" he asks, and I frown, following the sexy snake with my gaze.

"It was kind of like what my beast sounds like inside my head, but the voice was different. It sounded sibilant, lots of hissing."

He turns to face me swiftly, his eyes wide with surprise. Leaning in, he gives me a kiss. "Why don't you head to the hotel, and we will see you soon, okay?" He absently gives me another quick kiss before he hurries after his friend, his tentacles moving him hastily in the same direction.

I stare in the direction the two shifters went, but me going after them probably won't help.

What the fuck is wrong with me today?

"Ready?" Xavier's hand on my arm distracts me from my shitty thoughts and has me smiling at his mist-shrouded form as I turn to my warlock lover.

"Absolutely. I can't wait to get back so you can get rid of your disguise. I miss *you*. Let's go."

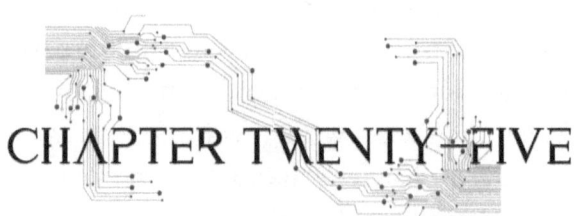

CHAPTER TWENTY-FIVE

Caspian

"Silac, hey, wait up!" I call after my friend who has shifted back into his humanoid form and is hurrying for our dressing room. I do the same, and when I finally catch up to him, he's wiping off his stage makeup and won't look at me when I come in.

"Hey! What was all that with Lila?" I ask him, and he still doesn't look at me.

"What was what?" He tries to sound unaffected, but it comes out strained. I know him well enough to know when he's bullshitting me.

"Your reaction to Lila. I was hoping you would like her as much as I do," I reply, and he sighs, puts down the makeup-covered wipe, and turns to me.

"Look, I guess I was surprised. I know we

haven't been a thing for a long time, and we agreed to just be friends, but when you called me to join the show, I thought you had finally changed your mind. When you said you had a surprise, I assumed it was because you wanted us to be together."

Fuck my life.

Seriously. How does this keep happening to me? Images of Dylan's tantrum and his threats toward Lila flash into my mind, and I start to get angry.

"You know very well neither of our beasts would accept each other as mates. I can't believe you're doing this to us. I thought you would be happy that I found her."

He brushes a frustrated hand across his cobra hood—in this form he has no hair—and hisses his annoyance at me.

"I know, but you can't blame a guy for getting his hopes up. I am happy for you, she really is something special. My beast was instantly attracted to her, which is why I picked her out of the audience. I hadn't even realized the brothers were on either side of her. It just kind of took over and forced it."

Fuck! Thank goodness it wasn't a random audience member. Silac won't look me in the eye, so I know there's something he's not telling me.

"I know exactly how you feel. My beast did the same thing the first day I met her. He tried to shove his way forward, but I managed to hold him back. We got stuck together in a pod during Earth takeoff, though, and she was open and accepting of my half form and we fooled around." I don't want to give him the details, that's for Lila and me only. "Before I knew it, my beast had her mated before we hit the moon's orbit."

I see the guilt in his eyes before I finish. "Fuck, man, I'm so sorry. Maybe it wasn't such a good idea for me to be here. I don't think my beast is going to get the memo that Lila is off limits. It would probably be better if you brought in someone else. I can recommend a family member if you still want a Naga."

I quickly shake my head. "Silac, the interest is not one-sided. Through our bond, I can feel that she was majorly turned on through the act, and even now, despite you being an ass, she was still emitting those fuck me vibes. Couldn't you feel them?"

"Yessss," he hisses, "but I was trying to ignore them."

"Why?" I ask, and he does a double take before hissing once more. "Why would you want me to be interested in your mate?"

"Lila is Skarrian. They are mostly polyamorous. She is also the intimate of a warlock, the blood rose to a Vilaxian, and has a cyborg boyfriend. There is also an Aquilian sniffing around, but I'll worry about him later." I look at my best friend and ex-lover's shoulder, but Lila's mark is not there—yet.

I know they are both warring with their feelings.

Silac is struggling because he knows Lila is my mate, and Lila is fighting it because she's worried that she's collecting more mates than she ever dreamed of. But I think if the two of them spent time together, it would quickly form. I just need my friend to show her how wonderful he is. I think the two of them would be perfect for one another, and I can't deny I want him to join our family because he deserves a chance at a happy life.

I see a range of emotions cross his face—intrigue, relief, and happiness followed by annoyance, anger, and guilt.

"Please, Cas, don't do me any favors, okay?"

"Ah, there you are." John Adams pushes into the dressing room, followed by his brothers. Shit, I hope they didn't hear what we were talking about, but I can tell by the looks on both William's and Eric's faces that they did. Both are frowning, but thankfully neither of them says anything, though that's not to say they won't later.

John carries on, oblivious to the tension in the room. "Today's show was magnificent, and I can't thank you all enough." He looks around and then frowns. "Where's Tirrian?"

"The others took him somewhere to cool off after he attacked Lila," I answer.

"Good, he's on thin ice already and he's only performed once. See to it that he doesn't fuck up again," William tells us both with a heavy sigh.

"Anyway, we want the show to be like that every

time. Involving Lila in the act was perfect. We're going to keep incorporating her into more and more, hopefully," John continues.

"Really?" I ask, sounding a little skeptical, even to myself. I don't know if I'll be able to handle her hanging from high wires or anything. I'd be constantly stressed about her falling.

"Yes. Lila has a background in gymnastics, so we're hoping once she becomes Saxon's blood rose, she may want to be involved in their act too. But for now, we will leave her with yours and the Aquilians'."

Eric chuckles. "She's going to be pissed, so how about you let her know about that, Caspian?" he says, and the brothers make a quick exit, not waiting to hear our opinion on any of it. Chicken shits.

Silac sighs and drapes himself across the couch, not looking at me.

"Look, man, I'm happy for you and all, but I kind of feel like you're pimping me out to your wife and... isn't that kind of weird? Why isn't your beast furious about it?"

I sit down on the couch, leaving enough distance between us so it doesn't look like I'm getting too cozy with him. "Lila is carrying our eggs," I tell him gently, unable to hide how thrilled I am, and his eyes widen before they soften with sadness.

"Ah, man, that's awesome. I'm so happy for you." He leans in and gives me a hug and a slap on the back. It's not like he would have touched me when we were lovers, more like a bro hug.

"My beast is so secure in our mating he now wants to play. He has already started propositioning Link, Lila's cyborg boyfriend, and he perked right up when I suggested you to the Adams as a replacement for Dylan."

"Dylan was the dragon Tirrian replaced? He attacked your mate?" he asks carefully, and I nod.

"Yup." I don't go any further. Telling Silac it was for the same reason that he's now upset about would not go over well.

Again, Silac sighs. "Look, man, I don't want to get caught between you and your wife. It sounds like she has enough males on her hands without throwing me in her path, but I would be honest with her if I were you."

I frown and sit back. I think Silac has gotten the wrong idea. Fucking hell.

"I didn't bring you here for me so I could have an illicit affair with you on the side. I brought you here because I thought you'd get a kick out of being in the circus. Your attraction to Lila, while not unexpected, has nothing to do with it, nor does our previous relationship. I didn't bring you here so I could have a side piece. I'm completely faithful to my mate, as is my beast, but he's also not opposed to having some fun with Lila's other mates, especially if she's sandwiched between us."

He's still frowning, his confusion evident.

"Look, all I'm saying is don't be afraid to explore your attraction to Lila. She's feisty and fun and a little crazy, and I think she's the perfect balance to your careful, trust nobody, let nobody in nature. If something does happen between the two of you, then that's amazing, but if nothing comes of it, that's okay too. I missed my best friend and am glad you're here."

I stand up, leaving my friend to think about what I just said.

"Okay, I'll see you later. Link and I are going to stay with Lila in her hotel room tonight."

He scrunches up his face and shudders. "With your human glamour?" he asks, sounding disgusted, and I shrug, changing into it.

"I want to clear something up. There's nothing Lila can ask of me that I won't do for her. This has all been a steep learning curve, and if she needs to touch base with what she is most familiar with, well, I'm certainly not going to get in her way. I'll see you tomorrow," I say and leave my friend with his thoughts on the couch. There's an air of sadness to him that wasn't there before, and I feel a little guilty for not telling him about Lila all week, but I really wanted to surprise him and thought he would be happy for me. Clearly not.

I hope he thinks about what I said, because I think Lila would be perfect for him, and I just want to see him as happy as I am.

"There you are." I finally find Link in his clinic after checking his pod quarters and the dining room. It had taken me a while because the crew was having dinner, and quite a few people stopped me to talk about the new act, complimenting me on it.

I saw Tirrian brooding in the corner, and he glared at me the whole time. He's been a complete asshole since he got onto the ship, but he knows he couldn't sabotage the show, otherwise he would have been in big trouble with both the Adams brothers and his father, who is trying to make up for Dylan's mistakes. I think he feels the circus is beneath him and he is being punished by being here. I will confront him about everything tomorrow. It can't go on like this.

"Ah, yeah, I was just checking over Saxon's vitals." Link sounds a little worried, and I can see why when I step up and have a look at the unconscious Vilaxian. He is normally pale, like fine Masovian china, but right now, he has a gray tinge to his skin, and his cheekbones look sunken in. His fingers are starting to curl into his palms, making them look like claws.

"He doesn't look so great."

"No. He's not responding to the blood as he should. I'm going to ask Lila for a pint of hers to keep him going until she's ready to bond. If I don't, he will be worse than feral when I wake him, and he may kill Lila in the bonding process."

"Will that seal the blood rose bond?" I ask with a bit of hesitation in my voice, and he shakes his head.

"No, I specifically called and spoke to the queen's physician, because this was a concern of mine too. He said that to seal a blood rose bond, they both need to drink each other's blood. Infusing it into him should be enough to sustain him physically, but it won't seal that bond."

I relax once he finishes speaking. "I think Lila is just waiting for her visit with Susie to be over, then she said she'll do it. She said she wasn't sure if it was a long process, and I think she's partly worried she won't survive it," I tell him, not hiding the concern in my voice or the frown on my face.

Link sighs, places his tablet to the side, and puts his hands on my shoulders. When I'm in human form, we're basically eye to eye, and this close, I notice how good he smells, and I feel my beast rumble with attraction.

"I promise you, Cas, I would not put your mate

at risk. From everything I've read, and with confirmation from the royal physician, the need for the blood rose to survive and flourish far outweighs the hunger, despite how feral he looks. But what makes this a little tricky is the time delay. While she's making her decision, his body is fading away, so the need to survive kicks in and it becomes more violent than a normal bonding. But we will do as they suggest to keep Lila safe and Saxon from slipping away. Okay?"

I nod, his hands heavy but comforting on my shoulders. I inhale deeply, drawing in his scent and letting it wrap around us. A purring sound comes out of my mouth, and his eyebrows jump in surprise. His silver eyes turn a little liquid before a blush spreads from his neck to his cheeks. That's so fucking cute. He's so sure and capable in some respects, but in others, he's a little shy and restrained. It's weird, considering he's the heir to Pleasure Bot Industries. One would think he'd have a whole range of sexual tricks up his sleeves. I look down at those sleeves, which are pushed backed, showcasing his sexy forearms. I start to lean toward him before I catch myself and stumble backward.

"Shit, sorry, my beast is attracted to you, and I won't deny that I'm not upset about it. He seems to be hellbent on making sure that Lila has all these strong men around her, and what better way to secure that than to seduce you as well." I shake my head. "I really don't know what he's thinking.

Every time I try to communicate with him, he growls, bares his teeth, and mimes biting like he wants to mate all of you too." I sit down on one of the chairs and place my head in my hands. "I'm so fucking confused, I have no idea what to do."

He takes a seat next to me and places a reassuring hand on my leg, but my cock jumps in my pants, a mind of its own.

"It's okay, really, but it's safe to assume that while Lila got some of your powers, she may have given you her Skarrian mating ways because she had nothing else to give you. Have you ever thought that you, too, may be polyamorous now, and his need to bite is his way to ensure you can seal that Skarrian mating bond with the people you are attracted to?"

I lift my head as my mouth drops open in surprise. "Holy shit! I never even thought about that. I've been so focused on her shifting that it didn't even dawn on me that I could have received Skarrian powers."

Link sits back, and I miss the feel of his hand on my leg. "It makes sense to me. Though I'm not sure how she's going to take it if you are interested in bringing other women into the bond. I doubt she's going to be upset if you're attracted to some of the same men she is though."

I think carefully about whether I want to mate with another woman, and my beast goes berserk inside. I groan in pain as I wrestle to keep control as he tries to burst out of my skin in anger. "Fuck."

Link jumps to his feet. "Shit, are you okay? Do you need me to check you over?" He sounds frantic, and I hold up my hand to stop him as he lifts his hand to scan me.

"It's okay. I think it's safe to say my beast is perfectly happy with Lila. The thought of another woman makes him beyond furious."

"Oh." Link calms down. "That's a good thing then." He pauses momentarily to collect his thoughts before continuing. "Look, I suggest you talk to her about it, and then talk about it with anyone your beast wants to mate with." He turns away from me and presses a couple of buttons on his tablet. "You might be surprised by their response."

He doesn't wait for me to answer before picking up a medical bag and walking out of the clinic, and I have to hurry to catch up. Before I can bring up what he just said, he presses a couple buttons on the wall outside the clinic in the reception area. "Okay, Saxon should be safe while we're away. I've got everything I need to take Lila's blood. Let's go have a late supper with our girl. I doubt she'll sleep much tonight with her friend arriving tomorrow."

Again, Link doesn't wait for me to respond before he heads out of the reception area and in the direction of the transport room. By the time I've recovered from his shocking announcement, I have to run to catch up with him. When I do, I leave the conversation alone for now. I need to discuss all of this with Lila first. I stay a step behind him once I catch up, because I have no shame staring at his ass while I wait.

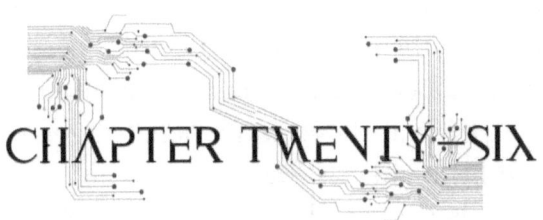

CHAPTER TWENTY-SIX

Lila

The boys and I had a late supper from room service, because I didn't want them to have to wear their glamours in public, and then we spent the evening just hanging out and watching movies. It was nice to just relax and have a bit of quiet. Once Link took a pint of my blood and stuck it in the fridge, they turned on the TV and quickly became completely enthralled with the *Tiger King* series. I went to bed alone, leaving them to binge watch it with beer and junk food. They barely even looked up from it as I kissed them all goodnight.

I can't say I didn't giggle about that for about ten minutes when I finally climbed into bed after brushing my teeth and washing my face. It's nice to see their amazement at new things for a change. I would have liked to stay up and watch with them, but Susie messaged and said she would be here by lunchtime, and I want to get some shopping done first thing in the morning.

John slipped a black Mastercard into my pocket before I left the show, and when I argued, he just held up his hand. "It was your parents' money and is your inheritance. The lawyer you saw arranged everything to be transferred into your name. I over-heard you telling Caspian the other day that you wanted to shop because we are leaving Earth for a little while and you need supplies. Buy what you need and have them deliver it to the front gate. The guards at the front gate will take the packages for you."

"Thank you." I wrapped my arms around him in a hug and his came up to embrace me too. The hug was comforting and something I hadn't realized I needed at that moment.

"I'm just sorry they are not here to see what an amazing woman you've grown into. They would be proud of you, Lila." He sounded choked up and quickly pulled away and took off, leaving Eric and William behind.

"Be patient with him. He has dramatic mood swings occasionally. At the moment, he's on a downward spiral," Eric said softly, the most serious I'd seen him since he yelled at me when he found out about my and Cas's mating.

"Is there anything I can do?" I asked, but

William just shook his head gently, sympathy shining in his eyes.

"No, but he'll be alright. And Lila, that card is spelled. It will change to the right card for the right planet we are on and access the funds from the galaxy wide bank account you have. It takes money from a different one on Earth."

So tomorrow I have some major shopping to do. I need more clothes, including pretty things for date nights with my guys, practical everyday things, workout wear, and underwear. I also need all the snacks that I'm not going to be able to get when I'm in space—Twizzlers, Snickers, Reese's Pieces, and Jolly Ranchers. I'm going to need craft stuff and boardgames as well, because I can't go that long without any of my things. Not to mention tampons and coffee. I don't know if alien species get periods, but I damn well do, and there's no way I'm going to get caught on a different planet when Aunt Flow arrives unexpectedly. I wonder if I will get my period now that I'm carrying Cas's eggs. I mean, technically they are not my fertilized eggs, so will I still need to shed my uterine lining monthly, or is that on hold because three little invaders have made a cozy nest out of it and have settled in for winter hibernation? It's something to ask Caspian or Link in the morning.

The last thing I want to do on my outing is go shopping for books. When I checked the account balance of the card John gave me, I choked on my drink and liquid flew out of my nose, hitting the laptop screen. There's no shortage of money in the account. In fact, it's safe to say I'm a fairly wealthy woman now, so I plan on buying a kindle and loading it up with thousands of books—monster porn, dark and dirty, reverse harem, alien abduction and breeding kinks, and anything that takes my interest.

Smiling, I close my eyes and pull my covers up, snuggling down. Maybe I can convince the guys to read with me. I know Link probably will. I wonder if I can persuade him to play out some of the scenes. I must remember to get some cyborg stories too.

The guys are still watching television when I wake up the next morning. They have moved on from Joe Exotic and are now watching something else with a lot of shouting in it.

"Hey." I slide into Xavier's lap. His eyes are heavy, and I can see him struggling to stay awake. "You know you can stop this and it will be here when you wake up, right?" I tell the three of them.

"Yes, we know, but I had no idea humans were so…" Link trails off.

"Depraved?" Xavier says dryly.

"Stupid?" Caspian adds, rubbing his hand over his face and yawning.

"No, *entertaining.*" Link snorts, throwing a kernel of popcorn up into the air and catching it in his mouth. He points at the screen, getting sucked into the drama again. "This woman didn't know who the father of her child was, so they went on TV so that everyone in the world could find out that this dude here is *not* the baby daddy."

I frown and look closer at what they are watching. Oh, for fuck's sake. Maury Povich. That's it. I stand up and search through the pile of wrappers and mountain of food containers until I find the remote. I aim it at the screen and turn it off.

"Right, off to bed," I tell Caspian and Xavier, who agree and stumble toward my room, even though the suite has two more bedrooms. I put my hands on my hips and look at Link who is wearing a fairly impressive pout. "Why aren't you as tired as the others?"

"My cyborg nanobot DNA allows me to regenerate. I don't need to sleep as often as someone with a fully organic body," he explains, putting down the bag of popcorn and dragging me into his lap. "Which means I can go on and on and on," he tells me, nipping at my neck and nuzzling his nose against my cheek.

Giggling, I push away from him and the pout comes back. "Sorry, Energizer Bunny, you're going to have to keep it in your pants for now. I have a mission. Care to join me?"

He jumps to his feet and sweeps me into his arms. "I am but your humble servant." He bends me backward and kisses me soundly before dragging me upright again and towing me out of the room. "But first, let me buy you breakfast."

"Whoa there," I say, digging in my feet. "You can't go out there looking like that."

He looks down at himself and back to me with a frown. "What's wrong with the way I look?"

"Nothing at all, you are most definitely smoking hot, but you shimmer like you're from the movie *Twilight*, and humans don't do that."

"Oh, okay." I watch in amazement as his skin changes color, starting at his forehead and washing down his body. Soon he looks just like a human, albeit a bit of a punk with his silver eyes and hair, but that's nothing that isn't explainable. "Is this okay now? What about what I'm wearing?"

I eye his sweat shorts and T-shirt and decide it's fine for shopping. I'd rather be comfortable than look fancy. Link just looks like a rock star or an A-list actor not trying too hard. His clothes are the last thing people are going to look at.

"You're perfect. Let's go!"

Link and I shop for the next few hours, and I have all my purchases sent to the circus to be put into my room there, except for a couple of things I want to wear when I go out for a late dinner with

Susie and Mark tonight after the show. I'm hoping we can hang out together with my three guys on the second night, maybe go to a club or something fun.

Link has been such a good sport, but I think he's also had fun looking at all the human stuff. I caught him picking up things and examining them closely.

"What exactly is this for?" Link holds up a brightly-colored plastic knitting loom while I'm shopping for craft supplies in Hobby Lobby. "Is it a torture device?" He runs his finger over the plastic hooks before cranking the handle and watching with amazement as it all moves.

Snorting in amusement, I take it from him and throw it into my cart. "No, it's for making garments. If you go over there and pick out what colors you like, I'll make you a scarf." I point to the aisle full of wool. "Maybe pick some for Xavier and Caspian too. I'll leave the colors up to you, but make it ten balls of each color." He happily walks away, leaving me to the rest of my shopping, and I breathe a sigh of relief. Shopping with him has been exhausting. Next time I'm leaving him behind. Thank goodness the others had been too tired to come.

Finally the text message I've been waiting for arrives, and I squeal with delight. "They are here," I tell Link, grabbing his arm and dragging him out of the shop after paying for our purchases.

I find us a cab, and before long, we arrive back at our hotel. I told Susie to wait in the foyer for us so I could take her up to the suite. I message Cas and Xavier to let them know we are coming up, and I remind them to put their human glamours on if they are still there.

When the cab drops us off, I see a familiar dark head standing next to a shiny pink Cadillac. Susie and Mark are lifting their luggage out of the trunk. Mark's normally stylish black hair is windswept, and he's looking a little wrinkled, but he's beaming at my girl.

"Hey, Link, is there any reason why Mark should make me feel icky?" I ask, remembering how I felt every time we touched in the past despite our awkward as fuck interactions.

He looks over to where my friends are standing. They haven't noticed us yet, and I'm okay with that because I don't want them to overhear what we are saying. "Probably because he's a taken man. Although he and Susie don't have a connection like Skarrians have, what they do have is obviously solid, and it's your body warning you that he's not available. It's a Skarrian thing."

A huge sense of relief washes over me. My body was protecting me and Susie without either of us knowing it. Not that I would have gone there anyway, but I guess not everyone has the same morals.

"Susie!" I shout, and she spins, dropping her bags and running for me. We slam together and hug in the middle of the valet parking area, oblivious to everything around us.

"Oh, girl, I missed you so much," she murmurs as I breathe in her familiar scent and finally relax for the first time since I got on that plane to London.

"You haven't got a clue," I respond, reluctant to pull away, but I know we need to move. Before I can, Susie tightens her arms, nearly squeezing me to death like Silac, although his was a more pleasant feeling.

"Holy fuck, Lila. Who is that tall silver drink of water with you? Please tell me he knows how to use his tongue."

I snort and then chuckle as we pull apart. Susie's worth measurement for men is whether or not they give oral and if they can give you an orgasm without needing a road map to your clit. It's what made her give Mark another chance after they had a quickie in the on-call room one day. That turned into many quickies, and eventually, they decided they liked each other as well.

"You have *no* idea. No fucking idea," I whisper quietly, and she holds her hand up for a high five. Her dark brown corkscrew curls bounce with the movement, and her warm chocolate eyes sparkle with delight.

"Hi, Lila." Mark joins us, carrying both his and Susie's luggage, and I see a valet driving away with their car.

"Hey, Mark. How was the drive?" I ask as we head toward Link.

"It was good, thanks." He smiles awkwardly, and I decide that I am going to find out what the fuck is going on with him. He and Susie are solid, and I need to make sure that we are too, even if I don't like what he has to say.

"Hey, guys, this is my boyfriend Link. Link, my bestie Susie and her partner Mark." I introduce them, and they greet one another politely before we head inside to reception.

"Lila, how about you take them to lunch? I know you must be starving, and I'll arrange for the luggage to go to our room before I grab the other two. We've got to get over to the circus for a little while," Link suggests, letting me have alone time with my friends.

"Other two?" Susie asks as her sculpted eyebrows almost jump into space.

"Sounds great, I'm starving. Let's try the restaurant here. I'm sure you guys are tired after your trip. We can grab some food, and then you can have a nap, because I have a big night planned. There's the show and then a late dinner with Link and a few of our friends." I ignore her question and give Link a kiss on the lips, whispering, "Thank you," to him.

He just smiles and says goodbye as I drag Mark and Susie to lunch.

A short time later, we're seated at one of the restaurants inside the hotel and Susie is bombarding me with questions about the circus, the performers, and my grandads. I skillfully answer all of it, but I feel guilty when I dodge the ones that dig deeper into the hows and whys of all of the acts. Luckily she's too excited to notice.

Mark sits quietly, holding her hand and listening and smiling, but he still won't look at me. My irritation at the dismissal is bothering me, and I can't help but feel relieved when I finally get the chance I've been waiting for.

"I just need to use the restroom before our food arrives," she tells us, standing up. "I'll be back shortly."

We watch her go, and once she leaves the dining room, I whirl on her boyfriend. "Okay, that's it. What the fuck is your problem with me? I've been nothing but nice to you, and you are awkward and shady, and I'm worried that maybe Susie isn't with such a good guy after all."

Mark blanches at my outburst, but for the first time ever, he holds my gaze, staring hard into my face. I don't blink, and he finally sighs and leans back in his chair.

"You really don't remember me, do you?"

Oh fuck! Did I sleep with Mark? Was he someone I brought home from the bar for a one-night stand and then hustled out the door the next morning before Susie woke? She'd kill me.

He chuckles when he sees the myriad of thoughts that just crossed my face. "No, Lila, we didn't fuck. Though I'm sad to hear you think I would be unmemorable. According to Susie, I have mad skills."

I roll my eyes at his tongue-in-cheek arrogance. "She would know," I mutter, and he stops laughing and takes a sip of his water.

"Do you remember wearing a glass of wine at work about eighteen months ago from an irate patron who thought you'd been flirting with his boyfriend?"

"Fuck yes. The man was batshit crazy. He said I kept fluttering my eyelashes at his partner and I should keep my whore ways to myself. It wasn't the first drink I wore, but it was certainly the most memorable because he screamed like a banshee. His boyfriend was so embar—" I break off as I think back to that night then gasp. "Holy shit! That was *you*. You were the boyfriend who helped me clean up and apologized profusely."

He nods, and a spark of relief shines in his eyes. "Yes, it was, and this whole time I've been thinking you remembered and were going to out me to Susie."

I shake my head, completely confused. "You're bi?" I guess with no judgment in my tone, and he nods again.

"Yes, and that was the problem with that date. He was gay as fuck and completely insecure. If I even spoke politely to a woman, he thought I was straying. I broke up with him later that night. I wasn't into him enough to put up with that kind of behavior."

"I don't blame you. That guy seemed like a jealous fucking dick. And Susie doesn't know?" I ask him pointedly, and I see him slump in his seat.

"No, I just haven't thought about the best way to bring it up. The quickie I had with her was a couple of days after that incident. I thought it was just rebound sex, but it happened again and again, and before I knew it, I was in love with her. It never came up." Regret flashes across his features, but he's got to man the fuck up.

"Dude, just tell her. Susie is going to be the last person who judges. She had her experimental phases too." I'm not outing her secrets, just reminding him that we've all been there at one time or another. She has no problem telling anyone she's fooled around with both sexes. "So that's why you've been so fucking awkward around me? You thought I'd let the cat out of the bag and ruin your relationship? Fuck, for a smart man, Mark, you're dumb as shit."

A small smile appears on his lips, his eyes looking less haunted. I just wish he would have said something sooner so we could have avoided all of this awkwardness.

"I know, I know. Do you forgive me?" he asks, and I grin, both because I'm glad we've gotten it out in the open and I can see Susie returning.

"Nothing to forgive, man, just tell her the

truth." And speaking of telling the truth… "Oh, and I need you to keep an open mind about some of the things I'm going to tell you both later."

His eyebrows jump, but he nods as Susie sits down. "Okay, so what did I miss?"

"Nothing, I was just asking Mark about the drive here," I tell her, lying, but he needs to be the one to tell her what we were talking about. He needs to trust that I'll keep my mouth shut, because this falls on him.

Susie bounces up and down in her chair and grabs his hand. "Did you tell her about the weird gothic mansion that was about an hour out of town? It was so odd. It was like it was built into the hill that was around it, and there were all these trees planted around it, but like fir trees or something, nothing native to the area, and it looked really strange in the middle of the desert. I made Mark pull over and we took some pictures." She pulls out her phone and swipes across the screen before handing it to me.

Sure enough, it's exactly how she described it. "I tried to look it up on Google, and all it said was it was called the Pleasure Inn. I'm thinking it's a bed-and-breakfast."

Just then our waitress arrives to take our order, and we spend the next two hours drinking and eating before we finally decide to go upstairs. When we get to our room, they both ooh and ahh about how fancy it is, and they find the bedroom Link put their luggage in. I leave them to get settled and have a nap, but fifteen minutes later, Susie joins me on the couch where I'd been lost in thought.

"Okay, spill," she demands, flopping down next to me with a bottle of champagne and two glasses in her hand. She makes quick work of the bottle and splashes some into each glass before handing me one. "You have been squirrely and twitchy since we got here, and that is not like you. What's going on? Do we need to make a grab at you and run as fast as we can? Is the circus full of freaks and weirdos?" She has no idea. "Give me something, a sign or a signal, and Mark will have us out of here faster than you can say alien."

Susie goes silent for a moment before pointing at her eyes after a single blink and shaking her head no. She repeats herself but with two blinks and nods her head yes. Then she starts doing some weird-ass hand gestures like she is trying to get me to read some code. I can't help but laugh at her brand of crazy.

"No, Susie, it's nothing like that. I promise." I try to ease her spiraling by reassuring her I'm fine. "But I have so much to tell you, and I need you to keep an open mind while I do, and by open, I mean Mariana Trench wide. Okay?"

Susie downs her glass of champagne and quickly fills it back up before reaching for the room phone. "Yes, can I get two bottles of champagne delivered to the penthouse and an assortment of snacks please?" She thanks the person on the other end and hangs up. "Okay, shoot."

"Okay, but before I start you need to make a choice. What I'm about to tell you is classified information. Like it's so secret it makes Area 51 look like a Starbucks. So you have two choices. I can tell you everything and then make it so you will still retain the knowledge but can't tell anyone about it. Or I can tell you everything, you can give me your thoughts, and then I'll have it all removed from your brain."

Susie's brow is so furrowed it's comical, and I would laugh if I wasn't so serious about this. "Removed? Like through hypnotism?" she asks, sounding skeptical.

"Hmm, yeah, kind of, I guess," I hedge, not really wanting to spill the beans too early.

"I need to decide this right now before I even know what the information is?" she whines, and I can see her point.

"No, I'll tell you, but you will have to make a decision. Don't make me have to make it for you," I warn her, and she swiftly agrees.

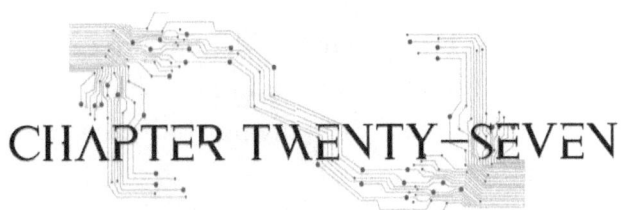

CHAPTER TWENTY-SEVEN

Lila

It takes me several hours and both bottles of champagne to tell Susie everything I've been through in the last two weeks. The expressions on her face have ranged from skeptical, to outraged, to downright disbelief, but I think I finally convince her when she faints after I shift into my half form.

Shifting back, I calmly drink my champagne and wait for her to wake up. I begin to worry when she doesn't immediately return to the land of the living, so I slap her face a couple of times, and she groans before jolting upright and scanning my body with intense scrutiny. She then looks down at the champagne and blinks a couple of times.

"I think I may have had too much to drink. I'm seeing things," she mutters, placing a hand to her forehead, trying to sort everything out, and I shake my head.

"Sorry to burst your bubble, but nope, it was all true." She blinks before nodding slowly like she understands what I'm saying but doesn't *really* understand.

"Okay, okay, alien circus, okay. And you're not human and… wow."

"Yup, could have knocked me over with a feather. But here we are. Still want to be my friend?" I look at her cautiously, studying her expression, because even though we're kinda sorta joking around about it right now, I'm not really sure if this will sit well with her. That makes me wonder what the outcome will be when she makes her decision.

She's quiet for a moment before a huge grin crosses her face. "Fuck yeah, Lila! You are the coolest bitch I know, and you have *tentacles*. Tentacles! That is fucking awesome." A sense of relief flows through me, and I sag against the seat. God! I was braced for rejection, and I know that Xavier could have removed everything from her mind, but I still would have known that she thought I was a freak.

"But I need you to tell me more about these men of yours. Holy shit, I love Mark and all, but I can't help but be jealous of the fact that you are getting three, soon to be four, different dicks daily.

And a vampire? I need all the deets on being bitten by one. Is it like the books say it is?"

"You know you can't tell anyone about this, right?"

Her gaze slides to the other room and she frowns. "I don't like keeping secrets from Mark, and this is fucking huge."

"I'm sorry, Susie, but I don't know if my grandpas will give me permission to share this information. There's more at stake than you realize."

"Maybe you better have your warlock remove all the details before we say goodbye. It would eat away at me if I knew and couldn't talk to him about it." A swift wave of sadness rolls over me, followed by one of understanding. I wouldn't want to keep a secret so big from my guys either, though the one about the orb is pretty huge. That, however, is a matter of galaxy wide security.

"Okay, but for now, let's go to the show with your memories intact so you can have the full experience. I can get Xavier to remove them after," I suggest, a little sad at her decision, but I completely understand. I hate having to hide the orb information from my guys too. Actually, that reminds me, now that Cas and I are mated, we can talk about it, and I make a note to do just that the next time we get a few moments alone.

Susie quickly agrees to my suggestion, excited to be able to watch the show while knowing how everything works.

"I need to head over to the circus. Why don't you go catch an hour or two with Mark before you need to get up and get ready for the show? I've arranged for a car to pick you up, and I'll meet you in the foyer and show you to my grandpas' front row seats." We hug it out and I head to the bedroom.

"Lila, why are you going to the bedroom? I thought you said you needed to go to the circus?" Susie asks suspiciously, and I turn and wink at her.

"Going to get my teleporting warlock boyfriend to come and get me."

Her mouth drops open at my nonchalance, and she shakes her head. "That is going to take some getting used to." She leaves me, and I continue on, sending Xavier a message from my watch. When I get to the room, he's already there, and he takes one look at my face and opens his arms.

"Oh, *phoeall*, I can feel everything. Come here so I can make you feel better." I allow him to wrap my arms around me and hold me while all my sadness and relief pour out of me and into him. He shudders as the power of the emotions hits him.

"Fuck, I hate that you feel this way, but God, it feels good and you fill me up like no one ever has before." His voice is ragged as he places a kiss against my hair.

"She wants to see the show, and then she would like you to take away everything I told her. She doesn't want to lie to her boyfriend, and I understand that," I explain, and he strokes a gentle hand over my back. "I'm just not sure how I'm going to explain being out of contact with her for so long. This has been the longest two weeks, and we were still on the same planet. I can't go for months without speaking to her."

The stress and anxiety of wiping away her memories eats at me more than I expected it to. But being with her today and finally getting to spill my secrets was a relief my psyche had been craving. I'm not sure I want to go back to how things were.

"We will work something out for you, sweetheart. Even if I have to charter a shuttle to bring us within calling distance of the Earth once a week while we are off planet, I will. I don't even have to charter one, I'll just steal my parents'. They won't care. You are their best friends' daughter and my intimate. They will do whatever they can to help. We might even be able to spell her phone to accept a warlock call to talk across the galaxy. Leave it with me, I will figure something out," he promises.

I hear a noise out in the living area and smile. I knew Susie wouldn't be able to resist coming to have a peek, but before she can, Xavier moves us to my quarters in the circus pod.

"Holy shit." I look around my room at all the bags piled onto every surface. "I didn't realize I bought so much stuff," I comment, picking up a bag from the bed and dumping it on the floor.

"Good thing my living space on the mothership

is big. We've got a couple of hours before I need to be down in the foyer. Want to nap with me since you don't have to be in the show and get ready?" I ask him, and a grin slides across his lips. "Well, not unless they decide to bring Vigolash out tonight," I quickly add, and the grin drops.

"Those fucking idiots. Your grandpas chewed their asses out, and they are lucky they even still have a spot in the show. I don't think it will happen again."

I strip down to my underwear, and Xavier's eyes light up, but before he can act on it, I slide between my blankets and pat the other side of the bed. "Come on, you insatiable warlock. I'm exhausted, come be the big spoon to my little spoon."

His brow wrinkles in confusion, and I chuckle as he steps toward the bed, but I wave a finger at him.

"Clothes are optional," I say, and in an instant, his are gone and he's just wearing a pair of boxer briefs. "That's better."

Fuck. Who am I kidding? It's *not* better. It's worse, much worse, because the fabric leaves nothing to the imagination.

He climbs in, and I roll over but pull him toward me so his front is against my back and we're spooning. "Now you are the big spoon, and I'm the little spoon," I explain, and his hard cock rubs against my ass.

"I'd rather you be the bun to my sausage," he

jokes, and I giggle but just pull his arm over my waist.

"Nap first, then we can discuss putting your meat in my taco."

He kisses my neck and rubs slow circles on my stomach with his hand, but he leaves me alone, and I drift off to sleep, all the worries about Susie and Mark just an echo in my mind now that Xavier fed from all the negative emotions.

I'm woken a little while later with the feel of Xavier's tongue swiping through my folds. Moaning, I look down and see my underwear is gone and my gorgeous warlock is between my legs. I thread my fingers through his long locks and grind my pussy into his face. If he didn't want that kind of reaction, he should have stayed away.

But it only encourages him, and he slides two fingers into my aching, soaking wet channel.

"Oh yeah." The sigh slips out of my mouth as I ride his fingers and face, my pants turning into moans and groans before I start begging for more. "Fuck yes, that feels good."

He chuckles and pulls away, his face glistening with my arousal as I growl at him.

"I love how into it you get. Your enthusiasm is

delicious," he says, his voice husky and seductive as he climbs up my body and thrusts his cock deep into my pussy, pushing me off the cliff. I dive into my orgasm, a scream leaving my mouth as his eyes lock onto mine and we free-fall together. He cycles the emotions and pleasure between us as he continues to fuck me, his thrusts getting harder and faster until I feel him stutter before his orgasm explodes out of him too. We orgasm over and over, my throat getting sore from how vocal I am. The sound of my name on his lips is pure heaven, and the fact that I can make this gorgeous, sexy man sound like he's praying to some warlock deity is a huge fucking rush.

Finally, he breaks his gaze away from mine and the cycling emotions and sensations ebb. He rolls off me, collapsing next to me on the bed where we both breathe hard for a few moments.

"Best wake-up call ever," I say once I get my breath back.

"I love a post nap quickie, but that was spectac-ular." He is still slightly breathless as well, and I give myself a mental pat on the back, but then I have a moment of panic and scramble off the bed. "Fuck! How many times was that?" I ask, my heart in my throat, and he frowns, losing his relaxed, freshly fucked glow.

"How many times was what?"

"How many times have we fucked or orgasmed or I don't know?" I run my hands through my hair, tugging on it with frustration, and the confusion leaves his face. There's a quick flash of hurt, and I suddenly feel like a bitch.

"We've fucked twice, you gave me a blow job, and we sixty nined on your grandpas' couch but didn't come simultaneously," he reels off flatly before rolling away from me, and I start to panic. Throwing myself back on the bed, I turn him to face me.

"Please, I didn't mean I was upset about it. I was worried my Skarrian biology was going to fuck with your intimate bond or process or ceremony thingy. That's even if my Skarrian biology would form that mate link. So far, my Skarrian shit is all messed up."

The hurt on his face disappears, and he pulls me to him. "I'm not actually sure, to be honest. There's never been a situation like ours before. I think your body needs to remember you're my intimate to do it the warlock way, but I'm guessing we would still mate the Skarrian way."

"You know what? Just to be sure, no more sex," I tell him, untangling myself from his body and sliding off the bed again.

His mouth drops open in shock, and he starts to stammer. "But…"

Ignoring him, I look at the clock, and my heart skips a beat when I see the time.

"Fuck! I'm going to be late." I hurry to the bathroom. I feel Xavier's release slide down my legs and moan. Some days you just don't have time for bodily fluids. I quickly pee and clean myself up with some wipes. I wash my face and tidy my hair the best I can before I rush out of the bathroom and toward my closet, but I don't make it there before I'm suddenly clothed. I spin around and raise an eyebrow at my boyfriend.

"Babe, you looked so panicked I thought I would help you out. Can we revisit the no sex mandate please?"

I launch myself onto the bed and kiss him hard, but I extract myself from his eagerly wandering hands. "You're the best, but no, not until we get to your planet and get my memories back. Oral's still fun, right?" I tell him. "I'll see you at intermission, okay?" I check to make sure he's going to be there to dry me, and he gives me a thumbs-up, still looking perplexed at everything that just occurred as I hurry out the door.

I'm only a few minutes late, but Susie looks at me with knowing eyes and a cheeky grin. "Well, I won't ask what kept you, it's obvious to see. Did you even look in the mirror before you came out here?" she scolds, tongue in cheek, as I pat my hair and smooth down my clothes that Xavier helped me with.

"That is quite a bruise on your neck there, Lila. Are you sure you don't want me to have a look at it? I can give you my professional opinion," Mark chimes in, joining Susie's teasing, and I roll my eyes.

Fucking Xavier. I asked him to hide the bruise from humans, but I guess he decided that he wants the world to see his mark. I'm glad I confronted Mark and we cleared the air. This is the most comfortable it's ever been between the three of us.

"Oh no, honey. Remember, one of Lila's lovers is a doctor as well, so I'm certain he can make sure she's okay." We agreed she could tell Mark about me being in a poly relationship, but not anything else. Otherwise, hanging out after the show might have been a little difficult.

I flip them both off and lead them to our seats. When we get there, I'm surprised to see William and John. Shit, I can't introduce them as my grandpas. Mark will know something is suspicious. But I don't need to worry, because after they introduce themselves as my grandpas, Susie nudges me in the side and whispers in my ear while Mark is talking to them. "I thought you said they looked young. All I see are a couple of handsome, older-looking dudes."

I breathe a sigh of relief. Xavier must have glamoured them for me. William must have heard her whisper, because he winks at me, and I realize just how much I love them. I don't know when it happened, but it happened. They are in my heart, and there's no removing them. I just have to make sure they know it. We're all each other has now for family, though I am slowly adding to it. Our family has already officially grown by one with another three in the works. I am going to be completely outnumbered by all the testosterone in this family. I just hope one or two of the babies I'm carrying has some estrogen in them. I hold my hand across my little bump for comfort. Susie sees it, and her eyes widen. Oh yeah, that's the one thing I didn't tell her about. I thought maybe knowing he was a shifter who mated me was enough. I didn't tell her that sometime in the future she was going to be an aunty too.

Before she can pounce on me, though, the house lights dim and the show begins with Eric appearing in a flash of light and smoke.

Thankfully the show is so mesmerizing, and even more so for her now that she knows the truth, she forgets about what she saw. Again, I'm dragged into the first act with Caspian and the other two shifters. Tirrian plays it up to the audience once more, but his eyes are cold and hard.

Cooling off yesterday did nothing to improve his attitude. Dick.

I also get dragged into the mermaid tank by a playful and horny Nikos, who whispers such filthy words to me when he's carrying me around the pool that my panties aren't just soaked from the water when I get back to my seat.

Thankfully I can avoid Susie's questions once more by going to get changed. Xavier is not pleased when I won't let him bend me over the couch while getting dry.

When I return, I'm grumpy and frustrated, but the rest of the show passes quickly and then it's over.

We walk out into the foyer with William and John while Susie and Mark gush over the performance.

"You didn't tell me you were going to be in it." Susie smacks my arm, and my grandpas chuckle.

"Oh yes, we plan to have her more involved in all the acts as we go on. She will take over from William and Eric eventually and become the ring-master," John explains.

"Well, at least then I won't get hauled around by a giant snake and ridiculous, horny dolphin," I mutter, and Mark shakes his head, his eyes wide with amazement.

"I can't even begin to guess how all of the special effects are created. It was so lifelike."

Susie hides a small smile as William tells Mark about the special effects and animatronic gurus we have on our team. It's a rehearsed speech that he uses with all humans and special guests who come to the show. That is something I'll have to memo-rize one day too.

The crowd flows out around us, their excited voices raving and speculating about the show.

"What are your plans now?" William asks as the crowd thins and only a few stragglers remain.

"We're going out to dinner. Xavier booked us a reservation somewhere," I reply.

"Would you like to join us?" Mark asks politely. I'm sure he'd love to grill them a little more about the show, but John shakes his head.

"No, I'm afraid it's late for us oldies. I'm ready to head to bed."

I roll my eyes, and Susie claps a hand over her mouth to hide her snicker.

"It's been a pleasure meeting you both." William shakes their hands and they take their leave as I usher Susie and Mark out of the circus tent.

"Come on, the car is waiting for us. The guys will meet us at the restaurant," I tell them as I lead them to the waiting limo.

"Now which performers are your boyfriends? I know you said that Link, whom we met earlier, is the show doctor, but what about the other two?" Mark is like a kid in a candy store. He could not take his eyes away from the show the whole entire time.

"Caspian was the juggler in the first act," I answer, and his eyes bug out.

"Do you think he will tell me how they change him into that costume so quickly?" he asks, and Susie snorts.

"Are you sure you want them to join us for dinner? Mark probably won't stop harassing them the whole time."

"I'm sure, and probably not," I reply, and he pouts. It's surprisingly cute. I like this new, open version of Mark. It's like I'm getting to know him all over again, and I can see why Susie loves him. "They all sign NDAs. My grandpas believe if people knew how it was all done, it would spoil the magic."

Mark sighs but nods. "Yeah, you're probably right."

"And the other boyfriend? I noticed you didn't say what he did," Susie presses, and I want to kick her, but she is asking the right questions as far as Mark knows.

"Xavier is part of special effects. He doesn't appear in any of the acts unless it's an emergency." I think back to last night's performance and how we managed to avoid a disaster with his quick actions. Thankfully Htaed was not brought out tonight.

The limo pulls up at the restaurant, and the three of us get out. The hostess welcomes us with a smile. "Hi, do you have a booking for tonight?"

"Yes we do, but I'm not sure if it's been placed under Galaxy Circus or Xavier Colest," I tell her, and her smile grows.

"Of course, right this way. Will the rest of the party be joining you still?" she asks, leading us to a table.

"Yes. The other three will be along soon. Can we get some drinks while we wait?" I inquire, and she hands us each a menu before placing one at the empty spots on the table.

"Of course, I'll send someone over to take your order in a bit."

We get our drinks, and Susie and Mark gush about the show. They had plans to do something else tomorrow night but beg me to let them come again, and of course I quickly agree. Having another night with my best friend is music to my ears, because I'm not ready for this to end yet.

The others arrive a short while later, and I introduce everyone. Susie doesn't hide her impressed expression, and I can't blame her. My men are rocking their sexy human glamours, and together, they look like they may be some of the cast from *Magic Mike*. We get a lot of envious looks from men and women alike at other tables.

Dinner is fun, with Susie doing her best to make me blush with questions about our sex life. Mark and Link seem to click, and they spend ages talking about doctor stuff. In fact, all four of the guys get on famously. It's like they have been friends for years, and I am so fucking grateful to my men for trying so hard for me.

After dinner we head back to the hotel suite for drinks and more conversation, but eventually we all need to go to bed. Susie and Mark want to do some sightseeing tomorrow.

Caspian heads to my room, and Link and Xavier are going to share the other room in the suite tonight, but before they can leave, I ask Mark to give me ten minutes with Susie, which he quickly agrees to before going into their room alone. I also ask Xavier to stay.

"It's time," I tell her when she looks at me quizzically, and her face falls.

"Yeah, okay. There's no way I wouldn't be able to tell Mark about any of this. He loved it so much, and he keeps talking about how you might have done it." She gives me a big hug, holding me tight. "I hope one day Xavier will be able to give me all our memories back and Mark can know too." I can hear the tears in her voice, and a lump sits in my throat. It's so big I can't answer her.

"How about I make you a deal. If you and Mark are still together the next time we come back to Earth, I will get permission from the Adams brothers for him to know, and then I can return your memories and make it so you can only talk to one another about it," Xavier suggests, and my heart swells with love for the man. That was the perfect way to deal with my pain.

"Deal," Susie says as we break apart and she wipes the tears from her eyes.

We take a seat, and I hold my best friend's hand as Xavier removes all traces of alien information. Susie will still know I'm in a three-way relationship, minus the Saxon knowledge, and she will know the circus will be out of the States for the next few months, but nothing else other than they had a fabulous time.

I watch as her expression transforms from one of pure sadness to sympathy. Her eyes no longer hold that knowing glimmer in them as she looks at

Xavier and me. My heart aches at the transformation, but we all know it's for the best.

"Oh, Lila, don't cry. It's only a few months, and we can talk on the phone all the time," Susie says, oblivious to what just happened.

"Yes, of course we can," I assure her, and she kisses my cheek and waves goodnight to us before heading to her room. Her door doesn't even close before Xavier is pulling me into his arms and holding me while I sob.

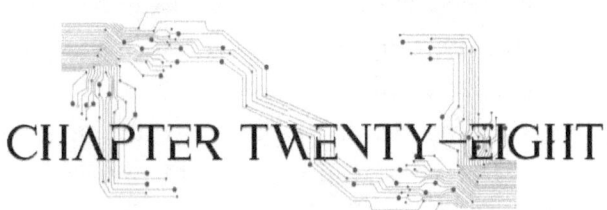

CHAPTER TWENTY-EIGHT

Lila

The two days I had with Susie passed in a blur of fun, friendship, and laughter, but soon it was time for her and Mark to return home.

After eating an early dinner, Mark finally manages to pry us apart, so I walk Mark and Susie out to the valet parking where their ridiculous hot pink convertible is waiting. I snort with amusement, but Susie waggles a finger at me.

"Oh no you don't. You know you want a ride in it. How about we give you a lift to the circus? It's on the way anyway, and I'm sure the strip looks amazing at night from the back of a convertible."

Laughing with her, I realize there's no point in arguing, so I agree. I was just going to go back to the room and have Xavier come get me. This will save him a trip. "Okay, sounds good."

Susie pulls a scarf out of her pocket, wraps it over her corkscrew curls, and sticks her tongue out at me. "It's the only one I have, and I need it more than you. Mark will drive slowly."

Shaking my head, I climb into the back seat of the old car. "Where did you find this thing anyway? It's gaudy as fuck. I hope it runs well," I comment as Mark pulls out of the valet parking and onto Las Vegas Boulevard. The hotel we stayed at is on the opposite end of the road from the circus, so we drive slowly, passing all the fantastic sights along the strip.

We suddenly come to a stop. "Huh, I wonder what's going on farther up," Mark says, undoing his belt and lifting up in the seat. People are running down the road, screaming in terror, and the bottom of my stomach drops out. Fuck, is it a terrorist attack or a mass shooting? "Oh shit, they must be filming a movie," he exclaims, and my panic abates as I unstrap and stand to get a look, but my dread returns in an instant. There, lumbering down the main street of Vegas, is Viggy.

Susie quickly joins us. "Isn't that the animatronic dinosaur from your show?" she asks, looking at me, and I slowly nod, hoping that I'm keeping my facial expression neutral.

"Oh cool, what a great publicity idea. Your grandpas are awesome," Mark comments. He developed quite a man crush on the guys, and they were thrilled, but I quickly latch on to his idea.

"Shit, I had forgotten all about it. I'm just going to jump out and go get involved. I love you both. Have a safe drive home," I tell them, giving them both a hug and a kiss on the cheek. "I'll speak to you soon."

"Call us and let us know how this goes," Mark replies, unaware that something is truly and terribly wrong.

I assure them I will and jump out, and they take a side street to get out of the path of the dinosaur. I quickly press my watch, calling the grandpas and Xavier.

"What's up, sweet pea?" Eric asks as I watch Viggy try to make friends with people, but they just run in terror. I startle slightly at the pet name, but quickly shake it off.

"Ah, did you guys know that Viggy is calmly walking down Las Vegas Boulevard, trying to convince someone to throw the palm tree he has in his mouth?"

I walk toward him, dodging the people fleeing in terror as he drops the palm tree, climbs the barriers that surround the pool in front of Treasure Island Hotel, and takes a long drink out of the pool the pirate ship is floating in.

It's such a ridiculous sight that I almost want to start laughing in disbelief, but as more and more people run, the idea of laughing seems ill-timed.

A litany of curses sounds out from my watch, so I'm guessing the answer is no. "I'm going to try to distract him, but Xavier, you need to get here as fast as you can."

They tell me they'll be here as soon as possible and just to stay calm. I look around, floundering with what to do to distract him. A lady passes me, going in the opposite direction, with a bunch of balloons tied to a stroller she's pushing. I grab her arm, stopping her.

"Can I borrow these?" I ask, shoving a hundred-dollar bill into her hand and untying the balloons.

She yanks her arm away. "Let me go, you crazy bitch. Can't you see the dinosaur?"

"Ma'am, don't stress. I work for the circus, and it's animatronic. He's a bit of promotion to drum up business. It's all a part of the act," I reassure her, and it seems to work. The panic in her eyes dies down, and she looks more curious now, her gaze shifting from me to Viggy.

"That one at the edge of town?" she asks, and I nod in response.

"Yup, just hang back and enjoy the show," I chirp, hoping that I'm not lying and she and the kid in the stroller don't get eaten. So far, he hasn't shown any interest in the silly humans as food. Thank fuck.

"Hey, Viggy, Viggy," I call, and I see the exact moment he spots the balloons above my head and hears me call his name. He's like a golden retriever who has finally been offered a treat. He bounds back over the barricade and comes running toward me, the sidewalk cracking under his weight. I contemplate turning and running, but I know there is no way I can outrun the giant beast, so I wait until he slides to a halt in front of me and brace myself to either be eaten or squashed, but he does neither.

"Sit," I command, and he does, plopping his butt down in the middle of Las Vegas Boulevard, the pavement vibrating with the abrupt action.

There's a small smattering of applause as more and more people catch on to the fact that this is a performance. Yeah, right, an emergency, last-minute, unplanned performance.

Xavier appears before me in a flash of light, his human glamour in place. Well, okay then, I guess we're not going for subtlety. Much to my surprise, there's an even bigger applause with gasps of disbelief and comments of, "How did they do that?"

"Alright, Lila, we have a plan. I'm going to put Viggy's harness and saddle on, and you're going to run up his back and sit in it. Then, when your grandpas get here with the Galaxy Circus promo car, they are going to lead the way back to the circus with you two following behind. Just a calm, fun day of promotional activities." Xavier runs his eyes over my body, making sure I am okay before pulling me into a quick hug. "Okay?"

"Ah, yeah, sure, I guess. Why didn't you bring

Fiona with you?" I ask out of the side of my mouth as Viggy's harness and basket appear on his back.

"Because the bitch is nowhere to be found, and neither is her brother. We're not even sure how Viggy got down here. He was supposed to be back in his habitat on the mothership."

"I'm just thankful Htaed wasn't transported too. That would have been carnage." I shudder at the thought of *Jurassic Park* becoming a real thing.

"You're not wrong," he replies, and there's a toot of a horn as the little clown van from the show and another bigger one with the Galaxy Circus logo on the side rolls up next to us.

"Okay, that's your cue. He's really easy. You just use the reins to steer him like a horse. Also, they have his favorite treats in the car and Eric is in charge of dropping them if he won't follow along calmly," Xavier informs me, guiding me to go around and climb up Viggy's back. With my stomach in my throat and my heart beating out of my chest, I do as he wants.

"Good, Viggy. Stay, Viggy," I say as I pull myself up onto his tail, his skin cold and dry underneath my hands. I use his ridges to climb up his back and sit in the saddle before grabbing the reins.

The now rather large crowd roars with applause and cheers, and I just smile and wave, smile and wave, before turning Viggy back in the direction he came. I breathe a sigh of relief when I squeeze my legs and he starts to walk calmly in the direction of the pod, following the clown and promo car.

Once back at the circus, we relocate Viggy to his habitat, and I collapse in exhaustion in my grandpas' office. Caspian is there to meet us, and he grabs me and does the same scan of my body Xavier did.

"Fuck, are you alright? Thank God you were there." He hugs me tight, leads me to a sofa, and helps me sit down next to the warlock before taking a seat himself, squishing me between them, which is perfect for now.

"Did anyone find our idiot niece and nephew?" William asks Cas, running a frustrated hand over his hair. It's grown slightly in the past two weeks and looks like it's ready for another buzz cut.

"Yes. They both claim they have no idea how it happened. They also have an alibi. They claim to have been visiting with Nambra and Lexus in their quarters since they have been confined to them. When I spoke to the transport operator, he was just as confused. The log shows the transport happened, but he doesn't remember doing it. I'd like both Link and Xavier to check him over," John informs us. He stayed behind when William and Eric rushed to help. I'm afraid it's all been too much for him recently. With his depressed mood and all the trouble with the performers, he's not the polished, well-kept man I met two weeks ago.

"Good thinking, but I would be the only one who could remove his memory like that. None of the other warlocks on this ship could do it now that Elyan has been stripped of her powers, and even if she had them, I don't think she could. The other four just don't have the juice. And yes, they are confined, but I thought they were aware they couldn't have visitors either," Xavier grumbles before putting an arm behind me and playing with my hair.

"Well, there has to be something somewhere. I'm going to go to the security room on the ship to see if anything shows up on the cameras," Eric says, standing up, but before he can go anywhere, the door to the room flies open, and Link rushes inside.

"Oh, you're here," he exclaims, staring at me with wide, panicked eyes. "Thank God."

"Yup, and all in one piece," I reassure him. "Viggy was the perfect gentleman."

He looks confused. "What about Viggy? You know what? Never mind. Someone got into my clinic and released Saxon from sedation. He's looking for you, Lila."

Link doesn't get a chance to step farther into the room before he's shoved to the side, and in the doorway appears a feral-looking Saxon. His eyes are blood-red, and his fangs are out for the world to see. There is not one ounce of humanity in him, and I can feel my heart start to beat faster as fear finally kicks in.

He looks around the room, and when his eyes lock with mine, I'm paralyzed physically and mentally. The hunter has finally caught his prey.

"Mine!" he growls as he lunges for me.

The end

GALAXY

CIRCUS

GLOSSARY

PLANET ICEEN

Lightning Cats

They are a shifter race that has two forms—a bipedal human form and their cat form. Their bipedal form is humanoid in shape, but they are covered in a soft downy fur except for the front of their torso and genital area. They have sharp teeth, big ears, and long tails in this form. Their animal form is similar to a saber-toothed tiger from Earth. They can shoot lightning from their tails, and it can be used for defense and attack.

They are a matriarchal society and live in family groups called streaks. They have alpha, beta, and omega distinctions, but there is always a female alpha who acts as head of the family.

Alphas have a rut and omegas have a heat. Only alpha and omegas can breed with one another, and betas can only breed with their own designation. There are male and female omegas. Both have breeding capabilities, but male omegas are rare. Most are killed once their designation is discovered to prevent competition with females for coveted positions within the streak.

The planet Iceen is a frozen tundra of caves and outcroppings, and the streaks usually have two dwellings—a cave for their animal form, and a dome-like, insulated glass building which they live in with their streaks.

Maxsim (Alpha Lightning Cat)

The leader of the streak of lightning cats that performs in the circus, despite it being a matriarchal society. Maxsim is a dark aqua blue that ombres out to snowy white in the legs, with black, tribal style markings across shoulders, chest, and arms. He has high cheekbones, cat ears, feline eyes, a tail, and fangs, which are bigger when in animal form, as well as a broad chest and well-defined arms. Fur covers his body when in humanoid form, except for a patch across his chest and down to his groin.

Maxsim keeps the rest of the streak safe from an aggressive Natalia.

Natalia (Beta Lightning Cat)

Only female in the group that performs in the circus. She is heir to her matriarchal streak, but is a beta designation. Natalia has pale blue fur all over, with long black hair, high cheekbones, cat ears, feline eyes, a tail, and fangs. She has small breasts, a slender, toned body, and a lean backside and legs. She has naked patch across her breasts and down to groin.

She wants to form a streak with Maxsim, Trace, Fuse, and Sim, but they are alphas and cannot breed with her. She took her omega sister's place, who was supposed to be the one performing with the circus.

Echo (Omega Lightning Cat)

He is a pure white lightning cat, with a smaller frame than Maxsim's, and built much more delicately. His designation is omega, and he has survived because he comes from a rare streak with a male omega. The streak, with help from the warlocks, protected him while growing up. They hid it, and he presents himself to the world as beta. He wants to form a streak with Maxsim, but not Natalia. She discovered he is an omega and keeps trying to kill him.

Other cats in the group
Trace (Alpha Lightning Cat)
Fuse (Alpha Lightning Cat)
Sim (Alpha Lightning Cat)

Yalani

An abominable snowman type creature with shaggy white and gray fur. They are good at blending into their surroundings. It is a hunter-gatherer species that lives in caves on Iceen. Eight to nine feet tall, they are an aggressive species that will attack if they feel threatened. They live solitary lives unless mated and raising a family.

PLANET SKARR

This planet is the birthplace of the human race. The original humans were exploring Skarrians who crashed on Earth, and because they no longer had access to the magical waters, lost all their supernatural abilities.

Skarrians are mostly polyamorous and have attraction marks that show up on both parties' bodies. If attraction wanes on either side, the marks disappear. Skarrians find themselves bonded to others after five rounds of sex, which requires them to orgasm simultaneously. Skarr is basically a sister planet to Earth in that it is made up of ten different land masses surrounded by pink oceans, but it has different species of plants and animals.

When reproducing, all bonded members of the family must participate to produce a child.

Lila Jenson (Liliana Adams)

Orphaned at a young age, she moved from foster family to foster family, never really fitting in anywhere, though nothing terrible happened to her. One family put her into gymnastic lessons and self-defense courses to keep her out of trouble. She has no real goal in life, but has always thought there must be something more than working in a bar and having the occasional one-night stand.

She is average height, with a curvy figure, long chestnut hair with turquoise streaks, golden skin, and green eyes.

Lila discovered she has grandparents who are still alive, and they invited her to learn their family business.

Currently, she has shown no signs of having Skarrian powers despite an impressive first showing.

John Adams, William Adams, and Eric Adams

Triplet brothers who appear to be in their late forties, they possess chestnut hair, tall, slender builds, and emerald green eyes.

They have been searching for Liliana, also known as Lila, for years, and are thrilled to have finally found her. They are also the CEOs of the Galaxy Circus and guardians of the power orb.

William has a buzz cut and is gruff.

Eric has long hair, which he wears in a man bun, and is the joker and tease in the family.

John has short, tousled hair and is the kind and

loving brother, but he is subject to spirals of depression.

Alina and Marcus Adams (Dec.)

Lila's parents moved to Earth in order to raise her in relative safety, but they were killed in a car accident. Alina had blonde hair and green eyes, and Marcus had brown eyes and the same chestnut hair as the grandpas and Lila.

Magenta

She is a performer in the circus. When on Earth, she uses the circus silks, but on other planets, she uses her levitation powers. Magenta has bright pink hair and pale skin. She is mid height with a slim build and light blue, almost gray, eyes. She has been a lifeline for Lila when it comes to all things alien.

Broderick Potter (Bubby)

Captain of the mothership and Marcus Adams' best friend. He has red hair and a red beard with crystal blue eyes. He's rugged and well-built and thrilled to meet Lila.

Phillip and Fiona

They are Lila's twin cousins, but not on the Adams' side of the family.

Fiona has long, curly red hair, brown eyes, and freckles with a tall, slim build.

Phillip's red hair is cropped short, and he has brown eyes and freckles with a tall, slim build.

They oversee the dinosaur act. The dinosaurs were hand raised in the zoo on Skarr.

Captain Lester

Captain Lester is an alternate captain for the mothership and circus pod. He has an abrasive personality and a voice like he smokes two packs of cigarettes a day.

PLANET EARTH

Susie

She is Lila's best friend, with dark, mahogany skin, melted chocolate colored eyes, and black corkscrew curls. She's a nurse and previously lived with Lila.

Mark

Mark is Susie's boyfriend. He has black hair and blue eyes, and works as an emergency room doctor. Mark is also bi.

PLANET FLUXX

Fluxx is a sister planet to Skarr, and its waters have magical properties too, but it gives its inhabitants the ability to shift into another creature. Fluxxians are animal shifters with three forms—humanoid while retaining coloration and some features of their animal, half form, and beast form. Fluxxians can use glamour to blend in and must do this when on Earth and in public. Fluxxians have fated mates, and their animal will dictate how they reproduce.

Caspian (Kraken Shifter, Lila's First Mate)

Caspian performs in the first act in the circus, shifting into half form and juggling multiple items with his tentacles.

He has mottled blue and purple skin, piercing stormy blue eyes, nipple rings, and vivid purple hair shaved on either side with a long section on top the drapes over one eye. His tentacles are purple and blue when in half form. Caspian's beast form is large. Male krakens implant their parents with their eggs via an ovipositor, and the womb then fertilizes the eggs, basically doing the opposite of a human. Fertilized eggs can lie dormant inside the female for a long time until she is ready to give birth. Drinking a large amount of the male kraken's cum tells the eggs that you are ready for babies. Four weeks later, they are born in kraken form. Two weeks after that, they are able to shift into their human form for the first time. Krakens can have anywhere between one and six babies at a time. Non-kraken mates will have their biology changed when given the mating bite. This allows them to carry a kraken's eggs for their partner.

Dylan (Dragon Shifter)

Dylan is in the first act of the show, which is a fire breathing act where he actually breathes fire.

He has ebony skin, wings, a metallic black shimmer to his scales, yellow and green reptilian eyes, and fangs. He also has sharp cheekbones, and his nose flattens slightly in half form.

Dylan is the man whore of the circus. He befriends Lila early on, only to betray her later and get kicked out of the circus for his act of aggression.

Silac (Naga Shifter)

Silac is one of the shifters who replaced Dylan in the first act. A Naga shifter, he has tousled emerald green hair in his humanoid form, with long, lean muscles and nipple rings. His eyes are orange and black. When he is in half form, he has a snake body from the waist down, with emerald green scales covered in horizontal orange stripes and black diamonds. Naga males have a hemipenis that hooks in to hold their partner close during copulation, and their mates give birth to live young.

Tirrian (Dragon Shifter)

Tirrian is the dragon shifter who replaced Dylan in the first act. Where Dylan was pitch black, he is more like an oil slick black. He has a shimmer to his skin that flickers from green and gold to pink and blue. He appears holographic depending on what angle you look at him from. In half form, his wings are the same color and his scales are holographic pink. He is tall, broad, and muscular. His hair is black with pink streaks in it, and his eyes are black with lines of pink in them. He's an asshole.

Dragons can only have young with female dragons or their mates. Once again, a mating bite will change a non-dragon shifter mate to allow them to lay eggs. Eggs are incubated by the couple for two months before being born. They must be kept at a certain temperature to ensure a live birth. Homosexual dragons can hire surrogates to help them with reproduction if they wish, and it is common practice for young dragons to offer this service as a way to start their own hoard before they wish to begin their own family. There is a website that can help facilitate this.

PLANET CYBERTRONIA

A technologically advanced planet inhabited by life forms that are half organic, half nanobot technology, allowing them to change their features at will. Reproduction occurs through intercourse, but parents program their respective organic matter with the traits and features they wish their babies to have. Once the baby is born, their source code is imprinted on a microchip, which is then deposited into a secret storage facility for safe keeping.

Pleasure Bot Industries is one of the main sources of employment for Cybertronia. They produce lifelike robots for sexual pleasure and are one of the galaxy's most popular purchases. Pleasure Bots are not like cyborgs, in that they are incapable of thoughts, feelings, or responses that have not been programmed into them.

Link (Cyborg)

Link is the ship doctor for the Galaxy Circus and is one of Lila's boyfriends. His skin tone is peach with a shimmer. He has silver hair and eyes. He is built like a swimmer, with long, lean lines, a tapered waist, and broad shoulders, and he is able to change his body parts at will. Cyborgs can't lie.

Josa Spears (Cyborg Nurse)

Josa is the nurse to Link's doctor, but he was hired by Link's mom to spy on him and the circus. He was promised Link's hand in marriage and a share of the Pleasure Bot Industries fortune if he complied. He has the same shimmery skin tone as Link, with metallic green hair and eyes. He has a slender, feminine frame and a dirty attitude.

PLANET VILAX

Vilax is home to a race of blood drinkers, the sanguinistas. Much like Earth's legend of vampires, this race is strong, fast, and has heightened senses. They can fly, and are very hard to kill. Their bodies will regenerate as long as their body parts are close to one another. To kill them, you need to burn both of their hearts. They are a warrior race and one of the fiercest in the galaxy. Military service is mandatory for all Vilaxians.

Vilax only gets five hours of sunlight a day, so while they are not allergic to the sun, they do prefer the dark. Sanguinistas drink blood because their bodies cannot process their own red blood cells. They have a fated mate called a blood rose, but not everyone finds them. They live in family clans, and blood sharing can be a sexual thing, but with children, it isn't.

Saxon (Sanguinista)

Saxon is part of the aerial troupe in the circus. He has magenta-colored eyes and thick, short black hair that's long enough to run your fingers through. His body is muscular and broad, and he has pale skin and fangs.

Hale (Sanguinista)

He is in the same troupe as Saxon and is

Saxon's best friend. He has blond hair, teal eyes, and fangs.

Radella (Sanguinista)

Estrella (Sanguinista)

Velorina (Sanguinista)

Xenos (Sanguinista)
Saxon's brother.

Dante (Sanguinista)

Kavita (Sanguinista)

PLANET WESTALIN

This is the warlocks' home planet. Warlock powers include, but are not limited to, mind manipulation and control, teleporting, and manifestation. Powerful warlocks have harems to feed from because they are psychic feeders who feed from strong emotions. Weaker warlocks and other creatures make up these harems. Weaker warlocks benefit from it, as they are able to feed off the stronger warlock at the same time and get a temporary boost in power. Members of the harem receive a wage and a comfortable position within the warlock's household. Powerful warlocks are able to absorb powers and life force, but it is frowned upon and is only used as a punishment. Warlocks have soulmates they call intimates. When a warlock finds their intimate, they no longer need a harem to feed from.

Xavier Colest (Crown Prince)

Xavier is one of the most powerful beings in the galaxy, only second to his parents. He is mostly with the circus because he gets bored easily. He helps with glamour to confuse the humans. He has purple/blue eyes and long indigo hair. His body is lean and muscular, and he has piercings in his ears, nose, and eyebrow. His ears are pointed, and he has lavender-colored skin with silver markings.

Xylene Colest

Queen of the Westalins and Xavier's mother. She was best friends with Alina and Marcus Adams, Lila's parents.

Cronus Colest

King of the Westalins and Xavier's father. He was best friends with Alina and Marcus Adams.

Elyan (Warlock, Head Harem Girl in Xavier's Harem)

Nambra (Warlock, Harem Member)
She has red hair and a voluptuous figure.

Lexus (Warlock, Harem Member)
She has short dark hair and a petite frame.

Ara (Warlock, Harem Member)

Ara has pale pink hair, eyes, and skin.

Jastia (Warlock, Harem Member)

Jastia possesses buttercup yellow hair, eyes, and skin.

Sinath (Rasque, Harem Member)

The Rasque is a humanoid race that looks like an Earth grasshopper. They have segmented arms and legs with plated body structure. Their penis is covered by plated sections, which retract when manipulated. Once the penis extends, claspers lock the copulating couple together.

Mithus (Milobar, Harem Member)

He has a stingray-shaped head and body, with arms, legs, and a barbed tail. Mithus has two penises, which both have barbs that activate during intercourse, locking them within their partner.

Zanorn (Morpheian, Harem Member)

A race of metamorphs, they are able to take any shape they desire. In natural form, they are like a blank slate with limited features and gray skin.

Topirey (Dionall, Harem Member)

Dionalls are plant creatures with two forms—one is an upright humanoid sentient form, and the other is a stationary plant form which is similar to the Earth's Venus flytrap, only a lot larger and it feeds on flesh. They have leafy foliage on their head and sharp teeth, and are able to grow their body parts at will.

PLANET AQUILIA

Aquilia is seventy-five percent water, and the Aquilians are an aquatic species with three forms—humanoid, mer, and beast form. In beast form, they resemble an Earth dolphin, but are scaled and have sharp teeth. They come in a variety of pastel colors. In half form and on two legs, they retain the pastel colors and cannot glamour. They require a glamour spell if they want to tour Earth. Family groups are called pods. Aquilians rarely leave their home planet, and if they do, they will return once they form a pod so that their young are born in their home waters.

Nikos (Aquilian Prince)

Nikos is one of the performers in the dolphin show in the circus. He is a member of the Aquilian royal family, but not in line to inherit. He is arrogant and horny. He has pastel green skin, and his scales are pastel green and gold. His hair and eyes are metallic gold.

Nixie (Aquilian princess)

Nixie is Nikos's sister and also a performer in the circus. She's friendly and fun and is interested in exploring the galaxy. She does not want to get trapped by being mated on Aquilia. Nixie is also open to trying relationships with other species. Her colors are pastel blue and gold, with metallic gold hair and eyes.

Galaxy Circus Pod Members
Joaquin
Nolani
Marin
Dorado

PLANET RILU

Rilu is a desert-like planet with small green oases dotted across its land surfaces. There are no above ground oceans or seas, but there are large underground ones which provide fresh water for the inhabitants of the planet. At each of the oases, which usually center around a small lake, are wells which provide fresh drinking water for travelers. Some of the larger lakes have permanent villages established for trade. The people of Rilu are nomadic tribes. They raise larnuks and are miners. Under the surface of Rilu are extensive gem mines, and the people of Rilu mine the gems for trade and to feed their larnuks.

Zala (Larnuk Mistress)

Zala is the larnuk mistress for the circus and is in charge of that portion of the show. She has exotic, Middle Eastern looks with darker skin and wavy, pitch-black hair with streaks of color in it from her horses. Her eyes are a pale blue, almost white, rimmed in kohl, and framed with long black lashes. She is tall and slim, and her body is covered in silvery scars from bonding with her horses. Five appear in the show, but she has more.

Larnuks

These are creatures much like Earth's Pegasus, possessing both wings and a horn. They come in the same colors as the gems that are mined on their planet—emerald, ruby, sapphire, gold, and amethyst. They eat gems and spout fire, and they have sharp, vicious teeth. They are bred and raised by a larnuk mistress or master who will bond with their herd. The larnuk will bite them, and a lock of their hair will turn the same color as the larnuk's. The more streaks a master or mistress has, the more larnuks they control.

Rilax

Rilax are berries that grow in the mines alongside the gems. The berries are used to make rilaxious, a pink alcoholic beverage popular across the galaxy. It is slightly bubbly with a thick, creamy consistency.

PLANET RECCEDEA

A lush, foliage-covered, tropical planet with frozen poles on either end. It is the birthplace of the dinosaurs found in the circus. Many species of dinosaurs that once roamed the Earth continue to survive and thrive on this planet.

Vigolash

Viggy is a red and black tyrannosaurus rex. He was trained from a baby, and acts just like a giant, overgrown golden retriever.

Htaed

Htaed is a yellow and orange velociraptor, who was also trained from a baby, but is unruly and kind of crazy.

OTHER ALIEN RACES

Unas

A race of highly intelligent, peaceful, powerful beings who created the power orb that the Galaxy Circus protects. The now extinct race had powers that were fueled through sexual energy. They didn't have mates or partners, it was just a free-for-all orgy.

Their war with the Aaz'ax dwindled their numbers until there were only a handful left. Their energy was absorbed into the orb when they turned it over to the Adams brothers. They used the Adams' ancestors' blood to link it to them, and if it leaves their line, anyone remaining will be absorbed too.

The power orb was supposed to be a clean, free source of energy capable of powering planets across the galaxy. It can be used as a weapon of mass destruction, but cannot be destroyed because the galaxy would implode.

Aaz'ax

The leadership of this race was cruel and vicious and wanted to use the orb to conquer other lands. They possessed it momentarily and laid waste to a number of planets, but the Unas were able to take it back. By then, the Aaz'ax weren't doing well. A mysterious illness had taken most of their women, and women of other races wanted nothing to do with the men. Their species has been on the brink of extinction and were finally able to dispose of their tyrannical leadership. Remaining survivors scattered to planets far and wide. The Aaz'ax are distant ancestors of the Vilaxians. Although they do not require blood, they can consume it, but it acts much like alcohol and drugs to a human. They have the ability to glamour, and their natural form is humanoid, but their shoulders and backs are covered in ridges and their body looks like they are covered in thorns. With their green skin and blood-red hair, they resemble a rose.

Telazions (Planet Telaz)

They sold the tech for the iPhone to Steve Jobs.

Nengh

They perform as clowns in the circus. They have detachable limbs and are able to adjust their body's size and mass. They are humanoid in shape, but they are orange with feathery tufts instead of hair. They use a glamour provided by Xavier to appear human when on Earth.

Jelliads

A race of gelatinous amorphic creatures. They are sentient and communicate via telepathy.

DICTIONARY

Phoeall (fo-all): Warlock for…

Vigolash: Obedient one in Aaz'axian

Sandar worm: native to the planet Westalin, they are large creatures that turn soil over in their paddocks between crops. They eat all organic matter left from past crops, leaving it free for farmers to plant the next crop.

Silax worm: Native to Rilu, it lives in the mines and is a pest. Their secretion kills the rilax berry plant. They are trapped, and their secretions are used to make achom.

Achom: A drink that is like a blend of coffee and chocolate with a chili vodka kick.

GIN: Galaxy Information Network.

Karta monster: A large, kaiju style creature the size of an elephant.

Cirillion: Little bundles of fluff with big eyes.

Lastovian hog: A long pig like creature with six legs, five eyes and a piercing squeal.

Saturn's Rings: A restaurant on the mothership.

Edalaxion Space Station: A space station with dodgy bars and meeting spaces for the dregs of the galaxy.

Celesian Brothel: A popular brothel if you want to have sex with living beings as opposed to sex bots.

Jaxa bird: A bird native to Westalin, it looks like a cross between a peacock and a phoenix. Its tail is a fanned bloom of fire.

Kala mouse: A marsupial found on Westalin.

Coolmy shell: This is a crustacean found in Aquilian waters.

THANK YOU FOR READING!

I hope you enjoyed the book. It would be super awesome if you could leave a review wherever you bought it, because I love to hear what you thought of the story.

Want to see what happen next for Lila and friends? Pre-order the third book in the Galaxy Circus series Whisperer

Also do you want to know what happened to Susie and Mark on their trip back from Vegas? Pre-order the Galaxy Circus Halloween Novella
A Night Most Wicked.
A Rocky Horror Picture Show retelling.

In the mean time why don't you check out one of my other series. You can find everything on my website at www.lexiewinston.com

ACKNOWLEDGMENTS

As always Grace and Hope. My throuple members, my author wife and PA, my best bitches. So glad I can feed your tentacle fetishes.

To Jillian and Kerry, the best alpha readers a girl could have, I love you guys.

To my super awesome beta team, your help is as always much appreciated.

To my cover designer Jessica, of Raven Ink Covers. Thank you for making the covers exactly what I envisioned, you nailed it.

Thank you to both Jess at Elemental Editing and Val at SCW Editing. My book is pretty and readable thanks to you guys.

Galaxy Circus is a real passion project for me. It's my least selling series but I'm so invested in the characters and I love seeing them come to life on the pages. If you love Lila and the guys, think about writing a review, or recommending it to other people. Share the awesomeness that is the Galaxy Circus.

And lastly to you guys the readers. I love what I do, and probably would do it regardless if anyone read them or not, but you guys make it that much sweeter so thank you.

Until next time, happy reading

Lexie